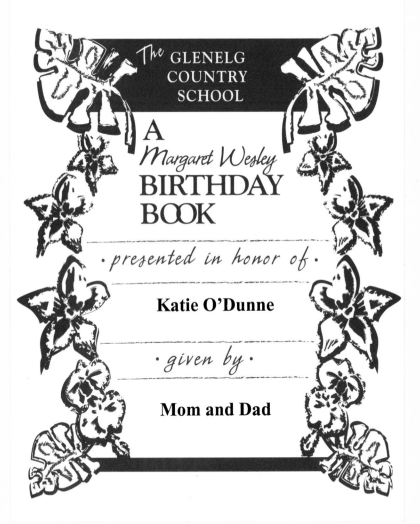

The GLENELG
COUNTRY
SCHOOL

A
Margaret Wesley
BIRTHDAY
BOOK

· *presented in honor of* ·

Katie O'Dunne

· *given by* ·

Mom and Dad

The Uses of Enchantment

The

Uses

of

Enchantment

A NOVEL

HEIDI JULAVITS

DOUBLEDAY / New York London Toronto Sydney Auckland

PUBLISHED BY DOUBLEDAY

Copyright © 2006 by Heidi Julavits

Published in the United States by Doubleday, an imprint of The Doubleday Broadway
Publishing Group, a division of Random House, Inc., New York.
www.doubleday.com

DOUBLEDAY and the portrayal of an anchor with a dolphin are
registered trademarks of Random House, Inc.

Book design by Jennifer Ann Daddio

Library of Congress Cataloging-in-Publication Data
Julavits, Heidi.
The uses of enchantment : a novel / Heidi Julavits.——1st ed.
p.   cm.
1. Teenage girls—Fiction. 2. Kidnapping—Fiction. 3. Psychologists—Fiction.
4. Psychological fiction. I. Title.
PS3560.U522U84 2006
813'.6—dc22   2006045434

ISBN-13: 978-0-385-51323-4
ISBN-10: 0-385-51323-2

PRINTED IN THE UNITED STATES OF AMERICA

1   3   5   7   9   10   8   6   4   2

First Edition

For Delia

Nobody tells fibs in Boston.

—HENRY JAMES

The girl would see, in locking minds with Freud,
how cruelly her own understanding had deceived her.

—PHILIP RIEFF, INTRODUCTION TO
DORA: AN ANALYSIS OF A CASE OF HYSTERIA

The Uses of Enchantment

What Might Have Happened

NOVEMBER 7, 1985

The following might have happened on a late-fall afternoon in the Boston suburb of West Salem. The afternoon in question was biting enough to suggest the early possibility of snow. The cloud cover made it seem later than the actual time of 3:35 p.m.

The girl was one of many girls in field hockey skirts, sweatpants, and ski shells, huddled together in the green lean-to emblazoned with Semmering Academy's scripted *S*. It had rained all morning and all afternoon; though the rain had temporarily ceased, the playing field remained a patchwork of brown grass and mud bordered by a rain-swept chalk line. Last month a Semmering wing had torn an ankle tendon in similarly poor conditions, but the referee refused to call the game until 4 p.m. because the preparatory school extracurricular activities rules and regulations handbook stipulated that "sporting events shall not be canceled due to weather until one hour past the official start time."

At 3:37, the rain recommenced. The girls whined and shivered while Coach Betsy glowered beneath the brim of her UMASS CREW baseball cap. These girls were not tough girls and they had little incentive, given their eight-game losing streak, to endure a rainy November afternoon.

At 3:42, the girl asked Coach Betsy if she could be excused to the field house. The girl did not say, but she implied that she had her period. Coach Betsy nodded her reluctant permission. The girl departed from the lean-to, unnoticed by her teammates.

Rain pattered over the grass as the girl traversed the empty field, her cleats suctioning in and out of the mud. She did not hurry. The man, she knew, would wait for her. Every afternoon the man parked across the street from the cemetery where she and her friends escaped after lunch to smoke cigarettes. At first they thought he was an undercover cop or a truant officer, someone hired by their headmaster Miss Pym to keep tabs on their forbidden roaming during school hours. But the man's car, a 1975 gray Mercedes, rendered this suspicion unlikely. He'd since been downgraded to probable pervert and treated by the girls as their mascot, rallying proof of their irresistibility. The girl made sure to pause each day in his line of vision to adjust her knee sock, or swing her Semmering-issue skirt around so that the rear knife pleats snapped back and forth like a school of fish when she walked. She had noticed that, as the weeks of fall progressed, as the trees became more and more naked and the humid tropical haze over the cemetery thinned to an astringent veneer, the man stopped watching in his non-watching way the anonymous passing of girls and focused on one girl in particular.

This should have been thrill enough.

The girl entered the new field house. She meandered down the empty halls with their long fluorescent tube lighting and glassed-in trophy cases, she pushed through the swinging olive-green door into the olive-green locker room with the olive-green tiles and the pervasive smell of pink hand soap. She stood in front of the mirror. She applied some lip balm but otherwise did nothing to improve her appearance. She was wet, she was bedraggled, and like all teenagers after a halfhearted day of French, trigonometry, study hall, drama, field hockey, she was in desperate need of a ride and a greasy meal, two very innocent things to want, even from a stranger.

She spun her locker combination, she propped her field hockey stick inside her locker and removed her book bag. Then she changed her mind, replacing her book bag, removing her stick. On her way toward the front doors of the field house, she stopped in front of the thirty-foot-long mural dominating the lobby. Miss Pym and the Semmering trustees, after securing the funds for the new field house, had announced a mural contest in which "entries should illustrate, with reference to our area's rich past, the trials, tribulations, and triumphs of New England women." The winning mural depicted women being chased by tomahawk-wielding Indians and women tied to stakes, their skirt hems blotted by flames fanning upward from crudely rendered piles of logs. The clouds above the heads of the soon-to-be-scalped-or-burned women transformed, with a little squinting and very little imagination, into faces that surveyed the scene with expressions commonly interpreted as enthusiasm. To the handful of actively feminist teachers at Semmering, these possibly enthusiastic clouds were read as a perverse endorsement of injustice against women by the school's trustees, who "noted" their complaint as a way to actively ignore it. The mural's official title—*The Disappearing Women*—was all but unknown among the student body, who referred to the thirty-foot wall painting as *The Grin-and-Bear-It Mural*; to them it aptly summed up the way they had been taught to approach the world by parents and teachers: to keep their sadness to themselves even as they were materially spoiled in this suburban enclave with its lurid history of torment.

The girl walked past *The Grin-and-Bear-It Mural*, heart beating at an average pace, the disappearing women gazing down at her with their irisless eyes. She exited the field house and walked three blocks north to the cemetery. She saw the man's gray Mercedes parked near the stone archway, the engine running, windshield wipers chick-chocking back and forth. The rain had increased its intensity, the patter giving way to pelting drops that formed puddles and then rivers as the water slooshed toward the leaf-clogged drains. The girl took her time. Water dripped from her nose and her chin and the hem of her skirt, soaking a perfect dark line across the thighs of her sweatpants. Her cleats made squinching noises as she walked. So little light seeped through the clouds at 3:59 p.m. that the streetlamps buzzed and ignited.

She sidled next to the Mercedes. By the car's interior light she could see the man's head bent over his newspaper. His hair fell longer than the collar of his scruffy trench coat and this slight unkemptness suggested that he was not indispensable to any job or anyone. The girl had decided that he was a banker or possibly a doctor but an undedicated one; she'd decided that he had enough family money that his profession was simply a decent way to keep his days occupied. There were plenty of men like this in her town; he was an identifiable and harmless type.

The girl paused in the ambient light shining through the Mercedes's window, illuminated, she imagined, like a beguiling specter.

The man pretended not to see her. How coy, she thought. It increased her fondness for him, the fact that he was treating this abduction like a formal courtship. Using the upturned goose head of her field hockey stick, she tapped on the glass.

The man stared at her. He reached over his newspaper to roll down the window.

The girl leaned into the car. She smelled old cigarette smoke and damp carpets. Close up, the man appeared more tired, more old, more possibly crazy.

She coughed, momentarily unsettled by the fact that this man might not be who she'd imagined him to be. She clamped her neck with the *U* formed by her thumb and forefinger the way her mother did when talking to someone she disliked at a cocktail party, squeezing her fingers tightly around her own throat.

The girl asked if he had a dime.

No response.

For the pay phone, she explained. Her ride had left without her, and home was too far a walk in the rain.

He responded with cautious politeness, which she read as bewildered gratitude to some unspecified higher power that this girl should walk into a trap he had yet to even set.

I'll drive you home, he said.

He unlocked the passenger-side door, sprung the latch.

The girl scurried through his headlights. She paused on the curb as the opposing team's athletic bus drove by—it was 4:05 by Semmering's steeple clock and the game had finally been postponed—to ensure that somebody might witness her getting into the car. Just in case, she dropped her field hockey stick into the gutter where it would be recovered and remarked upon by journalists and police, family, friends, teachers. She grasped the door handle and experienced a fleeting sensation of fear, an electrical charge that caused her fingers to retract into a self-protective claw. She imagined, because she was dramatically inclined, that the handle was burning hot; that her body was on fire; that she was immolating from within and her cells were being set individually ablaze because she, too, fancied herself to be a disappearing woman, her eyes a blank white stare.

West Salem

Once again, Mary Veal found herself the aggressively unnoticed guest at a tense social gathering at the house on Rumney Marsh. Once again, she wore a hand-me-down wool dress that itched horribly and smelled like a closet; her father was nowhere to be seen; the punch bowl provided the conversational focal point. Once again, her sisters were snubbing her. Once again, the hors d'oeuvres were lame.

Mum's funeral notwithstanding, she reflected, it felt just like old times.

From behind her plaid wingback redoubt, she watched as her older sister, Regina, ruddy hair yanked flat by a headband and thinner than her usual thin, listlessly orbited the downstairs. Her younger sister, Gaby, hunched on the piano bench, wearing a tight navy pantsuit that made her look like a down-and-out real estate agent. Gaby picked vacantly at her paper plate of grapes and salmon mousse Triscuits. She appeared, Mary thought, in need of an awkward social encounter with an estranged family member.

A wary Gaby clocked Mary's approach with her green-brown Mum eyes.

"Nice suit," Mary offered.

"Mum's," Gaby said through a mouthful of grape.

"It fits you," Mary said. She fingered the empty candy dish atop the piano, its circumference encircled by a green ribbon.

This elicited no response from Gaby.

"Except for the pants. And the jacket."

"Hmmppphh," said Gaby.

"It fits nicely around the wrists," Mary said.

The two of them wordlessly observed the arriving guests clot into special-interest groups around the punch bowl: Mum's sister, Helen, and their handful of local cousins; Mum's historical society co-workers; Mum's Wellesley College Alumnae Association friends; Mum's former Semmering Academy PTA colleagues. The wake felt uncomfortably overseen from the mantel by Mum herself, her ashes stowed in a Laotian dung vase forced upon them by Aunt Helen and flanked by two florist arrangements of pussy willows and weedy-looking filler plants.

Regina completed one last enervated rotation and dropped onto the piano bench beside Gaby. She folded her legs and coiled her left foot around her right ankle, a holdover gesture from adolescence; she'd claimed once to Mary that this tourniquet pose helped to stave off weight gain, at least in the leg area, which seemed about as reasonable as believing in the slimming powers of the electric massage belt.

Mary remained determined to forge an emotional connection with her sisters.

"How about that sermon?" Mary said, referring to Reverend Whittemore's selection from the New Testament—*For one believes he can eat all things, but he who is weak eats only vegetables*—offered, she suspected, as biblical proof that their mother's subsistence diet of white wine and pickles had been a more decisive element in her demise than the melanoma.

"He reads that sermon at every funeral," Regina said. "Once he called the dead person, who was a man, 'Beloved Phyllis.' "

Gaby yawned.

"Do you remember in junior choir how Reverend Whittemore smelled like embalming fluid?" Regina said. "The old perv was always hugging me after we sang 'Praise Him! Praise Him!' saying, 'How the heavens applaud you my dear!' "

"Blick," Gaby said through shards of Triscuit.

"At least Aunt Helen almost made it through her poem without crying," Mary said. She didn't mention Regina's poem, written specifically for Mum's funeral. The most truthful response she could muster, as she and Regina and Gaby waited for Dad to bring the car around after the service, had been: "It was so brave of you to read that."

"Or plugging her herbal grief tea," Regina said.

"I thought Healthy Acceptance filed for bankruptcy," Mary said.

"Dad bailed her out, which is why we have seventeen cases of grief tea in the attic," Regina said. "Where have you been? Oh right. You were *out West.*"

"When Aunt Helen cries," Mary said, ignoring the dig, "I wonder how anyone could ever appear convincingly sad."

"Which I guess explains why you didn't even bother to try," Regina said. "Gaby, where did you get that awful suit?"

"Mum's closet," Gaby said. "Is grief tea supposed to make you feel grief or make you not feel it?"

"Not feel grief," Mary said dully. "I think."

"That's not Mum's suit," Regina said. "Mum hated navy."

Gaby turned her suit coat inside out to reveal a green ribbon tied to the DRY CLEAN ONLY tag. Their father had donated the house's contents to the historical society for auctioning and an overly apologetic volunteer had come around the previous day to tag the desirable items with ribbons. To be safe, the volunteer had overdone the job, or maybe, given she knew the wake was to be held at 34 Rumney Marsh, she saw herself doubling as decorator for the occasion. All four legs of the couch were adorned with ribbon, both andirons, both candlesticks, the lamp bases and the lamp shades and even the spare box of light bulbs, every individual kitchen item (eggbeater, potato masher, potato peeler, wine key), the collection of circa 1979–1983 *Association of Descendants of the American Witch* newsletters stacked beneath the rattan coffee table.

"So," Regina said, "speaking of not feeling grief, has anyone checked on Dad recently?"

"I'll go," Mary offered, relieved to escape the hostile tedium of her sisters' company; it depressed her too intensely and made her feel abrased by an all-body loneliness. In the three years since Mary and Regina and Gaby had been together in the same room, nothing had changed. She tried to rekindle the heart-wrenching warmth she'd imagined feeling toward her sisters as she walked down the airplane exit ramp to their teary reunion, but instead found herself irked by Regina's self-centered prickliness and Gaby's wrathful apathy. Despite how she'd envisioned this homecoming—horribly sad, yes, stilted, yes, but glinting with the potential for everyone to recast themselves as expansively generous and affectionate people—the remaining Veal family members, herself included, hadn't really shown themselves capable of improvement.

Mary passed through the living room, her mobile presence registered only by the way the guests she neared strived to more actively ignore her. She split the curtains behind the punch table expecting to see her father, Clyde Veal, still stationed on the front lawn directing parking, but he'd abandoned his post; since his departure, guests had parked along the north side of the street, ignoring the fliers he'd taped to the streetlamps in order to avoid the territorial wrath of the neighbor Mum had christened Ye Olde Bastard. Eventually she found him, fingers pittering against his key-filled pockets, waiting in the foyer to receive coats, even though people had long since stopped arriving.

Dad, she started to say. But the two of them had pointedly arranged never to be alone without a chaperone since her arrival so, in fairness to him, she chose to "check on Dad" from behind the broken grandfather clock. He opened the door and peered down the street as if expecting a calvacade of mourners to turn onto Rumney Marsh and invade the house in desperate need of a coat-check attendant. Her father hadn't invited any of his work acquaintances from St. Hugh's today, nor any of his golf cronies from the public golf range, a nonselective, dress-code-free club overlooking a swamp that boasted, among its members, a gay couple and an acquitted child abuser. Her father maintained his connection with the local working-class community while respecting Mum's unspoken hope that these people never be invited to their house. So it was in deference to Mum, she assumed, that he'd failed to invite his friends. Or it was for some more complicated, self-defeating reason.

Mary knew without ever needing to be told: her father was a self-made lonely man.

She would tell her sisters, when they asked how he was: *Dad is Dad.* This diagnosis, transferably applicable to all of them, they would understand.

Mary returned to the living room, dodging the two hors d'oeuvres platters wielded at her neck height by the waspy widowed caterers. Did even *they* refuse to see her? How many years had it been? A stupid question. She knew how many years. Everyone in the room knew how many years. Fourteen years to the day. The waspy widowed caterers offered toothpicks and colored finger napkins to the guests, who seemed relieved to be interrupted from their non-conversations. People emptied their cups of gin punch so they could get a refill and have something to do. Not that funeral receptions were judged by the same standards as other social gatherings, but even given Mary's exceptionally low expectations for this event, it was proving to be a dud.

Though not a regular smoker, Mary needed a cigarette.

"Excuse me," Mary said to Fran Bigelow, Mum's tennis partner and a relentless chimney, currently hurrying past her en route to the bathroom. Mrs.

Bigelow—*Such hand-eye!* she remembered Mum marveling—sprung sideways as though Mary had attempted to stab her with an hors d'oeuvre fork; as Mrs. Bigelow continued to move in a diagonal vector at a near-tripping pace, her heel caught in the loop of green ribbon extending from the handle of the decorative coal hod. Her heel acted like a catapult; her next forward step hurled the coal hod into the fireplace, where the hod cleanly picked off both andirons and landed on its side with a deafening crash.

Conversations halted.

"Whoopsy!" Mrs. Bigelow said, staring damningly at Mary.

Mary froze. She, who had been previously so invisible, was suddenly aggressively seen. Mum's Wellesley College Alumnae Association friends, Mum's Semmering Academy PTA colleagues, Mum's historical society co-workers, the spouses, the distant cousins, all of them eyed her with a familiar blank probity. Exuberantly, she returned their gazes. She'd forgotten how enjoyable it was to dislike these people and was invigorated by the reminder. Cocktail parties notwithstanding, their preferred pastime was making others feel eternally shitty about themselves. These emotionally mummified, blank-eyed, sorry people. How easy it was to blame them for her troubles with her mother. How much easier it was to blame them than to blame a more deserving party: herself, for example.

She rewarded the lot of them with a grotesquely buoyant smile.

"Strike!" she said.

In the hallway, her father stifled a hiccup.

Aunt Helen—three, maybe four drinks deep into the afternoon—rushed from the kitchen, silk skirt thudding on her apparent wind as she pincered Mary by the elbow and steered her to a vacant space near the punch bowl.

A gossipy buzz engulfed them.

"Not recommended today?" Aunt Helen said. "Irreverence."

"I couldn't help it," Mary lied. "It's what Mum would have said."

Aunt Helen refilled her punch glass. Her wardrobe clashed as loudly as her interests in curative teas and gin drinks: a silk Ikat skirt blandified by a gum-colored twinset and a gold frog pin from the local purveyor of preppy, The House of Walsh.

"Also not recommended today?" she said. "Presuming to speak for your mother."

You're one to talk, Mary wanted to say, but didn't. Aunt Helen was a shadowy pro at expressing her own feelings by attributing them to others. Usually she employed her standard poodle, Weegee, for this purpose, to wit: *Weegee's feeling neglected today, isn't he?* But today Weegee was with her neighbors, and Aunt Helen needed a Weegee surrogate. Mary apparently fit the bill.

"Not that your extreme inappropriateness isn't understandable. You must be *devastated,*" said Aunt Helen. "Refusing to see you before she died. But that's just so *Paula,* isn't it? She didn't give two hoots about anyone's feelings except her own."

"What can you expect from terminally ill conflict avoiders?" Mary said lightly. The truth was, she'd been blindsided by her mother's refusal to see her, expecting, as inane as it sounded, to share some sort of pablum closure moment with her in the Lillian P. Rudy Memorial Cancer Wing, as the candy stripers wept and the oncologists did a mournful soft-shoe and her mother, the most pablum-free individual on the planet, clasped her hand and said . . . this is where the absurdity of her fantasy overrode the actual fantasy. Which didn't mean the failure of the fantasy to be met, to ever be met, hadn't left her feeling bludgeoned.

"You must be angry with her," Aunt Helen said. "I imagine you're very, very angry."

Aunt Helen widened her smudgy eyes tellingly, then shudder-gulped twice in rapid succession before appearing to cease breathing altogether. She released Mary's elbow and waved at her—Mary stared, bewildered, until she realized Aunt Helen wanted her cocktail napkin. Aunt Helen exhaled loudly, using the napkin to dab at her tearless face.

Across the room, Mary saw Regina and Gaby exchange a look that told her they were bonding over the hating of other people. Aunt Helen. Mary. Even their own father, who had excused himself from his nonexistent coat-check duties. Now he was playing with a second cousin's baby beneath the portrait of Mum's eighth great-grandmother, Abigail Lake, a suspected witch executed at Gallows Hill in 1692 and yet to be officially pardoned by the state of Massachusetts—and, notably, the only item in the living room without a green ribbon. Baby as grief shield, Mary thought, no funeral should be without a baby. Her father bounced the baby on his knee, he fake walked it across the carpet, he absentmindedly played with its left ear, squashing it in half and unsquashing it at seemingly intentional intervals as though he were sending Morse code to a guest across the room.

She watched as Regina approached their father and asked him if he'd like another punch. He smiled toward a longitude of unoccupied airspace; he'd been smiling at no one in particular since he woke up that morning, surrounded by an aggressively chipper force field that repelled all attempts at human connection.

Maxie and Susan, Mum's former Wellesley roommates, ladies-who-lunch vipers and the only two people Mary had been pointedly avoiding herself that afternoon, stood proprietorially to the left of the portrait of Abigail Lake. The portrait, frequent target of family scorn and the only item, according to her will, that Paula Abigail Bowden Veal had left to her three daughters, was painted to look like an antique but was in fact less than ten years old, inspired by a passage Mum found in a diary describing her great-great-great-great-great-great-great-great-grandmother's walk to the gallows. "Flatte and grey of eye," the diarist wrote. "Expressionless mouth, in which the words of a pretty devile lurk." The painting was a money-making scam, in Mary's opinion, cooked up by Susan's feminist artist daughter, a former classmate of Mary's at Semmering Academy, who offered, for an absurd fee, to paint portraits of the gallows victims "to honor those who have been so long dishonored." Susan's daughter had interpreted the diary description of Abigail Lake to produce a woman who, according to Regina and Gaby, resembled nobody so much as she resembled Mary in a bonnet.

Maxie held a paper plate of grapes; Susan nursed a sweating glass of seltzer. Both women were rickety and unseasonably brown, their chests and arms so sun-spotted they appeared upholstered in a miniature leopard print. They flashed Mary grins so intense that it only confirmed her formerly paranoid suspicion that they'd been discussing her.

"How's life in Montana?" asked Maxie.

"Oregon," corrected Susan.

"You moved to Oregon?" said Maxie.

"She's always lived in Oregon," said Susan.

"You're still a waitress?" asked Maxie.

"She's a secretary," said Susan.

"I work in the admissions office of a private girls school outside Portland," Mary said. *Work* was either an understatement or an overstatement. She was more of a professional calmer of buttoned-up hysterics, the bulk of her actual job consisting of talking down the mothers whose daughters were rejected from Beaverton's Grove School, mothers who charged into her office holding the "Due to the high quality of applicants" letter like a pair of damning panties pulled from a husband's blazer pocket. Like Semmering Academy, the Grove School was a gothic pile of bricks run by 1950s-era chalk drones, which maintained its cultural viability by perpetuating a weirdly seductive anxiety throughout its community. Mary herself was a victim of the seduction; despite the trying and repetitive emotional requirements of her job, she remained eternally fascinated by the wicker-thin girls and their wicker-thin mothers, all of them favoring dark wool skirts and macintoshes and unreadably faraway expressions; if she squinted, they could have emerged intact from any of the last seven decades. The past and the present ghosted together in the hallways of the Grove School, and maybe that was why she worked there—when the halls were abandoned for the day and the sound of rain thrumming on the slate roof blurred with the far-off screech of coaches' whistles, she could imagine she had herself been ghosted, that she'd been sucked back to a crucial crossroads in her own life and offered a second chance.

"I work at a private girls school," she repeated.

"Do you," said Maxie dryly.

"That's *odd*," said Susan.

Silence. All three looked at Clyde, holding the baby upside down by the ankles yelling, "Adios, little moonman!"

Then:

"Terrible about the obituary," said Susan.

Mary assumed they were referring to the headline—DAUGHTER OF EARLY AMERICAN WITCH DIES—she hadn't read more than that.

"Soooooo tasteless," said Maxie.

"Newspapers can't pass up an opportunity for scandal," said Susan. "Referring to her as 'Miriam's mother'—the *gall* of those people."

Mary blanched. *Miriam's mother.*

"That book ruined her life," Maxie said tonelessly.

"And such *exquisitely* bad timing for the funeral," Susan said.

"Fourteen years to the day," Maxie said. "Imagine the coincidence."

Susan's and Maxie's skulls quivered atop their reedy necks like the tips of dowsing rods, veering toward hidden watery areas under the green-ribboned Persian. Mary noticed people checking their watches and the other guests as if searching for a silently agreed-upon cue that they'd mourned enough in their bucked-up way and were allowed to go home for dinner.

Mary faked a coughing fit and pointed at her throat with one hand while miming a drinking gesture with the other. She escaped to the punch bowl where there was no more punch, and where her fake coughing fit intensified into an actual coughing fit. Eyes watering, Mary hurried toward the kitchen for a glass of water but was stopped in the foyer by Aunt Helen. "Weegee's tired," Aunt Helen announced, her words punch-shirred. She'd retrieved her vase from the mantel, having transferred her sister's ashes to the silverware drawer. After informing Mary of Paula's new whereabouts, she grasped Mary's wrist with a cadaverish hand.

"Mimsy," she said. When she pronounced it like that, *Mimsy*, nasal and high-pitched, Mary was reminded of Regina's favorite childhood goad—that her nickname was not a sweet diminutive inspired by her early-life littleness, in fact it came from Lewis Carroll's "Jabberwocky," and was a hybrid concoction of *flimsy* and *miserable*.

"After all this time, darling, you really shouldn't blame yourself," Aunt Helen said. "Your mother got over it—I mean *yes*, for many years she thought you did it to her on purpose. But you were young and unaware that anyone existed in the world but *you*. We all knew you didn't mean any *intentional* harm."

Outside, Mary heard the rhythmic swell and ebb of Ye Olde Bastard's leaf blower.

"I *mean* it," Aunt Helen slurred. "I think we can all stop catering to Paula's every little Paula whim now that she's . . . I mean look at your father, just look at the man, he hasn't had a whim of his own since he married her!"

If her father was a man impervious to whimsy, Mary thought, her mother could hardly be blamed. No two words less belonged in the same sentence than *whimsy* and *father*.

"Paula *did* have a talent for sucking up all the desire in the room. That's why everybody loved her, isn't it, because she was so commanding and grand and aristocratically needy while appearing to need nothing at all. It's no wonder my life is floundering, it's no wonder I never learned how to want with Paula as my older sister. But I forgive her. I mean I forgave her."

"So you had a talk with her," Mary said. "Before she died."

"Talk!" Aunt Helen cast a persecuted glance toward the living room. "Can I tell you a secret?"

Mary nodded even as she wondered, *Who says no to that question? And is the result ever worth the build-up?*

"Of course I loved her and forgave her all her controlling devious flaws, but Weegee knew better than anyone what a bitch she was, my darling. She pretended to love poodles but Weegee saw right through her. She was really a terrible liar, you know. Fooled absolutely no one, dear heart, except maybe you."

Aunt Helen held a finger to her rouged lips that were red now only in the creases; she smiled and the remaining color bloomed wide and Mary, in her slightly disoriented state, was made to think of the unexpectedly bright undersides of the wings of certain birds. Aunt Helen smothered her in a ginny embrace before teetering off toward her station wagon, parked beneath one of her father's DO NOT PARK fliers.

As the lingerers lingered, Mary stepped outside to smoke one of the two cigarettes she'd nicked from a guest's overcoat and walk around the neighborhood. She received a few sympathetic waves from neighbors out with their Yorkies but was ignored by Ye Olde Bastard, reversing out of his driveway in a beige Cadillac that featured a single bumper sticker: TAKE UMBRAGE! The sticker referred to the 1983 town council election between Harold Clarke and Sally Umbrage, an election handily taken by Clarke after a newspaper revealed that Umbrage's campaign was funded by a historical-amusement-park developer with his eye on West Salem's sleepy waterfront.

TAKE UMBRAGE!

Mary had seen this sticker hundreds of times and read nothing more than a clever campaign pun, but today, on this day, the day of her mother's funeral, Ye Olde Bastard's chrome bumper prickled with rebuke. She, Mary, was too accepting, too flimsy, and too miserable. A more committed sister would have appeared beseechingly weak in front of her

sisters and begged for the comfort she so clearly wanted from them. A
more committed daughter would have demanded to be seen by her dying
mother. A more committed griever would be wracked by the injustice,
she would have thrown herself atop the grave site (had there been a grave
site) and howled into the dirt until the medics arrived.

TAKE UMBRAGE!

She could not. She could not take umbrage. She was too long dull in
the heart.

Because it seemed like a fitting place to go on the day of a funeral,
Mary walked all the way to the West Salem Cemetery, a seven-acre square
of ill-tended grass and gravel paths pocked with tombstones scorched a
depressing carbon color, out of proper use since the eighteenth century but
favored by teenagers as a grisly locale in which to smoke pot or drink vodka
stolen from someone's parents' liquor cabinet or read faux-Victorian
pornographic novels procured in Boston by someone's older brother. She
and her friends, who used to escape to the cemetery for a between-class
smoke, delighted in finding the shredded pages on the grass with sentence
fragments such as "he resurrected his aching supplicant" and "languishing
her rose-red nonpareil." After entering the stone gate she found herself
searching the uncut grass, the piles of crimpled leaves, the evergreen shrubs
for a suggestive scrap of text from which she could extrapolate a beyond-
the-grave message from her mother. She'd assumed that Mum had refused
to see her in her final weeks because, in her dramatic and, yes, controlling
way, she'd intended to have somebody deliver a letter to Mary after she was
dead explaining why she'd refused to see her, claiming that she'd forgiven
her and wishing her well and maybe—just maybe—claiming to love her
despite it all. The assumption that such a letter existed had kept her from
panicking when she'd called her father to inform him she was coming to see
Mum, she didn't care what Mum wanted or didn't want, and her father had
responded, tonelessly, "Not now, Mimsy."

Thirty-eight hours later, her mother was dead.

During the cross-country flight home from West to East, as the ground beneath her turned from brown and bold to brown and flat to crimped and darkly wooded, the world felt unthreateningly alien; from this height she could let the scenery roll under her as a tourist might, without any defensiveness or fear because she did not belong to it, nor it to her. She found the most comfort in thinking that she and her mother were fellow travelers on this day; a chance existed that they could pass each other on the way to their respective new destinations. She examined the cumulus clouds, those speech bubbles of the traveling dead, for any message at all, even an insincere one benignly divorced from the events that colored her mother's feelings toward her while alive. *Goodbye,* she imagined the clouds were saying as she fell asleep, her cheek pressed against the window. *Goodbye.*

I t was dark by the time she returned to Rumney Marsh, all the downstairs lights, save for the kitchen light, extinguished. She sat on Ye Olde Bastard's curb and smoked her second cigarette, trying to observe the house as a perspective buyer might, as a box of happy potential and not as the saggy-floored, rotting-silled container she saw, listing slightly toward the scrubby rear yard, bogged down to a structural breaking point by her family's many material and emotional residues. In three days, her father would move to his golf condo. The historical society was coming with a truck to collect the auction items. Then the house would belong to her, at least until it sold. She would be its interim caretaker. She articulated her choice to live in the empty house to her quasi-boyfriend, a Beaverton cabinetmaker she'd been dating for seven months: *I feel badly for the house.* This was true. While she couldn't cry for her mother, she became idiotically tearful when she thought of the house abandoned by the people and the things that had afflicted it, lovingly, for the past thirty-two years, as a cool parade of buyers weighed its flaws against its promise.

She snuffed her cigarette into Ye Olde Bastard's tight-napped grass. Across the street, heels clicked along the sidewalk and up her family's

driveway. The automatic garage light snapped on, illuminating a famil-
iarly fuzzy-haired woman knocking with familiar impatience on the
kitchen door. The woman huffed and checked her watch. Mary heard the
kitchen screen yo-yo shut, she saw the woman struggle to fish a set of car
keys from her canvas bag.

Mary ducked behind the rear fender of the nearest parked car.

What the hell is she doing here, she thought. But her bewilderment was insincere. Though a psychologist, Roz Biedelman had never been one to
register the fact that a person hated her guts, even a person of her
mother's calculated lack of subtlety. Mary crouched lower. It had snowed
two days ago, and then it had rained, and then the temperature had
dropped below freezing, but the curb was still lined with a sooty, filigreed
crust that crunched noisily under her weight. Worse than Roz Biedelman
spotting her was Roz Biedelman spotting her crouched idiotically behind
a car. But Roz remained on the opposite side of the street and unlocked
the door to a green sedan parked in front of the Trevelyans' house. She
started the engine. She drove away.

Once Roz turned the corner, Mary sprinted for the house (noting,
curiously, that the automatic garage light failed to respond when she
crossed beneath it). She locked the door and flicked off the kitchen overhead, just in case Roz circled back (all paranoia was justified where Roz
was concerned). She removed her shoes and padded up the back staircase.
From down the hall she could hear Gaby and Regina in Regina's old bedroom, now a guest room, as Regina regaled Gaby with details about her
impending breakup from her third fiancé, Bill, the two of them
chortling in a ragged, sloppy way that indicated they were drunk.

Mary paused in the hallway. She needed to say good night to her sisters. She needed to engage in a polite post-funeral debrief. She wanted to
confer with them about the unexplained appearance of Roz Biedelman.
She decided to put it off.

Mary assumed that her father had gone to bed and so was surprised to spot him, as she passed the half-open door to the study-cum-second-guest-room, standing in the skinny triangle of light thrown downward by the desk lamp, reading a letter. The corners of his mouth spasmed as though his lips were being electrocuted toward a smile. From the doorway, she could see the letter's handwriting—her mother's—and she permitted herself a dopey surge of hope. *Of course.* Her mother had given a letter to her father, with instructions that he give it to Mary on the day of the funeral. The fact of this letter—the way her father held it, as if it were his but not his—relieved her for two reasons. The obvious reason involved her mother. The less obvious reason involved him, because the letter meant she could forgive her father his irritating and, yes, *hurtful* passivity. This trait of his she'd accepted without much resentment until his most recent failure to intercede on her behalf, acting as her mother's neutral spokesperson on the hospital phone and refusing, as he'd always refused, to go against his wife. Since Mum's death, her acceptance of his long suffering assumed a more spikey, wrathful tinge, at least until she arrived at the house full of pent-up angry words and he, numb-faced and too small for his own skin, showed her the photos of the charmless golf condo he'd bought, and tried, with a palpable neediness, to rally her enthusiasm for a life that sounded to her like just this side of death.

She stood quietly in the doorway to the study-cum-second-guest-room. Her father looked up from the letter long enough to register her own desperation, and to allow it to make him uncomfortable.

He turned back to the desk.

"Just catching up on some bills," her father said, folding up the letter and sliding it into his pants pocket. "Your mother left us quite a mess here."

He gestured toward a crisscrossed pile of envelopes.

"Quite a mess," he repeated.

He put his hands on his hips. He stared at the pile, as though willing it to ignite.

"I read an article about estate planning on the airplane," Mary said, after an awkward silence.

"We don't really own what you'd call an estate," her father said.

"It listed the top ten things people would do with their time if they knew they only had a week to live," she said.

"Ah," her father said, not listening.

"My point is that bill paying was pretty low on the list," she said.

Her father, she noticed, had taken the framed photographs down from the wall. This bothered her. Not that he had begun to strip the house of the few belongings he planned to take with him to the golf condo. She was bothered that she couldn't remember which picture had once hung above the couch bed.

"So is making lasagna noodles from scratch," she said. Was it the photo of their 1973 family waiting to board the Woods Hole ferry? "So is putting an old pet to sleep." Was it the photo of her parents straddling a tiny moped on their Bermuda honeymoon?

No, she thought. It was the framed letter from Governor Edward J. King in sympathetic reference to Abigail Lake. Or it was the photo of one long-ago Halloween, Regina dressed as a queen, Mary as a hand-me-down witch, and Gaby as a table.

"So is making amends with estranged family members," she said.

Her father didn't respond.

"Most people just want to get a manicure and go skydiving," she said.

Her father ground his teeth, producing a squeaky Styrofoam sound that meant he'd had quite enough of something.

"How's the boyfriend?" her father asked. "The one who makes shelves?"

As opposed to the one who makes recycled packaging out of old newspapers, she wanted to say. The one who makes deck chairs from a composite of unendangered hardwood pulp and natural glue. Her string of boyfriends were crafts-oriented people with a solid liking for the outdoors, an environmental business aesthetic, and a full head of hair; she'd met them all at the vegan bakery where she ate lunch every afternoon. She ate at the vegan bakery because it was the only place to eat within walking distance of the Grove School. They traveled distances to eat there aggressively on purpose, which partly explained why each of these relationships had failed, and maybe why her adult life, to this point, possessed a temporary feel. After a childhood spent plotting and attempting to assert control over the uncontrollable, she'd downsized her ambitions to practically nothing. Her attachments now, like her life in general, were a composite of pure, pure accidents.

But in fact she didn't know how the current boyfriend was. She hadn't called him once since she'd left. Nobody in her family knew his name (it was Dan), and thinking of him as *the boyfriend* had made it very easy not to call him. Her life—and it was a not bad life, not while she was in it— was suddenly reduced to a series of nouns to which she felt a very slim connection. *The boyfriend. The job. The West.*

"He's fine," she said. "I guess."

"Will he be coming to visit you while you're here?" her father said.

Implicit in this question was the fact that he assumed she was not staying. And she *wasn't* staying, not after the house sold. Was she? Still, she felt hurt by the fact that he didn't appear to care one way or the other.

"I'm not sure, Dad," she said. "I really barely know the guy, to be honest. He's more like—my buddy."

Her father nodded. "Buddies are good," he said. "Nothing wrong with a buddy."

"I guess not . . ."

"Your mum and I were never buddies. Not that I wanted her to be my buddy. That's what the golf course is for."

"Come on, Dad, Mum was your buddy," Mary said, not knowing what else to say. Other than *Father* and *whimsy*, no two words less belonged in the same sentence than *Mum* and *buddy*.

Her father seemed to appreciate the lie. He looked at her, really looked at her for the first time since she'd arrived five days ago. She took this opportunity to breach the unspoken contract.

"Did she know she was dying?" she said. "I mean I know she knew she was dying, but did she *know* she was dying?"

"We're going to have a dickens of a time straightening out things with the insurance," he said, returning his attention to the envelope pile. "We switched HMOs last spring and now there's some stickiness surrounding the preexisting condition."

"Because if she didn't *know*, as in *accept* that she was dying, that might explain why—"

"Your mother was not a stupid woman," her father said sharply.

"I was only wondering . . ."

"She was not a stupid woman," he repeated, more gently this time.

With a slap of his knees her father announced he was going to bed. He gave Mary a fraught-free peck on the cheek as though nothing out of the ordinary had transpired that week, that afternoon, that minute. He crossed the hall and shut his bedroom door; she heard the bedsprings creak as, presumably, he settled on the edge to untie his shoes, remove his socks, invert them into a ball as her mother had taught them to do before throwing them in the hamper.

Mary retired to her own bedroom, stung but then berating herself for feeling stung. She retreated again into the safety of nouns. *The man's wife just died*, she told herself. *Give the man a break.* She removed her dress and pulled on her high school–era robe, still hanging where it had always hung on the inside of her closet door. She took the back staircase to the kitchen to make some grief tea. They'd left the cleaning to the caterers, the two waspy widowed women Mum used for all her historical society events. The waspy widowed women had left a note on rose-dotted stationery leaning against a plate of leftover meringues. It read: *We are so sorry for you!!*

Mary read and reread the note as she fingered the tangle of Healthy

Acceptance tea bags in the tin. Grief tea, assuming it made a person not feel grief, was a beverage she might best avoid. Grief tea ran through her veins. She'd been raised on a diet of grief tea.

We are so sorry for you!!

She crumpled the note and put it in her robe pocket.

The kettle boiled.

Opening the silverware drawer to fetch a spoon, she noticed the plastic baggie—it was an actual plastic baggie with a ziplock top—containing her mother's ashes, folded neatly atop the knives. Her throat closed, her body fighting off a nausea that felt oddly divorced from the physical. *My mother is inside this baggie,* Mary thought, stunned by the queasy disconnect. *Her sister hid her in the silverware drawer.* In her mother's opinion open caskets were hideous, they were plain barbaric, and, yes, Mary understood her reasoning, but as a constipated mourner with intensely unmendable closure issues she sort of missed the open casket, she missed a concrete representation of death that was so mercilessly to the point.

You must be very, very angry with her.

Mary replaced the baggie atop the knives and shut the drawer, but not all the way. *Air,* she was thinking irrationally. It seemed insensitive to leave the kitchen in total darkness, so she flicked on the over-the-stove light. The light made a comforting humming sound.

She took the front stairs this time so that she would pass Regina's door and be forced to say good night to her drunk sisters. The pair of them sat side by side in Regina's skinny single bed, the duvet pulled up to their waists, the pillows mashed vertically against the headboard. Each held a water glass in their laps filled with something clear—vodka, gin, rum, evidently they'd stashed a bottle before the reception. They wore their old Lanz nightgowns, girlish be-flowered and be-hearted flannel things with eyelet lace at the collars and cuffs that made them look disturbingly older than their respective ages of thirty-one and twenty-eight. Regina in particular looked preternaturally ruined due to a combination of the lighting—the Itty Bitty Book Light clamped to the headboard ex-

posed the hollows under her eyes and the rumples around her mouth—
her resolute underweight-ness, and the physical toll exacted by her crash-
ingly doomed love life. In high school, Regina had been the only
functional Veal beauty, which did not mean that she'd been beautiful.
Since she exuded the composure and the sense of entitlement that typically accompanied beauty, many were charitably willing to concede her
the privileges. Mary, who was neither pretty nor its opposite, learned at
an early age that what beauty she might lay claim to was directly related
to the occasional moods that possessed her as a child and as an adolescent, and which now rarely did; a sense that her body did not matter and
her face did not matter, that when people looked at her they were struck
by a light that radiated from inside of her and was so entrancing as to
make her physical self irrelevant. But really it was Gaby who, despite her
alternately irate and affectless manner and her asexual-to-lesbian lean-
ings, had the most lovely moon face of the three, hidden behind a perpetual scrim of baby-fine, brown hair. Part of her allure could be
attributed to the fact that people felt self-congratulatory when they discovered it, as though this said something special about them and their
unique powers of perception.

Her sisters stopped talking when they saw Mary standing in the
doorway. They did not invite her into the room. Detached conversation
ensued. The kitchen was clean yes the waspy women were sweet yes and
even Aunt Helen was on her best behavior amazing how is Dad Dad is
fine Dad is Dad glad it's over now just glad it's over.

Silence.

Mary said good night. She did not try to kiss them or appear to need
to be kissed and they were clearly relieved about this.

"Yes, well, good night," she repeated.

Mary shut her bedroom door, surrounded now by the cabbage-rose
wallpaper she'd chosen as a ten-year-old, jail bars of pink-and-red flow-
ers. Regina's and Gaby's rooms had been stripped and repainted into the
guest room and the study-cum-second-guest-room respectively, while her

room—for possibly no more significant reason than that it was the smallest and the darkest—had been left intact, right down to the elementary-school swim-team ribbons pinned to the bulletin board and the robe in the closet. She sat on the edge of her dotty-coverleted bed and roughly worked her temples with her thumb and index finger, trying to poke away the effects of the day. She took a healthy gulp of Healthy Acceptance grief tea to maximize her attempts at relaxation.

Fuck.

She spat the scalding mouthful back into the mug. Her hand jiggled, spilling more tea and forcing her to drop the mug awkwardly on the bedside table. The mug overturned and grief tea splashed on the spines of the books in the nearby bookshelf and over the off-white carpet.

Fuck *fuck.*

She pulled the books from the shelf and one by one blotted them dry with her bathrobe sleeve. The worst hit, coincidentally, was her signed copy of *Trampled Ivy: How Abusive Marriages Happen to Smart Women* by Dr. Rosemary Biedelman. Mary removed the book's sheeny dust jacket (a crepuscular orangey-pink backdrop foregrounding a menacing silhouette of ivy) to swipe at the water droplets beneath it. The spine, stiff from never having been read, was nonetheless practiced at opening to this one page.

For Dora: We await your true story.

Beneath the ballpointed inscription was a scribble that might have read *Roz Biedelman* but had always looked more to Mary like *Skuz Bod.*

Her formerly treasured edition of *The Abduction and Captivity of Dorcas Hobbs by the Malygnant Savages of the Kenebek,* she noticed, though located on a shelf above the spill's Biedelman epicenter, had also been victim of the spray. She removed it gingerly and patted at the mildew-stained spine that might have been royal blue at one time, but was now a leeched-out violet with a tiny gold tomahawk glimmering in the center. The book's pages were compressed like a dense cake. Mary opened the front cover to read the full title of the book, which she'd once known by heart. *The Abduction and Captivity of Dorcas Hobbs by the Malygnant Savages of the Kenebek, A*

Compendium of Helish Tortores and Dreadfull Temtations and How an Innocent Young Girl Tastd Sine and Dancd with the Devill, Yet Was Still Savd by God and Returned to the People of York by the Corageous Mircy of Pastor Moses Vibber, Who Was Then Burned Under Suspicion for Committing Diabolical Acts of Wickedness and Wichcraft.

As Mum used to joke: "One need hardly read the book."

Neighboring *Dorcas Hobbs* was Mary's 1986–87 Semmering Academy yearbook, also vaguely splattered with grief tea. She wiped the spine and flipped through the foamy hair and atomized acne, the page after page after page of grinning girls in Fair Isle sweaters and easily decoded references to lost virginities ("D, platform tennis shack, 12/3/84"). There was no encrypted text under Mary's photo—for in fact there was no photo, just a uniform gray rectangle (IMAGE UNAVAILABLE) rising like a dead tooth between the countenances of Polly Vansykle and French exchange student Rosa Villeneuve. Mary hadn't attended school her senior year, she had missed the photo session and the deadlines for copy submission, she had ignored the pleas from yearbook editor Pansy Bittman who sent notes home with Gaby that grew increasingly threatening (Pansy took her job very, very seriously), and so it was partially to spite Pansy and her idiotic sense of self-importance that Mary refused to submit any copy. Beneath her gray rectangle, thus, was a listing of her meager Semmering accomplishments, compiled by one of Pansy's lower-school minions:

Field Hockey I & II (JV). Tennis I, II (JV). Local History Book Club II.

But what about junior and senior year? The observant person might ask. What did Mary "Mimsy" Veal do with herself? The observant person might think: *Something happened to her.* For that observant person, Mary had hidden three meticulously excised newspaper headlines in the back of her yearbook. LOCAL GIRL ABDUCTED AT FIELD HOCKEY MATCH. SEMMERING JUNIOR DISAPPEARS FROM FIELD HOUSE. NO LEADS ON VANISHED TEEN. She hadn't saved the articles, nor the dates that would have indicated these headlines were exactly fourteen years old. Let the observant person who finds this yearbook in a thrift store in seventy years wonder and deduce. Let them scrutinize the airbrushed expressions and speculate which smile disguised a slightly more sinister past, which girl was hiding more than a clove-cigarette habit or a penchant for stealing birth control pills from her friend's mother's bedside table drawer. Let them glide past the gray tombstone above her name (IMAGE UNAVAILABLE), more fascinated by the potential darkness obscured behind the happy faces that were available for scrutiny.

Mary returned the yearbook to the bookshelf. Instinctively, she began the methodical search for the book she'd searched for countless failed times, the book that, according to Maxie, had ruined her mother's life. Appropriately, her signed copy of *Miriam: The Disappearance of a New England Girl*, by Dr. E. Karl Hammer (*for "Miriam"* it said), had become, somewhere between college and her first three post-college apartments, unfindable. Still she'd managed to convince herself each time she slept in her bedroom that she'd simply overlooked it last Christmas, last summer. She felt the familiar disappointment rising as she ticked off each book spine with her eyes, head cocked to the left, the possibilities dwindling with each tick until she'd reached the end of the shelf.

The book, as usual, was gone.

Of course it was. Though she had no proof to support this conviction, she knew her mother had taken the book, an act of theft that Mary had clung to over the years as a sign of her mother's continuing if ambivalent affection for her. In truth, she realized, she'd looked for the book each time she visited home, not to find it, but to make certain it was still missing. And yet today its absence registered not as promising, but as devastating and permanent. On previous days her mother had been alive and angry and so it remained possible that, being both alive and angry, she could still forgive Mary—never directly, this was not the Veal family way, but through the simple reappearance of a long-vanished book.

Mary retrieved her overturned mug from the carpet, resting it on her lap. The mug pressed against her robe; she heard the crinkle of paper in the pocket. Despite herself she thought: *It's from her.* Her mother had left her a note in her robe before she died—of course she had—knowing that Mary would find it when she returned home for the funeral. Mary withdrew the note, heart thumping.

We are so sorry for you!!

Mary regarded the note wryly, pulse winding down to normal then past normal and dipping toward leathery fatigue, the dull beat of a girl whose dead mother has no intention of communicating with her from the beyond. She smoothed the flowered stationery, folded it in two, pressed it between the end pages of her yearbook alongside the headlines. It seemed the perfect, self-mocking addition.

Notes

My first session with Mary Veal took place on an overcast Tuesday afternoon. Mary had been referred to me by my suite mate Rosemary Biedelman, who had received the case from our mutual colleague Dr. Antoine Hicks-Flevill, chief psychiatrist at Mass General. I considered the fact that I'd inherited such a high-profile case an extremely lucky turn, not to mention a vote of professional confidence. Given my troubled record with teenage female patients, Roz was, as she didn't need to state as she handed me the file, *giving me a second chance*. No one in the city of Boston, in other words, less deserved this patient than I did, and yet Roz believed that my familiarity with her personality type, even if this familiarity was defined by failure, made me a natural, if counterintuitive, choice. Which is not to say that Roz was doing me a selfless good turn. Roz worked part-time as a mental health adviser at the prep school attended by the patient; she had complained to me more than once that she had had *quite enough of overprivileged non-traumas.* So we were doing each other a favor, Roz and I, with the debt weighing a bit more heavily on my side. It was an ongoing inequity to which I was accustomed.

In addition to basic biographical data and the summary notes made by H-F, Mary Veal's file included twenty pages of Xeroxed newspaper articles from the previous fall that factually recounted what had become, in and around Boston, the stuff of local legend. Before she became a local legend, however, Mary was a sixteen-year-old junior at Semmering Academy, a private girls school with an enrollment of two hundred students located in a wealthy Boston suburb. Described by peers and teachers as an emotionally reserved girl, Mary was frequently overshadowed by her two sisters, Regina and Gabrielle. Regina, a fledgling poet, possessed a dramatic and demanding temperament, could count few schoolmates among her friends, but nurtured intimate relationships with her female teachers. Gabrielle, Semmering's prized athlete in three sports, was a remotely charismatic girl and nearly expelled three times: twice for cheating, once for smoking marijuana on school property. Mary, by contrast, achieved average marks in all her classes; she had never posed a disciplinary problem; she had shown, according to her headmistress, "neither prowess nor passion." Until she disappeared, few of the teachers and students at her school even knew who she was.

The day Mary disappeared—November 7, 1985—was a perfect day to go missing. Her sister Gabrielle was checked into a hospital room at Mass General, recovering from a scheduled wisdom tooth extraction. Her sister Regina was in Portsmouth, New Hampshire, attending the annual meeting of the New England Prep School Scholastic Press Association. Her parents, Clyde and Paula, spent the afternoon at Mass General visiting Gabrielle before driving to a birthday party for Paula's sister in nearby Hulls Cove. They returned from the party after midnight; according to Clyde, the kitchen was a mess of dishes and crumbs, leading him and his wife to comfortably assume that both Regina and Mary had returned safely home. They went to bed without checking on either daughter.

The following morning, Clyde left the house at 6 a.m. for his Friday squash match at the public recreation center before driving two towns west to his job as a guidance counselor at St. Hugh's Academy. Paula laid out a cold breakfast for the girls and returned to bed with a headache. Regina awoke at her usual time (6:15), showered, dressed, and ate her breakfast alone, assuming that Mary had overslept. The girls were scheduled to be picked up that morning and driven to school by a neighboring girl's mother at 7:15.

At 7:10, Regina knocked on Mary's door.

It was later estimated that Mary was missing from approximately 3:35 p.m. on November 7, 1985, until 4:07 p.m. on December 31, 1985, when she was discovered by a student sitting in one of the rain shelters that line the Semmering sports fields. During that time, the only trace of Mary was to be found in the local newspapers, which ran her photo almost daily, or on the fliers that featured this same image—a foggily enlarged corner of her sophomore yearbook history club photograph—stapled around telephone poles. Under the photograph and the contact information, a single haunting word: GONE.

The girl who eventually materialized in my waiting room no longer resembled this grainy sophomore history club photo. Her face was thinner, her manner even more detached than her blurry history club photograph suggested. Mary was neither pretty nor not pretty; she was the sort of girl who had, as her file suggested, disappeared many times without her needing to go anywhere.

I invited Mary to enter my office. Aside from her hospital room sessions with H-F, Mary had never seen a psychiatrist or any other kind of mental health professional. Subsequently, she did not know where to sit. After a brief hesitation, she sat in my office chair. Not wanting to correct her, I sat on the couch.

According to the notes provided by H-F, Mary claimed to have been abducted by a strange man outside of her school. Because her case so closely resembled the famous case involving former Semmering Academy student Bettina Spencer, H-F was asked by the police to determine whether or not Mary, too, had faked her abduction. H-F was confident, after speaking with Mary ("not up to the mental challenge of such deviousness") in conjunction with the results of her medical exam, that she had not. While the medical exam did not, conclusively, prove that Mary had been raped by her abductor, it did conclusively prove that she was not a virgin. It remained possible, however, that she had been raped seven weeks earlier, at the initial point of her abduction, and that conclusive evidence of the crime had subsequently healed. The question of force, should it ever be settled, would have to be settled by the patient herself.

We began with a benign series of questions: How old are you. How many siblings do you have. What are their names. Where do you live.

Mary answered my questions neutrally. Her name was Mary. She had two siblings, Regina and Gabrielle.

Where, I asked, were you from November 7 until December 31.

I don't know, she said.

Do you remember whom you were with, I said.

She shook her head.

Pretend your skull is a dark closet, I said. Open the door. What do you see.

I see flashes of light? she said.

Flashes of light, I said. As from a fire.

No, she said. The flashes feel cold.

Her hand, formerly resting on her kneecap, clasped her neck, just below the chin.

Did these flashes cause you pain.

The flashes were hard, she said. There was a blunt side and a sharp side.

It sounds like you're describing a knife, I said.

She shook her head.

But it was hard and sharp, I said.

She didn't respond.

A saw, I said.

No response.

An ax, I said.

Her eyes skittered toward the window.

What is the ax called that Indians use to scalp people?

A tomahawk, I said, thinking that this was a peculiarly local variant on the usual subconscious symbols employed to represent male genitalia—sticks, umbrellas, poles, trees. Guns, pistols, revolvers, lances. Zeppelins. Hats.

But it was made of gold, she said. It was waving around and around. Through the air over my head.

Mary stood from my desk chair and whirled her arms back and forth. Her movements were languid rather than choppy, graceful rather than violent.

Like that, she said, sitting down again.

I might have been scared if I were you.

It was pretty, she said.

But he threatened to "cut" you, I said.

Who is he? she asked.

The man with the "tomahawk."

Nobody held it, she said. It moved on its own.

Mary attempted to clear her throat, failed, lapsed into a coughing fit. I waited for her to ask for a glass of water. She did not ask.

She blotted her mouth with her sweater cuff.

Help me understand something, I said. You cannot remember what happened to you because of the tomahawk. Would you agree that that is an accurate statement.

Yes, she croaked.

And yet, I said, there is something missing from this statement. What is missing?

The blood? Mary said.

Was there blood, I said, writing on my notepad *probable virgin prior to her abduction.*

No, she said.

Can you explain to me a possible connection between the tomahawk and your loss of memory?

Drugs? said Mary.

You were forced to take drugs, I said.

No, she said.

I wrote on my notepad *possible drug abuse.*

I don't know what the connection is, she said. Do you know what the connection is?

I don't "know" any more than you know, I said.

So why are you being paid? she said.

I'm being paid to locate possibilities, I said. The *possible* connection between the tomahawk and your loss of memory is that you knew you'd be "hurt" if you told anyone what happened to you. This warning has mutated into a form of amnesia. You can no longer "remember" because to remember could cause you pain.

Mary was overcome by a second coughing fit. I fetched her a paper cup of water from the waiting-room bubbler. She drank it furtively, taking tiny sips.

They told me if I stayed quiet there was nothing to be scared about.

Who is they? I asked.

Mary couldn't say. She did, however, recall that these voices weren't speaking English, in fact they didn't employ language at all, only sounds. Moaning. As if the people who belonged to the voices were in pain.

I paused to take more notes, and to give Mary a chance to recompose herself. During this series of questions, she'd become exaggeratedly animated even while her eyes remained glassy and remote.

I decided to return to the mundane. Where was her mother born. Where was her father born. What did her father do for a living.

Don't you want to hear more about the voices? Mary asked.

Do you have more you want to tell me about the voices, I said.

She withdrew from her coat pocket a makeup compact; she opened it to check her face. Not in a vain way. This action felt cursory, a matter of hygiene, a tick that appeared inherited, possibly from her mother. She dropped the hand holding the open compact into her lap. She stuck an index finger into the compact, swirling the tip over the mirror surface in an obsessive if distracted manner.

They sounded like . . . it's embarrassing, she said. She swirled her finger more furiously inside the compact.

Give me three words that describe the voices, I said.

Pained, she said. Happy, she said. Regretful, she said.

The voices sounded like two people having sex, I said.

Sort of, she said. Except louder.

The voices sounded like many people having sex, I said.

She stared at the carpet.

Yes, she said. It made me feel . . . sleepy.

Not ashamed, I said. Not scared.

They promised if I watched the tomahawk, I wouldn't feel scared. They said I would start to feel tired. That I would forget everything and become another person.

Did you become another person, I said.

I had another name, she said. My name was Ida.

Ida, I said. I wrote this name in large letters in my notebook. I rearranged the letters into *DIA, ADI, IAD, AID.*

Who gave you this name, I said.

I don't remember. I was told that Mary wasn't my real name. My real name was Ida.

I thought these people didn't speak English.

They didn't, Mary said. But after I fell asleep and woke up again, I could understand them.

I paused. Ever since the topic of sex had arisen, she'd continued to prod the interior of her compact with her finger. Should I point this out? Should I point out that "talking" to these people, speaking their language and understanding them, was tantamount to admitting she'd participated in an orgiastic manner with them? Or should I continue to permit her to inhabit her parallel universe and see what other suggestive similes emerged? "Give me a place to stand and I will move the earth," said Archimedes. Even if that place is an illusion, and that world a brilliant hoax the mind has flung upon itself.

If we are to accept your story on a literal level, I said, which I'm not necessarily suggesting we do, there is one obvious interpretation.

I was put under a spell? she said.

In a manner of speaking, I said. You were hypnotized.

Mary stared again at the carpet.

Have you ever been hypnotized before, I said.

Mary had not.

Hypnosis is something I regularly do with my patients, I said, when they believe they lack a memory that is simply hidden in a forgotten place. However, some people use hypnosis for less therapeutic reasons. They use it to brainwash people into forgetting the bad things that happened to them.

That could be a good thing, Mary said.

It could be, I said. But a shortcut to happiness is never synonymous with happiness.

Don't worry, she said. I'm not happy.

That's why you're here, I said. We're going to try to help you remember what happened to you.

She shook her head.

That won't be possible, she said.

Maybe not, I said. But it won't hurt for us try.

But I'm telling you we won't succeed. It's impossible.

Why is it impossible? I said.

Because of the spell.

You mean the hypnosis.

I mean the *spell*.

How did you know it was a spell? I asked. I recalled a biographical detail from Mary's file: her mother, a member of her local historical society, discovered that her family was distantly related to an accused witch who'd been hung and never pardoned by the state of Massachusetts. This relative had become an obsession for the mother; it had even been suggested by H-F's notes that the shame the mother felt toward this relative was ignited by the subconscious cultural perception that accused witches were, in fact, women of wild sexual proclivities.

I wrote on my pad *sexual shame is equated with witchcraft*.

What are you writing? Mary asked.

Notes, I said.

Notes about me, she said.

It will be my habit to make notes during our sessions, I explained. Later, with the help of the audiotape, I will draft these notes into a more fleshed-out composition. This activity will help me gain a multipoint perspective on your case.

Are you writing a novel about us? she said.

If I'm writing a novel about us, that would imply that you're a fictional character, I said.

It would also imply that you're a fictional character, she said.

Let's return to this "spell," I said.

She picked at her sweater cuff.

You seem irritated with me, I said.

Only because you're too busy writing to listen, she said, before succumbing to yet another coughing fit.

I thought I was listening, I said. What have you told me that I didn't hear?

Instead of listening to what really happened to me, you're trying to explain it away, she said. Her voice was hoarse.

It's like you don't believe me, she said.

Do you believe you? I asked.

That's a stupid question, she said.

Why is it a stupid question?

That's also a stupid question.

OK, I said. What's an example of a non-stupid question?

Mary didn't respond.

Let me put it this way, I said. What question would you most like to be asked?

She stared blankly at the carpet.

Mary? I said.

My end-of-session alarm beeped.

Mary closed her compact and returned it to her coat pocket. She rose from my desk chair and pulled on her gloves. I followed her to the door, opened it, waited for her to pass through into the waiting room. She paused at the threshold.

I would like to be asked if I enjoyed myself, she said.

What Might Have Happened

The man was a decent man. The girl could tell by the way he cautiously steered his Mercedes through the rainy streets of her town, as though she were endangered and required safeguarding against harm. He paused at a green light to allow a pedestrian, huddled under a tartan umbrella on the curb, to cross. He didn't speak to her except to ask directions.

Left here, the girl said. Now a right. Another right.

The man stopped across the street from a white colonial, its shutters appearing black in the rain. A station wagon was parked in the cobbled drive, the lawn neatly raked of leaves.

His car idled, the wipers tick-tocking across the windshield in which, the girl noticed, there was a very small starburst crack at eye level. When cars passed them in the opposite direction, their headlights struck the crack and it seemed to her that the intense brilliance alone might shatter the glass.

You have a crack in your windshield, the girl said, pressing a forefinger to it.

I know, he said. Apparently I've been meaning to fix it.

The girl inspected her house, looking for signs of people. With the exception the front-door light, which her father had put on a timer, the house was dark.

I had good intentions to fix it, the man said.

Another car passed them. The man's forehead gleamed sweaty in the headlights.

But I forgot to do it, the man said. I plumb forgot.

The girl saw, or thought she saw, a figure walking through her kitchen.

I plumb forgot, he repeated.

You forgot, she said distractedly. She was wondering if her sister was home, and if so, if she'd noted the car parked across from the house.

Yes yes it's embarrassing, he said.

Why is it embarrassing? she asked.

Excuse me?

Why is it embarrassing? Do you have amnesia or something? the girl said.

The man rotated the cartilege of his nose rapidly with the pad of his little finger.

Hello? I asked you if you had amnesia. Or have you already forgotten, she joked.

He cleared his throat and pulled a cigarette case from the inside pocket of his trench coat. The case was silver, it was tarnished, it was collapsed in the center and vaguely boat-shaped, as though it had been stomped upon.

Mint? he said, offering her the case. In the light of a passing car, she could see it was monogrammed with the single letter *K*.

She accepted a mint. It smelled of tobacco.

You don't smoke, the girl observed. Or did you used to? I mean before you got amnesia?

Smoking almost killed me, the man said.

You had lung cancer, the girl said.

Yes, the man said. I mean no.

You poor man, the girl said. Who are you?

The man stared through the windshield. From the side his naturally bulging eyes appeared fishlike, stupid.

I was trying to light a cigarette while crossing the street, he said slowly. It was a windy day.

Because it was windy, smoking almost killed you?

Because it was windy, I had my head down, I was cupping the match with my hands. I didn't see the car. So, yes. Because it was windy, smoking almost killed me.

How awful, the girl said.

Yes, the man said distantly. I suppose it was awful.

You don't remember the accident? the girl said.

I don't, he said. Apparently I'm not the same man I was.

According to whom?

According to whom. My grammarian ex-wife would be very impressed, the man said. According to the doctors. According to my ex-wife, who was my ex-wife before the accident. She claims I used to be taciturn and self-defeating, I used to be a trial lawyer who lacked animation, I used to be an uninspired dinner-party guest. I used to be a heavy sleeper. I used to detest shrimp.

Wow, the girl said. Do you miss yourself?

The man laughed bitterly.

It's hard to miss a man who married a woman I cannot imagine anyone finding attractive, he said.

The rain increased its intensity. The girl watched as a van pulled into her driveway; her older sister emerged from the passenger side, her school blazer pup-tented over her head. She ran for the side door and fumbled beneath an empty clay planter for the house key.

Her sister vanished inside the house.

It's getting late, the man said.

The girl reached down to grab her backpack, then remembered she'd left it in her locker.

I wonder, said the girl, if not knowing who you are—I mean, were—feels exciting or frightening.

Must it be one or the other? the man asked.

But you could be anybody now, the girl said. You might be a champion chess player or a famous artist. You might be a criminal.

The man gripped the steering wheel with his gloved hands. He wore black gloves, the sort of gloves, shiny and tight-fitting, that TV stranglers wear.

Exciting and frightening, the man said. Both, I'd say.

I'm hungry, the girl said. You?

The man didn't respond.

I'm in the mood for shrimp, the girl said.

One by one all the windows of her house ignited. Her sister was a nervous person, terrified of robbers, kidnappers, all-purpose intruders. She had yet to realize that the way to surmount your fears was to stalk them and invite them to dinner.

The man didn't say yes, he didn't say no. He put the car in drive and pulled away from the curb just as the girl's sister appeared in the living-room window, her body a silhouette framed by the curtains.

The man had a good sense of direction, or at least his new self did; he didn't ask the girl *left here?* or *right?* The rain had submerged the roads and driving the Mercedes appeared to be like steering an unwieldy scow; each slight turn of the man's wrist resulted in a delayed, and disproportionately large, directional shift. He slalomed out of the girl's neighborhood, a canopied tangle of poorly drained roads lined with very old houses close to the curb and very new houses built to look like very old houses set farther back in the woods. The girl's mother hated these new-old houses, these sentimental facsimiles with their suburban willow trees and their diagonal property sitings and their perfectly round ponds. Her mother volunteered at the historical society and the landmarks commission; she was in charge of maintaining the dignity of dead things.

The man turned south on Harbor Road. It was completely dark now, though only 5:46 p.m., according to the car clock. The girl did not ask *where are we going?* Possibly a restaurant. Possibly his house, where he now kept a freezerful of shrimp at his ready disposal. Possibly to his boat (if he had a boat), where he would offer her a beer and they would sit in the damp cabin and the sex, if they had it, would be the chafing kind that would leave friction burns in places he hadn't even touched her. Possibly to the woods, where he would rape and dismember her and promptly forget he'd even met her, because his short-term memory, too, might be compromised. She allowed these blacker possibilities to slide in and out of her consciousness without paying them any more attention than the blander ones; she did not want to seem nervous or immature to the man, because she knew his willingness to be seduced by her depended upon this.

The road got darker, the houses fewer and farther between. The girl shivered. Her sweatpants and her ski jacket were still damp, and the damp had transferred to her skin, then to the muscle layer beneath. The man, noticing, turned on the heat. The air from the vents smelled of many-times-burned things.

They passed a gas station, a marina sign, a reclining-chair store advertising a fire sale. Commerce began picking up, and the girl relaxed; at least she would be dismembered and raped in a neighborhood. Dying, even in the proximity of clueless strangers, seemed less terrifying than dying alone in the woods. They passed a dry cleaners, a plumbing supply store, the infamous day-care center run by two old women, now jailed and awaiting trial. These old women had been accused of doing unspeakable things involving toddlers and their own wrinkled bodies. They had been accused of riding broomsticks around the room. It was so unbelievable that it was totally and completely believable, at least to some people. But the girl needed only to glimpse the newspaper pictures of the two women—with their iron-colored hair, their drugstore reading glasses, their lumpy bodies in lumpy cardigans, their tiny gold crucifixes—to know there was nothing perverse or witchlike about these old ladies; the only potential crime they'd committed was to live their entire lives in an unimaginative way.

Eventually the man turned into the lot of a diner.

Tick-tock-tick-tock went the wipers.

Do they serve shrimp here? the girl asked.

The man squinted at the diner windows, trying to read the giant menu slanting from the ceiling.

I have no idea, he said. But I hear the food is good.

From whom? the girl said.

From whom, he said. From my ex-wife. According to her, this is where we came on our first date.

The girl tucked her chin into her ski coat collar. Rain splattered noisily on the car hood, the drops widely spaced and as heavy as nickels. The man exited the car, walked to her side, opened her door. He'd forgotten to put on a hat. His hair recoiled boyishly in the wet, encircling the lobes of his ears.

Perhaps we should be introduced, he said, holding out a hand.

OK, said the girl, palm pressed against his strangler's glove. I'm Ida. Who would you like to be?

West Salem

NOVEMBER 9, 1999

Mary awoke at 9 a.m. to the zippery sounds of packing tape and the hollow thumping of cardboard boxes. Downstairs she found Regina picking up cork coasters and ashtrays and other seemingly non-auctionable items that had nonetheless been tagged with green ribbon, huffing to herself *of all the tacky nerve*. Gaby, presumably in the process of sorting through the books on the shelves that flanked the fireplace, had become sidetracked by a paperback entitled *Famous Canadian Shipwrecks*; she'd since given up all pretenses of assisting Regina and was reclining on the sofa, reading. Their father appeared to have respected the well-meaning eviction notice issued to him by his daughters, who wished to spare him the packing ordeal. According to Gaby he gone to the diner for breakfast, after which he had plans to meet a friend at the golf course to spend the day chipping balls around the half-frozen scruff.

Regina emerged from the downstairs bathroom holding a be-ribboned, warped box of Kotex.

"They want an antique box of tampons?" she said.

The kitchen pantry items, Mary discovered as she searched for the jar of instant coffee, were similarly tagged.

Mary wandered back into the living room. Outside, it appeared to be sleeting.

"It's for the time capsule," Gaby called from the couch. Clearly she'd been sorting through her closet and thus, in a fit of nostalgia, had chosen to revisit the bizarrely layered uniform she'd favored during grades seven through twelve—a whale-patterned turtleneck covered by a pink Oxford button-down covered by a green Fair Isle sweater covered by a napless navy chamois shirt. On her feet she wore mukluks furred with an even coating of purply gray closet lint.

"The what?" Regina said.

"The Greene mausoleum got *raided by a vagrant*," Gaby said.

Regina tossed Mary a perplexedly irritated look.

"A *vagrant*," Gaby repeated.

"And the vagrant wants . . . I'm sorry. What does the vagrant want?" Regina said.

"Didn't you read the Semmering Alumnae Bulletin?" Gaby asked.

"It seems not as closely as you did," Regina said.

Gaby scuffled under the couch. She retrieved a newletter, ringleted with mug stains.

"'Miss Pym plans, with the help of the West Salem Historical Society to 'bury the past for the sake of the future,' " she read.

"An apt motto for Miss Pym," Mary said, yawning. She was still emerging from her blunt night of sleep. Her sisters hurt her brain.

"'Miss Pym convinced the Greenes to donate their mausoleum to the sixth graders to use as a receptacle for their yearlong cultural history study. 'Where once was death, there will now be life.' "

"Where once there were dead people, there will now be our trash," Mary said. "Is there any coffee?"

"There's no shortage of grief tea," Gaby said.

Regina glared at Mary.

"So it was *you*," she said accusingly.

"What," Mary said. "What was me."

"*You* told them they could have our tampons," Regina said.

Mary winced; without a few more minutes of awakeness under her belt, she hadn't had a chance to fortify herself against random Regina assaults. Mary didn't bother countering Regina's accusation with the obvious—that, due to her recent exile, she'd had zero involvement with the auction arrangements, or the real estate agent, or the funeral specifics. This defense, while true, would only introduce new areas for venomous critique.

"Sorry," she said. "I forgot you'd probably want them."

Gaby laughed from behind her paperback. Mary, for a quasi-instant, considered that Gaby, even while appearing to be a Regina disciple, might be a neutral party. Gaby had been to visit her in Beaverton last spring, just after Mum was officially diagnosed, and they'd spent the weekend smoking pot and eating the same re-microwaved tureen of chowder. She and Gaby, she'd believed, had a sibling closeness based on the unspoken agreement that they would never be close; this shared understanding of the limits of their relationship made it the easiest relationship Mary shared with anyone in her family.

Regina's eyes flared. Mary could see her teetering between states of increased or decreased or differently aimed rage.

"Well," she sniffed, her ire deflating into morbundity. "It's not like Mum left us anything else."

"Poor you," Gaby chided.

Regina checked her watch and ordered Gaby off the couch. They hurried into rubber boots and two of Mum's wool coats, hanging in the foyer.

"So it would be great if you could clean out Mum's study while we're gone," Regina said, consulting the to-do list on the credenza.

"Where are you going?" Mary asked.

"The auction truck's coming *tomorrow*," Regina said.

"Yes but we're not donating her personal files to the historical society..."

"Do you want to fight me on this?" Regina said. "Or do you want to help?"

It was too fucking early for this.

"Fine," Mary said. "Anything else you need? Should I repaper the hall? Do some stencil touch-ups?"

Regina put a line through an item on the list. She pointed the pencil at Mary.

"I did that while you were sleeping."

"And you're going where?" Mary asked a second time, trying to appear only passingly to care about the answer. But her disinterest masked her growing nervousness. When faced with the prospect she realized: she did not want to be left in the house alone.

"We have an appointment with Mr. Bolt," Regina replied, as though this explained anything.

"Who's Mr. Bolt," Mary said.

"Mr. Bolt? The art appraiser?" Regina feigned impatience. She knew damned well that Mary had no idea about any Mr. Bolt.

A familiar dullness descended over Mary. Though a presumably full-grown adult, she was still able to inhabit, quite instantly and quite viscerally and with quite a hefty dash of self-pity, the childhood terror of being left out of something.

"It's for the tax write-off," Regina said. "I can't stand here and explain it to you. We're late."

"What tax write-off?" said Mary.

Regina glanced toward the conspicuously blank space on the living-room wall where Abigail Lake used to hang.

"You're selling her?" Mary said, dumbfounded.

"We're getting her *appraised*. For the tax write-off."

"But how can we justify a tax write-off if . . ."

Mary noticed Gaby absently tweedling the green ribbon hanging from her coat's buttonhole.

"I've already spoken to Mrs. Bigelow," Regina said. "Abigail Lake *belongs* at the historical society."

"But the painting's only ten years old," Mary said.

"Last I checked, 1989 was still a part of history," Regina said. "At least in the reality I inhabit."

Her sisters departed. Mary returned to the box-strewn living room, nerves ignited. She sat on the couch in her pajamas, trying not to brood over the situation nor further freak herself out, even though the house creaked and rustled around her and she couldn't snuff out the irrational suspicion that she was somehow endangered.

To calm herself she stared at the space on the wall where Abigail Lake had once hung; the previously shaded portion of wall was paler than the wall around it and appeared, in this light, as a fossil-like depression in the plaster. The punted andirons, she noticed, had been stored safely inside the coal hod, which had been tucked inside the fireplace. After twenty-five years of out-of-service drafty space consumption, the fireplace's "working order" had finally been restored last month, its chimney a justifiable household expense only now that Dad was selling the house. Mary would have found this detail touchingly indicative of her family's penchant for parsimony where warmth, both literal and figurative, was concerned; but given the uncomfortably close parallel this act shared with her own last-minute attempts to restore working order, as it were, to her relationship with Mum, she viewed the new fireplace as further rebuke of her family's—of her own—self-defeating ways.

She returned her attention to the blank space on the wall. Poor Abigail Lake, she thought. Yes, she too was *disappointed* that her mother had left her nothing more meaningful than a painting she despised and was furthermore meant to share with her sisters, none of whom lived in the same town. But to take this disappointment out on Abigail Lake—to donate her along with the throw rugs and the andirons—struck Mary in that tender place she reserved for the outsize pity she experienced on behalf of inanimate objects. Easier to be ruined by the sight of a child's abandoned stuffed duck on the sidewalk. Easier to be ruined by the rejection suffered by a well-intentioned if misguided birthday gift—an ugly purple scarf. Easier to be ruined by "the pain" experienced by an ugly and unwanted purple scarf than the death, say, of one's own mother.

Returning to the foyer, Mary checked the to-do list on the credenza. Second on the list, beneath "M's Closet," was "M's Desk." An arrow traversed the paper and pointed to three keys on a ring with a masking-tape tag (KEYS TO DESK) resting on the credenza.

Looking at the keys, her immediate conviction was that she would find *Miriam* in one of her mother's desk drawers. Now, she realized, she just wanted to find the book, regardless of whether or not her mother meant her to find it. Then again (her un-caffeinated brain spun fuzzily), maybe her mother meant her to find it without consciously meaning her to find it. Meaning: Mary, when she'd packed up her belongings to move to Oregon for college, had neglected to take the book as an unconscious way to communicate to her mother—though she'd be hard-pressed to designate what, exactly, she'd been trying to say. One could argue that she had abandoned the book as a signal to her mother that she did not cherish nor self-centeredly fetishize her disappearance and its aftermath; she was, in fact, deeply ashamed of it, and wished to separate herself from it by inserting the span of a continent. But in that case, why not destroy the book? One could *thus* argue that her leaving it behind was an unconsciously aggressive maneuver and not an innocent, if misguided, mea culpa; that she could move across the country and symbolically leave behind her past for her mother to caretake was irresponsible and immature and even a little cruel. As was the possibility that she'd left the book behind as bait. Had she? Had she left it behind to test if her mother would take it?

Mary took the keys upstairs and unlocked the desk drawers, quickly surmising there were no books to be found, only sheets and sheets of disorganized paper. She diverted her disappointment through work, subdividing the drawer contents into five piles on the guest bed: PHOTOS, HISTORICAL SOCIETY, ABIGAIL LAKE, MISC. CORRESPONDENCE, MISC. JUNK. HISTORICAL SOCIETY became a jumble of press releases, meeting minutes, fund-raising pitches, unused letterhead. ABIGAIL LAKE included the sheaves of template responses Mum had received from governors and senators and local historians. *We are sorry but at this juncture,* they commenced, never ones to beat around the bush, those governors and senators and local historians. *We sympathize with your situation, however.* Many times Mary had found herself fascinated, but also perplexed, by Mum's obsession with clearing the name of poor long-dead Abigail Lake. For whose sake is this energy being expended, she had often wondered. For whose sake is this forgiveness being so single-mindedly sought.

MISC. CORRESPONDENCE was limited to European cathedral postcards from Maxie or Susan. MISC. JUNK included grocery receipts, a few dry cleaning tickets, fabric swatches and paint chips left over from the redecorating project Mum embarked upon after her daughters had left for college. PHOTOS became a repetitive pile of women in straw hats (summer) or loden coats (fall) stacked in neat unsmiling rows. Mum's left-leaning cursive identified the back of each photo. "Annual Beekman Plaza Luncheon," "West Salem Cemetery Restoration Committee," "Dibble Library Fund-raiser." After Abigail Lake, the Dibble Library was Mum's second-most-consuming pet project. Mrs. Dibble, a polio victim and fanatical collector of witch trial memorabilia, agreed to donate her collection to the historical society so long as it remained in her actual library, a miniature version of her larger stone house right down to the octagonal turret. The library had been moved from the Dibble Estate in

Hulls Cove to the grounds of the West Salem Historical Society in 1981. A giant portrait of a younger Mrs. Dibble hung in the Dibble Library foyer, her thin form flanked by a pair of coal-black Scotties, her leg braces hidden beneath a skirt. In the reading nook hung a second portrait, of a red-haired girl leaning on a decorative musket. Mum liked to tell potential donors that the Dibble daughter, at twenty, had hung herself from the library's chandelier while her parents were vacationing in Acapulco. Whether this was true or not, Mary never learned. But her mother claimed that the average donation to the library tripled after the donor had been told, in whispered tones, about the daughter's suicide.

Mary broke for a cup of grief tea, then returned to tackle her mother's filing cabinet. Bills, more letterhead, tax returns, a family tree that traced the Veal family back to Abigail Lake and very few other notables save a Nantucket whaling captain named Alonzo Veal. Alonzo Veal was the reason her mother had stipulated in her will that the family should go on a whale-watching trip on her next birthday, her sixtieth, and scatter her ashes at the first sight of a whale. Given her mother's practical allergies against powerboats and earnest poetic gestures, this request struck Mary as more than a bit peculiar; and again, while in the esteemed mahogany chambers of Harold "Buzz" Stanworth as he read droningly through the will's subsections, she had to remind herself how little she knew her mother anymore.

Mary shut the top two drawers and tried to shut the bottom drawer, but the bottom drawer would not shut. She jiggled the drawer, she semi-carelessly back-and-forthed it. From the muffled thunking noises this produced, she brilliantly concluded: something had slipped behind the drawer after she'd unlocked it. She muscled the drawer out of its slot and reached into the newly revealed space.

The object was palm-sized and made of metal, smooth save for the spidery-webbed engraving she could feel with her fingertip.

She knew what it was without having to look at it.

She placed the cigarette case—taped around its middle to a large manila envelope labeled decorator's estimates—on the floor by her feet, stupidly fearful of holding it. Though the case, like the book, had disappeared years ago, she'd always assumed that she'd simply misplaced it. She'd been careless with it, leaving it on her desk, stashing it in the odd drawer; she'd wanted it to go away, and was pleased to discover one day that it had. So she was surprised, and fairly unnerved, to discover her mother had been the thief.

Mary turned her attention to decorator's estimates. She slid the metal prongs through the gummed hole in the fold and slipped her hand inside, withdrawing a receipt torn from a generic sales slip pad. A rubber stamp had been pressed crookedly into the top: DEN OF ANTIQUITIES, it read, and beneath that, in black ballpoint:

engraved cigarette case $13 + .65 tax TOTAL $13.65

Mary stared at the receipt, uncomprehending. Stranger still was this: the receipt had been written by her mother. No doubt about it, the handwriting was her mother's.

Which made no sense at all.

Mary set the case and the receipt aside to examine the remaining items inside decorator's estimates. She pulled out a typewritten document, sawdusted with yellowed white-out.

Ida and the Arsonist, by Mary Veal
Ms. Wilkes, Period 2 English

10/01/85

Ida lived on a very dull block in a very dull town during a very dull time. On the dullest of dull days, she noticed a man hiding behind a tree in the neighbor's yard. She saw the man again hiding behind the gates of her school. One day she was late coming home. When she turned onto her street she saw that her house was on fire. The fireman told her that everyone inside the house was dead, including herself. The neighbors didn't recognize her. She said "I'm Ida!" and they told her not to play games with the dead. Then she saw the man in the crowd, flicking a lighter. Ida ran. She ran through the cemetery and across the golf course to the highway and caught a ride north with a bearded man in a truck. They drove into the mountains. They stopped for gas. The bearded man said "Stay here," but Ida followed him to the pay phone. She heard him say into the phone, "I've got her." Ida grabbed her knapsack and escaped into the woods. Pausing for breath on a rock, she heard the sound of a lighter behind her. Snap snap snap. Soon the leaves were ablaze. Ida ran until she was too tired to run anymore. She lay down to sleep, waiting to be burned alive. She awoke wet. It had rained. Around her, the trees sizzled. The man with the lighter sat on a charred stump, smoking a cigarette.

Ms. Wilkes, her ninth-grade English teacher, had noted in red felt pen, "Such imagination! but not really the assignment" in the margin, and given Mary a B.

Mary put "Ida and the Arsonist" in MISC. JUNK; it did nothing to help explain the receipt, and was embarrassing besides, a bit of self-satisfied youthfulness best relegated to the dung heap. She turned ~~decorator's estimates~~ upside down. Two envelopes dropped out, each embossed with a Semmering Academy shield, one perceptibly older than the other. She withdrew the letter from the older envelope first, noting the typed name below the signature. *Ms. Nadia Wilkes.* Ms. Wilkes, as academy protocol dictated, had written to Mary's mother on October 23, 1985, to inform her that Mary was currently failing fall semester English due to the following two reasons: 1) Mary refused to complete assignments properly (see as evidence Mary's enclosed "critical response" to Freud's *Dora: An Analysis of a Case of Hysteria*); 2) Mary had missed all but one of her deadlines for her fall English project, a letter-writing crusade "enacted on behalf of an unjustly accused or mistreated woman."

The wronged-woman project, Ms. Wilkes wrote, was Semmering Academy's most enduring rite of academic passage. Just last year a student's letter-writing campaign on behalf of a wrongly imprisoned babysitter had resulted in a reopening of the case. The point, Ms. Wilkes clarified, was not to make the news, the point was to "rescue" somebody with whom the student felt a deep personal connection, the idea being that the student "will discover within herself a wronged woman whom she herself has the power to exonerate." One African American student had chosen a slave girl from Georgia and written letters to the local elementary school, urging them to start a commemorative day in the slave girl's name; a girl whose father died before she was born wrote letters to Jason and his father, King Aeson, explaining Medea's actions and begging for a greater cultural understanding of the pressures endured by single mothers; some students had chosen, as had Mary's sister Regina, a family relative such as Abigail Lake, a woman accused of witchcraft and hanged.

Mary, however, had made a mockery of the assignment. She had chosen as her wronged woman Dora, Freud's famous patient. This was fine with Ms. Wilkes. What wasn't fine with Ms. Wilkes was that Mary, when asked to give an oral presentation on her subject, gave her oral presentation not on Dora but on Bettina Spencer (Semmering '74), a disturbed former student who had faked her disappearance, testified in court that she'd been abducted and sexually abused by Semmering's then field hockey coach, and burned down the Semmering Founder's Library. Ms. Wilkes, worried that Dora had mutated into a fraught topic for Mary, reassigned her to Charlotte Perkins Gilman. But Mary had failed to write her essay describing her personal attachment to Gilman. She had failed to submit her letter-writing campaign strategy, and the result she hoped her campaign would achieve. The project, due November 7, in two weeks' time, constituted 75 percent of her fall term grade.

"Unless unforeseen circumstances arise," Ms. Wilkes concluded, "I am afraid that I will have to give Mary a failing grade for junior fall English."

Mary folded the letter and returned it to its envelope. She couldn't

help but mildly gloat that Ms. Wilkes had been forced, due to "unforeseen circumstances," to give her an incomplete.

She withdrew the second, visibly newer letter postmarked four
months ago, the address written in someone's nearly illegible hand.

I've found something that might be of interest to you.

Skuz Bod

Mary coughed. Gently at first, then more desperately. Her throat felt
carpeted in a tickly fur, impossible to dislodge no matter how many times
she hacked into her hand.

She folded the letter, she returned it to the envelope, she placed it
atop MISC. JUNK. *This*, she thought *this is no road to pursue.* Her brain
whirred faster. She thought: *What's done was done.* She thought: *Where there
once were dead people there is now a future filled with our trashy past.* She thought:
What does the vagrant want? What does the vagrant want?

Outside, the sleet quieted down to nothing as it thickened into snow.
Outside, it was as dark as evening.

To Mary's knowledge her mother hadn't seen Roz Biedelman since
the one and only time the two had met, in April of 1987, some
three months after the publication of *Miriam*. Mary recalled with visceral
precision the dread she'd felt as through the window she watched Roz
struggling to free her canvas tote bag from the backseat of her Volvo.
Wearing an ankle-length kilim coat that lent her the hulking appearance
of a Mongol raider, Roz had led the way up the Veals' sidewalk that driz-
zly April morning followed by a skinny woman who wielded her umbrella
like a panicky lepidopterist with her net. Dr. Flood, an obvious anorexic,
was the third office member in Dr. Hammer and Roz's brownstone suite.

If Dr. Flood represented anything to Mary before this day, it was this: her anorexia had given Mary something mockable to offer her mother when she returned from her appointments with Dr. Hammer, and they had used the woman's evident misery as a bonding opportunity during a time when the two of them were otherwise lacking in bonding opportunities. Until Mary was face-to-face with this extracurricular version of Dr. Flood, skittishly trailing Roz Biedelman up Mary's own bricked walk, she had never seen any reason to find her behavior regrettable.

Her mother, cheeks and neck still greasy with unabsorbed face cream, greeted Roz and Dr. Flood at the door with the high, cheerful tones she reserved for the unwanted. She took their coats and ushered them into the living room and asked if anyone wanted coffee. Dr. Flood rescinded into the crook of the couch wordlessly while Roz pulled files from her tote bag and arranged them in a semicircular flare on the carpet. Her mother returned with coffee and some slabs of week-old coffee cake, leftovers from a historical society brunch she'd hosted.

Mary tried to catch her mother's eye numerous times. Her mother refused to look at her.

"So," Mum said. Just that: *so*.

Roz reflexively spooled off her CV: as she'd mentioned on the phone, she was a Harvard-trained psychologist and the author of the highly acclaimed book, *Trampled Ivy*. She volunteered as a mental health adviser at Semmering Academy though she had never treated Mary because Mary had never appeared to need treatment until her case was "beyond the legal purview of in-house counseling." She, Dr. Flood, and Dr. Hammer had, until the recent publication of Dr. Hammer's book *Miriam*, shared an office suite. In addition to being a colleague, she explained, Dr. Flood was also her "patient"; six months ago, Dr. Flood had joined Roz's encounter group, Radcliffe Women Against Needless Domestic Abuse.

"Is domestic abuse ever needful?" Mum inquired.

"Elizabeth and I have decided that we won't keep any secrets here,"

Roz said, gesturing toward Dr. Flood. "I don't want you to feel uncomfortable knowing about Elizabeth's RWANDA involvement, because Elizabeth isn't uncomfortable that you know this about her."

Roz looked to Dr. Flood for confirmation. Dr. Flood feigned transfixion with the fireplace.

"As long as you're not expecting an exchange of like confessions," Mum said. "And by the way," she said, turning to Mary, "you are not to say a word. Understand? Not one word to these people."

Mary nodded.

"I've had enough of their obfuscations," her mother said as much to herself as to anyone. "Quite enough."

"So much of Mary's story has been obfuscated," Roz said. "Which is why we feel it's important to get everything on the table. Or on the carpet, as it were."

Roz gestured toward the file folders.

"*Story*," Mum parroted sarcastically.

"That is the only word to use, I'm afraid," Roz said. "Your daughter's experience has been, to a highly unprofessional degree, fictionalized by Dr. Hammer."

From her bag she pulled a copy of *Miriam* and tossed it, with evident dismissiveness, onto the floor beside the file folders. She didn't need to explain that the book proposed the following: Mary, aka "Miriam," had faked her abduction and had successfully lied to everyone—family, friends, police, therapist, all of whom had believed her, at least until Dr. Hammer discovered the truth: Mary, he claimed, had never been abducted. She'd disappeared, yes, but not because someone had taken her. She had hidden herself away. He had even founded a theory after her called hyper radiance. A very pretty way of saying: she'd lied.

Flabbergasted, her mother searched for words. She stirred her coffee. She lifted the creamer and erased with her napkin the keloid, yellow-white ring that had accumulated beneath it.

"While I certainly appreciate your expert opinion," she replied finally, "every inhabitant of Greater Boston knows that Mary's story is *a story*. I'm relieved to know that it still comes as a newsflash to at least two people. But really, Dr. Biedelman—"

"Call me Roz. I'm not your doctor. I'm not Mary's doctor either."

"—Dr. Biedelman. We're a very tired family, in case you can't tell. We are tired, and we are—we're just tired."

Her mother lit a cigarette. She offered one to Dr. Flood, but not to Roz.

"I understand how tired you must be," Roz said, eyeing the excluding-cigarette exchange with a practiced brightness. Roz had clearly spent her life pretending not to be bothered by the fact that she was, in some globally recognized way, an irritating person.

"I don't see how your capacity to understand my exhaustion is of any relevance whatsoever," Mum said through an exhalation.

Roz rewarded the room with a powerful smile.

"Mrs. Veal," Roz said. "I understand—I do—I *understand* your resistance to traumatize what must feel like a healed wound. But Dr. Flood and myself have come to speak with you today because we think that Dr. Hammer has behaved . . . *ignobly* toward your daughter."

This caught her mother's attention.

"He took liberties," Roz said. "With her story, and for all we know . . . Well, let's not jump to any conclusions, shall we?"

Her mother drew on her cigarette so forcefully that her lips disappeared inside her mouth. Mary found herself the recipient of an unabashedly nasty look. She took a deep breath, intending to defend herself—then remembered her mother's request.

"I imagine you're dying to elaborate," Mum said.

Roz retrieved a file folder.

"I have it documented here in my report to the board," she said, flipping through the contents. "Dr. Hammer behaved in an unprofessional manner. To be specific: I saw Dr. Hammer and your daughter in his office wearing nothing but their underwear."

Her mother closed her eyes and pressed the palm of her hand, the one holding the cigarette, against her forehead. The lit end of the cigarette hovered dangerously near her hair.

Dr. Flood positioned herself on the edge of the couch, hands shaking. Her words shot out of her mouth as an anxious, pent-up jabber.

"Dr. Hammer claims this 'incident' occurred on the day of a big blizzard don't forget about the blizzard Roz."

"So for an hour my daughter sat on a couch with a man while the two of them were wearing underwear," Mum said. "And then he billed me."

"To be totally accurate he was wearing ski pants and Mary was wearing long johns so the word *underwear* is perhaps . . ."

"Regardless of who did what to whom," Roz interrupted, "it is unacceptable to counsel a patient in anything less than professional work attire."

Dr. Flood returned her jittery attention to the fireplace.

"Elizabeth and I agreed that Mary would be more comfortably able to tell us the truth if she knew the stress Elizabeth has lived under," Roz said. "Which is why I've brought her along. Elizabeth was abused by men from all corners. Professionally. Domestically. Much as Mary was abused from all corners. Also like Mary, Elizabeth has spent a lifetime being told by men what to think. Exactly what you hate most, am I right, Mary? Being told what to think? Like Elizabeth, you've never been able to take charge of telling your own story."

"Dr. Hammer helped Mary come to terms with what she'd done," Mum said.

"And what, exactly, Mrs. Veal, did Mary *do*?" Roz asked.

"Read the book, Dr. Biedelman," Mum said acidly.

"Exactly. *According to the book,* Mary was never abducted. *According to the book,* Mary made the whole thing up. But according to Mary, what really happened?"

"She made it up," her mother said.

"But not without some help," Roz said, retrieving a second folder from the carpet. "You should look at this."

Roz opened the folder on the coffee table.

"The highlighted sections are from Dr. Hammer's book. The page numbers in the margins correspond to a very famous book written by Dr. Sigmund Freud called *Dora: An Analysis of a Case of Hysteria*. I imagine you're familiar with this book," she said, turning to Mary.

Mary shrugged.

"In fact, I *know* that you're familiar with this book. I learned from a Mrs."—Roz rummaged through a second folder—"sorry, a *Ms.* Wilkes, that your English class studied *Dora* during the fall of your junior year. A month before you disappeared. Although you told Dr. Hammer during one of your sessions—highlighted there, Mrs. Veal—that you'd never read *Dora*, according to Ms. Wilkes's grade book, you received a B on the essay you wrote. That's a very high grade to receive for an essay on a book you've never read."

Mary glanced at her mother, a newly lit cigarette hanging between her first two fingers, her Pappagallo flats brushing back and forth on the carpet. The pile flashed dark, then silver, dark, then silver.

"We're particularly interested in how so many of the responses Mary supplied to Dr. Hammer's questions bear an uncanny resemblance to Dora's responses to Dr. Freud."

Roz enumerated Mary's offenses. The fact that her captor and presumed abuser was named "K." Her claimed "disinclination" for food. Her claim that her father had attempted to commit suicide in the woods, but was in fact having sex with his mistress who, along with her husband, was a close friend of the family.

"My husband doesn't have a mistress," her mother said.

"Exactly my point," said Roz.

She continued with her list. Mary's coughing fits, and the fact that they were caused by a sensation she likened to a feather tickling the back of her throat. The obsessive swirling of her index finger inside her makeup compact. The fact that she'd read, or claimed to have read, Mantegazza's *Physiology of Love*. Her dream about the burning house and the jewel case. Her response, *J'appelle un chat un chat*. Her later use of a second French term, *pour faire une omelette il faut casser des oeufs*. Her claim that she had decided to cease therapy "a fortnight" before she announced she was quitting. Her purported seduction by the husband of her father's mistress in his office building, in an empty file room with one window. The failure of the family to believe the story of this seduction. The fact that Mary reappeared on December 31, the same day that Dora terminated her treatment with Dr. Freud.

"Most damning, of course, is the fact that Mary claimed, while 'under a spell,' to have been given the name Ida. Dora, of course, was a pseudonym used by Freud. The real name of his patient was Ida Bauer."

Her mother stood. Ash from her cigarette landed on the carpet, on the plaid-upholstered wingback in which she'd been sitting. She claimed she had a headache and needed to lie down.

"Mrs. Veal," Roz said. "How familiar are you with the Dora case?"

"More familiar than I've ever been," Mum said, left thumb pressed into her left temple, eyes winnowed.

"What I mean is—how familiar are you with the critical response to Dora's case?"

"Dr. Biedelman," Mum said, "I actually do have a headache."

"Dora claimed she was molested by an adult male, and Dr. Freud didn't believe her. Why? Because he had his 'theories' to prove. According to him, Dora fantasized about an incident of abuse to express her own long-repressed sexual desire. But recent feminist scholarship suggest Dora was *not* fantasizing—"

"That's lovely," her mother said. "Do you need directions back to the highway?"

"Mrs. Veal," Roz persisted. "Do you think it's a coincidence that your daughter would choose to speak using the words of a girl whose own trauma had been discounted as fantasy by her male doctor?"

Her mother smiled, a sweet, tuned-out smile.

"I appreciate your coming here to inform us, or rather, *me*, that my daughter is not only a liar but a liar without a particularly good imagination. I thank you very much for this enlightening news, and now you both can go." Dr. Flood stood. Mary, hoping this meant the meeting was adjourned, also stood.

Roz remained seated.

"So I don't suppose you'd care to be reminded that we're not just talking about an abuse of narrative," Roz said quietly. "Mary's medical exam revealed the possibility that sexual abuse—"

"Dr. Biedelman," her mother said sharply. "You can go, now."

Nobody moved. Her mother stared at the two invaders to her house, weirdly powerless to rid herself of them.

"And if you refuse to go, then I will."

Her mother left the living room. The hallway stairs creaked irregularly as she made her pained way to her bedroom.

Roz refreshed her own coffee.

Mary checked her watch.

"I understand, Mary, why you'd feel the need to pretend your story was invented. If I had a mother like yours, I'd say anything to put her mind at ease. Please. Sit," Roz said.

Mary sat. Dr. Flood sat, too, but not in any way that indicated commitment. She balanced her pelvis on the couch arm and cast repeated glances toward the staircase.

"I should warn you that there's going to be an investigation into Dr. Hammer's book. He fabricated exchanges so that his own theories about a condition *he* invented—'hyper radiance,' which frankly is just the sexual drive theory and the Oedipus complex repackaged—were supported. He led you to incorrect conclusions. Worse still, he ignored your evident emotional distress. It's clear to many experts who have read his book that he misdiagnosed you, and in doing so is encouraging the misdiagnosis of many more girls like you."

Roz put her elbows on her knees, hunching down so that she was below Mary's eye level.

"You're a resilient girl, Mary. I can tell you have a gift for compartmentalizing, just as many intelligent women do. Take Elizabeth, for example. Elizabeth attended Radcliffe on a full scholarship at the age of sixteen; she triple-majored in psychology, French, and government and maintained a 4.0 average until her very public and very humiliating breakdown. And yet where did she put her childhood—a childhood rife with disturbances—as she succeeded in her daily life, seemingly *undistressed*? Where did she put her alcoholic father, her sexually abusive uncle? Where did she put these men?"

Mary watched as Dr. Flood took a final drag from her cigarette and casually ground the filter into the center of her untouched coffee cake.

"*She put them in a drawer*, Mary, a drawer deep inside her mind. But the drawer wasn't locked, and eventually she stumbled upon this drawer amid the clutter and detritus—maybe she was cleaning house, as people unconsciously do, looking at old memories, making space for new memories—and she forgot what she'd put inside of that drawer. She opened that drawer, that Pandora's box, and the evils of her past came surging out. The result? This brave woman, this brilliant and brave woman, was institutionalized for the better part of a year. This is what happens to women who compartmentalize. Instead of punishing the people who hurt them, they punish themselves. They deprive *themselves* of the full, happy life they deserve. And if you refuse to deal with *it*, Mary, *it* will deal with you. And deal with you and deal with you. Look at Elizabeth. A year in an institution wasn't enough. She had to marry a narcissist, she had to further deprive herself of happiness before she finally, *finally*, shoved her past not into a drawer but out into the world. She has reclaimed her story and signed her name to it. It can't do her any harm now."

Mary checked her watch again.

"But regardless," Roz said, collecting her various folders, "you'll need to prepare yourself. When this investigation gets under way, you're going to need an advocate, Mary."

Roz withdrew a business card from her vest.

"This is my new office. You'll call me, I hope, when you're ready to talk about *it*."

Roz nodded at Dr. Flood. They rose from the couch, pausing in the hallway, while Mary retrieved their coats.

Roz withdrew a book from her bag.

"My little Dora," she said, not without admiration. "I've inscribed it to you."

Finally, they left.

In the kitchen, Mary fetched three aspirin and a glass of water. As painful as she presumed her mother's headaches to be, they were also marvelously convenient. A cocktail party she didn't want to attend? Her headache would arrive just as she was applying her lipstick. A parent conference with the Semmering headmaster to discuss Gaby's pot smoking? Halfway to the car, she'd be seized with pain and return to her bed. A Wellesley alumnae luncheon where, as fund-raising chair, she was supposed to report on the delivery of the Christmas pecans she'd forgotten to order? Before the entrée was cleared, she'd be so afflicted that she'd need to be driven home by a friend.

But sometimes the headaches arrived when her mother was happy or simply flatlining through her days. These headaches were the most unsettling; Mary preferred it when her pain could be linked to a specific cause, like a flu that can be traced to this-or-that person who visited last week. Without cause, her pain felt invisibly contagious, unavoidable. Any one of them could be felled by it, and possibly worse, any one of them could be the cause.

Her parents' bedroom was dark, the only sound the erratic cricking of the baseboard heater. Her mother lay on the bed beneath a mohair throw. Her absolute stillness was proof that she wasn't asleep.

Mary put the mug on the bedside table and left, shutting the bed-room door loudly, to indicate that she knew her mother was faking it.

Downstairs, Mary bused the coffee tray into the kitchen and put the cups in the dishwasher. She left Dr. Flood's plate on the counter, her cig-arette filter protruding, bull's-eye style, from the center of the concentric cinnamon rings. It seemed the cleanest, most uncomplicated way to com-municate to her mother, who refused to let her talk and was feigning sleep and other unconvincing forms of denial: they were all about to get burned.

Notes

FEBRUARY 25, 1986

Mary's second visit occurred on the morning of a blizzard. The first flakes of snow began falling at 7 a.m., and by the time of Mary's appointment, at 10:30 a.m., nearly a foot had accumulated over Boston and its suburbs. Despite the adverse traveling conditions, Mary arrived ten minutes early for her appointment escorted by her father, Clyde. I knew from Mary's file that Clyde was a guidance counselor at the same prep school I attended as a boy. He and I spoke briefly about St. Hugh's newly appointed and radically minded headmaster without either of us belying an opinion about the man. Like many of his generation, Clyde appeared to distrust mental health professionals, or he at least appeared to distrust me; his aloofness made me wonder what rumors he'd heard, Boston being little more than a small town after all and the pair of us doubtless sharing more than a few acquaintances.

I gestured Mary into my office. Again, she sat in my office chair. This time I corrected her, and asked her to move to the couch. She complied.

She said nothing. For ninety seconds, I waited for her to speak. She did not speak.

I brought you some literature on hypnosis, I said to her. I handed her a pile of Xeroxed articles.

She flipped through the pages without comment.

Is there any particular place you'd like to begin today, I said.

She shook her head.

We don't have to talk about you, I said. You can tell me something notable you've observed since we last met.

No response.

Sometimes what a person notices can say a lot about that person, I said.

Mary rumpled her nose. Coughed.

You have bowlegs, she said finally. If I were you, I wouldn't wear tights. It calls attention to them.

These are ski pants, I said. I cross-country skied to the office today.

I wouldn't wear them, she said. Ever again.

Mary pulled harshly on a gold hoop earring, distending the lobe.

They'd be nice legs if they were straight, she persisted. Did you ever wish for that? Did you ever think your whole life would improve if only your legs were straight? My jeans are wet.

She stood and unbuttoned her fly, exposing the elastic waist of her long johns. Wriggling and kicking, she removed her jeans and slung the jeans over the radiator. She walked to the bookshelf—maybe interested in the books, possibly more interested in providing me with an adequate opportunity to examine her lower body. I attributed her exhibitionistic behavior to her relationship with her father; many girls who experience formal and unaffectionate relationships with their fathers—"rigid boundary respecters"—will often look to other paternal figures for a purely sexual validation that, in their minds, compensates for the emotional economizing they experience at home.

Mary withdrew a layman's 1948 book about psychiatry (*You and Psychiatry*, by William C. Menninger and Munro Leaf).

How's your appetite, I asked her.

I have some disinclination for food, she said, opening the book.

Disinclination, I said.

Disinclination, she said. That means I'm not hungry, right?

That's what it means in this context, I said.

Silence.

Are you familiar with Mr. Leaf, I said.

She was not familiar.

He's also the author of *The Story of Ferdinand*. It's a famous children's book about a bull.

That explains why there are a lot of entries under sex, she said. Have you ever read Mantegazza's *Physiology of Love*?

Have you?

K gave it to me, she said. She coughed.

Who is K, I said.

She coughed again.

Can I get you some water?

She shook her head, coughing into her palm.

No, she croaked. I'm fine.

I wrote *K* in my notebook. I underlined it four times.

She pushed her fingers into her Adam's apple, massaging it in small circles.

"Sex, education about," she read from the book's index. "Sex, psychoanalytic meaning of." Sex has a different meaning in psychoanalysis? "Sex, adjustments in marriage."

She raised her eyebrows, flipped to the referenced page, walked slowly back to the couch.

"Successful marriage blah blah . . . Through the ignorance or selfishness of the husband or the shyness of the wife or both, the wife never achieves the satisfaction of a climax to sexual intercourse—an orgasm. Often neither partner knows that she should!"

There really is an exclamation point, she said. I don't want you to think I'm mocking your profession. "Another restraining force is the strong indoctrination of girls in childhood of the attitude that sex is naughty and dirty. Too many wives, intelligent ones, too, believe that sexual relations are part of their 'marital duty'; they must give their husbands satisfaction, even though they feel that it is not 'nice' "—quotes there—"for them to have comparable pleasure."

She closed the book and clutched it vertically between her knees.

Does that seem at all true to you, I said.

Does what seem *at all true.*

Have you been taught that sex is naughty and dirty, I said.

She shrugged. Then: I'm here, aren't I?

Yes, I said. You are here.

Not because I want to be here.

No?

It's my mother's idea, she said.

Not your father's.

My father thinks you're probably more of a mental case than I am. Not you specifically. You as in all of you.

What do you think? I said.

She shrugged. Jury's still out, she said.

I'd like to return to your mother, I said.

Mary confessed to me that her mother was fanatical about virginity. This had been true even before Mary had disappeared. Her sister Regina, she told me, suffered from anemia due to frequent menstruation; it was recommended by a doctor that Regina be put on the birth control pill to modulate her cycle, but her mother had refused, fearing (according to Mary) that her daughter would now feel free to experiment sexually in ways that had formerly seemed too dangerous, given the risk of pregnancy.

How old was Regina, I said.

Mary couldn't remember. Twelve or thirteen, she speculated.

Perhaps your mother was simply unable to admit that her daughter was becoming a woman, I said.

She preferred that Regina stay sick than that Regina should get better, Mary said.

But her resistance could also be viewed as her attempt to protect Regina from the pains of adulthood.

Mary scowled. Just because she's paying you doesn't mean you have to take her side.

I'm trying to suggest there are fuller, oftentimes contradictory dimensions to every family conflict.

I had a dream, Mary said, changing the subject. It was nighttime and I was asleep in my room. I woke up and K was standing over me. "The house is on fire," he said. He rushed me out of bed and wrapped me in a coat. "We have to go and wake your sisters," he said. My sisters were asleep on the first floor, just past the dining room. Then my mother ran into the room and said, "We must save my jewel case!" She didn't seem to mind that the house was on fire. K got really mad at her and said, "I will not risk the lives of my three children so that you can save your stupid jewel case." We all ran outside, and then I woke up.

What do you think this means? I asked her, thinking that she'd settled on a very traditional subconscious symbol for female genitalia, typically represented in dreams by boxes, jars, bottles, coffins. Ships. Snails. Churches. Books.

The jewel case probably refers to my vagina, she said.

That's one interpretation, I said.

Does that embarrass you? she asked. That I said *vagina*?

Does it embarrass you?

J'appelle un chat un chat, she said. And don't you think it's notable that my mother wanted to save the jewel case, but K didn't want to save the jewel case?

Do you think it's notable?

Perhaps because he knew there was nothing left to save, she said.

Metaphorically speaking, then—you think the jewels had been stolen?

You want to know if my jewels have been stolen, she stated.

This is what you've just implied, I said.

But you want to know, don't you? About the jewels?

If you want to tell me, I said.

She stared out the window.

I think some jewels might be missing, she said.

Perhaps you should report this theft to the police. Give them a specific list of what's been taken from you.

But what for? Her eyes receded under her lids; her nose grew even redder. She started to cough.

I offered her a tissue.

Something keeps tickling the back of my throat. It feels like a very long feather. Rubbing at the back of my throat.

How about some water, I offered.

I opened the office door—the bubbler was in the waiting room—and ran into my suite mate, Rosemary Biedelman.

Who was that? Mary asked when I returned. She comes to my school sometimes.

Rosemary Biedelman. She does pro bono counseling with troubled kids at the local schools.

Troubled, Mary said skeptically.

Sometimes trouble isn't so hard to spot, I said.

Those are the least troubled troubled people.

How's the throat? I asked.

Still tickly, she said. She took a sip of water.

Should we talk about what's missing from the jewel case? I asked.

Her brows clenched.

I don't see what the point is, she said. What's gone is gone.

The question is, I said, whether or not what was stolen was never there to begin with.

That sounds like stupid shrink talk to me, she said. So don't you want to know who K is?

My end-of-session alarm sounded.

Yes, I said.

Good, she said, gathering her coat. So do I.

What Might Have Happened

The girl and the man sat opposite each other in a black vinyl booth. The girl ordered the fried shrimp basket. The man ordered a coffee. They didn't have much to say to each other. This made the girl feel more comfortable, more in control.

You're not much of a conversationalist, she said.

Never have been, according to my ex-wife, he said. He picked a creamer out of a small dish of water that used to be a small dish of ice. He held the creamer directly in front of his face as though he'd never before laid eyes on a creamer.

And another thing, he said. I used to be lactose intolerant.

He peeled back the paper top; he dumped the cream into his coffee.

The girl's food arrived. She offered the man some shrimp. He nibbled at one clinically.

I used to go into shock, the man said. My ex-wife told me recently about the time I almost died at her niece's wedding. We were sitting at a table next to a businessman my ex-wife wanted to impress—she's a stock analyst—and there was shrimp in the chicken bisque. Why would there be shrimp in the chicken bisque? My throat closed up and, in my panic, I dumped my bisque in the businessman's lap. Fortunately, there was a doctor at the next table with an EpiPen.

Wow, said the girl.

My ex-wife admitted to me that it was one of those moments in our marriage where she found herself hating me and wishing she were married to somebody else, because her life might have been completely different and in a good way different.

The man paused, took another bite of shrimp.

She tells me a lot of these stories in which she quietly suffered, he said. It's part of some women's therapy group she's involved with. "Reclamation therapy" it's called. She gets to take her story back from me.

You took her story? the girl asked.

Apparently I committed acts of domestic narrative abuse, the man said. Which is more damaging than just beating up a person. Regardless, spending time with me is very cathartic for her.

She wants to be forgiven, the girl said.

No, the man said. She wants recognition. She's never been able to tell anybody about these terrible thoughts of hers, and on a certain level she's proud of herself because it is absolutely not at all the way a Phi Beta Kappa Radcliffe graduate should think. She believes it makes her unique.

Hitler was unique, the girl said.

Are you studying Hitler? the man asked.

We're studying Freud, the girl said.

For a science class?

For English, the girl said. My teacher says that Freud is the greatest novelist of the twentieth century.

Huh, said the man.

I had to write a paper about this girl who was hysterical.

How'd it go? the man asked.

I got a B, the girl said.

That's not so bad, the man said.

A B from this teacher is like a D from any other teacher, the girl said. But I didn't really follow the assignment. I wrote a story instead about a young girl who's being chased by a man who burned her house down and killed her family, including her, or at least that's what everyone thinks. But she's still alive and the man is chasing her.

Sounds like a morbid story for a teenager to write, the man said.

I based it on a book I read as a kid. Or at least I think I read it. I've never been able to find the actual book. Sometimes I wonder if maybe I just made the whole story up myself. I mean, who would write a kid's book about an arsonist who kills a whole family and then tries to kill a little girl?

I read once that a decent percentage of children's book writers in fact hate children, the man said.

I wonder if she knew something, the girl said. Do you think maybe she knew something she didn't know she knew?

The real question is, the man said, pointing a half-eaten shrimp at her, if she has to be reminded that she knows something, does she really know it?

Maybe she blanked it out to save herself, the girl said. She knew if she knew this thing, that someone would try to pry it out of her.

Dessert? the man said, yawning.

Are you tired? the girl asked.

Prohibitively, the man said. I haven't slept for two days. Chronic insomnia.

Really, she said. From the amnesia?

It's a not unusual side effect of head trauma, he said. The brain is too rattled to doze off. A primitive response. Imagine the cave man who wanted to prevent his head from being bashed in by a rival. Insomnia was his friend. This is what I tell myself: insomnia is my friend.

The girl ordered pie, the man a coffee refill and a vanilla malted. By the neon pink clock over the cash register, it was five minutes to nine. Her parents would be home soon. They used to check on the girls, especially in the early days when they first began leaving them home alone without a babysitter. But by a certain age their safety seemed guaranteed. The girl had lain awake at night after her parents had returned home from a dinner party, she'd heard them switching off the downstairs lights and running water in the kitchen. She'd heard them come upstairs and shut their bedroom door without looking into their daughters' rooms. Soon the house would be dark and quiet; soon she could hear the muted snores her father made after he'd been drinking.

The man stirred his malted. The girl collapsed her pie crust with the backside of her spoon.

So what you're saying, the girl said, is that if you have amnesia, you know things you don't know. Or no. The reverse. You don't know things you do know.

I guess so, said the man.

Which could be kind of cool, the girl said. I mean if you're sick of your life and you get hit by a car. You can wake up and be a totally blank person.

True, the man said.

Like the girl in my story whom everybody believed was dead, the girl said. She could decide to be anyone.

But she's being chased by an arsonist, the man reminded her. He knows who she is.

If she escaped the arsonist, the girl said. Let's say she escaped. Let's say she moved to Paris and the arsonist forgot about her.

Memories are shoddy things, even under the best of circumstances, the man said.

Which makes me wonder, the girl said. Can you really trust this ex-wife of yours?

The man shrugged. *Trust,* he said.

I mean, she could be messing with you. I think that would be a lot of fun. To mess with a person's head like that.

How do you mean? the man said.

Maybe you were never allergic to shrimp. Maybe you weren't even a lawyer. Maybe you were something far, far worse.

Worse than a lawyer, the man said, trying to make a joke of her observation. But the girl could see she'd unnerved him.

Maybe she's not even your ex-wife, the girl said. She's just some deceitful nurse.

She showed me pictures of our wedding, the man said. We honeymooned in the Keys.

Still, the girl said, you can't be too trusting. For example, I could tell you something about yourself that you'd probably be tempted to believe.

Such as? the man said.

Such as, we used to be neighbors.

On Beacon Hill? the man asked.

Exactly, the girl said. Before my family moved to the suburbs.

OK, the man said slowly.

We lived in the brownstone across from your brownstone. You and I were fast friends. You took me to movies, you took me to restaurants. My parents didn't care because they were those sorts of parents, and I was a middle child, and they figured the extra attention was good for me. Plus they assumed my regular companionship eased the pain of the fact that your ex-wife couldn't have children.

My ex-wife didn't want children, the man said.

That's what she told you, the girl said. In fact, she was infertile. I overheard her confessing to my mother that she'd had an abortion when she was just out of college and dating around. She was ambitious, your ex-wife; she didn't want to be saddled with a husband and children before she'd had a chance to establish herself in the world of finance. The operation went badly. She probably told you all this before you married her, but you've forgotten. Now she's decided there's little point in divulging personal details to an ex-husband who doesn't remember the marriage anyway.

The man nodded, his face vaguely gray.

So. You and I, we were like a father and a daughter who never fought. I trusted you. Even after everything that happened, I trusted you.

After everything that happened, the man said.

You were ashamed, of course. That's why you burned down our house. Ask your wife if it's true—the family's house across the street burned down. An electrical fire, they determined. But I knew. You knew I knew.

This is obscene, the man said, signaling for the check.

Is it? the girl asked. Then why have you parked across from the cemetery every single school day this semester? Why have you been so interested in me?

You have a good imagination, I'll give you that, the man said, flapping open his billfold. He wedged too much money under his malted glass.

Maybe this isn't imagined, the girl said. Maybe I know something. I know something and you want to know what I know.

The man refused to look at her.

I'm taking you home, he said.

Outside, the rain had abated to a random spattering of drops, shaken loose from the nearby tree branches by the gusting wind. The man started the Mercedes, put the car in drive, then put the car in park again.

A person would remember, he said. A person would remember if he'd done a thing like that.

But you forget, the girl replied. Memories are shoddy things, even under the best of circumstances.

West Salem

NOVEMBER 9, 1999

Despite the house's state of festooned disarray, Mary found the phone book where the phone book had always been, fitted inside a roasting pan in the farthest right-hand kitchen cabinet. *Biedelman, Rosemary* was not listed in the Hulls Cove–West Salem–Massapoisset white pages; nor was she listed in the yellow pages under *psychiatrist, mental health professional, overzealous Freud-hater, feminist rabblerouser,* or *recurring life-disrupting nuisance.* Mary dialed the number for Semmering Academy; the switchboard operator speedily routed her to Roz's personal line.

She hung up before Roz's phone could ring.

Since Regina and Gaby had taken Mum's Peugeot to Boston and Dad had disappeared for the day with his American-generic sedan, Mary's transportation options were limited to feet or bike, neither of which was especially tempting given the weather. But the sleet-rain-snow had stopped; the moisture was in the process of being sucked back up to the sky and the air had warmed and thickened. Mary found three Semmering-era bikes leaning against the far wall of the garage behind a folded card table and a stack of equally old firewood, the remnants of a backyard maple her father had split and stacked in the early '80s on the assumption that their defunct fireplace chimney would soon be restored to working order.

Detangling the bikes from one another was like freeing a single coat hanger from a pile of coat hangers; the curled, raggedy-taped handlebars caught on the brake cables, the toothed pedals caught in the spokes. The first bike she freed was Regina's; were Regina home to witness Mary commandeering her bike (unridden for more than a decade), Mary would never have done so, since Regina remained viciously possessive over long-neglected objects well into her so-called adulthood. The color-coded belongings of childhood (bikes, hairbrushes, toothbrushes, mugs) were clung to like hard-won plastic checker pieces, forever reminding Mary that there was still a score being kept.

Mary found a bike pump and inflated the warped front wheel; she tested the arthritic brakes on the wet street, much to the evident irritation of Ye Olde Bastard, wearing a tam-o'-shanter and walking his miniature schnauzer back and forth across his lawn. She felt a momentary flush of affection for the man, his disgruntlement was so sincere and unconditional that he couldn't even quell it for politeness' sake, dead mother be damned. She far preferred it to the glassy courtesy of Mum's friends and the sundry neighbors who, in the days before the funeral, had stopped by with casseroles in foil pans or tin containers of cookies. They peered into the kitchen as though she weren't even there, perhaps hoping that her father or her sisters were nearby and might be recruited to dilute the encounter with the pretend invisible person at the door.

Mary biked past the Smiths' house, the Harringtons', the Ewings', the Pooles', dodging the icy snow remnants still condensed near the curbs and over the storm drains. She made a left on Neale Street and narrowly missed the pothole she'd hit at the age of twelve trying to turn the corner while standing on the bike pedals, arms outstretched and jerkily feathering the air. The barrette she'd been wearing at the time dug into her scalp and she'd suffered temporary amnesia, wandering the streets until a neighbor found her and drove her to the hospital. For three hours she didn't know who she was or why she was upset, but she knew definitively that something was wrong. It was a terrible sensation, and ironically, she could remember quite viscerally this experience of non-remembering, the sensation of knowing something while not knowing it at the same time.

She passed the West Salem Cemetery, its wrought-iron gate painted a wet seal black and glinting beneath the overcast sky. Three blocks later Mary passed through the Semmering Academy brick gates, past the marble plaque with the school's motto VOX IN DESERTO, "A Voice in the Wilderness," the "wilderness" part always a bit of a misnomer. Yes, there used to be farmland surrounding the Gothic Revival brick structure built in 1891 by the philanthropic Semmerings, but by the time Mary attended the motto had been colloquially rephrased as VOX IN SUBURBO, the farms having been sold off by impoverished heirs to subdividers, the fields replaced by cul-de-sacs that looked from the catwalk on the academy roof like a series of asphalt crop circles. Semmering Academy had been famously endowed by the Semmerings for the purpose of "educating the savages," of whom very few remained and those who did expressed little interest in learning French and geography; ten years later, the enrollment at three, the academy's mission shifted slightly from educating savages to educating girls.

Mary stashed her bike by the back Dumpster. She stood in the shadow of Semmering and reflected how much it resembled a sanitarium from this vantage point, with its barred rear windows and its ominous smokestack and its sinister industrial hum. The back door opened to expel a trio of girls, their skirts longer than in the days when Mary was a student, hanging nearly to mid-knee and so gaping around the waist that each hip-swaying step revealed flashes of stomach. They didn't notice Mary, standing by the Dumpster. They didn't even look glancingly in her direction. Mary slipped inside and walked the length of the fluorescent-lit basement hall, through the old cafeteria, now an empty art classroom. The room smelled of paint and glue, the walls papered with mooning charcoal self-portraits.

Mary walked up the north staircase, onto the main floor, past the main office and the bulletin board. Behind the closed doors of the classrooms she could hear the muted clacking of chalk, the incantatory drone of the teachers. She found her old locker, 4565. She spun the lock, still remembering the combination (13–23–12).

The locker opened.

Mary stared at the familiar interior, at the mushroom-painted metal, at the rust spot on the lower shelf in the shape of Alaska minus its archipelago tail. Part of her wanted to read this empty locker as an homage, but of course she knew the opposite to be true. The headmistress, Miss Pym, was famously thorough when it came to eradicating threats to her academy's reputation, a thoroughness that even took the form of forbidding the future assignation of Mary's locker to any Semmering student, just as she had forbidden the future assignation of Bettina Spencer's locker to any future Semmering student after Bettina burned down the library in 1972. Both stood as empty as the Greenes' mausoleum. But Miss Pym was less superstitious than she was wise to the ways that young girls infected one another, usually through silly coincidence, and with all the discerningness of pink eye in February. She wanted no new outbreaks of publicized bad conduct on her watch, and thus had gone out of her way to minimize contact between Mary and the girls who followed her.

So it was not out of any tenderness toward Mary that Miss Pym suggested, once Mary returned to school the fall of her senior year, that she eat her meals in an empty and unmonitored classroom. She allowed Mary to quit the history club without the usual hecticness of notes and signatures, she expressed no concern that Mary spent afternoons alone in the woodshop making three-peg coatracks and lidless boxes because that was all the shop teacher was willing to teach girls how to make. Mary was allowed by Miss Pym, in a school that prized distinction, to become un-notable to the point of invisibility.

Then *Miriam* was published in the winter term of Mary's senior year, and everything changed.

Within two weeks of its publication, *Miriam* became a best seller in Boston and the surrounding towns and was featured in the front window of every suburban bookstore, stacked beside a four-foot cardboard cutout of Dr. Hammer wearing a black turtleneck and looking more like a diet pioneer than a therapist. The Semmering students carried the book around school, reading passages aloud in the hallways and in the cafeteria. Miss Pym attempted to ban the book from the school grounds out of re-spect for Mary and her privacy, but in fact Mary knew that Miss Pym found the subject matter potentially inciting. Here was a girl—another Semmering student, no less—who had faked her abduction. Who had craftily engineered a situation in which she was not only a highly pitied victim (for a time) but had managed to star in her own pop psychology book, thereby securing her status as teenage idol of subversion. The teach-ers, however, were so excited that the students were treating with such rev-erence a *book* rather than a new slipcover for their Bermuda bag that they were hesitant to discourage this newfound, and presumably delicate, en-thrallment, for fear of scaring the girls off of books for good.

Instead of banning *Miriam*, Miss Pym offered to provide Mary with a private tutor so that she could study from home for the remainder of her senior year.

Mary accepted.

In retrospect, however, the tutor was a mistake. Mary's remove from the battering, equalizing social milieu of high school—where any person encountered on a daily basis becomes tiresome, no matter how many books are written about them—only heightened her mystique. Had Mary remained at Semmering, no doubt the furor and the reverence would have subsided much sooner. Instead it was as if she'd disappeared anew, and any Mary spottings were gathered like clues to a new mystery.

Miriam continued to be toted through the Semmering hallways in a talis-manic manner, much to Miss Pym's unarticulated misery.

But perhaps nobody suffered so much as her mother, who had at first tried in every way to minimize the reverberations of her daughter's ab-duction. Yet when *Miriam* was first published—a book that claimed Mary, despite what she'd implied, had been neither abducted nor sexually abused—her mother's enthusiasm to remove the "raped girl" suspicions overrode her formerly crazed need for privacy on the matter. Better a liar, her mother figured, better the disturbed perpetrator of a grand-scale hoax than an innocent victim of sexual assault. Though Mary's role in *Miriam* was supposed to remain anonymous, her mother told the women in the Boston Wellesley alumnae group. She told her former dorm mates who lived as far as away as Hong Kong, her historical society colleagues, the government officials to whom she made her monthly pardon phone call on behalf of Abigail Lake. While everyone within the Semmering community knew of Miriam's actual identity, Mary's alias was now guar-anteed to be known throughout Greater Boston and beyond.

While her mother succeeded in clearing her daughter of the "raped girl" suspicions, she simultaneously called far more public scrutiny upon her daughter and her family than before. In an effort to reverse these damages, her mother changed to an unlisted phone number, she posted a sign to the front gate threatening to sue interlopers for trespassing. This failed to intimidate anyone. In a fit of frustration, her mother listed 34 Rumney Marsh with a real estate agent and became tyrannical about the beds being made, the clothes being put away, the sink being kept clean of dishes. The first prospective buyer, a librarian-looking woman in her for-ties, peered around the house absently and inquired, "Isn't this the house where Miriam lives?" The house came off the market the next day.

Her mother, however, didn't know how good she'd had it, the months that *Miriam* ruled her life, before the whole family was ruled by Roz Biedelman's far more invasive investigations. Her mother had no idea how her attempts to control the details of Mary's abduction would come undone. Who could have known? Whoever would have guessed the extent to which a stranger will go to ruin a person's life under the guise of saving it?

Mary heard footfalls, the *squeak-suck squeak-suck* of sensible shoes. She closed the locker soundlessly and searched for a hiding place. She wasn't a student cutting class. She wasn't doing anything wrong, but she was, it was true, enjoying her illicit-feeling run of the place. She slid behind the door to an empty classroom—the very classroom, in fact, where she'd studied junior English with Ms. Wilkes who, judging from the posters (Plath, Sexton), was still in residence; either that or her successor was an equally fervent worshipper of locally suicidal female poets.

The *squeak-suck* paused, swiveled, continued toward Mary. Through the window in the door Mary saw a six-foot-tall woman wearing a thigh-length cardigan and a wool skirt, her neck curving up and then forward, her gray head dangling low like a heavy Christmas ornament from a too-slight branch. She swabbed at her nose with a tissue produced from her sweater cuff; a throat lozenge clicked against the insides of her teeth.

Squeak-suck squeak-suck squeak-suck.

Mary stepped from behind the door.

"Excuse me," she said.

Miss Pym didn't hear her.

"*Excuse me.*"

Miss Pym turned and glared disbelievingly at the woman who seemed to have stolen her own trick of materializing from nowhere.

Miss Pym raised a dryly inquiring eyebrow.

"I . . ." Mary walked closer to Miss Pym. Miss Pym's eyes watered, the blues a permanently irritated hay-fever blue.

"Did you sign in with the front desk? All visitors must sign in with Miss Vernon. Are you a prospective parent?"

She doesn't recognize me, Mary thought. Then: *Christ, do I really look that old?*

"I . . . no," Mary said.

"What can we do for you then?"

"I'm here to see Dr. Biedelman," Mary said.

"Dr. Biedelman's office is on the second floor," Miss Pym said. "Had you signed in at the front desk with Miss Vernon, *as visitors are clearly instructed to do,* she might have saved you the goose chase."

"I came in the back door," Mary said.

"What?" Miss Pym nearly screamed the word. She was going deaf, Mary thought, and no surprise—she had to be nearing eighty now, despite the fact that she didn't appear any more gray or hunched or desiccated by age than she had when Mary was a student. "The back door . . ." Mary repeated.

"So you said. How did you get in the back door? The back door is always locked."

"Some smokers," Mary offered, wondering if Miss Pym would think she was a tattletale.

Miss Pym hmmphed to herself, as though something she'd long suspected had been confirmed.

"Is Dr. Biedelman expecting you?" she asked.

"I called earlier but . . ."

"We're experiencing switchboard problems. I apologize on behalf of the local telephone company, 'run' by a consistent lot of underachievers. I'll take you to Dr. Biedelman's office."

Miss Pym led her back toward the main office—*She's going to make me sign in,* Mary thought. But Miss Pym took a left at the end of the hall, leading Mary up the main stairs to the second floor. Her palms prickled. Was she really going through with this? Miss Pym may not have recognized her, but there was little chance that Roz Biedelman wouldn't instantly know who she was. Miss Pym's brain had been inundated with girls for thirty years; her concern was only for their present selves, those selves technically under her watch, and unless they grew up to become distinguished in a field, in which case they would be contacted to appear at fund-raiser dinners, she was not terribly interested in what became of them after they left Semmering, particularly if they "failed to yield." Miss Pym delivered her famous "failure to yield" matriculation speech each fall, an accusatory exercise in inspiration that had always left Mary feeling like one of the neglected apple trees to the west of the Semmering playing fields, gnarled remnants from a long-ago-subdivided orchard, their only offering a handful of dense brown apples that rotted before they could mature.

"You're friends with Dr. Biedelman?" said Miss Pym, holding open the stairway door once they reached the second floor.

"Professional acquaintances," Mary said.

"Dr. Biedelman has proven a marvelous addition to the faculty. We've had no troubles with the students in years. I don't know how she does it."

"Pills?" Mary offered.

Miss Pym paused on the landing. "At Semmering, we believe that each girl has been given the tools by which to overcome her own obstacles. It merely takes a dedicated person to teach her how to best outwit her own worst tendencies. This is our pedagogical as well as our psychological approach, one that most parents subscribe to. Last year we had the highest application rate of any preparatory school in the Greater Boston area."

"Impressive," said Mary, wondering if Miss Pym had forgotten that she'd denied being a prospective parent.

"I'm not ashamed to boast, especially since it took nearly a decade to regain our status as the area's top school. Scandal does nothing for the admission numbers. Especially while we had the reputation for producing *disturbed mendicants*."

Mary was reminded of the so-called vagrant who had broken into the Greenes' mausoleum. Miss Pym had spent her life eradicating mendicants and vagrants, and yet when faced with a person accused of being both, Miss Pym was touchingly blind to this fact.

"Disturbed mendicants," said Mary lightly. "In a school like this?"

Miss Pym's face condensed into a wry smirk. "The school is hardly to blame. It's the mothers. If I had my way, Semmering would be a boarding school with limited parental visits. Mothers do not know how to raise girls. Boys, well, boys are like rubber balls. You can drop them and you can hurl them against a wall. You can resent them intensely. They are such dim creatures they don't even have the wherewithal to be ruined. But girls . . . girls, mishandled, are a menace."

Miss Pym blinked rapidly.

"I take it you don't have any daughters yourself," Mary said, knowing for a fact that Miss Pym was childless.

"I have hundreds of daughters," Miss Pym. "I do a perfect job of raising them. And do you know the trick of it?"

Mary shook her head.

"I don't love a single one," she said.

Miss Pym gazed directly at Mary. Mary gazed directly at Miss Pym. Miss Pym looked away.

"But consider the discussion of mendicants part of our buried past. Far be it from *me* to exhume it. By the way, Dr. Biedelman is often at the hospital in the mornings. But she should be back by now."

Mary trailed Miss Pym up the final stretch of stairs and onto the second-floor hallway. Miss Pym paused in front of a door with a pane of safety glass. The hall was noiseless, even the echoes of Miss Pym's footsteps had squeaked themselves down to nothing. As Miss Pym shook her hand free from her sweater, Mary experienced the world slowing to a near halt. Miss Pym's hand balled itself into a fist, preparing to knock. She cocked it back. Mary tensed, as though she herself were about to be struck. Just before Miss Pym's hand began its forward plunge, the end-of-class bell rang. Her hand jerked back. Four bomb-tickingly anticipatory seconds passed before the classroom doors blew open up and down the hall. Girls piled into the narrow corridor, their screeching and thundering accompanied by a deep structural rumble, the bricks threatening to collapse under their aggressive gaiety.

Mary found herself pushed against a row of lockers before being gradually sucked down the hallway as though by an undertow; she bucked against it, fighting her way back toward Miss Pym, who surveyed the hysteria disapprovingly from her naturally higher perch.

"Lunch!" she called out to Mary, now a good ten feet away.

Miss Pym lifted her oversized hand and, again, balled it into a fist. *I could just disappear*, Mary thought. She could relent to the tide of girls, she could turn around and allow herself to be sucked into the vortex. Within seconds she could be funneled down the staircase, tossed out the basement door and onto Regina's bicycle. Within seconds she could be pedalling home.

Mary played with the possibility; she allowed herself to be pulled even farther down the hall. But then she tensed herself, fighting her way back through the current. She watched as Miss Pym knocked on Roz's door. Once. Twice.

The door remained closed.

The crowd thinned and changed, the decibel level dropped, the deafening echo replaced by the angry rattle of a stuck locker door, the enervated shuffle of an acne-ridden loner.

Miss Pym knocked again. Three times. Four. She regarded her watch crossly.

"It seems Dr. Biedelman is still out," she said. "Would you like to leave her a note?"

"No thank you," Mary said.

"She might be at her office in the city," Miss Pym said. "I'll have Miss Vernon call for you."

"Really, it's not that important," Mary said.

Miss Pym shrugged disapprovingly. Clearly Mary was a woman without much desire or follow-through. Clearly she was a woman who had yet to learn how to outwit her own worst tendencies, who would fail to yield if she hadn't failed already.

Mary trailed Miss Pym through the doors, down the main staircase, to the main entranceway.

Miss Pym paused and waited, impatiently, for Mary to leave.

"Thanks," Mary said. "I appreciate your help."

"Not at all," said Miss Pym. "I like to help where I can. My opportunities, as you've surely heard, are numbered."

Mary started. She was dying, Miss Pym—of course she was. It explained her unusual melancholy, her willingness to talk civilly to a stranger who had broken her rules.

Miss Pym noted her mistaken assumption.

"My board wants new blood," she said. "Such a disgusting term. My board, previously unbeknownst to me, is a pack of vampires. I chose the people with the sharpest teeth, not foreseeing they'd one day use them to bite me in the neck."

Miss Pym scrutinized the filigreed copper chandelier overhead. Three of the bulbs had blown.

"I am," she said tonelessly, "a very stupid woman."

"I think," Mary said, "that this is the natural evolution of things."

Miss Pym sniffed. "Stupidity is not natural. Blindness is not natural. You must think I'm incapable of seeing the deception happening in front of my own eyes."

She leered at Mary meaningfully.

"I don't think that," Mary said.

"This is the price I pay for enjoying myself," said Miss Pym. "Did you know what I was doing when I met you today? I was *enjoying* myself. I like to walk the hallways during class. The girls think I'm trolling for truants. But the truth is I'm nearly brought to tears by the turbulent sensation of all that . . . potential."

Miss Pym's eyes remained hard and dry.

"You understand," she said. "You were one of those girls once."

Mary froze.

"I didn't grow up here," she offered hastily.

"But you were once a girl of potential," said Miss Pym wistfully. "Weren't you?"

Miss Pym unraveled the tissue from her cuff. She daubed her nose.

"I forgot," said Miss Pym. "Why did you say you were visiting Dr. Biedelman?"

"I didn't," Mary said numbly.

"Well. I don't imagine you'll find what you're looking for here. Next time, however, be sure to sign in with Miss Vernon."

Miss Pym vanished through the office doors, leaving Mary alone in the hall. Through the floorboards she could feel the vibration of the cafeteria activity and hear the hiss of the steam heat from the school's ancient radiators. Her arms began to sweat, her neck to itch. She fled through the front doors into the escalating cold. As she hurried over the flagstone walk, she experienced the unnerving sensation of being observed, a ribbony needle inserted between her shoulder blades. She glanced back at the school's façade. Miss Pym's dark ostrich shape watched her through the many-paned office window, her menacing figure seeming to Mary suddenly more frail and more transitory than the skeletal and half-frozen leaves that lined the walk. Mary raised a hand—a thank-you gesture, a regretful goodbye—but Miss Pym receded from the window without acknowledging her.

Notes

Mary was not my first patient to have attended Semmering Academy, an institution responsible for educating some of the area's most exceptional women. It was famously said in the 1930s, "Behind every successful Bostonian stands a Semmering woman." It has more recently been said that behind every Semmering woman stands its current headmaster, Miss Dorothy Pym.

Thanks to the tireless efforts of Miss Pym, Semmering became known as one of the most rigorous girls preparatory academies in New England, a status that remained uncontested until the events of 1971–72. In the fall of 1971, sophomore Bettina Spencer and her friend, Melanie Clark, mysteriously "disappeared" from the school grounds, causing considerable uproar within the community; two weeks later, the girls materialized in the parking lot of the Boston commuter train. Bettina, who became my patient, admitted early in the course of our work together that she had been drugged and forced to commit involuntary sexual acts by a masked man who bore an exact resemblance to the school's then field hockey coach.

After consulting with my colleagues, I made the difficult decision to break my patient-doctor privilege and report my suspicions to the police. The field hockey coach was arrested, charged, and awaiting trial when a photograph, sent by an anonymous source, appeared at the police station. The photo showed Bettina and Melanie standing in front of a horse-drawn carriage in New York's Central Park. Bettina smoked a cigarette while Melanie held up a *New York Post* and pointed to the date—October 29, four days after their so-called abduction by the field hockey coach. The field hockey coach was released and the exonerating photograph reprinted in the Boston paper. The girls were put through a rigorous drug therapy program and readmitted to Semmering. A month later, Bettina set fire to the school founder's library, destroying not only thousands of books but many original papers and other irreplaceable memorabilia entrusted to the school by the Semmerings. When questioned, Bettina claimed she'd been put under the spell of a witch, who had assumed the form of Miss Pym. She was, she insisted, only obeying her headmaster's instructions.

As is often the case with ludicrous accusations, this one contained a shred of suspicion that easily adhered to Miss Pym and her academy full of intelligent, capable women, her new field house built with funds miraculously seduced from the community's most notorious penny-pincher, its lobby adorned with a lurid mural commemorating the death of the Salem witches. The academy's reputation suffered throughout the early eighties; a far higher occurrence of eating disorders and general mental distress was reported among the student population. Miss Pym was accused of ruining young women by foisting unrealistic expectations upon their shoulders. Monthly weigh-ins were scheduled to monitor and catch early anorexic or bulimic behavior. Despite (or because of) these measures, applications dropped to their lowest rate since the school's inception in 1912, and had not yet fully recovered by the time Mary vanished in the fall of 1985.

Mary, unlike her myriad unhappy classmates, appeared to have been an averagely happy Semmering student; her marks were decent, she'd never been disciplined, there were no signs of physical distress noticed by the school nurse during her monthly weigh-in. Still, I found Mary's past hard to reconcile with her present self; the volatile young woman I'd met in very few ways resembled the invisible, obedient, and ultimately unremarkable girl evoked by her teachers and her report cards. This timid and inconsequential Mary (who also claimed to have been put under a spell) had effortlessly convinced Dr. Hicks-Flevill and the local police that there was no reason to believe her disappearance was in any way connected to the faked abduction masterminded by Bettina Spencer—which was precisely why I thought the connection worthy of deeper scrutiny.

Mary arrived at her third appointment in low spirits, her hair unwashed, her clothing clean yet rumpled. She moved with a manic brusqueness around my office, refusing to sit either in my office chair or on the couch.

Sit down, I said.

Mary did not sit.

I'm not going to strip for you this time, she announced. That was cruel of me. Regina said that was cruel of me to remind you that you're an old, old man and besides it's probably bad for your health.

How old do you think I am, I said.

Old is old, she said. Doesn't matter by how much.

She made direct eye contact with me—a confusing sign of ego defiance that did not coincide with the earlier abuse theory. Typically when a patient lashes out at her doctor, she does so without the ability to make concurrent eye contact; to do so would mean taking responsibility for her actions. But Mary suffered no shame; in fact she appeared exultant.

You seem to enjoy trying to offend me, I said.

I wasn't trying to offend you, she said. I was stating a fact.

You were co-opting me into a familiar and unresolved dynamic that means something to you but nothing to me. I need your help understanding this dynamic.

OK, Mary said dubiously.

Do you know what transference is? I asked.

Mary scowled. All I said was old is old and here you go turning it into some sick twisted thing.

Transference is neither sick nor twisted, I said. It's a natural by-product of the useful intimacy achieved between a patient and her doctor.

I thought that was called semen, she said.

I didn't respond.

She smiled.

I'm kidding, she said.

An implied sexual advance is no joking matter, I said.

She picked at her thighs through her wool tights. She withdrew her compact and checked her complexion, then resumed her unconscious habit of swirling her finger around the compact's interior.

I decided to take a more direct approach.

Was K old, I said.

K, she puzzled. Who's K?

K was the man in your dream. The man who didn't care about saving your jewel case.

I have no idea what you're talking about, she said. You must have me confused with another patient.

She stood and faced my bookshelf.

Have you read all these books? she asked.

Mary, I said.

She didn't respond.

Ida, I said.

She coughed.

Is it hot in here? she asked. I'm really burning up.

Mary pretended to be entranced by my bookshelves. I wondered if she suffered from "true amnesia"—gaps into which not only very old memories have fallen but recent events as well. Often "paramnesias" form to fill these gaps—stories that take the place of memory, memories which can conveniently disappear at the point a patient tries to put them into words. Often this disappearance is due to subverted shame—meaning that Mary's seemingly disingenuous forgetting could be the result of a force exerted by her unconscious.

Mary coughed again. So? she pressed. Have you read these books?

Most of them, I said. Do you not remember our conversation from last Tuesday?

It wasn't so memorable, she said. She removed a book from the bookcase. She turned the cover toward me, astonished.

She held in her hand my copy of *The Abduction and Captivity of Dorcas Hobbs by the Malygnant Savages of the Kenebek.*

I cannot believe you have this book, she said.

She opened the front cover.

"For Beaton," she read. Who's Beaton?

That copy was purchased at a used bookstore, I said.

"For Beaton," she read, "congrats on your (finally!) graduation from BU."

Mary cast an eye toward the wall above my desk where my diplomas hung.

You went to BU, Mary said.

For graduate school, I said.

I suppose that's just a coincidence, isn't it, Beaton? I see you also attended Oberlin.

It's in Ohio.

I know where Oberlin is, she said. All the hippie chicks who don't score well on their SATs go to Oberlin and pretend that they're really musical and Oberlin was their first choice when in fact they weren't smart enough to get into Brown.

She returned to the couch.

This couch sucks, she said. I bet you've had this couch since Oberlin. Which means you've probably had sex on it.

Do you always associate couches with sex, I asked her.

Do you always associate couches with sex?

Do you?

I associate couches with vomit. Once my sister Regina threw up on our couch and was too scared to tell our parents. She flipped the cushion over and thought no one would notice.

Mary extended her body over the length of the couch, her head hanging off the edge.

Did you also hide things from your parents? I asked.

Mary rumpled her left brow with her index finger, then smoothed it over. She repeated this action several times.

Dumb question, she said, righting herself on the couch and folding her legs Indian-style.

Did you hide things from *your* parents? she asked.

I'm not so old that certain universal childhood tendencies don't convey, I said.

Did you ever hide something on purpose because you wanted them to find it?

Hiding something because you want it to be found seems counterintuitive, I said.

What is less counterintuitive, she said. Hiding in plain sight?

Depends on how you define productive, I said. Do you want to be found, or don't you?

She didn't answer my question. She tapped a finger on the front cover of *Dorcas Hobbs*.

So, Beaton, have you read this or haven't you?

I didn't respond.

I wonder if you've read any of the books on your shelf, she said. Or maybe you're just one of those people who buys books because they make him look smart and interesting. For example, she said, hopping up again. Have you read this book?

She pulled Freud's *Dora: An Analysis of a Case of Hysteria* from the shelf.

Of course, I said. It's a classic.

A *classic*, she said, snapping the word off her tongue. When's the last time you read it?

Not since graduate school.

How many centuries ago was that?

I didn't respond.

Mary sighed.

You're a sad fellow, Beaton, she said, and not a very inspiring spokesperson for the benefits of emotional health. You should exercise more. That's what my mother would tell you. She thinks fat people should be deported on wood pallets to the tropics where they can provide food for the parasites. I'm not saying you're fat. Who gave this to you?

She'd returned to the inscription on the title page of *Dorcas Hobbs*.

As I said, it's a used book. The inscription was there when I acquired it.

Mary narrowed her eyes.

I felt my face reddening.

How am I supposed to trust you if you lie to me? she said. How can I be cured if I can't trust you? I'm sensing we're about to become victims of an ugly pointless circle, Beaton. We might as well terminate our relationship right now and save my parents the dough.

A former patient gave it to me, I said.

She sniffed, temporarily mollified. She dropped back onto the couch and paged roughly through *Dorcas Hobbs*, as though hoping to dislodge another scrap of information about me from its interior.

I didn't mean to pry, she said. It just seems unfair, you asking all these questions and I can't even expect one honest answer out of you. What was her name? I'm assuming it's a girl. Did you find her attractive? Is that why she gave you a present? To *thank* you for finding her attractive?

It's unethical for me to discuss my patients with you, I said.

You mean it's against your own best interests for you to discuss *you*. You're not supposed to reveal anything about yourself because then I might use it against you.

You must think I'm very paranoid, I said.

I think therapists in general are paranoid, she said. But we could make this about you if you want.

This isn't a chess game in which tactical errors can be made, I said.

No? she said. Then where's the fun? You should raise the stakes don't you think? Like in the witch-hunting days of Dorcas?

If they'd had therapists in the days of Dorcas, the unexplored subconscious would have been outed as the true evil.

Mary ignored me.

If you fail to make someone convincingly better, you get burned at the stake, she said. If you fail to make me better you should be burned, don't you think?

I think that the chances of you getting better are entirely dependent upon you taking this enterprise more seriously, I said.

Oh, she said, I *do* take it seriously. *Pour fair une omelette il faut casser des oeufs.*

You don't seem serious to me, I said. You're behaving in a manner I'm describing in my notes as "flippant" and "dismissive." Also, as a matter of factual accuracy, you should know that the witches weren't burned in Salem. No witches were burned in the colonies. They were hung.

Mary strived to look contrite. She continued to flip through *Dorcas*.

So, she said, pretending to absently read a page. Tell me about Dora.

Dora was a sexually repressed girl who lived in Vienna at the turn of the century who believed that her father's friend, Herr—

"Who is the one you chose to be your incubus?"

Excuse me?

It's a question from the appendix, she said, holding up *Dorcas Hobbs*. "Questions to Be Asked of a Witch." Originally printed in the *Malleus Malefactorum*.

Do you still want to hear about Dora?

Yes yes, she said.

Dora believed that she had been sexually abused, but Freud discovered that this "abuse" was actually a shameful fantasy of what she *wished* had occurred between herself and Herr—

What's an incubus?

Pardon?

An incubus.

An incubus is a male demon who was believed to have sexual intercourse with women while they slept. Figuratively speaking, it also refers to something that causes much worry or anxiety, such as a nightmare.

Huh, she said. I'm sorry. I interrupted you again.

Dora terminated her treatment prematurely, before Freud could cure her of her hysterical symptoms. Some people believe that she left because he refused her literal explanations of what happened to her, namely that she was sexually abused.

He sounds like a moron, said Mary. "What is the ointment with which you rub your broomstick?"

These same people believe that Freud was overly interested in confirming his theories of repression—more so than in actually listening to the patient, I said.

"How are you able to fly through the air?" "What do you make your plagues of pernicious creatures out of and how do you do it?" These questions are so leading. The people asking them weren't much interested in the answers, I bet.

As I said, if they'd known then what we know now about the subconscious—

Did you know that the *Malleus Malefactorum*, which was published in the 1400s, was one of the first international best sellers? Did you know that *Malleus Malefactorum* means "Hammer of Witches"?

She looked at me slyly.

Are you a Hammer of Witches? she asked.

Mary, I said.

Oops, she said. I forgot. *An implied sexual advance is no joking matter.*

She returned to the appendix. She stood and intoned in a deep voice "Who are the children on whom you have cast a spell?"

Mary, I said.

What, she said.

You're trying to derail this session by hiding behind that book.

Mary placed the book on the floor beside the couch. Resuming her cross-legged position, she bunched the fabric around the holes in her tights, jamming the bunched bit between her big toe and the neighboring toe until her feet appeared cloven.

I'm hiding in plain sight, Beaton, she said. Maybe a book is the best place to look.

What Might Have Happened

This is how the story might have ended: the man drove the girl home.

But as the man started to drive the girl home he realized that he was too curious to drive the girl home. Intensely, even shamefully curious, curious to the point of feeling erotically charged by his curiosity. Not that he believed the girl's insinuations that he had molested her—he didn't believe them for one second, and why should he? He didn't have amnesia—that lie had erupted from him because, well, he'd been accused of the same by the managing partner at his law firm who interviewed him for the purposes of "damage control." "Amnesia won't play well in this context," the general counsel had said when he'd refused to speak to him about the matter, claiming he didn't remember. But of course he remembered. He remembered peering down his nose in order to center the tip of his cigarette in the glowing bull's-eye of his car lighter, the heat warming his upper lip. He remembered the sound the body made as it glanced off his car, as though someone had hurled a giant bag of wet trash at the passenger-side door. He'd taken his eyes off the road for a millisecond, a fraction of a fraction of a fraction of time. His first reaction, when in his rearview mirror he saw the man tumbling along the breakdown lane and striking, with the floppiness of a rolled carpet, the guardrail, was one of dumbfounded amazement. *How has this never happened to me before?* he remembered thinking. He'd peered down his nose to light a cigarette while driving five or six times a day for ten years, taking special pleasure in landing the cigarette in the dead center of the lighter's concentric circles. He felt misled, cheated, as though he'd been seduced into casualness over a situation that required constant vigilance to prevent its turning tragic.

A crowd quickly gathered up and down the highway shoulder and gawked at him from a safe distance. He'd struck his head against the windshield when he slammed on his brakes; blood ran sideways over his temple, pooling in his ear, flowing over his earlobe and coagulating, finally, in a stalagtitelike drop. One of the gawkers was a physician. He kneeled by the heap of rolled rug and felt for a pulse. He rose to his feet with no urgency whatsoever.

The man was dead. The man had killed a man.

For less than thirty minutes, he contemplated the fact that he'd become the person his ex-wife claimed, in not so many words, to wish she'd married. He'd been cutting garlic for a salad dressing when she announced that she was leaving him for good. He turned quickly and without thinking, knife pointed outward, the point jabbing in and out of her arm—just a fraction of a millimeter—with the invisible quickness of a sewing machine needle. She bled a pinprick's worth of blood.

She met his gaze daringly. "Go on," she said. "Stab me again if you want me to stay." She didn't say: *You timid, depressive cipher.* She didn't say: *At least a man who stabs his wife gives a shit about something.* She didn't have to say these things.

He returned to chopping his garlic.

And so if he were honest with himself—he tried mostly to be—he'd have to admit that the initial numb horror he felt at killing a man was reprehensibly counterbalanced by an intoxicating sense of freedom, even of victory. Yes he'd suffered a mild concussion, yes he'd been in shock, but still this did not excuse the fact that his first impulse, as he stood watching the medics cover the dead man with a tarp, was to call his ex-wife and tell her: I have killed a man.

When it emerged, after a quick medical exam by the ambulance medics and an ID check by the police, that the man he'd killed was suicidal and mentally ill—he had escaped from a home south of the highway—he did not feel entirely relieved. He felt, instead, the deadweight of his boulder self redescend. He felt the strangulating tightness of his own skin. "Wrong place, wrong time," said the sympathetic officer who had, thirty minutes earlier, locked him in cuffs. "We understand your need to reassess after the tragedy that's befallen you," his partners wrote in response to the memo he sent, announcing his indefinite leave of absence from the firm. "This would only happen to you," his ex-wife said.

And so he found the girl refreshing. He found it refreshing to contemplate that he might be hiding a less pitiable victim of a person inside of himself. Of course, it was all a silly game. He reasoned that he could only find refreshing the possibility that he might have molested a young girl if the possibility were, in fact, impossible. He knew it was impossible. He'd spent his afternoons outside Semmering Academy reading his newspaper in his car because after he'd killed the suicidal man he'd thought: *I could be anybody now. Once a man has killed another man, even if unintentially, a world of options is open to him. I could be a molester of young girls.* He thought it wrong to cut himself off from this possibility, a refusal to fully self-realize, and so he'd stationed himself in a place where he would be most tempted. Sadly, he'd learned, he didn't much care for young girls, not at least as objects to desire. It was their noises he preferred; their screeches and their laughter so maniacal at the edges. They lived with the daily cognizance that they had no idea, despite their careful schooling and safe families, what they would become. Miserable lawyers? Adulterers? Alcoholic mothers? The future seems rife with failure when you're primed to succeed—this he recalled keenly from his own upbringing. When you are primed to succeed your failure looms like a certainty, at which you maniacally laugh as you skip class to smoke cigarettes in the cemetery. He felt comfortable amidst their pigeon squawking, which receded as they passed his car in search of a mausoleum behind which to crouch and prepare for their black futures. Failure was easier to accept, he knew, if there were seeds of its promise one could locate in an earlier time. There, you see. There is where it all began to go wrong.

Thus, he allowed himself to enjoy this girl in his passenger seat, because what was the risk? Certainly her imaginative rendering of his past made him a more intriguingly dark person than the version delivered to him by his ex-wife—now an active member of a women's encounter group—who had involved him in her urgently ridiculous need to *reclaim her own story*, as though he'd ever been the one in control. He accompanied her on trips revisiting their former house, their former vacation spots, their former favorite restaurants, while his ex-wife narrated her experience of being married to him into a handheld tape recorder. If he tried to correct her account, she'd raise her voice and state imperiously: "This is my story now." Generally speaking, her version of him could be summed up as follows: socially reticent, well-meaning, and killingly bland litigator afflicted by food allergies engages for years in loveless union with woman he finds repulsive but doesn't have the guts to leave.

It was not so terribly far off the mark.

He peered sideways at the girl, her feet on the dash, her chin resting between her knees and bouncing as he drove over the potholed road.

You're going to bite off your tongue, the man said.

Wouldn't you like that, the girl said.

No, in fact, the man said.

So, Mr. Amnesia, do you remember where my house is? the girl asked.

Which house? the man asked. The first house or the second house?

What do you mean, the first house, the girl said.

The house where we were neighbors, the man said.

The girl smiled into her knees.

And so it was that the man found himself actively awake at 9:55 p.m. and driving toward Boston in the company of a strange girl. This so-called Ida. She didn't feel like an Ida to him, any more than she felt like a total stranger. He allowed himself to consider; maybe he had been fol-lowing her for a reason. Maybe she did know something about him—was it so outlandish a notion? Not what she'd claimed, of course, but perhaps she possessed insight into him as a more fascinating person; like the sui-cidal man who chose him from a road's worth of death options, she too privileged other ways of perceiving him.

Soon the woods on either side peeled away to reveal office parks and malls, their brilliantly lit car lots empty of cars. These gave way to indus-trial wastelands of shipping containers and railway tracks, then ware-houses and the first shabby beginnings of the habitable city.

Do you remember where you're going? the girl asked.

The man nodded. He'd been to this house with his ex-wife too many times recently as part of her reclamation therapy, his unimaginative past shoved in his face in the name of her cure.

Good, the girl said. Because I haven't been here since I was little.

Are you scared? the man asked.

Are you scared? the girl asked.

A little, the man admitted.

No you're not, the girl said. You're excited. It's all that coffee you drink. You've always been a big coffee drinker.

I've become a big coffee drinker, he said. Since I have insomnia, it's nice to be alert.

You were always a coffee drinker and a smoker, the girl said. You sucked Sucrets so your wife wouldn't know. You hid a lot from your wife.

Could you blame me? the man asked.

The girl smiled sweetly. I've never blamed you, she said.

The man exited toward Storrow Drive, pinballing through the rotaries toward the house where he used to live. It was almost 11 p.m. by the time they pulled up outside the brownstone that he and his wife had sold in the late seventies for barely what they'd paid for it. Implicit in this fact, when recounted to him by his ex-wife, was this: He had been bad with money. He had been bad with investments. He had, due to his dislike of new people and new routines and his all-round timidity toward life—and this was confusing—*bullied* her into buying near their old apartment in the city (bad investment) rather than in the newly fashionable suburbs (good investment). He had forced her to become an angry and aggressive person; it was her only defense against becoming like him, against drifting out of existence as quietly as their money.

He pulled up in front of his former bad investment and put the Mercedes in park, leaving the engine running. The streets gleamed like a petroleum spill in the parchment yellow of the streetlamps. Brakelights and headlights bled red and white through the sheeny black, everything running together and jarring his sense of perspective and horizon until it was hard to tell where the ground was, where the sky.

This is it, the girl said, her chin still resting on her knees, eyes tilted up at the world, or what they could see of the world through his windshield.

She pointed at his old house.

But that's my house, he said.

I know, she said. Just testing you.

This time she pointed to a brownstone across the street.

I thought your house burned down, the man said. He'd been expecting a new glassy house slid between the brownstones like a vein of quartz through granite.

Burned down, the girl said, is a figure of speech. We sold the shell to a couple that wanted a fixer-upper. They were from Texas. Dad said they had a lot of *giddyap and go*.

The girl chewed on her sweatpants.

You seem nervous, said the man.

Just tired, the girl said.

It's late, the man said. After eleven. And it's a school night.

The girl fiddled with the Mercedes's lighter, pushing it in and then yanking it out, turning the dead heating coil toward her face.

This is broken, the girl said. Do you have any cigarettes?

I don't smoke anymore, he reminded her.

But you used to, the girl said. I bet there's a straggler in the seam of this seat.

She lifted her hips high, her field hockey skirt riding above her waist, her sweatpants pulling downward to expose the elastic band of her underwear.

Voilà, she said. She held up a flattened cigarette, the filter dangling by a tiny hinge of paper. She tore the filter free and dropped it onto the floor of the Mercedes.

Got a light?

No, I . . . the man fumbled.

You don't smoke, the girl said. Some advice: a lighter is a good prop for picking up women at bars.

I don't go to bars, the man said.

You just hang out across the street from an all-girls high school.

She was smiling as she said this.

Joking, she said.

Not funny, the man said.

Not funny but true, the girl said. I bet you have matches in this car.

She checked the glove box, underneath the floor mat. She found a book in the door pocket, wrapped in a desiccated woman's leather glove. His ex-wife's glove? Whose glove? He didn't have a clue. He felt suddenly threatened by the amnesia he'd only pretended to have.

One match left, she said. Should you do the honors or should I?

I'll do it, the man said.

There's a lot of pressure here, the girl said, holding up the last match. Think you can handle it?

The man removed the matchbook from her fingers, careful his skin didn't touch hers.

The flint had been scraped bare.

He struck the match on the first try. His hands were steady as he cupped the flame and extended it toward the girl's mouth.

She inhaled. Smiled.

They sat in silence.

There, she said, finally, pointing to a small window on the third floor of the man's former home. That's where it happened.

The man looked at the window, a bland and unsuggestive porthole into a past life that wasn't his.

Your wife was at work. You'd taken me rowing in the Commons. We were cold. You made us tea. Or maybe it was hot chocolate.

He watched as her eyes glazed over, her mind spinning and spinning, hooking images in far-off corners, pulling them forward and making them into words, sentences, a story for his benefit. He thought to himself, a not particularly original thought: What is the difference between one's memory and one's imagination in the end? What, really, is the difference?

Did you tell anyone, the man said.

The girl shook her head. No, she said. No, who would believe me?

Was it so unbelievable? the man said. Sadly it has happened before. Probably on this very street. Maybe in that very house. This is New England, after all.

The girl looked at him quizzically.

A joke, he explained.

There's nothing funny about implied child abuse, the girl said.

I'm not implying. You're implying.

I'm not implying, she said. I'm accusing.

I thought you said you'd never blamed me, the man said.

I didn't, she said. I don't.

You could if you wanted to, the man said. I can handle it.

How could I blame you? the girl said. After all, I enjoyed it.

West Salem

NOVEMBER 9, 1999

Mary pedaled the two miles back to Rumney Marsh in the rain. She'd stripped her damp sweater and jeans and was boiling water for grief tea when Regina and Gaby returned from the art appraiser's. The two of them blew into the kitchen along with some errant dead leaves and a jointly generated bad mood. Regina unwound her scarf and plucked leaves off her ballet flats, flinging them onto the linoleum floor where they stuck with a wet slapping sound. Gaby lugged the portrait of Abigail Lake by the piece of electrical tape that secured the pink bedsheet in which the painting was unlovingly wrapped. She banged the bottom corner against the door frame, she grimaced and groaned, kick-carrying Abigail Lake to the far side of the kitchen.

The bottom of the bedsheet was soaked. Clearly someone had propped Abigail Lake in a puddle while searching for meter money or the car keys.

"How was it?" Mary asked, biting back an impulse to criticize the handling of Abigail Lake. After all, she hated the painting too.

"Waste," Gaby said. She pulled the sickle-shaped remnant of a soft pretzel from her coat pocket. She tapped it with a fingernail, determining it inedible. She tossed it onto the counter.

Regina wiped her wet face crossly with a dish towel.

"It was not a *waste*," Regina said. "Mr. Bolt said the painting was 'an interesting novelty item.'"

"An interesting novelty item worth $100," Gaby said. "Not quite enough to cover his appraising fee and the ticket we got on Newbury Street because Regina parked in a handicap spot. What's for lunch?"

"We were grieving," Regina said. "We were handicapped by grief."

Gaby opened a cupboard door and faced off against the unopened jars of pickled onions, pickled fiddleheads, dilly beans, cornichons, olives.

"Gross," she said.

"*But he who is weak eats only vegetables*," quoted Mary.

"If she'd chosen to be embalmed, we could have saved some money," Regina said. "She'd been self-embalming for decades."

"I'm surprised we're not all anorexic," Mary said.

"We're not *not* all anorexic," Gaby said, shutting the cabinet in disgust, then reconsidering, opening it, withdrawing a jar of pickled onions.

"I have poor circulation," Regina said. "I also have a high metabolism."

"You don't eat anything," Gaby said. "How would you know what kind of metabolism you have?"

She opened the jar of pickled onions. The lid came loose with a wetly suctioning *pop!* sound. The kitchen filled with the needly stink of vinegar.

"So," Regina said to Mary, "any chance you came across my white ski hat with the blue-and-red pompon?"

"From high school?" Mary said.

"That one."

"I didn't," Mary said.

"Keep your eyes peeled," Regina urged. "Mum stole it. She asked if she could borrow it. I said no. The next day it disappeared."

"When was this?" Mary said.

Regina pushed on her cheekbone with her finger.

"Late eighties," she said.

"She was punishing you," Gaby said through a mouthful of onion.

"When we were at the beach last summer she touched my hair and said, 'I bet your head's cold, darling. Your head's been cold all these years.' "

"She meant that she finds you emotionally and creatively frigid," Gaby said.

"She meant me to have my hat back," Regina said.

"Speaking of lost things," Mary said, casually, "do either of you know where Mum put my signed copy of *Miriam*?"

Gaby stared at her blankly.

"Don't blame Mum if your silly book is missing," Regina said.

"I'm not blaming her," Mary said.

"You're accusing her."

"*You* just accused her of stealing your hat," Mary said.

"I don't know why you'd want that book anyway," Regina said. "Mum *despised* that book. Hyper radiance," she said. "What is 'hyper radiance' anyway?"

"It's a theory about—"

"I *know* what it is," Regina said. "I'm not stupid, I'm saying the theory is."

"These feel like little embalmed eyeballs," Gaby said, gazing at the onion she held between her thumb and forefinger.

"I just wish—" Mary began.

"*What*," snapped Regina.

"I just wish we could be a little warmer with one another," Mary said. "Don't you think that would make this easier?"

"Sorry to be such a disappointment to you," Regina said.

"I'm only suggesting that——"

"I wasn't the one who made a fool of herself in front of everybody at the wake yesterday. 'Strike!' You can't even be unironic about your own mother's death. How sad, Mary. No, really. I find it sad."

"It was your own mother's death too," Mary said quietly.

"And so what—you're accusing me of not grieving properly?" Regina said.

Gaby chucked another onion in her mouth.

"That's hilarious. That really is. I wrote a poem specifically for her funeral and you're accusing me of . . . forget it."

"Leave Mary alone," Gaby said.

Regina ballooned full of indignation.

"You," Regina warned, "you should stay out of this."

Gaby chewed, swallowed, winced, coughed.

"Mum hated your poems," Gaby said. "Your poems suck. Save your poems for someone who gives a shit."

"Hey," Mary said.

"*Don't* stick up for me," Regina snapped. She turned to Gaby. "You're right. Mum doesn't give a shit about my poems. She *gave* a shit. She's *dead.*"

Gaby's mouth twinged. She chewed furiously on another pickled onion. Her eyes watered. Regina and Mary diverted their attentions to distant quadrants of the kitchen. Gaby never cried, and when she did they knew it was wise to pretend she wasn't.

The telephone rang, its repeated peals echoing through the cardboard boxes and the bare walls and the ever emptier house.

Mary reached for the kitchen wall extension.

"Don't," Regina cautioned. "It's Aunt Helen."

"How do you know?"

"I know," she said.

The phone continued to ring until the kitchen felt like the inside of a bell, maddening and claustrophobic.

Finally, it stopped.

"I'm sorry," Regina said.

"You don't have to be sorry," Mary said.

"You're right. We should try to be nicer to one another."

"Wonderful," Mary said. "I'd like that. Really."

Gaby nodded.

Regina nodded.

The three of them stared at the linoleum.

"Did you clean out Mum's study?" Regina finally asked.

"I did," Mary said,

"Find any checks?"

"Checks for what?"

"Dad said he thought Mum had been squirreling away her insurance reimbursement checks."

"I didn't find any checks," Mary said. Then: "Do you remember Roz Biedelman?"

"Dr. Roz," Gaby said. "The school shrink. We got high once. In her office."

"You were involved with Dr. Biedelman?" Mary asked.

"I always suspected she was a lesbian," Regina said.

"She thought it made her seem cool to get high with me," Gaby said. "It kind of did."

"Dr. Biedelman never mentioned that you were her patient," Mary said.

"Lesbian-lesbian confidentiality," Regina said.

"It was medical marijuana," Gaby said.

"Right," Mary said, wondering if perhaps her mother had also been Roz's patient. Unlikely, given her mother's position on therapists, but

who knew what other whims possessed her toward the end? The nonre-
ligious seek out the priests. The fascistically mentally sound seek out the
shrinks. It would be unlikely, yes. But inconceivable?

Yes. No. The fact that she couldn't soundly gauge the level of incon-
ceivability only underscored how formal and unrevealing her relationship
with her mother had been for the past fourteen years.

"Did Mum have anything more to do with Dr. Biedelman that you
know?" Mary asked. "I mean, after we were out of high school?"

If so, Regina hadn't heard of it; neither had Gaby.

"Why do you ask?" Regina said.

Mary considered telling them about the letter, the cigarette case, the
antique store receipt—Regina, after all, could be helpful sometimes.
Regina could be sympathetic and even wise, and besides she might know
something. The chances of this occurring were probably less than one in
one thousand, but it was that slim possibility that continually fooled
Mary into trying.

"Actually—" Mary began.

"You look tired," Regina interrupted. "Doesn't she look tired, Gaby?"

Gaby shrugged.

"I am a little tired," Mary admitted. Regina rarely observed that a
person outside herself might be suffering. She appreciated that Regina
was trying to be nicer.

"I mean you *did* clean out her desk this morning, while Gaby and I
were wasting time in Boston. Isn't that what you did?"

"That's what I did," Mary confirmed. "She sure has some stuff."

"Huh," Regina said. "No doubt she does. You must be exhausted."

"Mentally, yes."

"But also physically."

"Not so much—"

"Have you been exercising?" Regina interrupted.

"Me?"

"I mean today."

"*Exercising?* No."

"Just wondering," Regina said. "Because did you notice that somebody recently rode my bike?"

She scrutinized Mary with a familiar look of victory.

"I hadn't noticed," Mary said, retreating up the back stairs with her tea.

R oz's Boston address was easy enough to find. A mode of transportation less so. Regina claimed that she could not be stranded without a car, it was absolutely not a possibility even though she had no plans and nowhere to go, even though Dad had promised to be home by five so they could have dinner together, probably terrible pizza ordered from the pizza place in the West Salem minimall, another historic anachronism that Mum had fought against and lost.

Gaby agreed to drive Mary to the train. She didn't ask Mary why she was going to Boston, not because she respected Mary's privacy but because she truly did not care enough about Mary's plans to ask her. The train, the 3:56, was empty save for three aggressively exuberant Semmering Academy students and a despondent domestic day worker. Clearly the Semmering girls saw their friendship as a sport where points are scored by making the spectators feel excluded and shitty. They laughed riotously and often, shedding their boots in the train aisle and giving one another foot massages, feeding one another orange sections, hitting one another with rolled-up magazines. After one artificially loud outburst, Mary and the domestic day worker exchanged a look of exasperation, but when Mary returned to the newspaper she was fake-reading she felt less exasperated than joyless and old.

The train arrived into North Station at just before rush hour. She hopped the T, emerging at ten minutes to five. Roz's office was still housed in a converted brownstone on a side street northwest of the commons, in the middle of a two-block concentration of mental health professionals whose tasteful black shingles covertly hung inside the first set of doors, below the buzzers and above the umbrella stands. The first time she'd met Roz at her new office she'd forgotten the business card Roz had given her and had wandered from building to building, each foyer identical to the next as though regulated by a mental health architectural board seeking to enforce a soothing, anonymous experience for its sheepish clientele. Implicit in the discreet placement of these shingles, of course, was the shame still associated in Boston with seeing a therapist. No one saw which bell you rang, no one, save those people already seeing a mental health professional, knew of the extremely high odds that anyone entering a brownstone on these two blocks was also en route to see a mental health professional. That explained the skulking quality to the pedestrians on this block, hats low and chins tucked, eyes tight to the bricks. They looked cold and put-upon, these people, as if walking headlong into an icy wind.

She checked her watch—5 p.m. to the minute. She assumed that the bulk of Roz's patients scheduled appointments at the end of the workday, since Roz's career focus remained educated women, an ever more-afflicted segment of the population according to an interview she'd read with Roz in *The Oregonian* last year. Roz toured the West Coast to promote her follow-up to *Trampled Ivy*, a book having to do with a seasonal depressive disorder that occurred among educated women during the holidays. It was called *The Tarnished Trivet* or *The Trivet Trigger*, at any rate something to do with trivets because according to the interview she'd read, Roz's own mother was institutionalized after the Thanksgiving dinner preparations one year when Roz was a teenager, the domestic detail that tweaked her mother for good being the last-minute need to polish an old trivet for a chafing dish of yams. Roz gave a reading at the northwest headquarters of the Daughters of the American Revolution, and Mary had been tempted to sit in the crowd or maybe even buy a book and wait in the signing line to see if Roz recognized her. But in the end, she hadn't gone to the reading. That was something the younger Mary would have done, and she was no longer the younger Mary.

The younger Mary had arrived at Roz's office that first time—the spring of 1987—without an appointment nor any clear sense of why she'd come. In the intervening two weeks since Roz called the meeting with her mother and Dr. Flood in her family's living room, another associate of Roz's had stopped by the house on Rumney Marsh. A mole-haired graduate student, he spoke of a lie detector test, he mentioned further therapy, he suggested Mary be deposed before a panel of psychiatric experts and her mother agreed to it. *You are not to say one word to these people.* But no longer. Now her mother was throwing her to the wolves.

And so this younger Mary rang the bell of Roz's new office and, partially to her relief, nobody answered. Thirty seconds later she heard the grinding honk-buzz-snap of the interior door's lock releasing. She stepped into the foyer's gloom, the door locking definitively behind her. Mary walked up the canted and depressingly gray-carpeted staircase to Roz's office on the third floor. She rang the buzzer and was admitted by a higher-pitched buzz. She walked down the narrow hallway (so narrow that the sides of her backpack rubbed against the walls), past a small bathroom, and into a waiting room furnished with a wicker couch and two matching chairs, all painted dark red, all decorated with generically ethnic-looking throw pillows. A white-noise machine fogged away beneath the scarred side table that abutted what she presumed to be Roz's office door. A framed photograph of a black woman pinning colorfully striped sheets to a laundry line hung on one wall, a poster from a primitives exhibit featuring a scary or miserable-looking wood mask hung on the opposite wall. She removed her backpack but not her anorak, sat on the wicker couch, and waited.

Thirty-five minutes later the door next to the scarred side table opened. A woman emerged, avoiding Mary's eyes as she struggled to don her coat in the narrow hall, her elbows thudding dully against the walls as she wrapped her head in a scarf.

"Come in," she heard Roz say.

Mary sat on the orange corduroy couch. A radiator sizzled in the corner; the neighboring windows were cracked open and Mary could see the waves of heat shimmying past the gap. She still didn't remove her anorak, even though the steam heat made her feel like her body was swelling to twice its normal size, a feeling of general discomfort unaided by the ceiling's track lighting, trained directly on the couch.

Roz's earrings, long silver-tentacled things, reached nearly to her shoulders. One was tangled in her hair like a helpless sea creature suspended in a tuna net.

"Hello," Roz said.

The radiator clanked in a distressed way. Mary shifted sweatily on the couch, her tights glued to her inner thighs.

"You've had a chance to think about our last meeting," Roz said. "I can see you've been thinking."

Mary wondered how the act of thinking made itself visible on a person.

"I appreciate that. I *appreciate* it, Mary." Roz placed a hand flat between her breasts, her cloisonné bangles making a tooth-clacking sound. "And I'm assuming, because you've come all this way to see me, that you've decided the best way out of this situation—for all involved—is to finally tell the truth."

Mary didn't respond.

"Mary?" she prodded.

"I'm not sure what you mean," Mary said.

"You're protecting Dr. Hammer, I know this, and while I admire your loyalty I want you to know that Dr. Hammer doesn't need your protection. He's an adult, and like many adults he's suffered an extremely misguided error in judgment. Nothing bad will happen to him—unless, of course, he's done something terrible to you that you want to tell me about. Did he do something terrible to you, Mary, that you'd like to tell me about?"

Mary shook her head.

"Well," Roz said. "Regardless I'm all ears."

What a strange saying, Mary thought. *All ears.* Roz's office felt like an interrogation room, with its overactive radiator and its track lights and its woman who was *all ears.* Worse than one of the Greek sirens Mary had been reading about with her tutor, Roz wasn't a person who would sing you to death—no no, Roz would *listen* you to death. She'd suck every thought and memory you'd ever had right out of your mouth, leaving you empty-headed, dry-tongued, identity-free, a husk.

A person might simply confess to untrue things just to be released from the situation with some of their actual person intact.

"I lied to Dr. Hammer," Mary said.

"You lied to *protect* yourself from him," Roz said. "Of course you did."

"I allowed him to believe things," Mary said.

"He put words in your mouth," Roz said. "He put ideas in your head."

Mary stared at Roz, flicking an octopus earring with her stout forefinger. For a so-called feminist, she was strangely quick to assign to women the most helpless of roles. *Who's to say,* she wanted to say, *that I didn't put ideas in his head?*

"He was not completely wrong in his assessment of me," Mary said evasively.

"But he was not completely right, either. An important distinction. Ultimately, he suppressed your own story with his theory."

"My story wasn't suppressed," Mary said. "My story was—in process."

"Of course it's in process. It's *still* in process. Given the subpar treatment you've received, you couldn't possibly claim to know what happened to you in any accurate way. Your past, you believe, could as easily be a product of your imagination. It's going to take some work, Mary, but together I know we can 'adhere,' as we say, your so-called fantasy life with your actual life. This is the only way that healing can begin, the only way that you can become the author of your own narrative. By accepting that the fantasy is not, in fact, a fantasy. In the meantime, however, you'll need to testify to how Dr. Hammer's . . . *enthusiasm* . . . for his theory posed, shall we say, a conflict to your own best interests as his patient."

Mary fiddled with the expired ski passes on her anorak's zipper.

Roz spun around in her armchair and opened her desk drawer, withdrawing what looked to Mary like a college catalog, with a glossy cover and a picture of a squat pillared building, a library or judicial court, flanked by two autumnal-leafed trees.

She handed it to Mary.

"The Massachusetts Mental Health Governing Board was founded in 1973 to protect people like you," Roz said. "People who have sought the help of a mental health professional and who have received *subpar* care. Most psychiatric licensing boards allow their members to re-up without checking their records or inspecting their performance. Many doctors and therapists don't even bother to renew their licenses in a timely manner. Dr. Hammer, during the months he saw you, was working with an expired license. Of course, Dr. Hammer isn't an actual *doctor*. He dropped out of his Ph.D. program. He isn't a trained psychiatrist. He studied therapeutic social work at Boston University and received his certificate by the skin of his teeth. He's been long associated with an experimental and uncertified school of therapy that borrows randomly from pop psychology and elementary psychoanalysis. Finally, though he was never officially indicted, while in graduate school he was brought up on dubious practice charges because of his mishandling of a sociopathic patient named Bettina Spencer. I presume you've heard of her. I've written a letter to your parents to this effect. I'm hoping your mother will now be able to direct her outrage toward the more deserving target."

Mary opened the brochure and was confronted with a blank white page and a Voltaire quote: Doubt is not a pleasant condition, but certainty is absurd.

"Of course I'm not underestimating what parents go through in these situations. True, it cannot compare to what you, the victim, experienced. But parents are especially hard hit by the limits of their own power—of their ability to effectively *protect* their children from harm. It's only natural that they should reject those who have their best interests at heart."

"Why did you share an office with him?" Mary said.

"Excuse me?"

"If you think Dr. Hammer's so dangerous. Why did you share an office with him?"

Roz smiled. "Would it predispose you toward me to know that I, too, have my weaknesses?"

"I doubt it," Mary said.

"Weak men are my weakness. I cannot help myself from helping pathetic men. But even I have my limits."

Mary closed the brochure. Also like a college catalog, it made her queasy about her future.

"Just because someone doesn't have a driver's license doesn't mean they don't know how to drive," Mary said.

Roz tented her fingers, the knuckles flexing inward like roof joists about to cave.

"A person who drives without a driver's license—to extend your own metaphor—tends to be a person who owes his landlord rent money, a person who doesn't make his alimony payments, a person who believes that the rules do not apply to him. Dr. Hammer did not believe that the rules applied to him. But the rules do apply."

Mary nodded. Her queasiness persisted. She'd made a mistake coming here.

"Our board has a remarkable record," Roz said. "One hundred percent of the wrongful treatment cases we've investigated have resulted in the successful prosecution of the doctor in question. Which is only to say: we do not waste our time chasing innocents. If a case has been brought to the board's attention, it's for a well-founded reason."

Doubt is not a pleasant condition, Mary thought, *but certainty is absurd.*

"But if I haven't yet . . . *adhered,*" Mary pointed out, "how can I testify that what Dr. Hammer wrote about me was false?"

"Some truths transcend adherence," Roz said. "Don't get fouled up by adherence."

"But if I don't remember what happened to me, how can he be wrong?"

Roz leaned her elbows on her knees, hunching so low that Mary could see the part running down the center of her head and the raised mole that protruded from the center of the part like a beetle or a drop of blood.

"I have a vested interest in you, Mary," she said. "You were supposed to be my patient. I passed you along to Dr. Hammer because I was busy with my book, and don't you think I feel *guilty* about that? Don't you think I feel guilty that my self-absorption meant that you've been made the object of psychiatric ridicule by a man I was trying to help emerge from a professional holding pattern? Post-traumatic amnesia, yes, it's in vogue right now, but if I'd been your doctor, here's what I would have said: You know what happened to you. You have the power and authority to tell your own story. And you know that I know that you know this. Isn't that why you've been avoiding me? Isn't that why you treat me as though I'm your enemy?"

Mary puzzled this out. *Roz knew that she knew that she knew* . . . And what did she, Mary, know exactly? She knew that she had ostensibly started this game as an imaginative way to complete a school assignment. But it was more complicated than even that—a complication that arose, in part, when she had been assigned, via sheer coincidence, to Bettina Spencer's former doctor. She had muddled Bettina and Dora and herself together so tightly that nobody's story felt distinct anymore. Dora had been kissed by Herr K; Bettina, so went the Semmering rumor, had been abused by an uncle, which explained, or was meant to explain, her troubledness. Mary had been kissed by her parents' friend Kurt Thatcher. A harmless enough event, the kiss had occurred while the two families were on vacation at the Cape and Kurt had been so drunk at the time that he was able to look Mary in the face the next day without any sense that a boundary had been trespassed. Mary, who was twelve, was ecstatic. She viewed the kiss—which was gently administered and almost fatherly, a just-this-side-of-too-long pressing of dry padded flesh against dry padded flesh—as confirmation that she was, or had the power to be, bewitching. That night in her bunk bed, still headily replaying that two-second snippet of the evening in her mind, she stupidly confided in Regina. Her mother cornered Mary the next day as the two of them were shopping for dinner in the local grocery: *Do not ever tell lies about our friends again.* She'd slapped Mary in full view of a college boy buying beer, and the boy had sheepishly abandoned them in the aisle to their shameful mother-daughter business. The kiss did not ruin her; her mother's slap did. And so years later, when she had read *Dora*, the book ignited a chain of electric connections. She thought of herself like a bulb in a string of Christmas lights; one bad bulb left the bulbs after it in darkness. So she ignited herself, and the string reached back and back and back, and she became emboldened not only by her own injustice but by a continum of injustices linking her to Bettina and Dora and Dorcas Hobbs and Abigail Lake and beyond. She'd begun playing games, games inside of games inside of games. But now when she tried to visualize that string of lights, all she could see was an expanding brightness that erased more than it revealed.

"I don't remember," Mary said. "And if I don't remember, then Dr. Hammer's version is as good as true."

She slung her backpack over her shoulder with a finality that implied *we're done here.*

Roz placed her hands on the arms of her chair, threatening to stand but remaining seated.

"This may sound like a cheap platitude," she said, "but I honestly believe that truth is what you make of it."

Mary rolled her eyes.

"I'm trying to encourage you to be a little more circumspect. A little less selfish."

"Selfish," Mary said.

"You might not be willing to come to terms with your own past. But girls like you need to be protected from men like Dr. Hammer."

"You want to make an example of him," Mary stated bluntly.

"As you well know," Roz said wryly, "*pour faire une omelette il faut casser des oeufs*. And what we will gain—what the innocent Marys of the world will gain—it will be immeasurable. You could be a part of this, Mary. We're involved in a narrative revolution here. The eradication of Freud's legacy of misogyny—Freud who, like Dr. Hammer, chose to overlook instances of actual patient sexual abuse to support his fantasy theories. The freeing of the stories of hundreds of women and girls, like your friend Ida Bauer, whose own versions were plowed under the dirt so that the careers of their male doctors could flourish in the sun."

Roz bloomed her hands in her lap.

"I'm asking you to help these women to reclaim their stories, Mary," she said, "these women are depending on *you*. Men like Dr. Hammer view girls like you as an absence that needs to be filled. You are the blankness that allows his phallocentric expression of ideas. Frankly, I thought you'd want to do something about it."

Mary nodded, wondering to herself, *How does anyone take this woman seriously?* But of course Roz's seeming absurdity went unchecked by her colleagues. Mary was equivalently dumbfounded by Regina's ability to convince the teachers at Semmering that she possessed a fragile poetic genius, but had soon come to realize that power was about believing you were powerful and insisting, to the point of silliness, that others believe it too. Most people are too polite to object, or simply too lazy to fight another's ludicrous misperceptions about their own importance, and so power was, through graciousness and laziness, conferred. Her colleagues didn't want the hassle of contradicting Roz Biedelman, so they let her have her way, assuming she'd eventually run up against her own mediocrities and retreat to her proper station in life. But this was never going to happen, and eventually Roz would be their superior. Mary suddenly saw Roz in a stark, allegorical light. Stupid people are the new smart people. An apt epigraph, she thought, for Roz's brochure.

"I'll think about it," Mary said.

"You've been thinking a long time already," Roz said. "In my practice, with my patients, I've started to set deadlines. Leave your husband by this date. Stop having affairs by this date. Maybe you would like a deadline," Roz offered.

"I'm busy studying for midterms," Mary said lamely.

"So you're no stranger to pressure." Roz flipped through her desk calendar, forward then backward. She wrote something on a pad, tore off the top sheet, handed it to Mary.

"I'll see you next week," she said.

Mary wadded the paper and shoved it into her anorak pocket.

She left, shutting Roz's office door behind her.

A girl about her age sat in Roz's waiting room. She wore glasses, one lens blanked out by a nude-colored medical patch. The girl appeared totally unself-conscious both about her eye patch and about finding herself in a therapist's waiting room. She met Mary's gaze with her one eye and smiled at her. Mary didn't smile back. She hurried down the narrow hall, her anorak rubbing against the wall, making a frantic hissing noise. She thought about saving that girl. *But from whom*, she wondered to herself. *From whom.*

Notes

Mary, it became clear to me after our third session, exhibited an atypical disclosure progression. Again I found myself struck by the discrepancy between the patient I'd received and the patient Hicks-Flevill had treated. H-F wrote in his transfer summary, "patient exhibits markedly average intelligence; is frequently confused by my questions, a confusion that is not, I fear, due to her distressed mental state; she truly struggles to keep pace with me; not up to the mental challenge of deviousness." How H-F could have found Mary, whose mental aptitude was so far above average that I felt, at times, intimidated by her, to be a girl of "markedly average intelligence" was deeply perplexing. Then again, our contradictory perceptions of Mary's mental capacities were in some—possibly significant—way consistent with my own contradictory session reports. Mary's first session indicated she suffered from paranoid delusions that might be due to an endemic disorder (like schizophrenia) but was more likely evidence that she suffered from a textbook case of post-traumatic stress. Her second session suggested she suffered from an obsessive-compulsive disorder (her repetitive act of swirling her finger in her compact), a mild anxiety disorder (evidenced by her coughing fits), and an intermittent explosive disorder with antisocial tendencies (her insensitive comments about my physique). The third session suggested that she suffered from amnesia and a mild-to-moderate bipolar disorder, leading her to experience alternating bouts of lethargy and manic intelligence. Her fascination with Dorcas Hobbs also indicated a possible imago issue involving her mother; her mother's commitment to clearing the name of her family's "witch" relative, and Mary's fascination with Dorcas Hobbs, suggested that Mary both revered her mother and over-identified with her, possibly to the point of wanting, subconsciously, to destroy her.

In short: Mary was an unusual case. The faked amnesia (regarding her claim that she had no recollection of discussing K during a previous session) became even more apparent to me after listening to our session tapes, and made me wonder how many of her other so-called amnesias, for example those involving the golden tomahawk and the "spell" and the suggested molestation by numerous unidentifiable individuals, had also been faked. In particular I noticed how Mary cut me off during my explanation of the Dora case at the precise moment I was about to pronounce the letter *K*. Clearly, despite her avowals, she had read this book before, and knew that her captor shared the same name as Dora's molester; perhaps she had even named him after Dora's K. Consciously or unconsciously, Mary was preventing *her* K from reappearing, "castrating" him from my sentences, which would, under normal circumstances, suggest that the patient had been abused in a sexual matter; but her golden-tomahawk fantasy, coupled with my prior experience with Bettina Spencer, encouraged me not to jump to easy conclusions before all the evidence was submitted and carefully, rationally scrutinized.

Mary's mood, on the day of our fourth session, was best described as elated confrontation. She slumped tensely in my waiting-room chair, her legs splayed open, her knees wipering back and forth in an agitated manner. She wore frayed jeans and a pair of mismatched wool socks into which her cuffs were partially tucked. Her hair was unwashed, her complexion splotchy, a constellation of blemishes on her chin worried into scabs.

Once inside my office, her agitation minimized slightly. She sat on the couch, she asked for a tissue. She blew her nose then dropped the soiled tissue to the floor.

You seem agitated, I said to her.

I have my period, she said.

Are you usually agitated by your menstrual cycle, I asked.

I didn't get my period until I was fifteen, she said. Regina got her period when she was twelve. So did Gaby.

Did that make you feel abnormal, I said. I was thinking: a girl's failure to menstruate in a timely manner—or any form of emmeniopathy, including primary dysmenorrhea and mittelschmerz—often indicates regressive emotional tendencies (not to mention literal or figurative impotence on par with the male castration complex) manifesting specifically as a failure to separate from the mother, a refusal to see herself as the mother's sexual competition, and an inability to acknowledge the increasingly sexualized dynamic with the father. I was reminded of Bettina. Also a late menstruator, also a girl with regressive emotional tendencies who unconsciously found her inability to act on her sexual impulses toward her father so loathsome, so damning, that she fabricated a sexual relationship with a father figure to fill the psychological void.

I faked it so my mother wouldn't be worried, she said.

How did you "fake it," I said.

The obvious way. I sprinkled red food coloring on my underwear and left it in the hamper where my mother would find it. That afternoon I found a box of pads on my bed and a pair of cameo earrings. This is how we communicate, my mother and I.

This form of communication creates a lot of space for misunderstandings, I observed.

It makes it easy to keep people happy without technically lying, she said.

You faked the commencement of your menstrual cycle to keep your mother happy, I said.

My grandmother gave me the pair of cameo earrings for my thirteenth birthday and my mother said: "No no, Mary isn't a woman yet. She isn't a *woman*." My mother kept the earrings and gave them to me after she found my underwear in the hamper.

Were your sisters given cameo earrings when they started to menstruate?

Mary nodded.

Did that make you envious?

They're ugly, Mary said. The earrings I mean.

Did you see these earrings as symbolic? I asked. I was thinking: what an unfortunate gift, one that subconsciously accentuates the teenage girl's classic bifurcated psyche, to literally imply that she is not one uncomplicated child anymore but has been split into two conflicting beings—a girl and a woman.

The first time I wore them I lost one, she said. Maybe that's symbolic? That fact that I lost one?

Losing an item can be a way of denying that item's inherent symbolism, I said. For example when a reluctant fiancée loses her engagement ring. She is denying the symbolism of the ring.

Meaning I don't love my mother, Mary said.

Your mother gave you a gift of two female faces, I said. Two halves of a woman that can never be whole.

It's just a stupid family tradition, Mary said.

Traditions do not spring from nowhere, I said. We don't celebrate Thanksgiving because we want an excuse to eat turkey.

You think my mother has a split personality, Mary said.

An unfortunate by-product of our cultural approach to women is that *many* women suffer from a type of psychic division, which complicates their happiness but does not qualify as a diagnosable personality disorder.

You think *I* have a split personality, Mary said.

I think your mother, as is the case with many mothers, put a great deal of emphasis on your commencing menstruation, for reasons that probably elude her.

Emphasizing it by not talking about it.

Emphasis through oversight is not an unheard-of tactic, I said.

You have an answer for everything, Mary said. You're so quick to be right that you don't notice when you're dead wrong.

What am I dead wrong about, I said.

The reason I faked my period to make my mother happy.

She was worried that you weren't developing normally, I said.

She was worried that I was pregnant.

That's a natural worry, I said.

Actually, she wasn't worried that I was pregnant. She was worried that I was having sex.

Because she didn't want you to become pregnant.

Because she didn't want me to enjoy myself, Mary said. She fired our landscaper's assistant because she was convinced he was having sex with Regina.

Was Regina having sex with the landscaper's assistant, I said.

Duh, Beaton, she said. He was a total fox.

The landscaper's assistant behaved in a predatorial manner toward your sister, I said.

Mary regarded me with undisguised scorn.

I'm saying he was cute, Beaton. It logically follows that he wouldn't touch Regina with a ten-foot rake.

Has Regina ever had sex, to your knowledge?

Not with the landscaper's assistant, Mary said.

A pause.

No, she said.

What about Gabrielle?

The last person Gaby kissed was a girl.

Does your mother know about Gabrielle's sexual preference for girls?

It's not a *sexual preference*, she said. She just kisses girls sometimes. It's harmless.

Do you consider lesbianism harmful, I said.

Mary didn't respond.

Or maybe I should rephrase: Do you consider consensual sexual contact between two same-sex people to be more harmful than, say, nonconsensual sexual contact between two people of a different sex?

You mean rape, she said.

Is that your interpretation, I said.

Mary toyed with her ponytail.

I was only saying that Gaby likes kissing girls, she said.

Maybe that question was too confusing for you, I said.

If you're going to ask a stupid question, at least get your stupid question right.

What's wrong with my question, I said.

What about consensual sex between two people of a different sex, she said.

Consensual sex, I said. Meaning that both parties are in agreement.

I know what consensual means, she said.

Mary gazed at me, calmly confrontational. It was a curious clarification. Was Mary saying that she'd had sex with K, and that the sex had been consensual? If so, this suggested a fourth yet completely divergent diagnosis—Mary suffered from a simple, easily manageable adjustment disorder, brought on by an intense experience of guilt. She'd engaged— perhaps willingly—in a sexual manner with her captor. I was reminded of Mary's final request at the conclusion of our first session: *I would like to know if I enjoyed myself.* Perhaps she already knew the answer: she *had* enjoyed herself, and was dealing with the emotional fallout of this illicit sexual pleasure that was so frowned upon by her mother.

Are you saying that you've engaged in consensual sex with a member of a different sex, I said.

Mary didn't respond.

So perhaps your mother's sex phobia isn't so irrational, I said.

Mary scoffed.

She can't enjoy what she's not having, she said.

You seem so certain about your mother's lack of sexual activity, I said. And yet you and your mother—as you've stated—do not communicate except through oversight.

I found a letter, she said. A letter my father wrote to Greta.

Who is Greta, I said.

Greta is the woman he loves, she said.

Mary explained her family's relationship to Greta Thatcher and her husband, Kurt, a couple with whom her parents had been close friends since college. Kurt was an executive at a frozen seafood company with an office overlooking Boston Harbor. Greta had grown up in Vienna. Greta and Kurt came along on most of their family holidays—to the Belgrade Lakes in Maine, to Vermont, to the Cape. At first it seemed natural that Greta and Kurt should accompany them—they were like an aunt and an uncle who drank too much and played card games until late at night and had no children of their own. But then it became clear to Mary that her mother deeply disliked Greta, she behaved badly around her, not-so-accidentally breaking plates and burning food. Even Kurt, a generally nonplussed man, began to drink more than his usual amount and punch their father with a jovial repetitiveness that verged on hostile. They last vacationed together when Mary was twelve years old, a cross-country ski trip to the Northeast Kingdom region of Vermont. Midway through the week, her parents stopped sharing a bedroom. On the final day at the ski house, Mary came downstairs to find her mother alone in the kitchen, crying. Mary's father, her mother told her, had gone off to the woods to commit suicide—and it was only through the brave intervention of Greta, who had chased after him in her bathrobe and boots, that he had been persuaded to spare his life for the sake of his family.

I believed her at the time, Mary said.

But then, Mary said, she found a letter from Greta to her father. The letter insisted that Mary's father shouldn't feel guilty about wanting to leave Mary's mother because Mary's mother and father never had sex anymore.

That's when I knew, said Mary.

What did you know, I said.

That my father hadn't tried to commit suicide, and Greta hadn't tried to stop him. They were off in the woods having sex. My mother lied to me.

It must feel terrible to be lied to, I said.

It must feel terrible to be such a fucking loser, Beaton.

You're still angry with your parents, I said.

Obviously my dad was just getting back at my mom for being an all-purpose bitch.

But you said that Greta was the woman your father loved, I reminded her.

He loved her in the way that you love people who give you leverage.

That's a very astute and mature observation, I said.

Thanks for the approval, Mary responded.

Notice that the moment I compliment you, you revert to flippancy. Note that such flippancy is a protective measure against being hurt.

Note taken, she said. Can we stop picking me apart?

I smiled.

Unfortunately, that's what we're here to do.

Is it? she mused, her manner darkening. I thought we were here to pick apart other people and how what they did to me in the past made me who I am.

That's a very victim-oriented approach, I said.

Like Kurt, she said. Kurt did something to me, she said.

OK, I said. Let's talk about what Kurt did to you.

Mary glowered at me.

Was that in quotes?

Was what in quotes, I said.

You just said *what Kurt "did" to you.*

If you think you heard quotes, then I respect what you think you heard.

That's an apology? she said.

No, I said. I am acknowledging that your perspective is valid even if I disagree with it.

You're a petty man, Beaton, Mary said chidingly.

Once again, you're diverting what could be an important topic toward a useless critique of me.

Sorry, she said. My parents didn't believe me, either.

I didn't say I didn't believe you, I said. You haven't told me anything to disbelieve.

Kurt told me that Greta would be there, Mary said, and that Greta would take me clothes shopping after lunch. We arranged to meet at his office.

But Greta wasn't there, I guessed.

Greta had a cold, she said.

What about Kurt's secretaries?

He'd sent them away. We were all alone. He asked me if I wanted to see the view from the conference room on the top floor. But instead he took me to a file room with a very small window. He drew the blinds and then he . . .

He touched you, I said.

Sort of, she said.

He made you touch him, I said.

He kissed me and hugged me and I could feel his . . .

His erection, I said.

I wrote in my notes *K = Kurt.*

Mary nodded.

I imagine you felt very betrayed, I said.

Mary shrugged. Whatever, she said. It was just Kurt.

Mary coughed.

But still, I said.

Mary was seized by a coughing fit. She waved her hands in front of her face apologetically.

I fetched a cup of water from the waiting-room bubbler. Mary drank the contents gulpingly.

Thanks, she said. There's a weird pressure—on my thorax. Every time I think of his—*you know*—pressing into my stomach I feel pressure on my thorax.

Calls a chat a chat, I wrote in my notes, *but not a penis.*

That's called displacement symptom formation, I said.

Mary coughed.

It's a common response to unwanted stimulus, I said.

Yeah, well, she said. You probably think I liked it.

I think you should tell me how it made you feel.

It made me feel tired, she said.

I was reminded of a remark Mary made during our first session, when she claimed that the "moaning sounds," which sounded like "group sex," had made her feel "sleepy."

You frequently respond to unwanted sexual stimulus with fatigue, I said. It's almost . . .

Postcoital, she said.

Excuse me?

I read that a decent number of convicted rapists are caught because they are so relaxed afterward they forget they've committed a crime.

But you're the raped girl in this equation, not the rapist.

That's a very victim-oriented approach, Beaton, she said.

Why don't you tell me what the raped girl feels, I said.

Her feelings do not matter, Mary said.

Why is that?

Because the raped girl is a liar, Mary said. Is that a bad thing to say?

Good and bad aren't words we value here, I said. Who says the raped girl is a liar.

Everyone says, Mary said.

"Everyone" includes you, I said.

Mary didn't answer.

If she's a liar, I said, why did she lie.

She lied, Mary said, because the truth is so clearly unbelievable.

What Might Have Happened

W hat might have happened next was nobody's fault. Looking back on it, the man could not allow himself to take responsibility, nor could he rightly blame the girl. *This is how things happen,* he imagined explaining to the policeman. *They happen by happening.* Sometimes explanations and blame do not exist. Sometimes a person's inability to have a firm feeling about a situation leads to situations in which there are only strong and complicated feelings. One minute the man and the girl were sitting in the Mercedes staring at the darkened third-floor window of his ex-brownstone, his former bad investment, the next minute—or so it felt—they were at a twenty-four-hour rest stop just over the New Hampshire border on 93 north, the man filling the Mercedes with diesel, the girl's head visible inside the illuminated convenience store above the aisles of potato chips and chewing tobacco and gum. The convenience store, the single visible object emerging from the lightless backdrop of trees, reminded the man of a globe filled with liquid and fake snow and tiny people. The girl was just a tiny fake person inside this globe and he thought to himself: this is the first step toward committing a crime. Dehumanizing the victim. She is just a piece of painted plastic, already drowned and entombed in a tacky shelf ornament flurried with artificial snow.

The man noticed that the girl had left her ski jacket in the back of the Mercedes. Checking her whereabouts—now she was standing before the beverage cooler—the man opened the back door and removed the jacket, in his guilty haste cutting himself on an expired ski-pass wire, bent at a malevolent angle. He stuck his finger in his mouth—the blood hot, at least in comparison to the air he'd been breathing—and flipped the coat inside out with his good hand.

No name, as he'd suspected there should be, young girls being fanatically proprietary creatures or so he remembered from his own childhood of three sisters, just a phone number and an instruction: If Found Please Call.

The man eyed the pay phone, angling from a plowed drift of snow and garbage. It had snowed north of Boston that day. Snow still sifted from the blackness above him like lazily falling stars.

Now the girl was talking to the cashier, invisible behind a blinking lotto display. *Turning him in*, he thought. But no. He saw the man hand her what looked to be a tire iron. *To defend herself. To cave in his skull.* But no. From the bottom of the tire iron dangled what he guessed to be a restroom key.

The girl unlocked and entered a door at the far end of the store.

The man scuttled toward the pay phone, her jacket in his hand. In his hurry he skidded on a patch of ice and felt a muscle deep inside his hip twinge, retract, tighten uncomfortably. He proceeded at a more cautious but still urgent pace. The pay phone had a dial tone, thank god, but distant, as though it were being cabled from the moon.

The man gave the operator his credit card number and the girl's home phone.

Silence, of the uninhabited kind. The man thought perhaps the connection had been severed, and of this inconvenience he was half relieved. What was he going to say when her mother, or her father, or possibly even the police, picked up the phone?

Help me, he would say. I've been kidnapped.

But that sounded pathetic and unbelievable. Was he really so out of control? Of course he wasn't. He was a man, he was confused, and he was lonely, and this girl had a key to him—a fake key, a toying key, like the restroom key it hung from the end of a tire iron with which she might cave in his skull—but still she represented *possibility* to him, whereas everyone else in his life represented shortcoming. *You're the man you've always been.* His ex-wife's favorite dismissive refrain.

In the same vein, thus, nobody had forced him to drive this girl home, nobody had forced him to take her out to dinner, to drive her to Boston, to drive her to his ex-wife's ski cabin in the mountains where god knows what would happen. (It would happen by happening.) Nobody had forced him to do any of this, and yet he still felt cornered, as though he weren't given a choice in the matter.

He heard a subtle change in the silence through the earpiece. Somewhere many miles east and south of him, a phone rang. Once. Twice.

A woman picked up the phone.

Hello, she said. She sounded angry or half drunk, not crazed with worry, not at all like a mother whose daughter has failed to come home from school.

Hello, the woman repeated.

The man didn't know what to say.

Hello, she said a third time. She was a smoker, he guessed.

I'm hanging up now, the woman said.

Wait, the man said. I've got her.

Got who? Who is this? Is this Preston?

I've got her, he repeated.

Your father's a cad, the woman said. Did you know he tried to kiss me at the Ives's Christmas party? Did you know that he's a hound for anything on two legs? What an embarrassment.

My father is dead, the man said.

You wish, the woman said. Your headmaster will be getting a phone call tomorrow. You can forget Harvard, young man. You can just forget it.

She hung up the phone.

The man stared at the receiver, dumbfounded. This was all a joke. He raised his head. The girl was staring at him though the convenience store window.

He shuttled back to the diesel pump and tossed the girl's coat into the backseat.

The girl returned with a paper bag.

Three kinds of potato chips and a two-liter jug of root beer, she announced. Who were you calling?

Huh? he said.

You were on the phone. Who were you calling?

My office, the man said.

You don't have an office.

My old office, he said. I still get messages through the service.

Why were you holding my jacket? she asked.

I . . . my hands were cold. I couldn't find my gloves in the dark.

The girl, not a moron, seemed unconvinced by this explanation.

Look, she said, holding up a foil bag. Shrimp flavored. Can you believe it?

I can't, the man said. I can't believe it.

He peered at his cut finger. In this light—from the dashboard, from the dirty fluorescents above the gas island—it appeared covered in a glossy tar. Blacktopped.

What happened, the girl said. Did you cut it on the gas pump?

She grabbed his hand. He pulled it back.

You should get a free tank of gas. You should at least get a free box of Band-Aids.

The man didn't answer her. He started the Mercedes and put it into drive. He accelerated quickly, careening too fast over the icy parking lot. He heard something bounce and roll in their wake. His heart nearly concussed itself on his Adam's apple. *Fuck.* He looked in the rearview mirror, expecting to see a sprawl of legs and arms. Then he remembered that he'd left the gas cap on the hood. Via his side mirror he could see the tank thrust perpendicular to the car and vibrating violently on its hinge.

Too late, he thought.

The back of the car fishtailed as they merged back onto the highway; the salt under the wheels made it sound as though they were driving over glass. Maybe they were. The man almost hoped that they were. Four flat tires would mean they'd have to stop the happening from happening, they'd have to spend the night in the convenience store playing cards with the cashier and eating shrimp chips, they would look like innocent victims of some bad automotive luck rather than a pair of mismatched strangers up to no good with each other.

You seem nervous, the girl observed. She opened the bag of shrimp chips. Immediately the interior of the car smelled like dried, aerated fish.

These, the girl pronounced, are disgusting.

Would you mind throwing those out the window? the man said. The fake stink was making him queasy.

But that would be littering, the girl said.

I don't give a shit, the man said, more harshly than he'd intended.

Jeez, the girl said. So-rry.

She unscrewed the cap to the ungainly jug of root beer resting between her thighs. As she lifted the jug with both hands and attached her mouth to the oversize opening, the Mercedes hit a pothole. He heard the plastic bottle strike her teeth. She pulled the bottle away, spilling root beer on her field hockey skirt.

She coughed gaggingly.

The man looked away, inexplicably embarrassed.

Ow, she said.

I just meant—it's food.

Huh? the girl said.

That's not littering. If you throw the shrimp chips out the window, but not the bag.

What's wrong with you, the girl said, her voice scratchy.

Nothing, the man said. I'm . . . tired.

You and me both, the girl said. She rolled down the window and pushed the bag of shrimp chips into the wall of cold wind; it sucked backward with a sharp, collapsed crackle. She reclined her seat, the window still open.

Roll up the window, the man said. The noise was deafening, the cold both invigorated him and caused within him surges of intense hopelessness.

The girl shut her eyes. Pretending to sleep.

Roll up the window, the man repeated.

The girl did not stir.

The man returned his attention to the empty road, gray asphalt scored with ribbons of salt and snow. His finger hurt more in the cold and he felt his brain unfurling and dissolving. It had turned into a caustic fume behind his eyebrows, useless for thinking. He felt poisoned by this organ of his, the poison spreading to the rest of his body, his aching hip, his injured finger. They would be healed and then readied for evil action, the synapses doped and then firing according to the pointed aims of this formerly complex brain of his, now reduced to a simple vapor, a collection of thoughtless molecules with nothing but science driving them toward an evil conclusion.

Among the many emotions he felt, empathy was strangely foremost in his mind. He'd spent a week in his former law firm packing up his office, a task that might have taken a day had he not read every dull piece of evidence and testimony, attempting to locate in this morass of paper a hint of what had drawn him to the law in the first place. The most upsetting file was a case against a babysitter, a junior college–educated woman of Italian heritage who had been accused, by a Beacon Hill banker and his wife, of sexually abusing their two children with wooden spoons, with curling irons, with crucifixes. The notes for his closing statement were appallingly exploitative—he had emphasized the fact that the woman, a lapsed Catholic, had a mother who ran a beauty parlor and a father who ran a pizza joint, thereby lending circumstantial, but emotionally compelling, relevance to her chosen tools of abuse. But really it had been an easy case, since everyone was abusing children these days— in groups, by Satan's minions, from the West Coast to New England; he had made a note to himself on a legal pad never to reference these other cases, but to make sure, subconsciously, that the jurors saw the woman's act as a continuum of malice sweeping the country. He'd brought up the Lilliputians, not that he'd read Swift since high school. What has a better chance of taking down an elephant—one spear thrown by one man, or millions of tiny spears thrown by millions of tiny people?

He had written a phrase in pencil, then sketched around the letters so that they appeared to spring from the lined page three-dimensionally: EMPOWER THE TINY PEOPLE.

He had won the case, a victory that affected him in his present head about as much as reading about the outcome of a tribal skirmish in Borneo.

What did affect him was the newspaper photo of the woman—the girl, really—being led away from the courtroom crying so intensely that her nose was a swollen blur of snot, her eyes two miserable slits, and the thought that such desires (assuming she was guilty—and he did, for the sake of his conscience, assume as much) could lurk in a girl like that, a girl who was so blandly, functionally average-seeming, such an exemplary representative of the blah American mean. But truth had a hard time adhering to logic these days; her guilt seemed the only possible choice to him because it seemed so impossible. And now the outlandish was happening to him, and he empathized with this poor Italian girl, whose brain had vaporized in a similar way and infiltrated her hands and fingers like a bad drug. He was—to his happiness and to his horror—becoming his own most impossible person.

The man shivered, his teeth so tightly gritted they caused his jaw muscles to cramp. The fucking cold, he thought. He glanced at the girl, still pretending to be asleep. Useless to ask her a third time to shut the window, she was clearly toying with him and enjoying it, or that's how he read the smile on her fake-sleeping face. He lunged across her body and wrenched the window handle around and around and around, leaning all his weight on her, his elbow jabbing into her rib cage with each rotation. He heard her gasp, which inspired him to extend his elbow farther into her midsection as he cranked. His left hand held the steering wheel loosely; with each lunging rotation he pulled the wheel slightly to the right until, just as he'd cranked the handle one final time, the window glass meeting the frame with the suction sound of a vaccum sealing, the car's rear end started to skid.

He jerked to an upright position and tried to recorrect the car's drift, really it was so casual, the car's gentle sideswiping, but the man's panicky left rotation worsened the problem into something decidedly not casual. Now the car was made of two independently moving parts, the rear of the car attempting to overtake the front of the car, and soon the car was perpendicular to the road, then facing backward, then perpendicular again, then forward. The man turned the wheel in the opposite direction of their spin and the car paused for a second, quivering violently, as though deciding between two equally desirous forces. The man won, or so for a split second it appeared. But his body, never such a reliable object, failed them. The car returned to a wobbly fishtailing motion, veered to the right, and buried its nose in the partially snow-obscured guardrail.

Metal against metal. The snapping lanyard sound of safety belts, the forced exhalations as both the man and the girl jerked forward then backward into their seats.

Silence.

The man looked at the girl. She was holding her stomach.

Are you OK? he said.

Her wide eyes fixated on the darkened dash. It took him a second to realize: she was hyperventilating.

Are you OK? he repeated, wanting to touch her but thinking: her neck could be broken. He knew this much from the television shows he watched all night long, night after crushingly dull night: do not shift a person with a possible spine injury. *Insomnia is my friend.*

Can I help you, the man said. Tell me. What can I do.

The girl shook her head—did he detect a touch of irritation?—still trying to catch her breath.

OK, he said. OK.

The girl glared at him. No doubt about it—she was irritated. Not terrified, not paralyzed—pissed off. The man fell back against his headrest. *It's over,* he thought to himself. Not the accident. But this night. This *happening.* The police would arrive. The tow truck would arrive. He and the girl would part, no harm done.

He massaged his left collarbone and his neck tendons, smarting from where the seat belt had near-garroted him upon impact. His eyes were closed, thus he was utterly unprepared for her attack. His stomach recoiled, his body pitched forward. He struck his chin on the steering wheel.

Jesus Christ! he said.

The girl glared at him.

That's for being a jerk, she said.

It was an *accident,* he wheezed.

I'm not talking about that, she said. You think I haven't been in a car accident before? You think I care about accidents?

The man massaged his diaphragm. It felt bruised. He imagined he could make out little individual swellings where her knuckles had made contact.

You knocked the wind out of me on purpose, the girl said. On purpose. While you were pretending to roll up the window.

The man didn't defend himself.

That's a lot of dishonest crap, the girl said. If you want to hit me you should just hit me.

Like you hit me, the man said. Out of nowhere. That's more honest.

The girl stared out the window at the woods. Steam rose from the hood of the car. The engine was dead—or had he turned it off?

Guess we're fucked, she said.

The man didn't reply. He felt like sobbing. The sky was turning colors as he watched. From gray to pinky-violet to a deep red-orange. Once light was shed upon this situation, he thought, it will become untenable. It would not hold up to the scrutiny of day. The girl would disappear like a ghost, and this impossible person he'd witnessed in himself would recede.

Is the engine dead? the girl asked.

The man shrugged. He assumed yes.

Try it, she said. Try the ignition.

The man turned the key.

The car started up.

No, he thought to himself. Not possible.

Amazing, the girl said. We are two very lucky people.

The man experienced a disorienting cramp of nausea; he turned his head to the left, closed his eyes. Maybe he just needed to sleep.

I'm sorry for hitting you, the girl said.

Don't worry, the man said. I deserved it, apparently.

The girl laughed. *Apparently*, she said. That's no fun.

What's no fun, the man said.

You should resent me for hitting you, she said.

Do you resent me for hitting you? the man asked.

The girl thought about this. No, she said. I was relieved.

You were relieved?

It gave me a good excuse, she said. It gave me a good excuse to hit you.

The man experienced a second vertigo twinge of sick. His ex-wife, during one of her reclamation therapy sessions, had admitted something uncannily similar. She'd wished for him to trip up in the final years of their marriage. She'd wished for him to stab her. Nothing gave her more pleasure than when he gave her a decent reason to hate him.

Look, the girl said, pointing out the window. The sunrise, now the pretty-scary intensity of a forest fire, made a million spears of the treetops; their black silhouettes appeared already burned.

Beautiful.

I have to pee, the girl said.

She pulled on her cleats without tying the laces.

Be right back, she said.

He watched her scale the modest snowbank into which they'd landed. The red-orange sunrise seemed capable of burning her up. Soon she disappeared from view, but he could hear the crunching of her shoes as she sank into the snow, en route to find a tree or some safe place to hide behind. Maybe she'll disappear, he thought. Maybe she'll disappear and wait for him to come looking for her. But he knew this was foolish thinking. He knew she was coming back without his needing to find her.

Boston

It was immature, Mary knew, it was inexcusable behavior for a thirty-year-old woman, but this did not stop her from tailing the red coat down Commonwealth Avenue. She kept a steady padding of four or five pedestrians between herself and the coat; at street crossings she paused to look into store windows as the coat waited for the light to change. She was feeling fairly proud of her technique until she momentarily lost her mark inside a scrum of school kids tumbling from the T exit, emerging from the pile just in time to see the coat disappear into a yellow-awninged store at the end of the block.

Mary feigned interest in a flyer taped to the window, uncertain how to proceed. Seven minutes earlier she'd been standing outside Roz's office, plotting her Roz approach. Should she ring the bell and identify herself and hope that Roz was still such a meddler that she'd welcome Mary into her office? Or wait until another client exited and sneak into the brownstone and then . . . the *then* had yet to be worked out in detail. Through the glass of the brownstone's front doors she had seen a woman in a red coat pulling on gloves and tensing her shoulders and generally readying herself for the cold. This was her chance; she would slide inside and then figure out what to do.

Yes. Perfect.

As the woman politely, if distractedly, held the door for her, Mary caught a narrow glimpse of nose and eyes, shuttered by the earflaps of a fur hunting cap. Just that glimpse was enough to be certain—fairly certain—that the face belonged to Bettina Spencer.

Mary watched the red coat until it was three stoops away, thinking *of course Roz sucked Bettina into her vampiric orbit*. She marveled at how youthful Bettina appeared, given that she was now in her early forties. She glowed in that rested, expensively moisturized, just-enough-sun way. In other words: she looked rich, and presumably she was rich now, at least according to Mary's research, conducted in the Grove library those weeks after she'd first learned of Mum's illness. These after-work spools through the microfiche provided her with her first inklings of what had happened to Dr. Hammer, because while his trial consumed the Boston papers she had pointedly avoided reading them. Soon thereafter she had left for college, she had spent four years in Ashland, Oregon, a town where people subscribed to crystal healing newsletters rather than reading pop psychology books when they had a yen for self-improvement. Nobody had heard of Miriam or Dr. E. Karl Hammer. She was young, and in the way that the young can be disturbingly self-exonerating, she was. Forgetting him was easy. Disappearing into the blank otherworldliness of the Northwest was easy, resuming her life as an unremarkable person was easy. But then Dr. Hammer and his uncertain fate had begun to needle her conscience, a conscience that grew exponentially more self-lacerating after Mum was diagnosed. Dr. Hammer became her obsession, a man whose fate she returned to night after night, watching his life unravel like the doomed protagonist of a freeze-frame TV miniseries (the Evil Hammer, *Malleus Male-factorum*), with obvious villains and an outcome that felt clunkily fore-shadowed.

And so she had learned: when Roz and her colleagues from the Mas-sachusetts Mental Health Governing Board started to circle Dr. Ham-mer, Bettina decided to sue Dr. Hammer for retroactive abuses. Dr. Hammer had volunteered as the Semmering mental health adviser while a graduate student at BU, a job he'd ceded to Roz after Miss Pym de-cided it would be more "seemly" for her girls to be counseled by a woman. He was Bettina's doctor after her mysterious reappearance. Bet-tina claimed Dr. Hammer had practically forced her to admit she'd been abducted by the field hockey coach. She'd been suggestible at the time, she conceded. But this did not excuse his taking advantage of her fragile mental state, this did not excuse his urging her to claim as her story a flight of his own imaginative fancy, which was his first, desperate attempt to make a name for himself.

Dr. Hammer denied it all.

Fourteen years later, viewed as sequential pieces of reporting, Bet-tina's case appeared ludicrously unwinnable and on its own would have probably amounted to little more than the empty accusations of a provenly troubled liar. But combined with the earlier assault led by Roz and her board and the general climate of paranoia surrounding minors and authority figures in the mid-to-late eighties, Dr. Hammer didn't stand a chance. His license, already suspended indefinitely, was perma-nently revoked. Soon thereafter he disappeared from the headlines and, presumably, from Boston.

There existed no photographs of Dr. Hammer entering or leaving the courtroom. Instead the papers printed and reprinted, with evident schadenfreude, his author photo, which, as his situation worsened, slowly transformed from a confident head shot to a cautionary portrait of hubris. The repetitive appearance of this one photo also had a slightly morbid feel to it, as though Dr. Hammer had gone missing and people were hopefully looking for him, even though everyone secretly presumed he was dead.

Mary had never been inside this particular storefront—a bookstore/stationery/notions/café that approximated the experience of stepping into somebody's wealthy grandmother's boudoir, a tensely desexed space that smelled headachingly of tea rose. The tables on which new books spiraled roofward in propeller-shaped piles were draped in toile tablecloths; the identical-looking saleswomen sported dark blond bowl cuts, pleated wide-wale corduroys, duck boots, and matching toile smocks; the square footage afforded the stationery area of packaged vellum greeting cards and wrapping papers and monogrammed desk sets far exceeded the square footage given over to books; the café was in fact a "tearoom," which was in fact a corner of the store with three tables and a small bar, cordoned off by a few gold posts and a thick swoop of nautical-looking rope.

Mary was assaulted by a perky middle-aged saleswoman wielding a pair of silver scissors and a bolt of kelly green grosgrain ribbon.

"Was it two yards you wanted?" The woman punctuated her question with two emphatic snips of her scissors.

"Excuse me?"

"Of ribbon," the woman said. "Two yards?"

"You've got me confused with another customer," Mary said.

The woman scanned the store with skittish irritation. Mary scanned along with her, noting that she and Bettina were the only customers under fifty. For the second time that day she found herself feeling wrongly seen, and wondered if in fact she had a mistaken sense of how she appeared to the rest of the world. Like a prospective Semmering parent with a high school–aged daughter. Like a preppily de-eroticized matriarch with a penchant for toile and kelly green ribbon.

Mary lurked behind the "Local Authors" table, grabbing for camouflage purposes the first book her hand encountered. She ruffled the pages while focusing on Bettina, partially hidden behind a freestanding shelf of greeting cards. The greeting-card area was organized by feeling rather than event, the calligraphied signs reading REJOICE! REGRET, SYMPATHY, EMPATHY, CLOSURE. Bettina picked up a card in LIMBO . . . before shifting her attention to FORGIVENESS. Mary partly suspected she was meeting someone, an older mustier someone—why else would she be in this store?—but she also suspected that Bettina didn't really have much of a purpose. In this store, in her life. In the grand sense, Bettina was purposeless. Unless skin care was a purpose. Unless she was up to something with Roz.

"Can I help you?"

A second middle-aged saleswoman with a blond bowl cut, indistinguishable from the first, flashed her a white-toothed grimace.

"Thanks, no," Mary said to the woman.

"Oh! Have you *read* that *book*?" the woman gushed nervously. She wore a name tag. ANNE. She held an uncapped glue stick. "She's one of our best-selling local authors."

Mary looked at the book she'd been fake-reading.

The Tarnished Trivet, by Rosemary Biedelman.

"Of course," Mary said, more bitchily than she intended.

Anne retracted inside her too-big smock.

"I mean, who hasn't read it?" Mary added to soften her remark.

"It's been one of our most dependable best sellers," said Anne, with mechanical enthusiasm. "I have customers who have read it four, five times."

Anne test-drove a second grimace-smile. Poor woman, Mary thought. Obviously the salespeople worked on commission here; obviously Anne's sales, given her rigor-mortised technique, were negligible to none.

Anne's agonized smile persisted while she struggled to find a conversational hook.

Mary decided to help her out.

"I know Rosemary Biedelman," she offered.

"You do!" said Anne.

"I do," Mary said.

"So do I!" said Anne.

Anne fiddled anxiously with her glue stick. She foundered.

"How do you know Roz," Mary said.

"She's a regular customer here. Which is why we have her books stacked so prominently. How do you know . . ."

Then something occurred to Anne. She reddened. Her attitude toward Mary, previously wary-to-fearful, shifted. Anne visibly calmed, as though she'd been awarded an upper hand in this mysteriously weighted transaction.

Mary understood—Anne assumed that Mary was one of Roz's patients, and Anne, clearly a self-loathing basket case, still clung to the only bit of flotsam left from her wreck of a life: only weak people went to therapy.

This assumption of Anne's made Mary unhappy. No, it made her quietly enraged.

"Actually, I'm a colleague of Roz's," Mary said. "I'm a psychotherapist."

"Oh!" Anne said.

"Yes indeed," said Mary.

"Then you definitely don't need to read self-help books do you?" Anne said.

"You know what they say about psychotherapists," Mary said. "The blinder leading the blind."

"Well, I wouldn't have any idea since I've never been in therapy," Anne said. "But as the book buyer for the store, I'm obliged to read all the self-help books. I don't subscribe to most of the nonsense. Which is not to say they're *all* nonsense," Anne said quickly.

"Some of them are well beyond the tasteful realm of nonsense," Mary said.

"Some of them speak to the soul. They're not about weakness, they're about *proud survival*. They're about *self-definition* and *human fortitude*."

"Also known as how-to denial manuals," Mary said.

Anne wasn't listening.

"I assume, since you know Roz, you've read this one?" she asked.

Anne hastened to a nearby bookshelf, her duck shoes suctioning across the varnished floor. She returned with a paperback copy of *Trampled Ivy: How Abusive Marriages Happen to Smart Women*.

Mary regarded it noncommittally.

"That was published before my time," Mary said, scanning the familiar cover. She watched as Bettina made her leisurely way from FORGIVE-NESS to the tearoom. She left her purse on a table while she ordered at the bar.

"You should read it. Your mother should read it. Every woman in your family should read it," Anne said fervently.

"That's quite an endorsement," Mary said.

"You'd be amazed how intelligent women put up with, well, with *less than ideal* situations, simply out of pride. We thought we were immune to that sort of working-class affliction, simply because we'd read Joyce and Proust. I went to Smith. Not technically an 'Ivy,' but as Dr. Biedelman explains in her introduction, the Seven Sisters are really considered Ivy League."

"I've always thought so," Mary said.

Mary turned the book over and flinched.

"Nice picture," Mary said. "Of course she looks nothing like this in person."

"Well," Anne said defensively, "the photo's quite old."

"In person she has a mole—actually, it's more like a wart—right here."

She pointed to Roz's nose.

"And a scar which you can really only see in certain lights. Of course this picture was taken before the cheek implants, which have turned out to be a disaster."

"Really?" said Anne. "That's strange. She just gave a reading here last weekend . . ."

"Stay away from silicon injections, that's my advice to you. They slide, and one of them's down around her chin now, rounding the horn, maybe coming up the other side for all we know."

"Huh!" said Anne.

Anne's front teeth, perfectly square and thick, reminded Mary of blank Scrabble tiles. They had been capped, clearly; unless she'd been a Smith College hockey goalie, her attachment to Roz's book made perfect sense.

"Well," Mary said contritely, "you're a persuasive salesperson. I'll take two copies."

Anne took the compliment hard. She blushed the crimson-red shade of her preholiday turtleneck. This made Mary hate herself all the more.

"Could you wrap one?" Mary said. "I'm going to give one to my mother for her birthday."

Anne offered to ring Mary up so she could continue browsing; Mary handed Anne her credit card.

"I'll be in the tearoom," she said.

Bettina had since returned to her table with a mug and a white plate on which a single chocolate truffle was centered. She'd taken a handful of greeting cards from the greeting-card section and absently wrote in one with a gold pen.

Mary sat at a table opposite Bettina. Though she'd never had an articulated plan, she'd loosely intended to introduce herself to Bettina as a reporter who was interested in writing a book about women's traumatic experiences with male therapists and she recognized Bettina from the papers and did she mind the intrusion and etc., etc. But she'd lost her appetite for pretending to be people she wasn't. She decided to leave the encounter to chance. Either Bettina would recognize her from Mary's own ages-ago newspaper photos and they might talk, or she wouldn't recognize her and nothing more would happen. Bettina would drink her tea and put on her red coat and leave. Mary would go home. In fact, she realized, she was extremely ready to go home. She was exhausted and she was starving in that exhausted starving way—starving but not in the least bit hungry.

Up close and without her hat, Bettina appeared older than Mary had originally thought—her eyes threatened by the fine concentric creases of skin surrounding them, her hair dyed a uniform chestnut color. She wore a stretchy black tunic over stretchy black pants. Mary watched as Bettina made an extended meal of her dusted truffle, pincering the tiny ball between two copper nails and taking tiny nips from it with her front teeth. Cocoa powder accumulated in the corners of her mouth unattractively like dried blood.

Mary tried to recall the strange power that Bettina, or rather the spectral story of Bettina, formerly exerted over her. Every study hall found Mary examining Bettina's yearbook photo in the new library wing, her averagely pretty face framed by her trademark braids and appearing all the more malice-tinged for seeming so unexceptional. Even her list of activities was unexceptional, especially by overachieving Semmering standards. FIELD HOCKEY I, II, III. ART CLUB I, II. The photo promised that Mary, too—another unexceptional girl—might harbor darker impulses beneath her plaid skirt and navy cardigan and iron-on school crest.

Mary narrowed her eyes, reducing Bettina to a hazy outline. She tried to recapture that shadowy side of Bettina, but couldn't. It saddened her, in the way the fog-shrouded coastline that used to evoke in her a sense of spooky promise and now left her dull saddened her. She couldn't even summon the logic that allowed her to view Bettina as a wronged girl, a New England Dora whose stories were dismissed by the authorities as fantasy—or worse, lies. Bettina wasn't a victim. The shame Mary endured while spinning through the microfiche in the Grove library convinced her that in her quest to avenge, in some misguided and unarticulated way, Bettina Spencer, she'd only wrongly involved more innocent people. So now, appropriately, Mary was unable to discern within Bettina a shred of her former enchantment. Again, the weighty feeling of age dropped over her. She was too old to be piqued by mistaken teenage fervor. She was too old to locate in another flawed being the seeds of her own bewitching potential.

Despite the increasing level of scrutiny Mary lavished upon her, Bettina remained unwittingly engrossed in her truffle and her greeting cards. Mary coughed. In an attempt to influence chance, she tried to catch Bettina's attention, but Bettina, when she did glance up, was only interested in tracking the harried trajectories of the interchangeable saleswomen.

Anne approached Mary with a bag. "Here you are," she said. She waited while Mary signed her credit card receipt.

"Thank you," Mary said loudly. Bettina still had not noticed her.

"Excuse me for prying," Mary said. "But didn't you teach at Semmering Academy?"

"Me?" Anne said.

"Semmering Academy," Mary repeated. "You look so familiar. I used to be a student at Semmering Academy."

Bettina glanced up from her greeting cards; she stared intently at Anne's face.

"No, I'm sorry, I never had a job until this one," said Anne.

Mary watched as Bettina, eyes still locked firmly on Anne, slipped the greeting cards she'd yet to pay for into her purse.

It was all Mary could do not to laugh. Brilliant, she thought. Add shoplifting to a list that already included arson and perjury. (ARSON I, II. PERJURY III, IV. SHOPLIFTING II.)

"My mistake," Mary said. She watched as Bettina donned her gloves with the languidness of a practiced thief. She even possessed the nerviness to pause by the door and ask the cashier for the time.

She was gone.

Mary put on her coat and returned Anne's covertly enthusiastic wave, her hand tucked close to her chest, vibrating more than waving. Out on the street the temperature had dropped to the predicted low, the shock of the unseasonable chill lessened by the fake fir boughs and illuminated plastic berries already strung from the streetlamps, even though it was still seven weeks to Christmas. She walked with a very specific destination, listening to the rhythmic crunching of her boot soles on the salted sidewalk and the crinkle of the paper bag under her arm. She remained dogged by guilt and could not shake from her head Anne's blushing face, her capped teeth. Shame wrapped around her heart and squeezed it even smaller than its already paltry size.

Soon Mary found herself in front of Roz's office brownstone again. She rang the bell and stated quite firmly and clearly when asked to identify herself: "Mary Veal. It's Mary Veal, here."

Notes

The statistics on child molestation in the suburbs of Boston are astonishingly high given the area's comparative per capita wealth, a topic to which many psychiatric papers are dedicated at the annual Massachusetts Association of Mental Health Professionals Convention. The stricter Freudians among my colleagues presume this number to be wildly inflated by the recent influx of feminist psychoanalysts (most, but not all, are women) who insist on giving literal credence to abuse incidents formerly chalked up to sexual fantasy. I sympathized with the feminist psychoanalysts to a point; if ever there were a culture upon which the Freudians would have an unquestioned lock, it would be a repressive culture like New England. However, in a culture of inculcated repression, a backlash of equally distorted proportions must be expected. While a graduate student at BU I found myself caught unawares by exactly this sort of equalizing dynamic. As the resident mental health adviser at Semmering

Academy, a position I held from the fall of 1971 until the spring of 1972, my job primarily involved counseling the student body—an intelligent if highly strung collection of adolescent girls, prone to suffering from illnesses rarely more serious that the side effects of overachievement. To say that I was, initially, less than sympathetic to their suffering would be an understatement; so unmoved was I by their traumas that I soon warranted a visit from the headmistress, Dorothy Pym, who memorably informed me that girls, like horses, needed apples as much as they needed the crop.

And so I fed them apples. I considered every B plus a world-threatening tragedy. I was empathic to a saintly degree. Which was possibly why I allowed myself to be duped by the school's then most infamous student, Bettina Spencer.

Following my reprimand from Miss Pym, I possibly became lazy in the face of simple plausibility; I became an enabler, and I enabled Bettina Spencer to temporarily derail the life of an innocent man by failing to see that the girl suffered from an easily diagnosable cluster B personality disorder—more precisely, she was a pathological liar and a narcissist who exhibited grandiose tendencies. Bettina, I later came to learn, had been abused by an uncle when she was twelve years old. Always an imaginative girl with a tendency toward exaggeration, Bettina's accusations were dismissed by her mother as a more malignant strain of her usual tall tales. Thus exaggeration mutated into mendacity, and Bettina, seeking a way to right a wrong she believed she'd suffered at the hands of doubting adults, decided to fabricate a more believable situation of abuse. This did not excuse the burning of the library, nor the accusations directed at Miss Pym, nor various other injustices visited upon the innocent by Bettina's desire to make a name for herself through the destruction of property and other people. But I take responsibility for failing to diagnose Bettina's illness in the early stages; had I done so, perhaps the old library would still be intact, as would the lives of her victims. As Plutarch said, "It is worse to be sick in soul than in body, for those afflicted in body only suffer, but those afflicted in soul both suffer and do ill."

Which was why Mary's confession regarding her abuse at the hands of Kurt, and her family's failure to believe her, seemed of linchpin importance. It also explained why Mary's diagnosis failed, up to this point, to cohere. If, as I suspected, Mary's mental status belonged to cluster B, then this would explain her erratic, dramatic, and nongenuine emotional behavior; it would explain the vagueness of her answers and her generally evasive temperament; it would explain her love of open-ended questions and florid, if often contradictory, responses. It would explain her flirtatiousness, which often took the form of hostility or cruelty. And it would explain my general sense of disorientation, for such is the danger of treating grandiose narcissists—they are expert mimics, able to inhabit the disorder profiles of many competing illnesses so that the bewildered doctor finds him- or herself taking wrong turn after wrong turn at the bottom of many pointless rabbit holes.

Subsequently, my next appointment with Mary felt extremely crucial, the fulcrum meeting upon which the rest of our work together would teeter. I was reminded of a conversation Mary and I had had during the third session, during which I'd claimed that therapy wasn't a chess game in which tactical errors could be made. I couldn't have been more wrong.

I began our next session, our fifth, with a game.

What kind of game, Mary said. She arrived again in a hostile mood. Her complexion had improved, however; she even appeared, to my eye, prettier than I'd ever before given her credit for being. She admitted that she'd been to a tanning booth on a lark with her sister Regina, that she hadn't worn underwear and thus didn't have a tan line. She offered to show me this lack of a tan line, and even stood up and began unbuttoning her jeans, expecting me to stop her. She slowed her fingers, watching me intently, waiting for me to object.

I did not object.

You're such a pervert, Beaton, she said, rebuttoning her jeans and dropping back onto the couch. What would your colleagues say? Encouraging a patient to undress in front of you. Next you'll be begging for a striptease.

I didn't encourage you to do anything, I said.

Not making a decision is a decision, Mary said.

I was allowing you to act on an impulse that consumed you.

I wasn't *consumed*, she said. What are you writing?

More notes, I said.

Who cares about you and your notes? she said. Nobody reads them.

That's not true, I said. I'm part of a weekly workshop in which my performance is reviewed and critiqued by colleagues.

Reviewed how, she said.

They read my notes. They listen, if there's a reason to listen, to these tapes. It's done anonymously, of course. Your name will never be disclosed.

Mary regarded the tape recorder.

Huh, she said. So they'll be listening to my voice?

I nodded.

Huh, she said again. Maybe I should tell them how I really feel about you.

You may say whatever you like, I said.

An endorsement, she said. You can use it on your book.

What book, I said.

Mary smiled. The book you're going to write about us.

Mary pulled out her compact, she checked her lips. She dropped the compact into her lap but failed to insert the obsessive swirling finger.

I need to jot this down, she said. Can I have a piece of paper?

I tore a sheet of paper from my pad.

A pencil?

I handed her a pen.

I need a pencil, she said.

I fetched a pencil from my desk drawer. She stared at my face as she passed the pencil back and forth over the sheet of paper.

What are you doing, I said.

Sketching you, she said. You have a very high forehead. Have you ever studied phrenology?

Have you? I asked.

A high forehead means you are well suited to public speaking and occupations involving water.

Is that your endorsement of me, I asked.

No, she said, this is my endorsement of you. "Dr. Hammer is a man endowed with incredible intellectual and physical resources. His obsession with genitals is a source of constant stimulation for both doctor and patient. I feel thoroughly explored by this man, if scarcely understood."

Mary smiled. Would you like to see my sketch?

If you would like to show it to me, I said.

Mary turned the sheet of notebook paper to face me. She had shaded in the top half with the pencil; in doing so she had revealed the depression caused by my pen as I had written my notes about her.

Can't believe you fell for that old trick, Beaton, she said.

Maybe I wanted you to know what I thought about you, I said.

Nice try, she said. What's faked anterograde memory disturbance?

Do you know what paramnesia is, I said.

No, she said.

Paramnesia is a term for the story a patient creates to explain their lives. They've substituted what they've forgotten with a new memory, I said.

Why don't you just call them liars, she said.

Because it's more complicated than lying.

Lying is complicated, Mary said.

It can be, I said.

She pointed to the upper left-hand corner of the paper on which I had written "BS Connection?" and circled it.

You think I'm bullshitting you, she said.

That's your interpretation, I said, relieved that she hadn't interpreted the notation correctly as "Bettina Spencer."

So you think I'm a liar, she said.

Do you think you're a liar, I said.

If I say no and I'm a liar, then I might be a liar; then again I might be telling the truth.

And if you say yes?

If I say yes and I'm a liar, then that means I'm not a liar. And yet I've lied to you.

I'm still curious how you'd diagnose yourself, I said. Presuming you would tell the truth in this one instance.

Never presume. It makes a pre out of sue and me. And besides, she said, I'm not the doctor.

How would you like to be the doctor, I said.

What do you mean, she said.

You'll be me, and I'll be you.

This is the game, she said.

This is the game, I said.

She tried to appear skeptical of this suggestion, but I could sense it excited her.

I think this will be harder for you than it will be for me, she said. I just have to repeat everything you say and ask obvious stupid questions. You need to be creative.

I'll have to try my best, I said.

Can I wear your coat? Can I sit at your desk?

I'll be in the waiting room, I said.

I retreated to the waiting room. Two minutes later the door opened.

Come in, Mary said.

I entered the office. She was seated in my swivel desk chair, facing the window.

Lie on the couch, she said.

You want me to lie down?

Facing away from me. You're so tense, she said. I want you to relax. I want you to forget I'm even here.

I lay on the couch. I heard the squeak of my desk chair.

So, she said, you think you have problems.

No, I said.

No? she said.

I've been told I have problems, I said. It's not the same thing as believing I have problems.

Who told you that you have problems? Mary said.

My mother.

I doubt that, Mary said. She's not able to recognize, much less articulate, her feelings about me. About you, I mean.

She telegraphs her disapproval in other ways.

So she disapproves of you, Mary said.

She disapproves of anyone with problems, I said.

Mary didn't respond. I turned my head toward her but she reprimanded me.

No absolutely not, she said.

You didn't respond, I said.

I nodded, she said.

I can't see you nodding, I said.

Good point, she said. I'm nodding again.

I've thought about telling my mother that I can sense her disapproval, I said.

That would be a waste of breath, Mary said. In my professional opinion.

But as I've learned from my mother, there are ways to communicate that don't involve talking.

Such as? Mary said.

Actions, I said. Actions that involve deceit.

Interesting, Mary said. Is this being tape-recorded?

Of course, I said. If I'm paying for this session I want there to be a record of our work.

Maybe I should take notes, Mary said. Just to be safe.

Whatever you need to do, I said. You're the doctor.

I heard Mary rummaging through my desk drawer.

OK, she said. I'm ready now. What was it you just said?

I said that one could communicate using actions involving deceit.

Nice, she said. I think we're nearing a breakthrough.

Really?

I think of breakthroughs in a sexual manner. They can be extremely erotic. I need a cigarette.

I heard the snip of a lighter, smelled cigarette smoke.

You're not supposed to smoke in here, I said.

There's no smoke detector, she said. Unless you rat me out, nobody will be the wiser.

I'm not here to rat you out, I said.

Huh, she said. Somehow I doubt that.

You're very paranoid for a doctor, I said.

I'm not paranoid, she said. I am *paying attention to you*. You are paying me to pay attention to you.

I'm not here to rat you out, I repeated. I thought you were here to rat me out.

To whom? she said. To your mother? All she wants is a doctor's note claiming that you weren't raped. You could agree to let me tell her that, in my professional opinion, you weren't raped, and then we could stop this therapy I-care-about-you-a-total-stranger bullshit. Because I *don't* care about you. I'm just trying to further my career.

How will this further your career?

Mary exhaled.

A white girl disappears from a white prep school in a white suburb. Nobody knows what happened to her. The overall whiteness of the world is threatened. This must be resolved by whatever means possible.

You're going to lie to further your career, I said.

Telling assumption, she said. Do you remember writing English papers in high school?

I'm still in high school, I reminded her.

Sorry, she said. You seem so mature for your age.

Thank you, I said.

Did you happen to notice where I hid my ashtray? she asked.

I think you hid it in the top left drawer, under the file folders.

What I meant was, when I was in high school so very very very very very long ago, I realized that I could take any book and pair it with a thesis—let's say I wanted to show that Hawthorne in *The Scarlet Letter* advocated genital mutilation—and I could write a paper proving that thesis. Then I could write an equally convincing paper proving that *The Scarlet Letter* was a scree against genital mutilation. Truth is created through logic, and logic can be used to prove that anything is true. In which case, truth seems a waste of time. Right?

Truth has always been a slippery fish, I said.

Which is why we might as well just give up on this whole "truth" thing, which is what every person learns the first time they get stoned. Why look for something that doesn't exist? It's like spending your life in search of Big Foot. Fun, maybe, you get to travel and collect a lot of cool tracking equipment. But at the end of the day you'll have wasted your life on something that was never there to begin with.

If we're not looking for truth, I said, what are we looking for?

I'm looking for a way to further my career.

And me?

You're looking for the same thing.

I'm looking to further my career, I said.

We can help each other out, she said. I think that's why you're here.

I thought I was here because I needed help. Not you.

Mary laughed. People only help people when it helps them to do so.

That's a very cynical worldview you've got, I observed.

That's why you pay me the big bucks, she said.

Let's say I agree with you, I said. Let's say that I also think that truth is a waste of time if you want to get your point across. Let's say I prefer, as already stated, acts of deceit.

Deceit is different than giving up on truth, she said. But go on.

Or not deceit, I said. But a situation that, logically, appears true. Let's say that I tried to tell the truth and nobody heard me. Let's say, then, that I've decided telling the truth got me nowhere. If I want anyone to listen to me, I have to construct a scenario that appears true, but isn't.

That sounds like a lot of work, she said.

Maybe it's worth it, I said. Maybe I want to be believed, even if I'm believed under false pretenses. Maybe being believed is that important to me.

I think you should try to care less about what other people think of you, she said. Who cares what they believe?

I'm in high school, I reminded her. I care about what other people think. Besides, I've been hurt. I've been hurt and I want my revenge. But it's not for the reason you think.

Don't tell me what I think. Mary said. I'm the doctor. I don't need you telling me what to think.

It would be *understandable* if you thought that the hurt I was referring to was the incident with Kurt. The actual incident of sexual abuse.

Sexual abuse. How dramatic.

Isn't that what you'd call it? You doctors are always categorizing every little kiss as sexual abuse.

That's because we're bored, Mary said. But Kurt is a sad man. I suspect he was impotent in his marriage.

So Kurt *is* a sad man, I said. You understand this.

Mary didn't respond.

Doctor?

I'm nodding, she said.

So you agree. You understand how Kurt couldn't really inflict hurt upon me. After all, I'm a grown girl. If a man makes a pass at me, I might take it for flattery. As proof that I was desirable and attractive.

You are *incredibly* desirable and attractive, Mary said.

So the question is, *why am I hurt*, I said.

I'm asking the questions here, Mary said.

But don't you agree that's the question?

Mary didn't answer.

Don't you agree?

I'm shrugging, she said. I have a dubious look on my face.

Why dubious?

I feel trapped, she said. I feel like you've trapped me.

Ah, I said. I am an expert at trapping people. I thought you'd figured that out by now. Which is why, when I was hurt that my family didn't believe me about the Kurt incident, I decided to trap them. I decided to trap them by playing on their worst fear.

What is their worst fear?

Their worst fear is losing me, I said. But they hide this fear behind more shallow concerns. They pretend to care about my purity. My unsoiledness. The overall whiteness of the world is threatened.

This must be resolved by whatever means possible, Mary said.

Exactly, I said.

I have an idea, Mary said.

You do, I said.

You have to close your eyes, she said.

They're closed, I said.

Wait until I tell you to open them.

I heard the groan of the office chair, the near-soundless padding of her feet.

OK, she said. Open them.

Mary stood next to the couch wearing my suit coat, which she held open like a flasher. She had removed all other items of her own clothing except her socks, bra, and underwear.

Are you cured? she asked.

Put your clothes on, Mary.

That's "Doctor" to you, she said.

I'm leaving the room now. Please put your clothes back on.

Score one point for the patient, Mary said.

Are we keeping score, I said.

Mary laughed.

It's a game, she said. Of course we're keeping score.

What Might Have Happened

When the girl woke up, she was alone. The sun, a bleach stain upon the overcast sky, had nearly cleared the tops of the pine trees that closed in on her from all directions save the direction of the very narrow road.

Still half asleep, she turned her groggy attention to the mess at her feet—potato chips ground into the Mercedes's carpet, a skull-shaped stain of spilled root beer. She could see her breath, which meant the man had abandoned her some time ago. He hadn't left the car running, nor the heat. How inconsiderate, the girl thought to herself. Her man wasn't shaping up as she'd hoped.

She opened the door and stepped into four inches of snow covering a partially frozen puddle. Immediately her field hockey cleats filled with icy water. Her calves and ankles tingled.

Hello, the girl called out.

Overhead, the trees sounded like brushes slipping through somebody's coarse, heavenly hair.

Her anger turned to worry. To just up and leave her to freeze to death in her field hockey uniform did not seem like him. To leave her to be gnawed to death by wolves, discovered by a depraved snowmobile rider who would take liberties with her stiff if still inviting cadaver.

She circled the car, spotted footprints leading through the woods. To the left of the footprints, every four or five steps, was a minuscule drop of blood.

So he was hurt, she concluded, but not badly. His finger, most likely; he'd reopened his wound. He had gone into the woods, simply to pee. Again she called out, to save him any potential embarrassment. Again all she heard was the sound of brushing hair.

She followed the footprints through a parting in the trees, tracing the vague suggestion of what might, in snowless times, be a path. As the cold intensified, so did her earlier dismissed anger. How could he leave her like this? Alone, in the woods, without the car key, without access to heat? She cycled back to the possibility that he was seriously injured. Now she *hoped* that he was seriously injured. She hoped he was gradually bleeding to death beneath a boulder that had landed on his leg. She hoped his foot had sprung a bear trap, that he'd been mistaken for a deer by a bow hunter. Nothing else would excuse his abandoning her.

Soon the path became a clearing, the clearing became a meadow. The footprints continued across the snow-blown expanse and entered the woods on the opposite side. *Where was he?* Her wet feet, now starting to freeze, throbbed in a prickly way and she started to cry, the tears freezing and shrinking and pulling at her skin like glue. She was thirsty, hungry—when had she last eaten? The diner, and then, after the gas station stop, she'd eaten a bag of vinegar chips that left her stomach raw and the insides of her cheeks fuzzy with canker sores. The people she and the man had been at the diner were hard to connect to the people they were now. Mere hours after exchanging their first actual words they had en-

tered a black hole in which time no longer had any bearing on their behavior. In theory they were still newish strangers; in theory a certain
politeness should still regulate, in a safe and predictable way, their inter-
actions. Callousness, indifference, had not yet set in. But somewhere—
maybe on the highway, maybe earlier—a meniscus had been pierced, and
now anything could happen. He could come back and rescue her. He
could leave her in the woods to die.

As the girl crossed a stream and another narrower meadow, it occurred to her that she'd made a mistake. These prints didn't belong to the
man. Maybe these prints belonged to a hunter who had discovered the
Mercedes, who had seen a girl sleeping inside and left her there undis-
turbed because he was the type who trusted the general arrangement of
things, even when peculiar.

The girl stopped. She closed her eyes and listened to the brushing
of the heavenly hair. She felt sleepy now, almost peaceful. The first signs
of hypothermia. You fall asleep. No pain. No suffering. Like lobsters in
a pot of slowly boiled water. Death, the experts assure you, is no more
traumatic than submitting to a nap.

The girl lowered herself into a snowbank. She curled into a ball, listening to the hair-brushing sounds. But she was kept awake by the sharp
rumblings, like liquid convulsions, roiling about the interior of her rib
cage as the blood surrounded her organs, abandoning the lesser parts of
her body—hands, feet—to whatever was fated to befall them. Her body
had made a decision, and it was enacting its plan without any consulta-
tion with her brain.

Fine, she thought. Her brain was clearly unreliable, hardly worth consulting in matters of her own survival. She reflected on the person she
was at the diner. Who was that person? Difficult, hours later, to recall.
What a fool. What an idiot, thinking she could toy with her own life.
She would get what she'd secretly wished for—she was going to die. She'd
imagined her family gathered around the phone as her father was informed of her mysterious demise, her sisters huddled beneath his raised

elbow, her mother watching over his shoulder. Woods. Body. Mercedes. No suspects. No explanation. That would be the worst for her family— that she, the dead girl, presumably knew what happened to her, but they would not. More than her death, she imagined this curiosity would be the lasting trauma.

But in the current scenario, *she* didn't have the answer either. She would die curious, and this would haunt her in the afterlife, a state about which she'd given little actual thought. She'd have visiting privileges with this world, this much she'd assumed; she'd be able to screen from above and gloat and possibly even, once she was feeling more generous, leave her family helpful clues hinting to her demise. But if *she* didn't know what had happened to her, the afterlife scenario grew less appealing. She'd waste her energy haunting the man and interpreting his every action. *Did you do this to me?* she'd ask him by swirling the winds around his ears, by dropping sticks at his feet. *Did you?*

The girl extracted her hand from her sleeve and examined her fingernails. They were purple-blue, the exact shade of purple-blue they turned after she'd swum too long in the ocean. She raised herself to her knees, stuttered onto her feet. The prickling had receded, now her feet felt numbly compressed and cushioned, as though they were bound in rags. She forced herself to lift her legs and run for ten steps. Her lungs blazed, her bones unsteady and sick, nauseous in the marrow. *My bones are nauseous,* she thought to herself, *I am sick in the bones.* She alternated resting and running until she'd crossed the first large meadow and reentered the original woods. Darker clouds blotted out the peaked sun completely; though it was probably only 11 a.m., the woodsy shadows and the clouds made it feel like dusk, the dark approaching, the animals convening, the cold, the fear, the end.

This sequence—*the cold the fear the end*—she repeated to herself over and over, her marching orders. *The cold the fear the end the cold the fear the end.* She ran until the trees thinned and she could see the road, the tire tracks, she could hear the engine of a car.

The engine of a car.

She exited the woods to see the Mercedes's tailpipe expelling weak puffs of exhaust smoke. Her first response, illogical, absurd, was this: *The hunter is stealing the car.* The hunter, who had become as real to her as the man had become unreal, the hunter who accepted the peculiar arrangement of things, had returned with poor intentions. Hauling his crossbow through the woods he'd cut a deal with fortune: If the girl is in the car when I return, I will have my way with her. Not a decision, simply a response to circumstance or even a decree. But finding the car empty, the hunter decided to steal the car. The girl couldn't explain where he'd found the keys—he was a man with a crossbow, he was a tamer of the woods, an ingenious, superior human for whom keys, for whom logic, for whom actual existence was not an obstacle. *The hunter is driving away*, she thought. He'd have his way with her or he would not—but in either case her ride was leaving. She yelled in a voice not recognizably her own. She put a hand on the door handle, as though she could restrain the car's forward motion employing the steel intensity of her terror.

She opened the door—her whole body was required to overcome the hinges's stiffness—and threw herself into the passenger seat. Her hip bone struck the gearshift, a dull and unimportant pain, not equal to her overall numbness.

The man sat in the driver's seat, smoking.

Shut the door, he said.

She shut the door. She pressed her hands, curled in her sleeves, against the heater vents on either side of the glove box. Her nose ran profusely. She blotted it with her shoulder.

The man smoked, said nothing.

You're smoking again, the girl said, her heart beyond wild. *Show him nothing.*

The man nodded. Apparently, he said.

Amazing, the girl thought. As though nothing had happened. *The cold the fear the end.* But she could beat him at this game of pretending nothing had happened.

Apparently, the girl said, struggling to keep the rattle from her voice. You like that word.

Do I? the man said.

You use it a lot.

Huh, the man said.

I guess because you don't agree with a statement even if all facts point in that direction.

It's the privilege of an amnesiac, he said.

You can't be an amnesiac about the present, girl said.

No? the man said. Is there a rule about when a person can start forgetting?

You know what I mean, the girl said.

He held up a hand in a gesture of apology, or a call for a truce, or a warning to back off.

This made the girl angry. She had almost died, for fuck's sake, she wanted to yell.

She did not yell.

I thought you didn't have any cigarettes, the girl said, recalling their interaction—what was it, two years ago? ten?—while parked in front of his brownstone.

I lied, the man said. An ex-smoker always has cigarettes. For those situations that are beyond him.

Can I have one? the girl asked.

The man jutted his chin toward the dash. He made no move to knock a cigarette from the pack. He made no move to light it with his blue plastic lighter.

She removed her frozen hands from her sleeves. Her toes and fingers were burning back to life and all sensations were amplified. Flicking the lighter felt equivalent to running her thumb pad over a serrated knife blade.

For those situations that are beyond me, the man repeated. I am beyond.

Really, the girl said.

I am beyond beyond, he said.

Is that why you disappeared?

I disappeared, he said.

You disappeared, she said.

I was behind that boulder, the man said, gesturing with his cigarette to a lumpy granite flank emerging from between two large trunks. I was relieving myself.

For a long time, the girl said.

What?

The car was cold. I could see my breath. You didn't just leave to "relieve yourself."

I was thinking, the man said.

You turned off the car and the heat, the girl said.

I took the keys, he admitted. I didn't mean to leave you without heat. I only meant to leave you without keys.

You thought I would steal your car, the girl said.

The man didn't answer. Then he said: Do you know what's at the end of this road?

Not a rainbow, the girl said caustically.

At the end of this road is a sixty-foot drop-off. It comes without warning. If you were driving and you didn't know any better, you'd drive right over the edge.

The girl must have appeared skeptical, because the man put the Mercedes in drive and continued down the two-rut road, the ice and snow sawing at the undercarriage. He slowed around a turn. The woods evaporated.

The man put the Mercedes in park.

A quarry, the man said. Filled with water now, and eels apparently. I mean, filled with eels without question if you believe what people tell you. It's a swimming hole in the summer. When I was married to my ex-wife, she invited a couple to our ski house. The couple's marriage was in bad straits. The wife was a drinker. The husband was indifferent.

Indifferent to her drinking?

Indifferent to her period, the man said. The wife got drunk, her husband remained indifferent, and the two of them had a fight over dinner. The woman began to cry and the man yawned, so the woman drove off in their car. We didn't think she'd end up on this road.

She drove into the quarry, the girl said, thinking *the cold the fear the end.*

Some ice fishermen called the police to report the hole in the ice, right around the time the man learned from his neighbor in Boston that his wife hadn't driven home as he'd suspected she had. The rescue team found the car but it was empty. They had to wait until spring when they could send more divers.

How did they know she was dead? the girl asked. I mean, how did they know for sure that she was in the quarry?

They didn't, the man said. The indifferent husband, who was a little bit less indifferent after this, received an unsigned postcard from a cruise ship six weeks after her car was found. Her handwriting, or so he thought. He told everyone she was having an affair, that she'd left him for another man. Five months later they found her body in the quarry.

I bet he felt like a dick, the girl said.

I don't know how he felt, the man said. He was my wife's friend, apparently.

Apparently, the girl said.

Sorry, the man said.

He carefully turned the car around, making sure to leave plenty of clearance between the car and the edge of the quarry. The girl was reminded of her initial impression of him—he was a cautious caretaker of a man.

So, he said. Where did you go?

Me? she said. I was following you.

But I was behind that boulder.

They had reached the place where they'd previously been parked.

I was following the tracks, the girl said.

Tracks, the man said. There were no tracks.

They must have been a hunter's tracks, the girl said.

The man didn't want to disagree with her, she could tell. He was beyond beyond.

There was only one set of tracks, he said firmly. Your tracks.

And you didn't follow them, the girl said.

The man nodded.

Yes you didn't follow them or yes you followed them.

Yes I didn't follow them.

Huh, the girl said.

I knew you'd come back, he said.

But what if I had been kidnapped? she asked. By the hunter?

What hunter? he said.

Or whoever it was. The tracks. I was following somebody's tracks.

The man stopped the car. He walked over to the place in the woods where she'd emerged.

He returned to the car.

See for yourself, he said.

The girl didn't want to get out of the car; she was warm now, and vulnerable anew to a chill.

I believe you, she said.

See for yourself, he said.

I don't need to see for myself.

Yes, he said. You do. Later I don't want you to say *apparently*.

Apparently?

Apparently there was only one set of tracks. That is what you will say.

Reluctantly, the girl exited the car. The footprints had softened in the wind to tiny bluish depressions. One set headed into the woods. One set returned. She felt dizzy, her body in a state of sleepless, hungry shock.

The sight of the single footprints—clearly her own, and only her own—disoriented her, made her feel like the man was playing games with her, or possibly that she was playing games with herself. Yes, like the man and his amnesia, she was fracturing off from some core person, and the two of them were proceeding forward in the same body with very different designs on the world.

See, the man said. Did you see.

The girl grabbed another cigarette from the dash with her shaking fingers.

Apparently, she said, smiling, trying to make light of it all. Apparently you were right.

Mary Chapter

Mary couldn't believe, all these years later, that the same mask poster hung on the wall in Roz's waiting room, that she had the same wicker furniture with the same throw pillows, that she even had the same fake ficus, its green leaves now faded to the generic paraffin hue of old plastic. She'd entered a minutely preserved time capsule, maintained in pristine condition like her own bedroom. Or maybe she had, via some trick fold in the universe, returned to her teenage self, the past fourteen years had been nothing but a fantasy she'd pursued past the usual boundary, in her usual way, yet another fantasy brought too finely to life that had cycled back to haunt her.

She eyed the pile of magazines on the coffee table, heart tumbling beneath her coat. What if she picked up the magazines and they, too, dated back to the mid-eighties? What if? All roads led back to this waiting room—no matter what believable construct she'd fashioned, her adult self would eventually become curious about its own unresolved past. It would wonder about the fates of this or that person. It would land her in front of the mask poster and it would all begin again.

So wound up was she that she didn't hear the office door open. The polite cough made her jump.

Roz—a discernibly aged, statelier Roz—stared at her from behind a pair of purple plastic glasses.

Thank god thank fucking god.

"Is this a good time?" Mary said.

"For you, it's always a good time," Roz said.

Like her waiting room, Mary reflected wryly, Roz hadn't changed one bit; she still had the capacity to make displays of emotional capaciousness seem belittling in the extreme.

Roz gestured Mary into her office, which, Mary noted as she shed her coat, *had* changed. The room was painted a pale violet color that she registered as new, even while she couldn't remember the wall color it replaced. Roz's couch had been reupholstered, the orange corduroy traded in for a dark red velour. Roz herself appeared to have been reupholstered, her hemp layers sloughed away, leaving her clad in a navy dress with lapels and double-breasted gold buttons made of a shiny wool-ish material. Roz had traded in her earth-mother hippie-academic look for a corporate-librarian look. *The touring,* Mary imagined Roz explaining. *Need to travel light. Permanent press so much easier when you're on the road.*

Roz remained at her desk, writing. "Just let me finish these notes," she said to the desk, over which hung her framed book-jacket covers, her diplomas, and a photo of her shaking hands with a tall Indian woman in a sari. A long fish tank gurgled and spat like somebody drowning in the corner. Three fat brown fish lazed at the bottom, mulish faces pointed outward.

"So," Roz said, swiveling her chair toward Mary. "No surprise to see you."

"Is it not?" Mary asked. She smiled woodenly. She tried to keep her tone civil, but found herself squeezed by a familiar mood vise. Roz was like family in that way; Mary's brain experienced the equivalent of an evolutionary setback when it encountered her, regressing to a reptilian thuggishness.

"I knew you'd be here. The question was when."

"That's why you're the doctor," Mary said jokingly. *I'm not your doctor,* Mary imagined her saying. Say that, Mary thought, and I will punch you dead center in the suit dress.

Roz removed her reading glasses and propped them on her knee, making a little face of it. Age had softened Roz; her skin had a dull wind-burned appearance, it had not so much wrinkled in the intervening years as lost its structural integrity like an overripe fruit. It slumped, dragging her mouth wider, her eyes bigger. Her wild hair had whitened around her forehead; she looked blizzarded, Roz did. A woman just in from a blizzard. The effect was appealing. Had Roz always been pretty? Mary wondered. Had she despised the woman too much to notice? Maybe. Maybe not. She'd found, as she'd begun to age herself, that she was more prone to locate in decimated faces some shred of former prettiness made more apparent by the sags and the wrinkling, by these tricks of distortion.

"I'd hoped, of course, that you'd come to me before your mother died."

"I almost went to hear you read once," Mary offered. "In Oregon. But the whole point of my life out there is—"

"Is that it isn't your life here."

"Correct," Mary said.

"What an honest statement," Roz said.

"Actually, you said it," Mary said.

"Too bad you couldn't have found it in yourself to be honest with me before your mother died. Now your visit to me appears self-serving."

"I thought that's why people came to therapy," Mary said.

"I know that's what *you* think," Roz said.

Mary gripped her thighs.

"I'd like to point out," Mary began cautiously. *I'd like to point out that you've gone zero to bitch in less than three minutes.* But no. She retooled her approach, flexed her reverted-to-lizard brain.

"However much my behavior might be an ongoing disappointment to you, I think, under the current circumstances, I deserve to be cut a little slack."

Roz's expression shifted from stony to stock sympathetic. Her face was like those old View-Masters Mary and her sisters used to fight over; a flick of a lever and you've rotated from the Grand Canyon to the Bering Strait, from Victoria Falls to the bat caves of Zulu National Park.

"I am sorry about your mother," Roz said.

"Thank you," Mary said. "It's been harder than I expected."

"You expected it to be easy?"

"I expected it to seem inevitable," Mary said. "She'd been sick."

"Not for long," Roz said. "Certainly not long enough for it to seem inevitable to her."

Mary's gut shifted queasily. With guilt, yes, but also with resentful bewilderment. That this woman should know more about how her mother felt before she died was, well, *ironic* in the least bitter of terms.

"Your mother became a different woman," Roz said. "She changed."

"I suppose you take credit for that," Mary said.

Roz chuckled. She swiveled back and forth in her chair.

"You're so distrusting," she said.

"Of you," Mary said.

"Because I stumbled on the truth? For that I'm to be distrusted?"

"You're to be distrusted because your motives were . . . suspect."

"I was doing my job," Roz said. "You were sexually abused by a man and you were given permission by your therapist to pretend that you weren't. Not only did he give you permission—he made you famous. But you don't distrust me. The problem, Mary, is that you find my entire profession suspect."

Mary stared at the floor—at the new carpet that was a tastefully old

carpet, a threadbare brown and orange and purple kilim—and experienced a shot of sudden clarity about a very shallow thing. Not an
epiphany, since the subject matter was so banal. A baniphany, then. Her
baniphany was this: Roz had hired a decorator. The office colors—
orange, purple, dark red—were the sort of colors no amateur would dare
toss together. It required a guild-validated pro to assemble something so
confidently hideous. Roz had hired a decorator and maybe she'd even
hired a personal publicist, one who had suggested that she exchange her
hemp layers for the more subdued and mainstream-ugly suit dress. As-
sertive without being overtly feminist. Authoritative but not dykey. Cul-
tured but not elitist.

"Isn't that true?" Roz pushed.

Mary met the single eye of a mule-faced fish. Her blood felt thin and
oxygenless, as though she were trying to breathe at a very high altitude.

"Without sounding disrespectful," Mary said, "I think your profession shares more in common with fiction than with science."

"Psychoanalysis is a shared creative endeavor," Roz said. "Some schol-
ars believe that Freud was more artist than scientist."

"I thought you hated Freud," Mary said.

"I 'hate' Freud in the way that I 'hate' any father figure—as a useful
and ultimately healthy means of transcending the implied authority he
has over me."

Mary scoffed.

"What," Roz said.

"You have an answer for everything," Mary said.

"It's that kind of knee-jerk defensiveness that prevents you from
wrestling with your root conflict," Roz said. "Something your mother finally came to understand."

Mary's eyeballs burned. Her mother, she was dying to point out, *despised* Roz Biedelman. Yet her mother had refused her daughter's overtures
and turned to . . . Roz? It didn't make any sense.

"Here," Roz said.

Mary, her vision asway, tried to focus on Roz's extended hand, offering her a tissue.

"What," Mary said. "I don't need that."

"Yes you do," Roz said. "You're crying."

"I'm not *crying*," Mary said.

"Don't worry," Roz said. "I won't consider it a sign of anything."

"Of weakness? Of defeat?" Mary made brutal swipes at her cheeks.

"You're bereaved," Roz said.

I'm enraged, Mary thought. How dare she allow herself to cry in front of this woman? How dare she be unable to cry at her mother's funeral, only to dissolve in front of Roz fucking Biedelman?

"Because of your lack of closure with your mother, you're unable to mourn her."

Apparently not, Mary thought to herself as her eyes leaked in an undifferentiated stream.

"Guilt has a way of transforming into rage, which can prohibit the grieving process indefinitely. Which is why I'm happy you decided to find me, even if it is too late to make things right with your mother in person."

"Bluntly put," Mary said.

"I'm stating a fact," Roz said. "Your mother is dead. What you failed to tell her while she was alive is what she will always fail to know from you. But there are other ways of knowing things. After all, you may not have been the most reliable source of information."

Mary blew her nose, wiped her eyes, wadded the tissue, shoved the evidence of her breakdown into her coat pocket.

"I'm so tired . . ." Mary began.

"Of course you are," Roz said.

"I'm so tired of *circumlocution*," Mary said. "Is there some kind of therapist protocol against speaking in plain language? *Say what you mean.*"

"Fine," Roz said. "What would you like me to say? You seem to already know what you'd like me to say."

"Tell me that my mother came to see you."

"Your mother came to see me," Roz said.

"As your friend? As your patient?"

"I can't really answer that question."

"Of course you can't," Mary said bitterly.

"This may be difficult for you to accept," Roz said. "But sometimes the only person who can understand what you're going through is a person who has shared that experience. I know that contradicts what I'm supposed to believe is therapeutically possible as an unbiased observer— but I can admit that some relationships are more predisposed to succeed due to a familiarity with the material."

"*The material.*"

"With you."

Mary experienced a numbing sensation beginning at her temples, spreading under her forehead. This wasn't rage; this was shame, pure and simple. Shame that her mother had confessed to Roz Biedelman feelings she'd never been able to express to Mary, or to anyone else in their family. Mary would have felt betrayed if she didn't believe, on some level, that she deserved it.

"You mother came to me after she learned that she was sick," Roz continued.

Mary stared at Roz, the numbing sensation subsiding.

"She came to you," Mary said.

Roz nodded.

"Out of the blue," Roz said. "Trust me, I was as surprised as you are now."

"Out of the blue," Mary said, her shame loosening further as she touched the letter in her pocket. *Roz, as usual, was full of shit.* "She just picked up the phone and called you."

"Your mother was a complicated woman, I don't need to tell you that."

"Right," Mary said. "Do you know why I'm here out of the blue?"

"What matters is that *you* know why you're here."

Mary nodded. "I think I can answer that question."

Mary withdrew the letter from her coat pocket. She handed it to Roz.

Roz did not take the letter. It dangled between them, shuddering in a draft from the partially opened windows.

"I wonder which out of the blue came first," Mary said. "My mother's phone call to you, or the letter you sent to her."

Roz still refused to take the letter.

"Read it," Mary said.

"I don't have to read it," Roz said.

"No?" Mary said.

"No," Roz said. "Does that make me guilty of something in your mind?"

"Me, and my perception of things, are not the issues here."

"Fine," Roz said. "What are the issues?"

"Despite how you've characterized my mother's actions, in fact you were the one who contacted her first."

Roz nodded in a tolerant way that Mary did not for a second mistake for agreement. Roz, Mary realized, was as attached—if not more attached—to vagueness than she was. Her approach to therapy was about obfuscating every obvious thing. Maybe it was nothing more—or less—cynical than a business survival technique she learned in graduate school. A way to ensure a consistent patient base. Shy away from anything concrete; shatter it into a diffuse powder. Maintain the mystery above all else.

"I had a very good reason to contact your mother," Roz said.

"A good enough reason to lie to me, apparently."

"I had a good reason," Roz repeated.

"Does it have anything to do with Bettina Spencer?"

Roz removed the glasses from her knee, breathed on the left lens and scrubbed it on her sleeve, returned the glasses to her face.

"Bettina Spencer-Weeks," Roz said. "What do you know about Bettina?"

"That she left your office building today at five. That she had tea at the bookstore you bully into selling your books. That she shoplifted some greeting cards."

"You were spying on her," Roz said.

"I was coming to see you and I saw Bettina. I followed her."

"How curious," Roz said. "In all senses of the word. You've obviously chosen the wrong profession—you're a high-school gym teacher?"

"I work for the admissions department."

"Your talents for subterfuge are going to waste."

"As are your talents for career counseling," Mary said.

Roz flashed Mary a bemused grin. She enjoys this, Mary thought. This sort of tinged-with-hostility repartee was Roz's idea of a great way to pass the early evening.

"But about Bettina," Mary said.

"What about Bettina? She remains a narcissist with a minor shoplifting problem."

"It's an improvement over a sociopath who burns down libraries."

"She recently set fire to the potting shed of a neighbor she dislikes. By the way this is not to leave this room, this information."

"You think I'll trust you because you've shown trust in me."

"I'm satisfying your curiosity about Bettina."

"But you've broken another person's trust so that I'll trust you. Eventually I'll put two and two together and realize that you'll break my trust in order to gain the trust of another. A risky gambit."

"One that, with you, will pay off."

"You're so confident?"

Roz shrugged. "You dislike me, Mary. I'm appealing to your sense of curiosity, which is the only thing I can appeal to. I have information that you need."

Mary didn't respond. Roz was irritating. She was not stupid.

"Bettina suffers from a personality disorder that most in my field consider incurable."

"Which doesn't prevent you from taking her money every week," Mary said.

"Narcissists can't be cured, but they should be managed. They can cause a lot of harm otherwise—as Bettina has already proven."

The fish tank emitted a loud belch.

"I suppose you're referring to Bettina's lawsuit against Dr. Hammer," Mary said.

"Actually, I was referring to the arson incident."

"But still, if she's a harm-causing narcissist, then there's a good chance that her case against Dr. Hammer was just another opportunity to make her mark via destruction of an innocent person, right?"

"Dr. Hammer was not an innocent person," Roz said.

"So you maintain. But of course you would have to, given you aligned yourself with Bettina during the court case."

"*Aligned*," Roz said. "You make me sound so sinister."

"You aligned yourself with Bettina."

"My lawyer's idea," Roz said, swiveling away from Mary to attend to a non-important diversionary something on her desk.

"Which couldn't have pleased you more. You hated him."

Roz flipped through her date book; she uncapped a pen and copied something onto a notepad. She swiveled back toward Mary.

"If you don't mind me telling you a few things about yourself, Mary: You cling to an extremely simplistic and infantile way of viewing the world, and the people in it. You're unforgiving. A grudge holder. In my business, we might say that you haven't properly separated from your parents. In your case specifically, your mother."

On the contrary, Mary thought. She'd never been so separated from a person.

"You still haven't explained why Bettina is your patient."

"I thought I just explained her problems in detail."

"Why *you*," Mary said. "If that's not a conflict of interest . . ."

"Bettina and I were engaged in a patient-doctor relationship long before the lawsuit," Roz said. "Read through the code of conduct manual published by the Massachusetts Psychiatric Board. I've violated not a single subsection."

"I'm sure Dr. Hammer wouldn't feel violated to know you're still seeing his most infamous patient."

"You're so protective of him," Roz observed. "You must think he needs protecting."

"Exactly," Mary said. "Which should tell you something."

"It tells me that your mother's not the only person from whom you're seeking forgiveness," Roz said. "Fortunately for you, Dr. Hammer is still alive. It's not to late to find him and set things right."

"What it should tell you is that I lied to him about being abducted," Mary said. "And he correctly wrote a book detailing how I fabricated the whole thing. Then his life was ruined."

"How powerful you must believe yourself to be," Roz said. "A sixteen-year-old girl ruining the life of an adult man."

"I didn't ruin his life," Mary said. "You did."

"Really," Roz said. "I didn't see you rushing to his defense when it counted. When I claimed that your fabrications weren't fabrications at all. When I claimed that you had actually been sexually abused by an adult man. If I was wrong, Mary, why didn't you say so?"

Mary grew light-headed. "It was—a difficult choice," she said. "I was young. I didn't realize what would come of it."

"Only good things could have come of it," Roz said. "Dr. Hammer's career would have been saved. And your mother—nobody was more invested in Dr. Hammer's theory than your mother. She wanted *so desperately* to believe that you'd been lying. That you'd never been abducted or sexually molested, that you merely suffered from an overactive imagination. So I find it hard to accept, Mary, given the many benefits of testifying on behalf of Dr. Hammer, that you couldn't bring yourself to do so. Where was this 'choice'?"

Mary locked eyes again with a stone-faced fish. *Exactly*, the fish seconded. *Where was this choice?* From this distance—fourteen years—she was having a hard time recapturing the difficulty of the choice. It seemed so obvious in retrospect. Testify that Dr. Hammer was right. He had rightly created his hyper radiance theory, about girls who come of age in a sexually repressed society, girls who fabricate abduction and abuses because they're unable to act out in a directly sexual way without risking cultural shame. He had spun her testimony into a theory involving adolescent girls in New England and regardless of what you thought of his theory, it had been based on this supposed truth: she'd lied.

"I can see this conversation is upsetting you," Roz said.

"I'm fine," Mary said.

"Maybe we should return to your original reason for coming here tonight."

"My original, selfish reason."

Roz View-Mastered from defensive to sympathetic.

"Seeking closure is selfish business. That doesn't make it unworthy. Just don't expect too much solace to come of it. While Dr. Hammer might yet forgive you, your mother never will."

"But you said she'd changed..."

"She may have forgiven you in her lifetime—I'm not at liberty to say. But what good would it do you, even if I could say 'Yes, Mary, your mother forgave you'? The fact remains that you will never be forgiven *by* her. That's what I meant when I said I was sad not to have seen you before she died. I wasn't accusing you of anything."

"You accused me of being selfish," Mary said.

"Yes," Roz said. "You're being selfish. And what an improvement that is."

Mary's face and neck grew hot—as if she'd received a compliment for something she hadn't realized it was good to be good at.

"I should go," Mary said.

"But I haven't given you what you came for."

"What was that?" Mary said. She was too muddle-brained to remember why she'd come.

"That good reason your mother had for contacting me," Roz said. "The letter you found in her desk. Aren't you curious?"

"Maybe not anymore," Mary said. She was embarrassed, suddenly, by her quest. How silly it was, as Roz wisely pointed out. How pointless and silly. It was as pointless and silly as her own mother's obsession with clearing the name of Abigail Lake. Abigail Lake was dead—so very, very dead, she was three hundred years worth of dead, her body nothing but a black lichen imprint on the bottom of a pine box. Forgiveness being sought for the dead, or from them—a vain endeavor. Vain, pointless, selfish. She should return to the West Salem living room and learn how to be sad. Sad that her mother was dead. Sad that she'd blown all opportunities to rectify their relationship while her mother was alive. A classic example of "failure to yield."

Roz tore a sheet of paper from the pad on her desk. She folded it in two. Mary shoved the paper into her pocket without reading it. Uncertain how to end things, she extended her hand.

Roz took her hand but did not shake it. She held onto it with the firm-yet-light grip of a psychic trying to get a surreptitious read off a stranger.

"Maybe I'll see you again," Roz said. "But I'm guessing I won't."

"OK," Mary said dumbly.

"You have a chance to set things right for yourself, Mary," Roz said. "Don't screw it up."

Mary found herself fighting back a second humiliating bout of tears as Roz's office door shut behind her with a scarcely audible click. She stood in the tiny hallway, made smaller by the space-consuming exhalations of the white-noise machine. How unportentious it all seemed, Mary thought. No definitive slamming of doors. No flickering streetlamps. No bolts of lightning. All these years of hating Roz Biedelman, and now the woman was—possibly—gone from her life for good. How many times a day do such disappearances occur without a person noticing? These final meetings between two ambivalent humans. The last opportunity she might ever have to speak her mind to Roz Biedelman. The last opportunity to apologize to Miss Pym for her "failure to yield." The last opportunity to ask Bettina Spencer-Weeks why she did what she'd done to Dr. Hammer. Just like that, people are eradicated from your life, without any cosmic fanfare accompanying that final handshake, that final glance. It seemed useless to even *remember* a person like Roz Biedelman; what was the point? The Roz portion of her brain could be erased now. Forget the bad feelings. Utilize that nubbly area for something more productive. Amnesia was not a disease, it was a practical use of storage space.

Mary waited until she'd reached the lobby before withdrawing the folded paper from her pocket.

48 Water Street
Chadwick
He will want to see you.

Notes

I would not be the first person to suggest a similarity between the job of a psychiatrist treating a patient faking a severe anterograde memory disturbance and that of a prosecutor cross-examining a witness of dubious integrity. This similarity was suggested by H-F in a paper entitled " 'Cross-examination' and the Faked Severe Anterograde Memory Disturbance" that he delivered at the 1982 New England Psychiatric Conference. As H-F learned from studying prosecutorial techniques, abrupt transitions during the interrogation phase with the defendant—"the patient"—can reveal inconsistencies in his or her story; as the ground shifts, the defendant/patient does not have the opportunity to recalibrate his or her position, and the effect is as revealing as any lie detector.

Had I been more attuned to the similarities between a perjurer and a patient, I might not have been so easily duped by Bettina Spencer's "false memory"—that she had been abducted and abused by her field hockey coach. In fact, had I been privy to her police testimony—at the time, such documents were off-limits to a psychiatric volunteer—I might have more immediately identified Bettina's confabulation pattern and been able, thus, to treat her more effectively.

Call it curiosity, call it a hunch, or call it, as my own analyst might be inclined to call it, an attempt to rectify a past mistake. Regardless, after my fifth session with Mary, I thought it might be helpful to read the transcript from Bettina's questioning by the police after she reappeared on November 7, 1971. (*November 7.* A brief glance at Mary's file confirmed: she had disappeared on the exact same day that Bettina had reappeared, fourteen years earlier.) The transcripts were available through the the Massachusetts Mental Health Governing Board, the same board that assigned a caseworker to investigate my methods and procedures after I testified on Bettina's behalf in a preliminary court hearing against her field hockey coach. Curiously, the revealing transcript had nothing to do with Bettina's disappearance. Appendix F: Interrogation Transcript May 19, 1972, included the entirety of the conversation between Bettina and a police detective named Morse after she was arrested on suspicion of setting fire to the Semmering library. The relevant part of the exchange went as follows:

> MORSE: You say you were not responsible for your
> own actions.
> BETTINA: That's what I said.
> MORSE: Because you were under a spell.
> BETTINA: Yes.
> MORSE: And you claim that your headmistress, Miss Pym, cast
> this spell on you.
> BETTINA: That's what happened.
> MORSE: Can you describe this spell to me?
> BETTINA: No.

MORSE: No?

BETTINA: I can't remember.

MORSE: But you know you were under a spell. You remember
　　　that much.

BETTINA: The last thing I remember was a bright flash.

MORSE: What kind of flash?

BETTINA: The flash came from a solid object. An ax. Like those
　　　axes Indians use.

MORSE: A tomahawk.

BETTINA: Yes. A tomahawk. But it was made of gold.

A golden tomahawk. A coincidence? Impossible, unless you believe in
spells—and even more impossible when you consider the corresponding
dates of appearance/disappearance. The question was, how had Mary
gained access to this exchange between Bettina and Morse? I phoned
Miss Pym and was informed: Semmering sponsored an after-school in-
ternship program with the Massachusetts Mental Health Governing
Board; the previous spring, Mary Veal had been one of these interns.

Now I had proof, even if circumstantial, that Mary's "story" was a
fabrication—or an unconscious confabulation—and that she was either
hiding something by lying or that she was simply, like Bettina, suffering
from an antisocial personality disorder. The latter diagnosis would be
the more troubling, from both a recovery and a treatment perspective;
the antisocial personality disorder patient will "play along" only so long
as you do not resist their manipulations. Any attempt to confront
them or criticize them typically results in the patient terminating treatment. A therapeutic alliance can only be formed by presenting yourself
as an ally; a tone of accusation or judgment must be avoided at all costs,
unless you wish to lose the patient's cooperation. At the same time, a
doctor must be careful not to condone the actions of an antisocial sociopath, for fear of becoming an enabler. The difference between an enabler and an ally, of course, is a difficult line to walk. And since I had

been an enabler in the past, I was more than a little leery of making that misstep again.

Despite my best intentions—to restrain from judgmental or confrontational behavior—Mary's own behavior at our next appointment made it difficult to respect these intentions. She appeared wearing a Semmering field hockey jacket, her hair in two braids. As the session progressed, and Mary's hostility toward me mounted, I could no longer chalk up to coincidence the fact that Mary resembled, to an uncanny degree, one of the much-circulated photos of the missing Bettina Spencer. It was as if she had intuited my discovery of the Bettina Spencer transcript and was flaunting her total lack of intimidation.

Atypically, it was she who began the conversation.

I had fun last week, she said.

Good, I said. We strive to make the process of self-discovery an enjoyably challenging one.

You're a fun bunch all right, Mary said. Did you know that my last shrink tried to kiss me?

I know Dr. Hicks-Flevill extremely well. He's not . . .

He's not the kissing type, she said.

He's professional above all else, I said.

He's professional above sexual, she said. He's professional above residential.

Are you warm? I asked her. You haven't removed your jacket.

She peered at her jacket.

Do you know where I found this? In a storage room at school. It must date back to the mid-seventies.

Interesting that you should pick that date, I said.

I've seen the yearbooks, she said. And the girls used to wear their hair like this.

She gestured toward her head.

Did you know girls look at girls more than guys? she said.

Homoeroticism, even when unrealized—

It's not because they're lesbians, she interrupted. It's because they desire inspiration.

You find other girls inspiring, I said.

Oh yes, she said. I am very inspired by other girls. I doubt I've ever had a single original thought of my own. I'm not the creative one in the family. "Regina," my mother loves to say, "is a poet. She writes poetry at night by flashlight under an afghan." Which isn't true. She did it once, under the afghan like that, because she knew Mum would find her and repeat the story to everyone. *Regina writes poetry at night under an afghan!* How brilliant and odd!

Does that bother you, I said.

The fact that the afghan thing was staged?

The fact that your mother believes your sister is the poet in the family.

She *is* the poet in the family, Mary said. She's just a really shitty one.

But you're not even a shitty poet, according to your mother, I said.

I'm a slut, she said.

Why are you a slut?

Because I disappeared and can't remember what happened to me.

So your misfortune reflects poorly on your mother, I said.

Mary rose from the couch and walked to the window. She put her hands into the back pockets of her jeans, collapsing her shoulder blades; the S on the back of her field hockey jacket coiled, springlike. From the rear, with her hair in braids and wearing this jacket, her resemblance to Bettina evolved from uncanny to distressing.

She sighed. We've been over this before. It's boring.

I must insist you sit down, I said. And remove your coat.

I'm cold, she said.

Are you sick?

Can't a person just be cold?

It's plenty warm in here, I said. Please sit down and take off your coat. Stay a while, I added, trying to appear jovial. I did not feel jovial. I feared, irrationally, that time had collapsed and I was experiencing the worst professional mistake of my life anew.

I'll sit down, she said. But you can't make me take off my coat.

Fine. Returning to your mother, I said. Her egocentrism.

Snoozeville, Beaton, she said.

But the issue persistently arises, I said. So obviously your mother's tendency to internalize your misfortune upsets you.

Can we switch places again? Mary asked. I really like your chair.

Not today, I said.

How about if we switch places but you could still be you and I could still be me.

I don't understand, I said.

I could ask you questions, say, about your former patients. It might feel good to unload. I'm an impartial listener. Unlike your own therapist.

My analyst, I corrected.

Whatever. Your *analyst* has issues with you as a professional. He will want to prove to you that he's better than you.

And you won't want to prove you're better than me, I said.

That's different, she said.

How is it different?

Because if I'm better than you, I'll be the only one who knows it.

How is that possible?

Because I'll make it so, Mary said. Haven't you ever had the satisfaction of besting somebody who didn't know they were bested by you?

Give me an example of what you're talking about, I said.

Mary fiddled with her braid. Another habit of Bettina's. Bettina, who was medicated for a hyperactive disorder as a young girl, still had a tendency to fidget unconsciously as a teenager and even as an adult; she was persistently pulling at the split ends of her hair or turning a spot on her face into a small bloody hole; she'd once, during a particularly tense session, pulled out her eyelashes one by one.

Mary yanked a strand of hair across her lips and into her mouth. Her tongue waggled suggestively as it attempted to tie the hair into a knot.

An example, I reminded her.

I'm thinking, she said. Let's say that I have a sister who's a very shitty poet. Let's say that she values, above all other things, a prize given out by the poetry journal at Semmering. And let's say that I say to myself, any idiot with a pencil could win that prize. For example: I know that the committee prefers poems that connect school activities—like the pumpkin pie bake sale to raise money for poor people who can't afford a holiday turkey—to historical events, such as the first Thanksgiving. This poem should furthermore be written in a style reminiscent of Edna St. Vincent Millay's "Renaissance" since that's the poem that Ms. Wilkes, who is the only person on the committee, recites each September, by heart, on the first day of class. Let's say I write a poem called "Bake Sale 1621," in which I compare the Indians to the high-school girls making pies, and I slip in the school's motto, *Vox in Deserto*, "A Voice in the Wilderness." Our ancestors, the pilgrims, are like the poor people receiving the help. I blend the lines between girl and Indian, poor person and ancestor. And then I show, via some very sappy imagery—say, withered kernels of corn being blown by the wind and taking root far and wide over this great and generous land of ours—how this impulse to help those who are less fortunate than us by feeding them locally raised foods is now the inborn duty of every Semmering student, because every Semmering student understands that she is no different from an Indian or a poor person. Let's say the concluding couplet, which might be something like "And as these golden kernels doth widely blow, no winds abandon the hungry to heartless snow," are only slightly different from a poem that won the competition ten years earlier, and thus it rings familiar to

Ms. Wilkes, who is too daft to remember the poems that win from year to year.

This is a very complicated example, I said. But I still don't see how you've bested your sister without her knowing it.

I'm not finished, Mary said. Let's say I submit this poem using the name of a girl whose father is an English professor at St. Hugh's. Let's say this girl is dyslexic and can barely read a comic book. Let's say her father spends gazillions of dollars on an after-school tutor because he can't accept the fact that his daughter isn't "Yale material." Let's say I am confident that, should her poem win the competition, she will never tell anyone that she was not the author of the poem because her father, for the first time in her whole underachieving life, will be proud of her. He'll call his relatives, he'll throw her a party, he'll send copies of the school newspaper article announcing her win to the Yale admissions office. And now, let's say the poem, "Bake Sale 1621," wins and my sister takes second place to a dyslexic girl who can barely read a comic book.

Mary replaced the strand of hair in her mouth. Her tongue darted around and around in repeated figure-eight movements outside her mouth as she attempted again to tie the hair into a knot.

I used to be really good at this, she said, referring, I assumed, to her tongue exertions.

Fortunately you have other talents, I said. Like writing poetry under a pseudonym.

Regina's the only poet in the family.

So your example, I said. It's just an example.

You asked for "an example." I gave you an example.

So you didn't write a poem called "Bake Sale 1621."

It's a masterpiece languishing in the ether, she said. But I've fantasized about writing it.

Clearly, I said. Your fantasy life is very detailed.

Dad always says I'm "hatching a plan." Because I don't talk much at home. Mum will say "she's so quiet" and Dad will say "she's hatching a plan." Of course he doesn't believe I'm doing anything more than day-dreaming.

Which is another "example."

Example of . . .

Besting somebody without his or her knowledge. You *are* hatching plans, but you don't let your father or mother know that you are. You al-low them to believe that you're pointlessly daydreaming.

About sex, she said.

You like to be perceived by people as less than who you really are.

What they don't know won't hurt them, Mary said.

What they don't know won't hurt *you*, I said. Isn't this a self-protective tendency?

Maybe I'm modest, Mary said. Maybe I'm shy.

Others might interpret your behavior as deceitful.

You mean *you* think it's deceitful.

I didn't say that, I said.

Though she had a point. I *was* feeling judgmental toward her; I was feeling ungenerous, and these feelings initiated from a threatened place. The similarities between her case and Bettina's case made me feel as though I was the one who needed to protect myself against her and the detailed manner in which her mind processed these alternate realities. For in essence, this was what her "example" revealed to me: she was an inhab-itor of an alternate reality. She lived in one world, while in her mind she manipulated that world, to a minute and pragmatically detailed de-gree, to achieve different outcomes. Of course there was nothing unusual about this; there was nothing even pathological about this, if experi-enced on the level of fantasy and acknowledged by the mind as such. My worry was that Mary, given the level of detailed thought accom-panying these fantasies, was no longer able to distinguish between fan-tasy and life. Or worse—she could no longer discriminate between fantasy and life because, in some way, she had imposed this fantasy onto her life. Her fantasies really were the hatchings of plans, and she did not permit these good ideas to go to waste. Like Bettina, she implemented them.

In that case, Mary said, every thought you have and don't share is deceitful.

You have a point, I said.

So you take it back. About being deceitful.

I apologize if I sounded as if I were passing judgment on you, I said.

Apology accepted, she said. I like it when you apologize.

So today I had an idea, I said. I'd like to ask you some questions.

A departure from the usual, she said.

Different questions. More free associative kind of questions.

Great, she said. Shoot.

What does K look like?

K? she said.

K, I said.

I'm not sure to whom you're referring, she said cautiously.

K is the man who abducted you, I said. K is the man you mentioned during our second session. I can replay the tape if you like.

That's OK, she said.

So you recall mentioning him, I said.

If you say I mentioned him, I guess I mentioned him, she said.

What did he look like? I said.

I told you I don't remember, she said.

But you remember his name, I said.

K is not exactly a name.

But that's what you called him.

It's a nickname, she said. Like Beaton.

How do you feel about undercooked meat, I said.

Gross, she said.

Did K cook for you, I said.

I have no idea, she said.

How long have you been a witch, I said.

Huh?

Answer the question.

I'm not a witch.

Who is the one you chose to be your incubus?

Is this a game? she said.

Answer the question.

Can you remind me what an incubus is?

What about K, I said. Where did K live.

I can't remember, she said.

Who are the children on whom you have cast a spell?

Mary laughed.

Answer the question, I said.

I didn't cast any spells on any children, she said.

Interesting, I said.

What's interesting, she said.

Your mother was right. About your lacking creativity. When K undercooked your meat, did you tell him you'd prefer it better cooked?

He didn't cook, she said. He preferred takeout.

Where did he live, I asked.

In a cabin in the woods, she said.

What kind of takeout is available in a cabin in the woods, I said.

Mary grew flustered. I don't know, she said. I'm—trying to be creative.

You're not doing a very good job, I said. Even creativity must respect
the confines of plausibility.

We bought food and made sandwiches.

Where did you buy the food, I said.

At the store, she said. There was a store not too far down the road.

I didn't respond.

Even in the woods there are stores, she said defensively.

What music was played there, and what dances did you dance.

There was no stereo. We didn't dance. K wasn't the dancing type.

What type of a person was he?

He was . . . sad, she said.

Sad, I said. Do you mean remorseful?

Remorseful? she said.

Did he suffer from feelings of shame and guilt.

Not at first, she said. He hadn't done anything yet.

No? I said.

She shook her head.

He'd abducted you, I pointed out.

Mary reddened.

That's a crime, I said. Don't you consider that a crime?

It depends, she said.

Depends on what?

It depends on how hard he had to try.

How hard he had to try . . . to abduct you, I said. You mean he didn't take you by force.

Mary gazed toward my bookshelf.

I still can't believe you have this book, she said, walking to the shelf and removing *Dorcas Hobbs*.

What is it about that book you find so special, I said.

She shrugged. Then:

Did you know Bettina Spencer was obsessed with this book?

Was she, I said.

To some people, Bettina's a hero.

She destroyed school property. She lied.

Maybe hero's the wrong word, Mary said. She was fascinating the way witches are fascinating. Bettina was a kind of witch.

Do you mean because she was wrongly accused of something and wrongly punished, I said.

No, I mean like real witches.

There were no real witches, I said.

But if there were real witches. She was like a real witch. She made people do uncharacteristic things. Like her friend Melanie Clark.

Maybe Melanie Clark has a hard time taking responsibility for her own actions, I said.

Mary frowned.

Did I say something wrong, I said.

No, she said. Forget it.

What did I say, I said.

I'm trying to tell you something, she said. I'm trying to describe a feeling that I have, and that a lot of girls have, and you're resistant to the idea of this feeling.

I apologize, I said. What is this feeling you're describing.

It's a feeling of . . . wanting to be somebody other than yourself, she said. Of looking up to somebody who's a bad influence, but who's a good influence too.

How could Bettina be a good influence, I said.

Mary shrugged. I think that's why Bettina liked *Dorcas Hobbs*. All these girls form a long chain of influence.

Again—to claim an "influence" is often to fail to take responsibility, I said.

Did you know that she stole this book from the library before she burned the library down?

I didn't know that, I said.

She and I both looked toward my bookshelf.

After the library was rebuilt, the school replaced the book but the book kept disappearing, Mary said.

Girls were stealing the book, I said.

Probably, she said. But the rumor was that Bettina was a witch, and she could make the book disappear. The librarian stopped replacing the book because according to Miss Pym it turned girls into thieves.

It *is* a cautionary tale about how human hysteria can override human rationality.

Books can be evil, Mary said. They can give people ideas.

They stimulate thinking, I said.

Not all thinking is good, Mary said. I know you disagree.

I believe all thinking is worthy of scrutiny, I said.

That sounds tiring, she said. I'm tired. I was up late last night.

You had insomnia, I said.

Dorcas Hobbs kept me awake, she said. There's something about that book.

What is it, I said.

Mary shrugged.

Does it have to do with Bettina, I asked.

Now you want to talk about Bettina, she said.

It's reasonable to ask about Bettina in connection to this book, I said. So what do you see as the connection between Dorcas and Bettina.

Bettina wanted to be Dorcas, Mary said.

She wanted to be abducted by Indians and cause the death of an innocent man, I said.

Mary rolled her eyes.

You're so literal, Beaton.

So you've said. Multiple times.

So open your eyes and look! Mary said. Why do you think Bettina wanted to be like Dorcas?

I'm unable to comment on the wants of Bettina, I said.

Mary pulled on her braid.

Bettina wanted somebody to write a book about her. Look at Anne Frank. Every girl wants to be Anne Frank. I mean, minus the dying part. But how exciting, to be locked in an attic like that. If you didn't have to die, you know? That's why it's such a great read. Because the bad stuff happens outside of the book.

Some pretty bad stuff happens inside the book, I said.

But she doesn't die. Not in the actual book. Only in the preface.

Yes, I said. But that's missing the point. To an almost amoral degree, that's missing the point of her life entirely.

Her life didn't have a *point*, Mary said. She was just a girl. Girls' lives don't have points. That's why they do what they do.

What do you mean, I said.

That's why they obsess over books like *Dorcas Hobbs*.

Obsess, I said. How many times have you read this book?

I've never read it. Not in the way that you've read all of these books. She gestured at my bookshelf.

You think I read differently from you?

I've never read it straight through, from beginning to end.

Because you find it boring, I said.

No, she said. It's more complicated than that.

Can you try to explain it to me, I said.

It depends, she said. Earlier today you didn't care about my feelings.

I do care, I said. Why haven't you read *Dorcas Hobbs*.

Because, she said. I'm afraid to ruin what I've imagined is a really good story.

What Might Have Happened

They stopped for lunch in a small town not far from the quarry. Their second diner meal together in as many days of knowing each other, the girl observed.

Actually, the man said. We've barely known each other a full day. Not even twenty-four hours.

The girl poured four creamers into her coffee cup until the liquid came even with the rim. Her thawing hands still smarted; tearing open the sodden paper creamer tops, she feared her fingernails might bleed.

Depends on what you think of as a day, she said. Let's say your doctor tells you that you shouldn't drink more than three cups of coffee a day. How do you know when one day is over and the next has begun?

Usually when you go to sleep, the man said. Which is why I count in hours. Sometimes I don't sleep for six consecutive twenty-four-hour periods. Which could be construed as the same long day.

Your ex-wife wanted you to try meditation, the girl said. She claimed you were anxious.

I'm sure she did, the man said. My ex-wife believes if you die from cancer it's your own fault.

You can also die from lack of sleep. Did you know there's a Jewish family in Bologna who has a hereditary sleep condition? Starting near the age of thirty their bodies stop making a protein and they can no longer sleep. They stay awake for seven years, then they die.

Being awake for seven years is like being alive for fifteen years, the man said.

They did age more quickly, the girl said. I saw pictures. Did you notice that sign as we were driving last night?

What sign, the man said.

The sign that said "Next Gas: 23 Days, 37 Nights."

What about that sign, the man said.

I thought it was funny, the girl said. To measure the distance of gas in days and nights.

Those were mileages based on—

I know, the girl said. But I misunderstood it for a moment. It made me think of Scheherazade and the *Thousand and One Nights*.

Is that how you see yourself? the man said. You are my Scheherazade?

I'm a teenager, she said. It's my prerogative to see myself reflected everywhere throughout the ages. You're not eating.

I should eat more protein, the man said. Sleep is a protein. It can be found in eggs.

Of course the real reason you can't sleep is because of me, the girl said.

You.

The terrible guilt you feel, the girl said. Before it was a part of your daily life. But now that you've "forgotten" the guilt, it keeps you awake at night. You must come to terms with who you were, and then you'll sleep like a baby.

The man laughed. He jammed his fork into his eggs, shoveled the quivering jumble into his mouth.

The girl cringed. He was ugly when he ate.

He clanged his egg-messy fork on the Formica tabletop.

You need to start coming up with some different story lines, Scheherazade, he said. I'm getting sick of this one.

The man paid the check while the girl visited the restroom. In the milky mirror she could see that she'd aged, too, like the sleepless Jewish family from Bologna. Fifteen years in one night. Her cheekbones were more mounded, her mouth wider and resting more flatly on her teeth. She was so tired that her eyes felt like balls of lint, incapable of locating contours or anything more specific than the gross outlines of things. Everything seemed very far away—her exhaustion, her vinegar-chip canker sores, her need to pee. She knew that she must not sleep before the man did. She vowed to herself that she would not. They were having a parallel experience that would be disrupted if she abandoned him like that.

The man drove them to a small general store that was, he said, only three miles from the cabin.

Supplies, he said. What do you like to eat?

Nothing in particular, she said. Should I come in?

All the same to me, he said, turning off the Mercedes and pocketing the key.

Won't they know you here? she said.

These people up here love to not know me, he said.

She followed him into the ancient store, the floorboards cupped, the front door weighted with a Diet-Rite can on a dirty string. The old woman behind the glass deli case aggressively did not notice them.

The food here dates back to about the mid-century, the man said, not out of earshot of the old woman. He showed the girl a box of cereal, its front sun bleached to a puke-beige color. The man picked up a carton of milk, a dozen eggs, a cardboard flat of bacon. The girl added a packet of dried biscuit mix and some black tea to their basket. The man struck off in search of toilet paper, leaving her alone beside the chips display.

Hello, she heard a woman say.

Hello, she heard the man say.

Fancy meeting you here, the woman said.

Fancy that, the man said.

I didn't know you and Laura were still together. I heard you split.

We—we did split, the man said.

Oh. So then—

But it was an amicable split. From a property perspective. I have visiting rights with the house.

The woman laughed. Those are the best kind of divorces, she said. I had one of those with my first husband. Did you know that my cabin here originally belonged to his family?

I didn't know that, the man said.

It's the truth, the woman said, as though she'd asked him to believe something very unbelievable. Are you alone?

The woman's voice sounded mockingly hopeful.

The man paused. The girl poked her head out from the aisle in which she was eavesdropping.

No, the man said, spotting her.

Hello, said the girl.

Hello, said the woman. The woman was hyper-blond with a faceful of orange makeup.

Who is this? The woman's eyebrow raised as though she expected a delicious answer.

I'm his daughter, the girl said.

But I though you and Laura—

From a previous marriage, the girl said.

Ah, said the hyper-blonde.

Actually, the girl said, he and my mother were never married.

Really, said the hyper-blonde.

She was so clearly a gossip, the girl thought. Clearly she saw herself in her own mind repeating this story to great acclaim. This was how she best envisioned herself. This was when her image of herself came most colorfully to life.

Now now, the man said, his tone sweet and chiding. No need to air our dirty laundry in public.

He smiled fake-tensely at the hyper-blonde.

He didn't have a clue I existed until last year, the girl said. My mother never told him.

This is just our little get-to-know-you father-daughter trip, the man said. Did you find what you needed in the bread aisle, sweetie?

Even though we got to know each other pretty well already on the camping trip, the girl said.

The camping trip, said the hyper-blonde.

With our church group. He was my leader. We almost made a very large mistake because we thought we were strangers. We realized at the last minute that we were related.

Huh! the hyper-blonde exclaimed.

We mistook our attraction to one another as sexual, the girl said. In fact it was familial. He was attracted to me because I reminded him of a lost part of himself. It's easy to confuse those attractions.

There are some very confused people in this world, the man said.

The hyper-blonde licked her teeth.

I have to meet Alain, she said. But it's been great seeing you. And meeting—I'm sorry, what was your name, dear?

Ida, said the girl.

Great to meet you, Ida. You're a beguiling young lady.

She smiled approvingly at the man and told him to give her best to Laura—*whoops I mean*, she struggled.

No problem, said the man.

The woman tucked her chip bags under her fitted parka and headed toward the cash register.

The man and the girl hid in the beer aisle until they heard the rise and fall of the Diet-Rite can.

The man paid for the groceries with cash, of which he had very little remaining.

Do you know who that was, the girl asked, after he'd pulled the Mercedes out of the parking lot.

Of course, the man said. I mean . . . a friend of my ex-wife's I'm guessing.

And of yours, the girl said.

I doubt that, the man said.

She was always hitting on you. Trying to make you cheat on your ex-wife.

Her? the man said. Surely I'm not her type.

Exactly, the girl said. She liked you because you were a dullard with a shrimp allergy. If only she knew.

She's beginning to know, the man said. Nice tale spinning, Scheherazade.

The girl took this as a compliment. She was pretty certain it was meant as a compliment.

Her advances made you uncomfortable, the girl continued. She pretended to be your ex-wife's closest friend. Also, you found her physically repulsive.

That remains true, he said. Why did I tell you this?

Because it's easy to confuse attractions, the girl said.

Ah, the man said. Am I confused?

You were confused. And yes. You are confused.

Before I was confused . . .

Before you were confused because you were a father figure who experienced sexual feelings toward his daughter figure. Now you're confused because I may or may not have information about you, and this desire to know the truth—this curiosity—has evolved into an erotic attraction.

Interesting interpretation, the man said.

I'm not wrong, the girl said. Do you want to know why I know I'm not wrong?

Does it involve more terrible secrets about my past?

No, it involves terrible secrets about my past.

Absolutely, then. I want to know why you know you're not wrong.

I know I'm not wrong, the girl said, because I had a best friend when we were neighbors.

Did I know her?

The girl shook her head. I was worried you might decide you'd rather be sexually attracted to her as a daughter figure.

Did I really seem so fickle to you?

This story isn't about you, she said. It's about me.

Sorry, the man said.

You really are a hog, the girl said. I've been spoiling you with all these stories about yourself.

I said I was sorry, the man said.

This friend, the girl said, moved to Michigan when I was ten. We lost touch. I didn't see her again until last year, when I was sixteen. We were both attending a weeklong field hockey camp in Virginia.

What a fun coincidence, the man said.

Unfortunately she sprained her ankle the first day of camp and had to go home, the girl said. So I spent that night talking to her until two a.m. in her dorm room. Finally she asked me to leave so she could sleep, and I felt the most unbearable urge to kiss her.

Did you? the man said. Kiss her?

No! the girl said. But I wanted to kiss her. This disturbed me very much. I worried I was becoming a lesbian.

Late-onset lesbianism, the man said.

The girl stiffened in the passenger seat.

Sorry, the man said. Is irreverence off-limits suddenly?

For the rest of this story it is, the girl said.

Sorry, the man said. So you worried you were a lesbian.

But then I realized that I wanted to kiss her not because I was attracted to *her* but because I wanted some physical way to make contact with a former version of myself. She reminded me of a part of my life for which I had no memory touchstones. We no longer lived in the house. Our photos and belongings had burned. She was the only remnant of that part of my life.

There's me, the man said.

OK but—until you, the girl said. She was the only remnant.

So the point of this story?

You mean, the girl said, as it pertains to you?

Since all things must pertain to me, the man said.

The point is that you feel attracted to me because I am your memory touchstone. You think you're attracted to *me*, but in truth you're attracted to a lost part of yourself. That's why you want to kiss me. You're trying to get it back.

The man jammed on the Mercedes's breaks. The car snaked and slid to a stop.

Jesus, the girl said.

I missed the turn, the man said.

So do you agree?

Do I agree with what?

That you want to kiss me so that you can get back a lost part of yourself.

Who says I want to kiss you, the man said. The road onto which they'd turned was badly plowed and required all of the man's concentration. The girl could see only trees—to the sides of them, ahead of them, even behind them now that they'd rounded a corner and the main road became lost from view. She should have been scared, but instead, because she was so obliteratingly tired, she felt happy and resigned. This was what it was like to be boiled alive, to freeze to death. Yes yes she understood it now, the drifting-off that equals submission to one's circumstances. She was no longer responsible for what happened to her. She had positioned herself in the path of the inevitable.

The Mercedes struck a rock and bounced to the right. The front tire embedded itself in a snowdrift. The man pumped the accelerator. He slapped the wheel with both hands, not angrily.

That's it, he said. Looks like we're walking. Leave the groceries. I'll come back with the sledge.

The girl and the man started down the road, each of them huddled inside their own inadequate clothing. After about five hundred feet the road took a dogleg turn to the right. She could see a cabin, the shutters pulled over the windows as if it were asleep.

So you don't want to kiss me, the girl said. She had to hurry to keep up with the man, who was suddenly walking very fast.

Not really, the man said.

You've gone through quite a bit of trouble in that case. What's your reason for bringing me here?

Reason? the man said. Do I need a reason?

Just because you have amnesia doesn't mean you're an all-purpose idiot, the girl said.

OK then, the man said. My reason.

He kicked his boots against the outside wall of the cabin. He unhooked the nearest shutter and pulled a key from a nail on the windowsill. He opened the front door and stood aside to allow her to pass first.

He smiled at the girl as she brushed past him.

I've brought you here, he said, because this is our little get-to-know-you father-daughter trip.

West Salem

NOVEMBER 9, 1999

M ary called from the train station.

"It's eight o'clock, where have you *been*?" Regina said.

"I need someone to pick me up," Mary said.

No answer.

"Hello?" Mary said.

Regina inhaled audibly. Weegee barked in the background, indicating Aunt Helen was somewhere in the background, too.

The connection terminated.

Mary stared at the dead receiver, uncertain if something had happened to Regina (*Weegee's feeling homicidal*), or if Regina intended to pick her up, or if Regina expected Mary to call back and plead for a ride. She chose optimism: Regina was unharmed and en route. She rechecked her pocket—as she had every few minutes—for the scrap of paper with Dr. Hammer's address in Chadwick. Strange that he would have remained in the Boston area—then again, she reasoned, since he was no longer a therapist, he didn't require a new city for his new start after the trial. The owners of hedges wouldn't hold his past against him if he'd become a landscaper. The buyers of kitchen tiles wouldn't care if their salesman was a defrocked shrink.

To keep warm, Mary kicked at the hardened disks of dirty snow that hemmed the base of each streetlamp, slowly chipping them away with her boot heel. Across the street and through the bare woods, the perfect squares of house windows blinked as their inhabitants walked past. She smelled burning wood, could see the chimney smoke rising above the tree line. A delicious melancholy overtook her as she recalled the many nights she'd waited to be picked up at the train station by her mother who was always, at least until Mary disappeared, late. She'd huddle in her never-warm-enough coat and search hopefully for headlights illuminating the black gap through the trees that was Old Bellows Road. The headlights would round the horseshoe and drive straight toward the train platform. *Here she is*, she'd tell herself, and she'd experience the hopeful chest lift of a lost skier who hears the distant rumble of an avalanche and chooses to mistake it for a snowmobile. She'd feel a little less cold, her shoulders would unwinch. Then the car, at the very last second, would take the second sharp turn in Old Bellows Road, missing the parking lot, the sound of its engine fading more quickly than it had intensified upon approach. Her heart would drop, and the cold would attack her exposed neck with renewed fervor, and she would grow self-pityingly enraged. *How could she be late again.* The rage would mutate from incendiary to a dull, pragmatic thudding. Soon a vengeful possibility would overtake her; she would hide. She would stick out her thumb and accept a ride from the next car that passed. She would simply, soundlessly vanish.

This plotting kept her warm.

Once, when her mother was fifty-three minutes late, a record even for her, Mary had gone so far as to act; she'd tried to hitchhike, but no cars passed. When the headlights of her mother's Peugeot rounded the horseshoe, she slid along the side of the station steps and crouched behind the Dumpster, fenced off with lattice. She gripped the lattice with her gloved fingers and wondered how long she would let her mother's panic build. Three minutes, perhaps. Three minutes to check the station waiting area and the station restroom and the train platform seemed a generously brief amount of time, given that her mother had kept her waiting in the cold for nearly an hour.

Her mother pulled into the parking lot and sat in the idling car, peering upward through the windshield at the clock on the station's exterior wall. She squinted toward the empty train platform, again at the clock. Mary waited for her to honk. She waited for her to emerge from the car and search the platform. But her mother did neither of these things. One minute and twenty-three seconds after arriving, her mother put the Peugeot in gear and, without a backward glance, drove away.

Mary stared at the Peugeot's brake lights, dumbfounded. Her coat pockets were empty of change so she called home collect, trying to keep the outraged teariness from her voice as she gave her name to the operator. Her father appeared within seven minutes, smelling of gin and peanuts. Her mother, when Mary arrived home, stood at the kitchen counter cutting onions. *Strange*, her mother said. *I looked for you everywhere.*

Mary heard the screech of tires as the Peugeot—the same Peugeot—careered into the parking lot. Classical music blared behind the windshield, the entire car pulsing like a salt-rusted cocoon about to pop a bombastic insect.

She slid into the passenger seat, cringing against the wall of sound.

Regina pulled recklessly back onto Old Bellows Road. She looked awful, the lights from the dashboard transforming her face into a haggard landscape of sinkholes and fault lines.

The humid smell of pizza pressed against Mary's cold nose. The closeness of the air plus the decibel level of the music made her feel sweatily claustrophobic.

"Can I turn this down?" she asked.

Regina didn't respond.

"Do you mind?" Mary asked. "I have a headache."

"*You* have a headache," Regina said. "You didn't have to spend the past two hours with Aunt Helen. Did you know you broke her vase?"

"I didn't break it," Mary said.

"She found a hairline crack," Regina said. "It's worthless now."

"Too bad," Mary said.

Regina didn't respond.

"I bet Weegee's upset."

Regina didn't laugh.

"That was funny," Mary said.

"What?"

"That was funny. You should laugh."

"*Hah hah hah*," said Regina.

Regina glared through the windshield. Clearly she was in a bad mood, which probably exempted her, in her own mind, from her promise to *be nicer*. But Mary was feeling vulnerable, not to mention giddy, after her visit with Roz Biedelman. If selfishness were a virtue, than she would persist in being selfish. She would selfishly force her sister into a confiding, kindly relationship with her even though Regina was not in a headspace that made provisions for sisterly bonding opportunities.

"So," Mary said. "You look tired."

"I am tired," Regina said.

"Have you been exercising?" Mary asked. She couldn't help herself.

"Me?" Regina said.

"I mean—what I mean is, how are you?"

"I'm fine," Regina said. "And by the way I picked up the pizzas for dinner. I paid for them myself."

"I'll pay you back," Mary said.

"Don't worry. It cost $50, including the tip. But really don't worry about it. It's my treat."

A pinched silence descended.

"I'm sorry about Bill," Mary said.

Regina sniffed.

"It must be hard dealing with a breakup on top of Mum and everything else."

What Mary didn't say was *it must be hard to lose three fiancés in four years.* By which she would mean emotionally hard, but also impressively difficult to accomplish. Then again, Regina's first two fiancés were fuss-potty men who Gaby suspected, somewhat predictably, to be gay; Regina's first fiancé, Jim, was a cruddified preppy from Concord and the sort of man who wrote on the endpapers of novels the date he finished reading said novel and where he was at that historically momentous instant; Perry, an urban planner, was such a tedious expert at the obvious that he earned the nickname "Perry Is Perry." (After the breakup, Gaby renamed him "Perry Was Perry.") Bill, according to Gaby the most promising of the bunch, ran a domestic abuse hotline in Somerville.

"You never even met Bill," Regina said, half accusingly.

"Gaby liked him," Mary said. "Gaby said he was her favorite."

"And you consider Gaby, who's never had a boyfriend, a reliable judge of fiancés."

Mary considered this. "I do," she said. "She's . . . unbiased."

Regina snorted.

"Seriously though," Mary persisted. "Do you feel like talking about what happened?"

Regina took her eyes from the road long enough to gauge her sister's sincerity. Apparently, Mary appeared convincingly sincere.

"What always happens?" Regina said. "I exhaust people." She tried to say this boastfully, as though to imply that "people" were pathetic and lacked stamina. But Mary could tell that she was more destabilized by this realization than proud of it.

Mary nodded. "You do have a certain intensity," she said. "Someday you'll find a person who treasures that side of you."

Regina cocked her head. "Do you think that would make a difference?"

"I do," Mary said.

"Bill was that person. He treasured all my worst qualities."

"That's rare," Mary said. "That's the mark of a keeper."

"Except that he broke up with me."

"Still," Mary said. "As a type, maybe you can see Bill as . . . an improvement. I mean over the long haul. You're trending upward, I guess is what I'm saying."

"Is a person who treasures your worst qualities a keeper," Regina asked, "or is he a doormat?"

"One person's doormat . . ." Mary offered.

"I exhausted Bill, but he was determined to love me. Not some future improved person. *Me.*"

"Like Dad did with Mum. That's not a bad thing," Mary said. As a vision of her slack-faced father flashed through her mind, she realized that she did not believe this.

"Nobody told me that I need to calm down, or get rational, or stop being so self-obsessed. He practically *encouraged* me to misbehave. And so I became Myself Plus Plus. It was unbearable. Not for him. Or not only for him. It was unbearable for me."

"What an honest statement," Mary said, immediately regretting her knee-jerk Roz-ism. She meant the comment in a sincere, not a patronizing, way. She truly was impressed with Regina's sudden onslaught of self-knowledge—as perhaps, she reflected, Roz had been sincerely impressed with hers.

Fortunately Regina took her comment in the manner it was intended; she smiled appreciatively, and Mary glimpsed behind her listless features, a touching flicker of the plain girl who could convince people that she was beautiful. She had to stifle an urge to put her hand on her sister's arm.

"I've been doing some soul-searching," Regina said. "And I've been writing a lot. I'm assembling the more polished poems into a chapbook."

"That's great," Mary said encouragingly. "It's about time somebody published you."

"It's self-published," Regina said.

"Oh," Mary said. "Well. You're somebody."

"Maybe you can fly out for my publication party," Regina said.

"I'd like that," Mary said.

"Have you ever tried writing poetry?" Regina asked. "It's very therapeutic, so long as you don't worry about rhyme. Or meter."

"I don't think I'd be very good at writing poetry," Mary said, her face heating up. "Bake Sale 1621" wasn't the covertly mocking success she'd hoped it would be. She'd written the poem but it hadn't won the Semmering Poetry Contest. Regina's poem hadn't won either. Nothing had unfolded as she'd planned and she should have learned something from the experience. She had not.

"Do you see a therapist?" Regina asked.

"Me?" Mary said, relieved that the topic had shifted. "Who would have me?"

Regina laughed. "Now *that's* funny."

Out her window, Mary clocked the familiar beginnings of the Semmering grounds—the sharp-tipped, wrought-iron fence that lassoed the entire 110 acres and was as much intended to keep its students within as to prevent the much-feared vagrants from invading. The sports fields swept like an unreflecting black sea up to the school itself. As the building emerged from the dark, Mary imagined that Miss Pym stood in one of the windows, spookily observing them as they drove by.

Regina, similarly transfixed, pulled her foot off the accelerator. As the car slowed, the fence's metal bars transformed from a translucent black blur into the ever slowing tick of individual spokes.

The Peugeot coasted to a stop before the school's entry arch.

"*Vox in Suburbo*," Regina announced.

Mary said nothing. She wanted Regina to continue driving, to allow the building to recede back into the night, but didn't want to call attention to this desire. She worried it might imply something damning about her, the fact that this place could still unnerve her so.

"Do you remember the Semmering fight song?" Regina asked.

"Kind of," Mary lied.

"Give a roar, give a roar, for the feisty Semmering whores . . ." Regina tapped on the steering wheel. "They will suck out all your blood, they will nah nah nah nah nah . . ."

Regina peered at her expectantly. Mary perceived a slight barometric change inside the car, the formerly chummy atmosphere tensing into one more potentially hazardous.

"I guess I don't remember it," Mary said.

Regina laughed. "*Really? You* don't remember?"

"You didn't even play sports," Mary said. "Why do you care about the stupid fight song?"

"Because I feel overcome by team spirit," Regina said. "Don't you? Don't you feel overcome by team spirit? Or possibly you're just overcome by spirits in general. Tomahawk-waving rapist witch spirits. How about it, Mimsy. Do you feel like *talking about it?*"

Mary didn't respond.

Regina pushed the Peugeot's gear shift into drive and floored the accelerator. A good half-second later, the Peugeot's tortoise engine lurched to life. Then the two back wheels spun grudgingly to attention and the rusted body swayed back and forth as though threatening to capsize. The car hurled itself downward, the bumper grinding against the asphalt until the shocks retracted and the car pitched dopily forward.

"Feel better?" Mary asked dryly.

"Much," Regina said.

"Good," Mary said.

"So," Regina said, "while we're baring our sisterly all. I thought you should know that Gaby thinks you went to Boston to see Dr. Hammer."

"Why would she think that?" Mary said.

"She thinks that Mum's death is prompting you to have a moment of castigating self-reflection, and that this is making you act secretively again."

Mary reached into her pocket to touch the piece of paper Roz had given her.

"That's idiotic," Mary said. "Besides, he's been disbarred. Or whatever the equivalent is for therapists. De-couched."

They passed the cemetery. As they neared the spot where the Mercedes used to park, Regina jerked the wheel to the right; the car's tires ground along the shoulder, kicking gravel against the undercarriage and creating an unmelodious series of *pings*.

"Watch it!" Mary said.

Regina returned to the road.

"I was avoiding the dog," she said innocently.

"What dog?" Mary turned around. There's been no dog.

"In addition to being nicer to one another," Regina said, ignoring Mary's bewilderment, "we also need to start being honest with one another. The way I was honest with you."

"Obviously," Mary, still distractedly searching for the dog over her shoulder.

"You agree," Regina said.

Mary refused to reconfirm this.

"So then you'll tell me what you were doing in Boston. I mean if you weren't meeting Dr. Hammer."

"I was following a lead," Mary said.

The windshield fogged. Regina poked the Peugeot's DEMIST button.

"How euphemistic," she said tightly.

"Sorry," Mary said. "I went to Boston to see Dr. Biedelman."

Regina cast her a sidelong withering look.

"Don't insult me, Mimsy," she said.

"I went to see Dr. Biedelman," Mary repeated.

"I know you probably think that one dishonest turn deserves another. That's how you're rationalizing your behavior, am I right? We went behind your back so, you think, it's justified that you go behind ours."

Mary didn't respond.

"So what did Mr. Bolt tell you?"

"Who's Mr. Bolt?" Mary said.

"*Please.* The painting's worth a lot more, as you obviously discovered."

Mary fingered the DEMIST button. When she was younger, she'd thought DEMIST was a French word, she hadn't realized it was the English word for getting rid of mist.

"I hope you know it wasn't my idea to try to cheat you out of your share of the money. Gaby doesn't think you deserve anything from Mum's estate. Because, as Gaby sees it, you're the reason Mum got cancer and died."

Mary's vision turned white, then black, then white again. She thought she was having a stroke then realized they were driving past St. Hugh's new outdoor hockey rink, with its blinding, distantly spaced overhead lights.

"How about you? Is that how you see it?" Mary said.

"It doesn't matter how I see it," Regina said. "Everything's always about *you.* We even had to have Mum's funeral on the anniversary of your disappearance."

Mary's heart was beating inside her face. Hot and staccato, just under her cheeks.

"Dad insisted on the date," Mary said. "Because of Reverend Whittemore's schedule."

"So you say," Regina said.

"It was a coincidence," Mary said. "A really, really shitty one." *For me too* she refrained from adding. She didn't want to sound self-pitying.

Regina wasn't listening.

"Even *Dad* blames you for Mum's death. He'd never admit it, but don't for a second think that Mum was the only person who didn't want you coming to the hospital last week."

This stung. More than anything else, this stung, and made Mary feel not only alone but stupid and naïve and alone.

"I think we should leave Dad out of this," Mary said quietly. "I'd also suggest leaving all speculative causes of terminal diseases out of this."

Regina sniffed. "I was only telling you how Gaby felt."

"Gaby actually *said* that?"

"Don't act surprised. If you knew your sister you'd understand: Gaby is a steel-mouthed bitch."

Regina hit the last straightaway before Rumney Marsh and floored the Peugeot again, filling the car with the stink of diesel and vaporized salt.

"So?" she said.

"So what?"

"Now you know we tried to cheat you out of your inheritance. What do you have to say to that?"

Mary fingered the scrap of paper in her pocket. She had nothing to say for herself. Nothing at all.

"Weegee's tired," she said tightly, staring at the lightless woods.

A unt Helen's station wagon was still parked in front of the house. "She's going to be too drunk to drive home," Regina said.

"She can stay in the guest room," said Mary coldly.

"She cannot stay in the guest room. I am staying in the guest room."

"I thought you were staying in your room."

"My room is the guest room," Regina said.

"I guess I meant the study," Mary said.

"She can't stay there. Weegee will eat all of Mum's stuff, which you left in piles on the floor."

"I'm still sorting," Mary lied.

"Whatever. Aunt Helen is not staying in the study."

"Fine," Mary said. "We'll just let her drive home and kill herself."

Regina opened the door and, in her haste, dropped the car keys; Mary heard them skitter off to a distant shadowy place.

"*Damnit,*" Regina said. "Will you jump around? I need some light over here."

Mary positioned herself directly under the motion-sensitive light angling from the garage eaves. She jumped up and down. She waved her arms. Nothing happened.

"Come *on,*" Regina said.

"I'm *trying.* It's broken."

"It's not broken," Regina said.

"Maybe I'm invisible," Mary said, feeling suddenly quite worried about this possibility. It wouldn't have been the first time that day.

"Don't flatter yourself. You're just retarded when it comes to very basic activities."

Regina waved frantically at the eaves. The light clicked on.

"See?" she said.

The side door opened.

"What are you doing?" said Gaby.

"Mimsy can't find the car keys," Regina said.

"You lost the car keys?" Gaby said to Mary.

"I'm looking for the car keys," Mary said. "Which does not mean that I lost them."

"We'll find them in the morning," Regina said, and then added somewhat ominously: "Nobody's going anywhere tonight."

"Dad got a hole in one," Gaby said.

Mary pushed past her younger sister, looking falsely innocent in her raggedy Semmering field hockey team sweats. She wore the cuffs like a pair of gloves, her thumbs extruding from two large holes, the sleeves stretched long and covering her fingers. Mary felt far more betrayed by Gaby than by Regina, but then, she reasoned, what right did she have to feel betrayed? One sisterly weekend with Gaby in three years did not count as knowing someone. She had no one to blame but herself if she was feeling emotionally swindled by a person who was, in essence, a stranger to her.

Aunt Helen sprawled in the breakfast nook, one scrawny leg snaked around the other scrawny leg, bobbling a large scotch in her two palms. The overhead fluorescents rendered Aunt Helen even more skeletal and translucent than her usual skeletal translucence. When drinking, her veins became prominent and she resembled the giant diagrams of the human vascular system that used to hang on the wall of the Semmering biology lab.

Weegee appeared from the mud room wearing a red dog sweater, the phrase CA VA? knit into the pattern with white yarn. He burrowed his muzzle into Mary's crotch.

"Weegee was so worried about you," Aunt Helen observed.

"It's nice to be missed," Mary said.

"Mary went to Boston to have Abigail Lake appraised," Regina said. She stared meaningfully at Gaby.

"Did you," said Aunt Helen.

"Apparently I did," said Mary, no longer caring what anyone thought.

"Thinking of selling the painting," Aunt Helen said, eyebrow raised. "Of your own ancestor."

"It's a painting of Mimsy in a bonnet," said Gaby. "*Regardons*. Weegee has a hard-on."

"Can I refresh your drink?" Mary asked Aunt Helen as a way to further agitate Regina.

"Well!" Aunt Helen said, handing Mary her glass without actually looking at her. "I'm glad I came over. I had plans to eat at the club but I thought no way should you girls be alone tonight. People *will* make some poor decisions after a funeral."

"Did Dad go to bed?" Mary asked.

Aunt Helen nodded. "It's all been a bit *too-too* for Clyde. He's not a coper, your father. Your mother was fine with that, of course. She preferred to be the one in control. Weegee! Don't be so aggressive!"

"It's OK," Mary said. "My crotch isn't seeing a lot of action this week."

"Grief will kill the libido," Aunt Helen said. "Look at me."

"But don't look at Weegee," Gaby said. "*Ca va?*"

"I'm still grieving over my divorce," said Aunt Helen.

"Tom left you twelve years ago," Regina said. "Do you want any pizza? You should probably have some pizza."

"I don't eat pizza, Regina. And twelve years is not such a long time when your husband was sleeping with the golf pro."

"I didn't know Tom was *gay*," Regina said.

"The golf pro was a young woman from Saugus," Aunt Helen said. "What a sexist assumption. And speaking of gay, how's your divorce from Bill going? You know your mother thought he was a homosexual. I'm sure she was very relieved to hear you were getting divorced a third time."

"He was my third fiancé," Regina corrected. "I've never been married."

"Not that I expected to be invited to the wedding," Aunt Helen said. "You've made it quite clear how you feel about me."

"I'm eating in the living room," Gaby said.

"Your mother hated it when you ate in the living room," Aunt Helen said.

"Which is why I'll enjoy doing it," Gaby said.

Mary and Regina followed Gaby into the living room. They sat quietly on the couch and ate with plates on their knees. Gaby balanced her pizza on her thumbs and knuckles. With her fingernail Regina pried the mushrooms from the cold cheese, ignoring the rest of her slice. Weegee wedged himself under the coffee table and whined for a hand-out. Mary couldn't eat. Minutes later, Aunt Helen joined them with a freshened drink and no plate. Regina was right: Aunt Helen was drinking her way toward becoming an obligatory houseguest.

"So!" said Aunt Helen. "When would you girls like me to pick up my painting?"

"What painting?" Regina said.

"What painting! The painting of Abigail Lake."

"Abigail Lake belongs to us," Regina said.

"Did you read the will's fine print?" asked Aunt Helen.

"There was no fine print," Regina said. "Mum left the painting to us."

"She left you the painting *so long as you didn't sell it.* The fine print states that if you decide to sell it, the painting's ownership would revert to me. Probably because I have a graduate degree in fine arts and can appreciate Abigail Lake as valuable in terms not involving cash."

"But Mr. Stanworth read us the will," Regina said. "There was nothing about ownership reverting or whatever you just said."

"He was ordered not to read that subsection. Your mother wanted to see whether or not you were sentimentally attached to the only thing she left you."

"She was testing us?" Regina said.

"You could interpret it that way," Aunt Helen said. "I certainly would."

Gaby laughed.

"You find this funny?" Aunt Helen said.

"Mum is dead," Gaby said. "Whatever we decide to do with the painting, it's none of her fucking business."

Aunt Helen's already scotched face blushed a shade darker.

"*Ca va!*" Gaby yelled at her.

Aunt Helen jumped.

Gaby widened her eyes psychotically.

"You're such a quietly angry girl, Gabrielle," Aunt Helen said. "You've always been angry. It killed your mother to see you so angry. And to what end? Where has rage ever gotten you?"

"I'm glad to know I'm not the only one who killed Mum," Mary said.

"I was speaking figuratively, Mimsy," Aunt Helen said.

"Not everybody's been speaking figuratively," Mary said. "Gaby thinks that I'm the reason that Mum got cancer and died, don't you Gaby?"

Gaby looked at Regina, dumbstruck.

"That's a terrible thing to say!" Aunt Helen said.

"I'm just repeating what I heard," Mary said.

"It's what you think, even if you've never articulated it," Regina said defensively.

"I didn't have to articulate it," Gaby said. "*You* articulated it."

Aunt Helen appeared stricken. "You girls are so cruel," she said. "What is it about sisters that makes them behave so hideously toward one another? Your mother was an expert at hideous behavior. Do you remember when she went to that doctor of yours, Mimsy—what was his name?"

"Dr. Hammer," Mary said.

"She went to Dr. Hammer and pretended to be me so she could wheedle information about you. What a lark! What an absolute riot! Weegee knew what a bitch she could be, didn't you Weegee? She *hated* Weegee."

"Spare us the victim monologue," Gaby said.

"Can I get anyone another slice of pizza?" asked Mary.

"I'm not the one with the rage problem," Aunt Helen said. "Where does rage initiate from, Gabrielle, but from a sense that one is a perpetual victim? Hmmm? You think about that. But about the painting. Of course I understand why you'd want to sell it, especially you, Regina. You've always been jealous of your sister. She proved to be the most imaginative one in the family, didn't she? And of course Mimsy wants to sell the painting because it reminds her of how much her own misdeeds wounded—perhaps *mortally* wounded—your mother. Paula was so wounded by her own daughter that she wasted her adult life trying to exonerate a long-dead lice-ridden *chambermaid*. Talk about poorly redirected energies. Which couldn't have helped her cancer any. I'm not saying it was the cause."

"Abigail Lake was not a chambermaid," Mary said numbly.

"Darling, they were *all* chambermaids. And those were the classy ones."

Weegee, previously dozing under the coffee table, let out a high-pitched yelp. He skittered, tail tucked, into the front hall and up the stairs.

"Weegee!" She looked accusingly at Gaby. "What did you do to him?"

"He caught his pecker in a rug loop."

"You're disgusting," Aunt Helen said. She stood unsteadily, bony hand propped against the door molding for balance.

"Maybe you should go home, Aunt Helen," Mary said.

"Home! You're trying to get rid of me? When I'm too weakened by grief to carry the painting that *lawfully* belongs to me?"

"We've all had a very long day," Mary said.

"I'm sure you have. Nobody's asked me what kind of day I had."

Nobody spoke.

Aunt Helen raised her voice. "*Nobody's* wondered what it's been like for me to lose my older sister."

Aunt Helen started to cry.

Mary put a hand on her elbow. "We know you're suffering in a highly unique way," she said.

"I *am* suffering. My older sister is gone. Who shall death come for next, but me?"

She turned her eyes toward the space on the wall where Abigail Lake used to hang. Then she lurched into the hall.

"Where are you going?" Mary called after her.

"I need to find Weegee," she said. "He's hurt and he's scared. You girls are beasts. You've always been hideous little beasts. And ugly, too. Why do you think no one will marry you? You ugly, ugly girls."

Aunt Helen bobbled precariously up the plush stairs.

"Go follow her!" Regina hissed.

"Me?" Mary said.

"She might end up in Dad's room! Dad will blow his stack if she wakes him up."

"Dad took sleeping pills and he's never blown his stack in his life." Gaby cocked her wrists and made motions with her fingers in the air as though she were snapping a pair of castanets. "*Ca va!*" she yelled at Regina.

"Be quiet!" Regina yelled back. "But thank god she can still drive home. The only thing worse than Aunt Helen drunk is Aunt Helen hungover."

"I'll clean up the kitchen," Mary said.

"No, we'll clean up the kitchen," said Regina. "You go get Aunt Helen. She needs to start driving before they set up the police roadblock."

"What police roadblock?" Mary said.

"To catch drunk drivers," Regina said. "She'd never pass a Breathalyzer. But she's fine to drive. She's an old pro."

Old pro or not, Mary worried that Aunt Helen had exceeded the point of functional drunk and would land her station wagon in the living room of one of the faux-colonial elderly apartments built stupidly close to her exit ramp. But she kept her worry to herself, in part because she didn't want to spark another disagreement, in part because she too wanted Aunt Helen gone. Aunt Helen's presence wasn't merely an annoyance, it was unsettling, not to mention heart-wrenching, to catch glimpses of Mum in Aunt Helen's face as it shifted gears between distinctly Aunt Helen–like expressions; during these split-second moments of slack repose, Mum's face became fleetingly visible—her denatured, uninhabited, glum, dead face. Because of this Mary was willing to pretend, like her sisters, that Aunt Helen was perfectly fine to drive.

The upstairs was creepily quiet and dark—perhaps Aunt Helen *had* found her way into their father's room. She opened her father's door and heard the weighty, underwater sounds of his drugged sleep. No sign of Aunt Helen, no sign of Weegee. Nor was Aunt Helen in the guest room, study-cum-second-guest-room, or the bathroom. Which left only one possibility.

In the pyramid splash of hallway light she could see Aunt Helen's sweater set and pants folded on her desk chair along with Weegee's dog sweater. Aunt Helen's shiny-beige bra straps curved over her shoulders, emerging from the top of Mary's duvet. Weegee had made a bed of Mary's bathrobe and towel, wadded into a nest at the foot of her bed. His head was tucked under his flank and he, as well as Aunt Helen, was snoring.

Mary might have been angry if the scene, slapstick and pathetic as it was, didn't tweak her in a deeply familiar way. If she squinted to the point of practically closing her eyes she could almost fool herself into thinking the woman in her bed was Mum—a deeply ironic misidentification given that Mum, on several occasions, had succeeded as Helen more readily than Helen might have done. In the summer of 1960, if Mum's version was to be believed, Aunt Helen found a job as an intern at the Lesley College Archaeology Department, but awoke her first morning of work with chicken pox. Mum, a Wellesley student on grade probation, drove to the department to fill in for her sister so that Helen wouldn't lose the job. Surrounded by canoe-length mandibles and children's skulls the size of teacups, her mother decided that a job at the Archaeology Department was a far preferable way to pass the summer than selling fudge and tulips to cranky matrons at a clapboarded roadside stand in Concord. Within a week she'd worked her way from filing department-meeting minutes in a windowless file closet to replacing the department head's assistant, away on a temple dig in Sri Lanka. Aunt Helen, once she learned that her sister had stolen her job, insisted that she confess. Mum did; the department head, remarkably, didn't care. Aunt Helen took her rightful place as a filing intern in the windowless closet while her sister enjoyed her own office with a view of the quad.

There were other incidents as well; her mother, already married, had gone on a blind date as a "placeholder" for Aunt Helen, stuck in the Philadelphia airport due to a blizzard. Before she could properly identify herself to the architect as his blind date's sister, he kissed her on the cheek and addressed her as "Helen." She remained Helen for the evening. The architect wrote letters to Aunt Helen when, humiliated, she refused to return his calls. The architect grew increasingly besotted. What could Aunt Helen do? Her potential husband had fallen in love with the wrong Helen. To show her face now would be to spend another metaphorical summer in the file closet.

Which was not to say that her mother was a malicious or even deceitful person. Mary interpreted her mother's admittedly questionable behavior this way: she was unable to disappoint strangers. She flexibly transformed herself into a file clerk, an assistant, a potential wife. Or, to dig more deeply into the thicket of her mother's psyche, maybe some chronic dissatisfaction made slipping into another's person skin and body and life a welcome diversion. Given the chance, her identity was prone to wander.

Mary relaxed her eyes and her mother disappeared from her bed. She noticed that Aunt Helen had placed her car keys on the bedside table. This struck Mary as a fair exchange—her bed for Aunt Helen's station wagon. Besides, given the slip of paper in her pocket, there was no way she was sleeping tonight.

Notes

Before my next meeting with Mary, I received a phone call from her mother's sister, Helen, informing me of a discovery made in Mary's bedroom. On principle, I do not allow family members to intrude upon my therapeutic dyad with a patient unless convinced that the discovery concerns a life-or-death matter. I explained this policy to Mary's aunt over the phone; she insisted nonetheless that I meet with her, while refusing to reveal the nature of her discovery. She would only say it was of "extraordinary significance." I doubted very much the extraordinary significance of her discovery; it was possible, even likely, that Mary's aunt and mother suffered from a hysterical condition or similar cluster B personality disorder, these things being hereditary.

I agreed to the meeting.

Helen, an extremely thin woman with short blond hair and lively dark eyes, arrived late to our scheduled appointment. We spent the first few minutes determining what sort of rate I'd charge for the visit, since her older sister's insurance didn't pay for second-party consultations. I asked her if money was an issue for her sister, and if so we could negotiate a rate that would be agreeable to all. Her hands clenched and unclenched in her lap. She said that no, money wasn't the issue, it was a matter of her sister's insurance policy and what it would and would not cover. I told her that if money wasn't an issue, than neither was the insurance policy. She became flustered by logical attempts to solve her concern, unable to mount an articulate defense of her fixation while remaining stubbornly fixated.

Eventually, she let the matter drop and produced, from her purse, a dented silver cigarette case engraved on its front with the letter *K*.

The engraving glinted beneath my office lights like a mangled rebuke. My scalp began to sweat; my peripheral vision darkened and constricted until I was staring down what seemed like a virtual optical nerve at that single letter. Only one conclusion could be drawn from it: *K existed.* I experienced what my own analyst calls the Rosenthal effect kickback—and I realized, as Helen and I stared unspeakingly at the cigarette case in her lap, that I had decided absolutely, without consciously acknowledging the absoluteness of this decision, that Mary had fabricated the story of her abduction, just as Bettina had fabricated her story. I had begun unquestioningly to see them as parallel cases, and planned to do with Mary all that I had failed to do with Bettina, thereby rectifying my past mistakes and, additionally, restoring my own faith in myself as a therapist. The cigarette case, thus, served not only to undermine this certainty—it called into question my own therapeutic methods, and suggested that either my methods were faulty or my relationship with my past remained so unresolved that I was unable to objectively assess situations with my new patients. I had, in classic Rosenthal effect fashion, conflated Mary and Bettina—for understandably circumstantial reasons. But my deeper analytic self had cut itself off from nuance—not to mention the possibility that Mary, after all, had been telling the truth.

This first Rosenthal effect kickback was followed by a second, more distasteful realization: I was depending upon this assumption for professional as well as personal reasons. I had begun to generate an idea for a book about a new adolescent disorder I'd been calling, in my own casual thoughts, hyper radiance. Literally, hyper radiants were Parisian lenses created in 1822 by Augustin Fresnel and used by lighthouses; a single thousand-watt lightbulb is condensed and magnified by the hyper radiant so that its beam can be seen eighteen miles away. This struck me as a fitting metaphor, so I'd adopted the term "hyper radiance" to describe the morbid appeal of the Salem witch trials and the need for young girls, especially those girls raised in the repressive culture of New England, to "magnify" themselves as the victims of spells and devilry at the very moment they come of sexual age; since the abduction of one's personality and soul were no longer viable claims, these girls insist that they have *literally* been abducted. Their soul does not go missing; their body does, through a complicated self-engineered process that may, or may not, be "known" to the hyper radiant. Both, however, were fabricated situations created in response to fear—in the case of the girls who claimed to be spellbound in 1692, such fear was later seen as a mutated terror of Indian abduction combined with intense sexual repression. Though hyper radiance enjoyed a certain local potency due to the proximity to the source myth, there was little doubt in my mind that hyper radiance threatened to become a nationwide phenomenon. On my more confident days, I believed this theory would prove a tremendously influential discovery, and would result in a book that would, in turn, make my reputation among my colleagues. On my less confident days, I was reminded of something Mary herself once said about high-school English papers, and her ability to prove competing theses using *The Scarlet Letter*, her point being that one can find what one wants to find, which does not necessarily means that what one finds is actually there.

I'm assuming this is the important item you wished to discuss with me, I said, finally, to Helen.

It is, Helen said. Paula found it in the top drawer of Mary's bureau.

Is your sister in the habit of opening Mary's drawers, I said.

The top drawer is the place Mary hides the objects she wants Paula to find.

That's quite a roundabout means of communication, I said.

It's a classic mother-daughter non-relationship, Dr. Hammer, Helen said. Surely you've encountered the phenomenon before.

Helen didn't smile; her demeanor remained caustic toward me, but her hostility possessed a glumly erotic component.

But if Mary's mother found the cigarette case, I said, why are you here?

Paula doesn't want to be perceived as a meddler, said Helen.

One person's meddler is another person's nurse, I said, my mind still distractedly spinning through the dismal implications of the cigarette case. I had the strongest desire to snatch the case from Helen's lap and throw it into the Charles, to remove it permanently from the world. A part of me actually considered the fact that if I could destroy this case, then my theories about Mary and Bettina would still be true.

Helen, as though reading my mind, flashed me a strangely complicit smile; I was struck in that instant by an uncanny resemblance to her niece. Feature for feature, they shared nothing; but I sensed a deeper psychic resemblance, a prevailing caution that mutes the spirit's instinctive ebullience and causes, in effect, a constant inner tension that can be read, by certain receptive members of the opposite sex, as profoundly sexual in nature.

Her mother's desire to appear a non-meddler might be misread as a failure to care, I clarified.

A failure to care might be misread as a failure to care, said Helen.

How would you describe your relationship to your niece, I said.

Mary is an impossible girl to know, Helen said. I have tried. I have given up. So has her mother.

Mary's mother has given up on Mary, I said. That's quite an extreme statement.

Helen blinked owlishly.

Don't you agree? I said. To give up on one's own daughter? Especially when her daughter was abducted and possibly raped?

I said this for my own benefit as much as for Helen's. Trying out the sound of this new story: *Mary was abducted. She was possibly raped.*

Helen winced.

I didn't come here to make excuses for Paula, Helen began.

To this I said nothing.

What I meant when I said she'd given up . . .

Helen paused, retooled her response.

Paula is struck, she said, on a daily basis, by the fact that this child, who was once so uncomplicated and loving toward her, has become a vindictive stranger.

She stared at me meaningfully.

Clearly Paula has suffered, I said.

Let's say it's been a *uniquely trying experience*, Helen said.

I don't know how *unique* it is, I said. Isn't what you're describing in Mary the textbook definition of adolescence?

Helen's expression wavered momentarily before turning scornful.

Most adolescents don't fake their abductions, said Helen. Most adolescents don't torment their families by letting them wonder, for weeks, whether or not they're dead.

But the cigarette case . . . I began. I was confused. Wasn't the cigarette case proof of just the opposite? Mary *had* been abducted. She was a victim; she hadn't tormented her family on purpose.

Exactly, Helen said. The cigarette case.

You've lost me, I said.

Helen didn't reply.

To me, I continued, the cigarette case suggests a very different interpretation.

That's because you're easily stunned by the obvious, said Helen.

Helen reached into her purse and withdrew a compact. She checked her nose, she checked both cheekbones, she snapped it shut, she rested it in her lap. Her index finger, I noticed, drew vague spirals over the faux-tortoiseshell cover.

Let's start again, I said, trying to maintain my patience. To whom does it belong?

The cigarette case? she asked.

I bit back my annoyance.

Yes, I said. The cigarette case. Isn't that what we're discussing?

Presumably we're *meant* to believe that it belongs to K, Helen said. Hasn't she told you about K? What do you two talk about?

Helen crosshatched an insect bite on her wrist with her thumbnail.

I have a policy, I said.

You have a lot of policies, said Helen.

My policy is never to divulge details about a patient's treatment to another person, particularly a family member.

Your policy is to play dumb so that you can trick me into revealing what I know, she said.

I grew testy.

You would not be the first family member who came to my office claiming a discovery of "extraordinary significance," but who in fact wanted to fool me into violating the confidence of my patient by asking leading questions such as "Hasn't she told you she's in love with Todd?"

I glared at Helen.

I see, she said contritely.

Do you? I asked.

I do, she said. We need say no more about "Todd."

Excellent, I said.

I don't want to violate anything, she said.

I appreciate your sensitivity to this sensitive situation, I said. Many family members feel threatened by the access a total stranger is afforded to a relative, especially when their own access has been blocked.

Cuttingly put, Helen said. Are you always so gentle with your patients?

You're not my patient, I reminded her.

Yet here I am paying for the pleasure to talk to you, said Helen.

She smiled insincerely.

I smiled insincerely.

Why don't you explain to me the significance of the cigarette
case, I said.

It has no significance, she said. That's the significance.

Helen withdrew a slip of paper from her purse and handed it to me.
She was nervous as she did this, as though trying to pass off a counter-
feit bill. The piece of paper was a receipt—handwritten on a green
restaurant pad—rubber-stamped at the top with a store logo and the
name DEN OF ANTIQUITY. According to this receipt, a silver cigarette case
had been purchased three months earlier for $13.65 cash.

Despite myself, I again felt "easily stunned by the obvious."

You look unwell, said Helen.

I'm fine, I said. It's warm in here.

I opened the window above the radiator.

You understand what this means, said Helen.

You suspect that Mary purchased this cigarette case.

I think that's a reasonable suspicion, don't you?

A reasonable *suspicion*, yes, I said.

She's planting evidence. This means that there is no K. And if there
is no K, then there was no abduction. If there was no abduction, there
was no rape. If there was no rape, then she's not a victim. She's just a very
selfish and needy little girl.

That's a reasonable suspicion, I repeated dumbly.

Helen cocked an eyebrow.

A circumstantial *leap*, I cautioned, though of course I was thinking exactly what she was thinking, and as a result was feeling, inexplicably, sick-

ened. Can one feel sick from relief? I did, like the nausea one experiences after an adrenaline rush.

Really I think we cannot make that assumption, I said.

Helen twisted her neck, stretching it from left to right, trying to release a tightness.

You realize that this cigarette case has put Paula in a terrible position, Helen said.

Of course, I said.

She's been given the choice between a daughter who's been raped and a daughter who is a liar, Helen said.

Choice, I said. That's a strangely empowered way for Paula to view her daughter's possible trauma.

It isn't about *empowerment*, Helen said. It's about coping. Paula will cling to whatever conclusion makes her most comfortable. That is her right as a mother.

Not if she's aware that it's her right. If she is aware it is her right, then she is obligated to overcome that sense of "entitlement"—also known, in my profession, as denial.

This is why she does not go to therapy, said Helen, sighing again.

Her leg continued to bob in its casual/noncasual way, clearly a practiced façade meant to disguise her anxiety. I suspected that Paula had been rejected early as an infant—her mirroring phase had clearly been disrupted—and she subsequently suffered from a mild narcissistic disorder. Her daughter's situation could only be viewed in terms of how it affected her.

It's a shame Paula won't consider therapy during this stressful time, I said. She might find the experience enlightening.

You think she needs enlightening? Helen said nervously.

When it comes to ourselves, I said, we are never blinder.

Therapy would be a futile exercise for her, she said. Trust me. I've known her longer than anyone.

Many people, before they begin treatment, share those exact feelings, I said.

Paula is completely aware of her shortcomings as a parent and a person. But awareness does not mean a person can change the way she intrinsically is.

That is true, I said. Awareness is just the first step.

For some. For most, however, awareness is the end point. Honestly, Dr. Hammer, how many patients have you "cured"?

We don't use terms like "cured," I said. We respect the process over results. To be result-oriented—

Would mean getting results, Helen said.

Helen's hostility levels, I noticed, had increased dramatically; the underpinning erotic aspect of this hostility, however, was muffled by an almost palpable distress—a sense of true emptiness and of loss. I wondered if perhaps she was hiding a deeper hurt or rejection—possibly the hurt existed between herself and Paula. Maybe she and Paula had had a falling out, or an act of deceit or betrayal had cleaved them apart. Regardless, I sensed there was more to Helen's story than she was telling me.

You and your sister think very little of psychologists, I said. It's strange she would choose to send her daughter to one, given her low opinion.

She's aware of the contradiction, she insisted fervently. See? She's *aware* of it, but that doesn't mean she has the power, or the desire, to behave in a more consistent manner. She knows she's a flawed person. She remains a flawed person who lives, in your opinion, *in denial.* That does not mean that she is impervious to emotion. That does not mean that she is incapable of being ruined.

As I said, I began, awareness is just the first step.

Awareness is a taunt to the people in your life who share your poor opinion of yourself, Helen said bitterly, her eyes rising to meet mine. They were greenish brown gray, the noncolor of the ocean on a poor day.

What is the taunt, I said.

Since you know your shortcomings, the assumption is that you will change them. And how often does that happen?

People do change, I said.

I'm sure they do, said Helen. But should they? That is a different question.

A person is not an island, I said. Denial is a disease; it infects entire families. Denial is also linked to an inability to take responsibility for one's actions, and the shifting of blame onto innocent parties. It is linked to depression. It is linked to a higher divorce rate among adults, and suicide attempts among adolescents.

Helen, clearly, was not listening to me.

But if a person lives in denial, she said, don't you think there could be a decent reason why she does?

Of course, I said. Denial is, in the short term, an easier way to manage emotional stress.

Some people are not built for emotional clarity. Some people thrive best, emotionally speaking, on confusion.

Then a few of us will have to take responsibility for the shortcomings of the happily confused, I said.

Really? she said, appearing sadly bemused.

Really, I said.

My end-of-session alarm sounded.

Well, Helen said. Paula will appreciate your taking the time to see me. She'll be eager to hear what we've discussed.

I'd prefer that you didn't speak to Paula about this meeting, I said.

Oh? she said.

If Paula wants to see me, Paula will come to see me.

But I need to tell her that you understand, she said. How did you phrase it? About "the shifting of blame onto innocent parties."

Understand, I said.

What Mary has tried to do to you.

Helen, moving mechanically, replaced her compact in her purse, along with the cigarette case and the receipt. She stood from the couch, coat slung over her forearm.

To me, I said.

Of course, Helen said, her expression lifeless. For all we know, you are her intended victim.

My next session with Mary followed a lengthy session with my own analyst. I had come to the conclusion, after a restless night, that Mary, her aunt, and Bettina Spencer were involved in a plot to destroy me; that they were attempting to enact revenge on me via a stealthy psychological game. His assessment of the situation was, of course, moderate and logical, so moderate and logical that I lost my temper. Not that I believed my own story—but I wanted validation that my perceived scenario was a plausible one. My analyst accused me of suffering from a metaphorical case of *penis captivus* and forced me to admit that my own unresolved issues with my mother—a passive aggressor who suffered from lifelong premorbidity—had led to my failure with Bettina and were threatening to destroy my professional relationship with another patient. He made me repeat the words *gray, watch, daisy, justice,* as he does when I am beset by paranoiac feelings related to my mother. I left his office with the phrases *gray watch* and *daisy justice* riding on the coattails of every brain wave, these two phrases coming to represent to me, in her chilly abstraction, my now dead mother.

Mary arrived at my office, four days after Helen's visit, as her usual, moderately unkempt self.

You look terrible, Beaton, said Mary. Did you catch the flu?

I feel fine, I said.

Hmmmm, said Mary. She stood by my bookshelf, fingering my bric-a-brac.

What is this? she said.

A Chinese cricket cage, I said.

And how about these? She pointed to a series of increasingly smaller brass chickens.

Opium weights, I said. A souvenir from Thailand.

Did you know that Freud was a coke fiend?

Cocaine was once used for medicinal purposes, I said.

He was a coke fiend. Did you ever go to Thailand or China?

It sounds like you're interested in travel, I said.

It sounds like you're avoiding the question, she said.

I have never been to either place, I said.

Gifts? she said. From your devoted former patient? The girl who gives you the books? Have you ever played the game props?

I'm unfamiliar with that game, I said curtly.

Do you want to play? I like it better when we play games.

Why is that?

You're less anxious, she said.

You find me anxious?

Do you find yourself anxious? Mary said.

Then she laughed.

Just kidding, Beaton. Trying to beat you at your own game.

Tell me about *your* game, I said.

First I need a piece of paper, she said.

I handed her a piece of paper from the bottom of my pad. She tore the paper and handed half to me.

Here's how it works, she said. You write a list of seven "props" that might be used in a play. Normally you're limited to objects in the room, but you don't have enough weird stuff in here so we may have to cheat.

Fine, I said. Then what happens?

Make the list first, she said.

Where did you learn this game? I asked.

My sisters and I used to play it when we visited people we didn't want to visit. My grandparents, for example.

Where do your grandparents live, I said.

Revere, she said. They have a salt and pepper shaker collection and use famous paddleboats placemats. They share an oxygen tank.

So you make a list of items in a room, I said.

The point is to choose seven incompatible objects that must be used plausibly in a single story. In order to create a scenario that makes "sense" of the props, you have to make up a really wild story.

A wild story that makes sense, I said.

And that really wild story makes the depressing place where you are seem interesting.

So the point of the game is to take control of a situation in which you have no control, I said.

Mary regarded me queerly.

The point of the game is to win, she said.

So we'll both make lists of things in this room.

No, she said. You list things in this room. I'll list some things randomly, to give you an idea of the game.

OK, I said.

Go, she said.

I wrote down the seven most obvious objects in the room: my BU diploma, my opium weights, my cricket cage, my copy of *Dorcas Hobbs*, the pink tissue-box cozy knitted for me by my depressed sister, my bronze scarab paper-clip container, my Boston Red Sox coffee mug.

Done, I said.

I'm still thinking, she said. This is harder when you don't have objects right in front of you.

Understandable, I said.

If only I were more imaginative, she said.

I think you're plenty imaginative, I said.

Mary scowled happily. She either did not catch my deeper meaning—*I am onto you*—or chose not to acknowledge it. Outside my office door I heard the sounds of Maura, our suite cleaning lady, vacuuming.

Maura was an enthusiastic vacuumer, banging the head of the vacuum against the door so forcefully that it sounded as though she were trying to break it down. The noise inspired a tenseness in my temples, signaling the possible beginning of a headache. My side vision became flecked with white confetti blinkers.

You know, Mary said, chewing her pencil, you don't look so fine.

I lifted my head. It buzzed and throbbed.

Excuse me?

You said you were fine. But you don't look it. I think something happened to you since our last meeting, she said. Maybe you look terrible because you met my mother.

Your mother?

She has that effect on people.

Mary scrutinized my face, as I scrutinized hers. I was not so disoriented that I didn't understand what was happening. She was baiting me, just as Helen had baited me.

My head throbbed harder.

Did your mother tell you she was meeting with me, I said.

What did she want to talk to you about? Mary said, avoiding my question.

In the waiting room, Maura muscled the chairs around; she whacked the plastic hose nozzle against the floor molding.

I know what you're doing, I said.

Huh?

You're trying to trick me into telling you that your mother came to visit me, I said.

I'm not tricking you, Mary said. I'm asking.

I regarded her sternly.

I don't get this, she said. Are you mad at me about something?

I want you to acknowledge that you behaved in a deceitful way.

Mary laughed.

That is not an acceptable response, I said.

OK, she said. Whatever. I'm sorry.

I didn't respond.

I *apologized*, she said. What else do you want?

You did not apologize, I said. You withdrew from the conversation. That is not the same as apologizing. In order to apologize you would first have to take responsibility for your actions.

Mary held up her hands in a gesture of sarcastic surrender.

I take responsibility for my actions. *Jeez.*

So you admit that you tried to trick me, I said.

If I say yes, I tried to trick you, then you'll lay off, right? *God.* You're as bad as my sister Regina. You can be really psychotic sometimes.

Because I hold you to an honest behavioral standard I'm psychotic, I said wryly.

Because you're a nitpicker, Mary said. You nitpick.

I'm doing my job, I said.

Well then, Mary said. I guess I know what Regina should be when she grows up.

We lapsed into silence. Mary scratched furiously at her pilled sweater. I felt my face redden and tried, mentally, to reverse the blood flow to my head. The mind can slow the pulse, the mind can control the sweating of the palms, the spiking of the temperature. This is crucial knowledge for a therapist who is on the brink of losing a patient to his own unauthoritative show of humanity.

I took a deep breath. I was clearly still rattled after the visit with Mary's aunt.

I thought Regina was planning to be a shitty poet, I said.

Mary fiddled with one of the black rubber bangles she wore on her right wrist.

Huh?

Regina, I said. When she grew up. Had plans to be a shitty poet.

Was that a joke, Beaton?

I didn't respond.

It's premature to make a joke after being such a tool, she said. You must really be ashamed of your behavior.

Who's nitpicking now? I observed lightly. Maybe you're the one for whom my profession calls.

I can't care enough about other people's problems, she said.

Hardly a prerequisite, I said.

Another joke, she said. You really feel like crap, huh?

I didn't respond.

You could have admitted that you were in a bad way when I originally asked you, and all of this could have been avoided.

Good point, I said.

I'm just holding you to an honest behavioral standard, she said.

Fair enough, I said.

She smiled.

I smiled.

So, she said. Honestly. What did you think of my mother?

Honestly, I said, you should rephrase your question.

Rephrase how?

What you want to know is whether or not your mother came to see me, and if so, why.

I know why she came to see you, Mary said. She can't stand the fact that I tell you stuff I'll never tell her.

I'm pleased you've come to trust me so much, I said.

Mary frowned.

It's less a measure of how much I like you and more a measure of how much I don't like her, said Mary.

She withdrew her compact and, with brutal movements, opened it to examine her reflection.

Interesting, I said.

What's interesting, she said, snapping the compact shut and tossing it onto the adjoining couch cushion. I hate it when you say *interesting*. What does it mean, Beaton? *Interesting. Interesting.*

As I've observed before, you cannot make a statement that would imply emotional dependence. Such a statement must be imploded and converted into an insult that hurts the very person you meant to compliment.

I didn't mean to compliment anyone, she said. What's with you today? Is this some new kind of therapy you're trying out? Because I'd like it noted on my customer comment card that it sucks.

I can't understand why you refuse to admit you *do* care why your mother would come to see me—if in fact she did.

I *don't* care, she said. Whatever she told you, it's a lie.

Your mother didn't tell me anything, I said truthfully.

So why did she meet with you?

Why don't you tell me why you *think* your mother came to see me, I said. Let's speak in hypotheticals. Why *might* your mother come to see me?

That's obvious, she said. She wanted to tell you about Kurt Thatcher.

Kurt Thatcher, I said.

How she threw a drink in his face last weekend. At Barbara Thorne-Hill's wedding.

Tell me about this, I said.

Sixty-seven people at the wedding got botulism. They had to be hospitalized, including the groom, whom Barbara's mother hates because he's Polish.

Botulism, I said.

From the week-old crab cakes. Everyone was too busy bad-mouthing the cheapwad Thorne-Hills to remember that Mum attacked Kurt with her gin and tonic.

Why did your mother attack Kurt, I said.

Mum accused Kurt of kidnapping me last fall. Then she accused him of being a pedophile and molesting me when I was younger. Then she threw her gin and tonic in his face.

How did you learn about this, I said.

From the bartender, who is also my dad's favorite caddy at the range. "Mike" is his name. With quotes. Dad and I call him "Mike." Because he's more than just a Mike. He's a "Mike."

You and Mike are in regular contact, I said.

I saw him at the arcade in the mini-mall two days ago.

How old is Mike, I said.

Old, Mary said. Like maybe thirty.

But he still plays video games.

He wins all the time, Mary said, by way of explanation.

One important development is suggested by your mother's outburst, I said. She believes you now. About Kurt trying to kiss you when you were twelve.

Mary shrugged. Whatever. She was drunk when she came home from the wedding and she passed out in my bed.

What's the connection? I said.

Maybe she forgives me, Mary said.

For what? I said.

Threatening the overall whiteness of the world.

Mary's eyes grew hazy, as they frequently did when she began to disassociate from our conversation.

But enough about *me*, she said. Let's return to our game. What've you got?

She grabbed my list and handed me her paper scrap, on which she had written the following seven items:

1) Dented Silver Cigarette Case
2) Broken Car Lighter
3) Shrimp-Flavored Potato Cips
4) Very Old Pack of Cigarettes
5) Very Old Movies of Meerkats
6) Movie Projector
7) Blindfold

I read through the list three times in numerical succession. My paranoia rebounded; these little trinkets—the dented silver cigarette case—were just more clues to a meaningless scavenger hunt, meant only to scramble my sense of direction while falsely reinforcing my notion that I was onto something. I was not getting closer to the truth—I was being toyed with and led strategically astray.

In my head I repeated: *gray watch, daisy justice*.

This worked. My heart rate decreased as I retreated from the paranoid and sought refuge in the logical. Clearly, I told myself, Mary *knew* why her mother—or rather her aunt—had come to see me; she *knew* her mother had found the cigarette case and the receipt. Thus she *knew* that in order to regain the reins, so to speak, she needed to confound my sense of having discovered something about her without her knowledge. By introducing the possibility that the cigarette case was part of a game, she was engaging me on my own turf—she was telling me, in no uncertain terms, that she had fabricated her abduction, that the story of her abduction was her way of assembling these disparate artifacts to make her dull or depressing life feel interesting and, more to the point, the game was her way of taking control of a situation over which she had no control.

This list, in other words, was nothing short of a confession.

Well? said Mary.

As I observed earlier, I said. I think you have a plenty active imagination.

What Might Have Happened

As was usually the case with a cabin in the woods, the man reflected, the journey was the only fun to be had. No wonder in movies the arrival at the cabin in the woods marks the beginning of the end. The dead come alive. People are inhabited by malingering spirits and behead their lovers with any old ax. The anticipation of arriving, the luxury of sitting in a dark car and talking to the person in the passenger seat without needing to deal with their actual face—this was the pleasantly relaxing prelude to a bludgeoning in a cabin in the woods.

Now that the man and the girl had arrived at the cabin, now that he had pulled the sledge down the road to the Mercedes and fetched their groceries, now that he had built a fire in the fireplace and heated the girl a can of soup, now that the two of them were seated on the sagging couch with the afghan crocheted by his wife's dead sister, both of them staring into the fire and pretending to be consumed by a "comfortable silence," now that these various things had occurred his ashy many nights' exhaustion overtook him and he wanted to be alone. He wanted to be rid of her. He was reminded of those days as an undergraduate at Boston University when he decided to become a coke addict for the sake of a cute, jagged-out oboist in his chemistry lab. He had paid good money to stay in close proximity to this oboist, and eventually the investment paid off; after three days of mindless inhalation, he had awoken beside her in a Lowell hotel room. Her skin was taupe; she smelled like new vomit. The distant fun they'd had wasn't enough to erase the disgust he felt looking at her skeletal pelvis, the white blisters on her fingertips, the chafing between her upper lip and nose. Some days he just wanted to retreat inside himself, with no external people to remind him of the person he was. He needed to regroup without the assistance of myriad fucked-up others.

That girl—this girl—he wanted her gone.

But this girl was going nowhere without considerable effort on his part. Where the hell would she go? The process of getting rid of her involved hours and hours of preparation: a call to the local tow-truck company run by a notoriously unreliable pair of alcoholic half brothers who might or might not show up before dark the following day. Then the hours-long drive back to Boston, the discussion of the "story" such as they would both agree to represent it to anyone who asked. The actual goodbye.

The girl sipped her soup from a coffee mug. She was still wearing her sweatpants, her field hockey skirt, but she'd removed her cleats and her socks. She'd found a pair of his ex-wife's shearling slippers beneath the bobbled drape of the guest-bed coverlet. She appeared tense to him, her lips had all but disappeared inside her mouth; maybe it was the lack of sleep. Insomnia, after all, was something for which one trained for years. And yet she refused to sleep, she insisted that she wanted to keep him company, that she wanted to experience what he experienced.

Appropriately, then, she looked unhappy.

Yes, he thought, no doubt about it, *she looked unhappy*. And why wouldn't she be unhappy? If he was perfectly aware of how hard it would be to get rid of her, she didn't even have the privilege of such specific knowledge. For all she knew there *were* no alcoholic half brothers who towed cars when they damned well felt like it; there were no buses, there was no phone, she was as stuck as an Eskimo in a blizzard without his dogs. *Stuck as an Eskimo in a blizzard without his dogs.* A strange metaphor, the man thought, until he realized he had, last week, during an insomniac 4 a.m. space-out before the television, "taken in" a documentary about Eskimos. (He used that phrase now when he was watching but not watching; "taking in" a movie. "Taking in" the weather report. He "took things in" and these things rolled around in his head, stray bits of information that failed to adhere to anything resembling a thought.) Yes, these Eskimos were a spontaneous bunch, they hopped in and out of their kayaks and could industriously build an igloo from scratch in gale-force winds, but that didn't mean that they weren't struck dumb by their own isolation once they'd barricaded themselves inside and had nothing to do but stare at the semitranslucent walls and wait out the storm. The Eskimo husband was stoic and grumpy until his wife refused to feed the crying baby. Clearly she was too depressed even to feed the baby. It flailed on a snow mound as the wife stared at it, uncaring. Then, the man could tell, the Eskimo husband's whole shitty world dropped out from under his sealskin boots, and he started to smile.

The girl hid her face in her soup mug. It appeared to him that she was trying very hard not to cry.

This girl. This strange girl. He had—inadvertently, advertently—made her cry.

Suddenly the man stopped wanting the girl gone. No, no, he wanted her to *stay*. Not because he wanted her to *stay* exactly but because, well, worse than his own desire to be alone was his fear that the girl, too, wanted to be alone. That would be worse, he decided. If the girl wanted to be alone because he made her unhappy. Thus he determined that he must stay in the living room with her and ensure that she was happy.

Happy, he thought. Yes yes. Then, scoffingly, he caught himself, as he was now prone to do—"catching himself" meaning not that one hand grabbed the other hand, either literally or figuratively, but "catching himself" as in catching a glimpse of himself, as though he were an unbiased stranger observing his behavior on a train. His internal stranger on a train scoffed and said: Here is a girl who has kidnapped you—or gotten herself kidnapped—and you are concerned for her happiness? I find this ridiculous. And I will laugh at you, a little dismissive cough of a laugh.

Hah.

What's so funny, the girl said. She was playing with the tassel on his ex-wife's shearling slipper, trying to appear nonchalant, but he heard the tightness in her throat. It destroyed him, that tightness. He was a criminal, a potential abuser of minors, a crusher of innocents. His little Scheherazade, she was too unhappy even to tell him stories. How was it that the real Scheherazade never let on that she was scared out of her mind? How was it that her sultan, or her king, or whomever it was who wanted to kill her, how was it that this sultan or king was so wooed by her stories that he did not hear the occasional tightness in her voice and recoil, forced to reconsider his bloody plan?

What's funny, she repeated. She wiped her nose. She attempted a wan, transparently miserable smile.

I was wondering to what degree you would consider yourself happy, he said.

Happy, she said. She moved from an averagely happy smile to the insanely happy grin of a person about to break into sobs. Had he done the right thing by asking? Showing his tender, caring side? Or had he only reminded her, rubbed her face in the fact that the last thing she was at this moment was happy? Soon he would know, she would begin to cry and he would know.

But instead she pulled back from the precipice of total dissolution and retreated behind her teenager's mask of skeptical ennui.

Is this the kind of thing you wonder about in the woods? she asked with an efficient *I'm fine* toss of her dirtying hair.

The woods might have something to do with it, the man said. *I am relieved*, he thought. *The last thing I need is a crying girl on my hands.* But he also wanted to know what she was thinking. He wanted to ask her if she was disappointed in him. He had taken her to a cabin in the woods with fake wood paneling and a distinctive mold smell. His fire was lame. She had imagined an outcome and he had failed to deliver it.

You weren't wondering if I was happy in the diner, she said. You weren't wondering if I was happy at the rest stop.

On principle I don't express wonder, the man said. Which doesn't mean I'm not wondering every second of every day.

A piece of bark on a burning log exploded. The girl jumped, spilling soup on her sweatpants.

Whoops, she said, her composure jostled.

Cry now, the man thought to himself. *Cry now.*

But she didn't cry. She efficiently blotted the soup spill with her napkin.

I'm thinking this cabin depresses the heck out of you, she said.

The girl rolled the shearling slipper tassel between her thumb and forefinger.

The moment, he realized. The moment was gone.

Tough, he thought, not without a fair bit of admiration. This girl was tough.

What's up with that poster in the guest room? She asked. The one that says WE ARE MEERKATS!

What's up with it? the man said. My ex-wife's former brother-in-law was a solar engineer.

The man jerked his head toward the rafters, his attention snagged by a shifting piece of air. The dark overhead rippled imperceptibly like the skin of a pudding. A bat, he thought. A goddamned family of bats.

The girl picked at her slipper, clearly confused.

My ex-wife's former brother-in-law. Her sister's ex-husband, he explained, trying not to eye the ceiling. My twice former brother-in-law.

I got that, she said.

Oh, said the man, understanding now. The meerkat is the solar panel of the animal world, and thus my twice former brother-in-law the solar engineer's favorite animal. He believed his rarified enthusiasms were shared by the masses. Thus, for such an otherwise eccentricity-free household, we have a lot of meerkat tchotchkes.

The man pointed to a Meerkat Society ashtray; the meerkat bookends on the fireplace mantel; the meerkat andirons.

The meerkat rolls onto its back and raises its body temperature by exposing its black stomach to the sun, the man continued. The meerkat is a member of the mongoose family. It usually travels in a "mob" or a "gang" of thirty. That pretty much exhausts my knowledge about meerkats. We have some films upstairs of my twice former brother-in-law on safari in the Kalahari, if you're still curious.

For someone with amnesia, the girl said, you remember a lot.

The man reddened.

My ex-wife and I took a trip here after the accident, he said quickly. She wanted to help me remember. We walked around the cabin and she told me stories relating to every needlepoint cushion and piece of ski-house junk. This was cathartic for her.

I bet it was cathartic for her, the girl said. Lying through her teeth.

She wasn't lying to me, the man said. He felt defensive on behalf of his ex-wife, suddenly. They had actually shared a tender weekend and he had slept with her. A woman whom he found nearly as repugnant as the woman from the general store.

What could be more *cathartic*, the girl said, than to mess around with the head of the man who had messed around with *her* head. Who had loved *girls*, while pretending to be her devoted husband. Who lost her money on a crappy brownstone. Who embarrassed her at weddings.

That's enough, the man said, thinking he wanted the unhappy girl back. The quiet, unhappy girl. He started to connect her stories with her hostility; her stories were not made to entertain, they were made to derail him. They were weapons of self-defense.

The girl dropped her empty soup mug on the floor; it tipped onto its side, rolled under the couch.

She did not lie to me, the man said.

You don't know that, the girl said. I wouldn't be here if you knew that for sure.

The man nodded. Right, he thought. That's why she believed he was here. But that didn't explain why *she* was here. Why she had engineered to be abducted by him? What was in it for her? She should be scared of him, if she were a normal girl of seventeen. She should be fearing for her life. If he were to take a step back, if he were to allow his stranger-on-a-train self to view his actual self, the oddness of his predicament was blazingly apparent. Who the fuck was this girl?

You wouldn't be here if I knew, the man said. Which still doesn't exactly explain why you're here.

The girl smiled. Doesn't it? she said.

I don't think so, the man said.

Oh, she said. You're right.

So then, the man said. Why are you here?

A good question, the girl said. I'm surprised it's taken you so long to ask it.

There hasn't really been . . . the need, he said. What he meant was: It had happened. Things happen by happening.

True, said the girl. But now there is a need.

There is, he said.

Something understood between us has been destroyed, she said.

Not necessarily, the man said.

No, that's what you think.

OK, the man agreed. That's what I think.

Your back is against a wall and you're wondering why. Why would you let yourself be backed against a wall by a person you don't even know?

Can't I be backed against a wall by a stranger?

You're backed against a wall when you know what the other person wants and this conflicts with what you want and there's no satisfying the both of you. But you don't know what I want, and this is starting to frustrate you. Or this is how I'm reading your take on the situation.

My take on the situation, the man thought to himself, is that you are a disturbingly odd girl, and despite the fact that I am older than you and outweigh you by eighty pounds, I feel endangered in your presence.

Maybe, the girl said, maybe, like your ex-wife, I'm also out for revenge.

That makes no sense, the man said. I've never done anything to you.

Actually you have, the girl said. But I don't blame you, as I've said. I'm not out for revenge against *you*.

Ah, the man said, relaxing slightly. You're using me to get revenge on another person.

The girl made an angry cross-hatch with her thumbnail, impressing a red X onto her ankle. Her ankle, the man noted, was as small around as any normal person's wrist and scarred—not a pretty ankle—but something about its evident bones and its scars made it, and her, unspeakably alluring.

It's OK if you are, the man said. Using me for revenge.

If I *am* using you, well, at least I'm offering you something in return.

What's that again? the man asked.

I'm offering you your lousy forgotten life back.

The electric cuckoo clock on the wall commenced its hourly foolishness. Four o'clock. Thank god, the man thought. Though, as an insomniac, the idea of night usually made him anxious, in fact he couldn't wait for this day to end.

I suppose that's a fair exchange, the man said.

So you admit that your wife lied to you, the girl said.

The man ran his hands through his hair and stared at the meerkat andirons, their squirrel-like arms raised in clawed confrontation across an abyss of smoking logs. What was the point in disagreeing with her?

Chadwick

NOVEMBER 9, 1999

The roads were empty, the temperature now well below freezing, and the prior rain seized into an even slick of ice. The stress of the poor driving conditions winched Mary's shoulders as high as her chin. She lowered the volume of the distantly live symphony performance on the radio, but found the noise of the wheels leaving the patches of salted road for the soundless swaths of friction-free ice deeply unsettling. She re-cued the symphony. Eventually she spotted the beetled form of a salt truck ahead of her, its load rising humplike above its orange metal container. She followed it, not minding that it kicked a salinated slush onto her windshield smoothed by her wipers to gauzy streaks, creating a prism through which the truck's rear lights were stretched and multiplied like a hundred bug eyes.

It was 10:42 p.m.

She'd once known a shortcut to Chadwick—a series of badly lit back roads, each turn a potential failed vector that would deposit her in a tree trunk, a mailbox, a six-foot-thick wall of arbor vitae—and though there was no need for a shortcut at 10:42 on an icy November week night, shortcuts were ingrained in her by her father, a man for whom finding a good shortcut was like stealing a game of golf from an opponent with a far snazzier set of clubs. Each shortcut he discovered between the wealthy suburbs was further proof of the superiority of his working-class street smarts, his way of tunneling more stealthily through this foreign world he called home. So she'd taken the short cut, turning off the lit and salted route onto a side street so narrow it might have been someone's private drive, she'd negotiated the potholes and the stretches of icy road where it seemed that her aunt's station wagon had been converted to an unsteerable hovercraft, the brakes flurrying the air like a pair of useless rudders. Eventually the road looped back to the main highway—a place she had no intention of ending up, a place she found herself relieved to be.

As she approached the town limits of Chadwick, her mood began to shift, from vaguely anxious to self-castigating and hopeless. It was late. For all she knew Dr. Hammer had a wife now, he had young children who had been in bed for hours and whose early waking curtailed his evenings, making it impossible for him to reach ten o'clock in the evening without nodding off over his book or TV program.

But even assuming Dr. Hammer *was* still awake at 10:55 p.m., what guarantee did she have that he would talk to her? She struggled to remember the last time she'd seen Dr. Hammer but couldn't recall the specifics or even the nonspecifics because the meeting, whenever it had been, had failed to preannounce itself as final. Logic told her that the meeting took place on Beacon Street at Dr. Hammer's publishing house, located in a three-story brick house with a functioning dumbwaiter that the secretary used to move files and sandwiches between floors. After she'd terminated her treatment she'd met Dr. Hammer only three or so times, and always in the company of her father and the editorial assistant, to go over the *Miriam* manuscript. Hard facts were unthinkingly changed—her name, the street on which she lived—while more slippery ones had to be verified and reverified, as the editorial assistant flipped through the page proofs with his pencil, erasing marks next to the fact-checker's queries. It was a confusing business; she was asked to swear as accurate, for example, her statements that Dr. Hammer claimed to be untrue. *Yes*, she'd agreed. *It is true that that is a lie. Everything is correctly false.*

But maybe there'd been something more celebratory to mark their final meeting, a lunch she'd forgotten, at which he'd handed her the finished book and written his inscription (*For "Miriam"*). Or had the book quietly arrived by mail, already inscribed? She didn't remember. The book was so long lost that its arrival, too, had been obscured.

But what most needled her at the moment was this recent meeting (she presumed there had been a meeting) between her mother and Dr. Hammer. Roz had sent her mother to Dr. Hammer armed with the same address—wasn't this the thing "of interest" she'd used to tempt her mother into her office? Still, the many unknowns nagged her. Her mother, after all, had never technically met Dr. Hammer. Of course she'd *met* the man, but not so far as he knew. Had she appeared to him, these many years later, still pretending to be her own sister? Or had she appeared as herself? *Of course*, he would respond. *Of course you weren't who you said you were.* He would invite her into his house, where there would or would not be a wife, children, etc. And they would talk about . . . what? *The material. Some relationships are more predisposed to succeed due to a familiarity with the material.* Years after the fact, Mum and Dr. Hammer had sat in matching armchairs flanking a table with cups of tea or maybe, depending on Dr. Hammer's extracurricular vices, a glass of scotch, white wine, some gummy half-congealed coffee liqueur he'd been dragging around since graduate school. They had stayed up all night and, because her mother's self was prone to wander, she had discovered, as Mary had discovered, her natural ability to be Dr. Hammer's most perfect patient. She had confirmed all the self-fortifying suspicions that kept him awake at night. *Yes*, her daughter had lied to him—and then lied about lying. *No*, he had not been a bad doctor, a devastatingly wrong judge of character, a plain old sucker. He had been betrayed by a young girl who, they both chose to agree from this more charitable distance, was more to be pitied than blamed. She craved attention; once one avenue had been exhausted she'd done a U-turn and, with Roz's help, reinvigorated interest in her case. And then—nothing. She had faded into obscurity, she had moved to the Northwest, she had failed to yield. Hyper radiant that she was, she had burned herself out before she was even twenty.

A gristly possibility, Mary thought. A years-later postmortem that effectively rendered her unnecessary. No wonder her mother had refused to see her; the closure her mother had required was attained without any help from her. Mary *was* Miriam, the hyper radiant, her mother might have concluded; she'd inhabited her imagination's crafty geography as a way to refute the confused call of adolescent sexuality, which meant she was neither a liar nor a slut; she was an *artist*. Roz's investigation, the inquiry by the Massachussetts Mental Health Governing Board, the court case—none of this discounted what her mother and Dr. Hammer resurrected as the real story. Together they assured themselves: Mary's abduction was, as Dr. Hammer originally claimed it was, all in Mary's head. Together they'd agreed to forgive her. Closure all around. The end.

So easy.

Mary pinballed recklessly through three rotaries, she ignored the CAUTION signs that admonished her to reduce her speed now that she was approaching the Village of Chadwick. Main Street quickly corroded into increasingly crimped and hobbit-size storefronts before lapsing into wall- and hedge-lined blackness. Here Water Street picked up the thread as an unlit and unassuming artery wiggling off the main drag, its erratic zig-zags approximating the shape of the invisible coast. As with most Water Streets, no water was visible from the street.

Mary peered at the walls for house numbers as she drove, slowly now, her desire not to overshoot her mark deflating her sense of recklessness. A stone wall gave way to a newish brick wall, then a hedge, then another stone wall. Dr. Hammer's number—48—was plainly visible on a generic black metal mailbox that emerged from the ground at a thirty degree angle, victim of repeated batterings by the winter plow. His driveway slid through a narrow gap in the brick.

The problem with rich people, Mary thought, *is that they're impossible to stun.* She stopped in the middle of the street, not wanting to turn into Dr. Hammer's driveway. Her headlights would pique him, give him crucial seconds to wonder *what the hell* as she parked her car, walked to the door, rang the bell, predispose him to categorize her visit as an unwelcome surprise. Nor was there any shoulder on Water Street where she could leave her car. So her only choice, as she saw it, was the least noble one: turn off her headlights and drive up to the house in the dark.

Mary extinguished her headlights and instantly the space in the brick into which she was turning extinguished as well. But she had already begun her turn and so, trusting that she'd aimed properly, she confidently drove Aunt Helen's station wagon into what she abstractly experienced as a hardened piece of night.

Her skull hurled toward the windshield, spared a concussion by the just-in-time retraction of her seat belt. Outside, a mini avalanche of brick bits and mortar ricocheted off the station wagon's hood. Mary remained in the driver's seat, stunned to near fury by her stupidity. She opened her door and stepped into the dark, instantly tripping over a long, pipe-like something—her axle?—and pitching clumsily forward onto her hands and knees. From this humbled position, she surveyed the damage. The front of Aunt Helen's car was so badly crushed it appeared to have been swallowed by the brick wall. The mailbox and its now broken post, over which she'd tripped, had caught in the car's undercarriage; it now protruded at a perpendicular angle from behind the front wheels. Attached to the mailbox—by a severed chain—was a carved wood sign, the gilded cursive wriggingly alive in the glow cast from the car's interior light: WANDERSLORE.

She looked toward Dr. Hammer's house, tensed against the explosion of dog barks or the sudden blazing of porch lights—but nothing. No one had heard the sound of Aunt Helen's car striking their brick wall, or they'd heard it and attributed the noise to a more likely source, like the salt truck hitting a pothole.

Her earlier desire to speak with Dr. Hammer was replaced by an overwhelming impulse to flee the scene. Better to simply disappear and allow the situation to resolve itself, however inaccurately; she could approach him again in a few days, maybe even a week, and she would either confess to running into his wall or she would not. The station wagon she could return to the spot in front of her house from which she'd removed it. She could allow Aunt Helen to believe that she'd drunkenly hit a parked car on her way to see her nieces. Aunt Helen, once properly saturated, forgot the majority of her pre-drunk day. She would view the crushed front half of her car, she would quietly slip the key into her ignition and drive home, operating on the theory that the fewer people who knew about her accident, the less chance of being caught, the less chance of her insurance premiums skyrocketing, the less chance that the world would have to publicly acknowledge that she was a drunk. What dismayed Mary, as she played out this scenario in her head, was how stupidly easy it was to be dishonest. People needed to be more vigilant. People needed to be more paranoid. People needed to realize that the least probable explanation was the most probable explanation. *My niece stole my car to drive to see her former therapist, she ran into a brick wall trying to take him by surprise, and then she tried to gaslight me.* But if Aunt Helen weren't such a shirker then Mary wouldn't be able to be a shirker either. Dishonesties bred dishonesties. Lies encouraged tiny epidemics. She should know.

As she indulged her theoretical regret over the ease with which she could, once again, disappear, she realized that, in fact, there was no escaping this situation. As her eyes adjusted better to the poorly lit gloom she registered that the station wagon's bumper had in fact wedged itself *into* the brick wall; so many bricks had been knocked out by the impact that the wall dipped and swelled above the car's hood. It didn't take a structural engineer to deduce that Aunt Helen's station wagon was the only thing standing between the wall's tenuous existence and its partial collapse.

Mary brushed the crushed stones from her pants and hands and started down the driveway. The house too was brick, set on a diagonal to the drive. The upstairs windows remained dark, the downstairs windows as well, but she could see large rectangles of light spreading across the backyard. So he was awake, she thought, unsure if this improved her situation or worsened it.

Mary, she would say when he answered the door. *It's Mary Veal here.*

She climbed the steps expecting a sensored porch light to announce her approach, but she proved to be as invisible here as she was in West Salem. And so it was in relative darkness that she reached for the bell. It was in relative darkness that he answered the door seconds after the pad of her finger touched the protruding bronze button, almost as if he'd known she'd be standing at his threshold.

His hair was still too long for a lawyer's hair, even an ex-lawyer's hair, curling upward where it struck his collar.

She stared at the man, stunned.

Hello, Scheherazade, the man said. I've been expecting you.

Notes

The morning following my most recent session with Mary, I awoke in a confident mood. I awoke confident that my hyper radiance theory was both relevant in this particular case and likely of greater psychological consequence. I awoke confident that, like Roz, I could secure a patron to fund my research and assist my publishing aspirations. So it was serendipity, coincidence, or my own fate-altering sense of deserved good fortune that prompted Roz to accept a last-minute invitation extended by a local live radio show producer to discuss her new book, *Trampled Ivy*. She was thus unable to attend a fund-raiser for the Dibble Library in West Salem with her patron and editor, Craig Hoppin, that evening. I was perhaps too eager to attend in her place.

I had met Hoppin, a newspaper heir in his late sixties with a Tourettic capacity for rapid-fire rudeness, upward of seven times. That he'd never remembered me didn't lessen my enthusiasm to accompany him to the fund-raiser. I waited by the name-tags table for ten minutes until Hoppin, a compact bulldog of a man, arrived in his usual tweed suit and bow tie. There hadn't been time to call ahead for a replacement name tag; I extended a hand and introduced myself jokily as Roz. I offered to get him a drink from the bar. Fifteen minutes later I relocated him with Mary's Aunt Helen, the two of them stationed before a portrait of a young girl leaning on a single crutch. Helen noticed my approach and whispered to Hoppin. He nodded, two fingers pittering along the nose-guard of his wire rims.

Do you two know each other? Helen said loudly. As is typical behavior for a patient suffering from a confused intimacy disorder, Helen's facial expression discouraged me from advancing even while she beckoned me toward her with her hand.

Roz Biedelman, I reminded Hoppin, handing him his watery drink.

Hoppin glared at his drink.

I don't know about you, said Hoppin, but I am eroticized by sadness.

I can get you another, I offered.

We're talking about how this space exudes a palpable, and almost *sexual*, despair, explained Helen. Did you know that Mrs. Dibble's daughter—Helen pointed to a portrait they'd been examining—hung herself from the chandelier?

Her eyes gestured overhead toward a cast-iron light fixture, its sharp extremities punctuated with flame-shaped bulbs.

How tragic, I said.

The foreshadowing of the musket, said Hoppin, dipping his eyes toward what I'd interpreted, tellingly, as a crutch. It's delicious.

Helen smiled, apparently thrilled to share the experience with a recent convert to ghoulishness.

How does Mrs. Dibble feel about your treating her family tragedy as cocktail party chitchat? I chided Helen, trying to mimic her hostile-flirtatious tone and sounding instead like a drab scold.

Mrs. Dibble's in a home, she said. Stroke. The third in as many years.

When life has been reduced to bedpans and IV-drip dinners, it's time to consider "abandoning the manse," as my grandmother used to say.

"Abandoning the manse," Hoppin said. I like that. Or maybe it works better as a command. *Abandon the manse!*

Works better as what? Helen said.

I'm funding a documentary that examines the delusional tendencies of the elderly and the astronomical cost to taxpayers. It's called *The Immortal Dead*. But maybe *Abandon the Manse!* has a more self-mockingly patrician ear-feel.

Ear-feel. Helen squirmed girlishly inside her beaded sweater.

She and Hoppin exchanged a look that made me wonder whether the two of them were having an affair. Hoppin, as his name either suggested or dictated, suffered from hyperactivity. He rocked rapidly back and forth on the soles of his loafers. As we lapsed into a tense silence, I recalled what Roz had counseled that afternoon: If you run out of things to say to Hoppin, disagree with him. According to Roz, Hoppin's insecurity among doctors, academics, and artists explained his interest in funding them and thereby "purchasing" the upper hand. He loved a fight because it indicated a presumed equality between the opponents. If you challenge him, Roz said, he'll take it as flattery.

You believe the elderly are medically overindulged? I said.

I'm a euthanasia man myself, said Hoppin. The first time I crap myself my wife has instructions to smother me with a couch pillow.

What about the curing properties of optimism? I said.

New Age lunacy, said Hoppin. Are you some type of healer?

He's a therapist, said Helen. He's treating my niece.

Is she troubled? said Hoppin.

Not especially, said Helen. *That's* her trouble. You should pay someone to write a book exploring the tragic lives of the untragic. Am I right, Dr. Hammer?

Funny you should mention that, I said.

A great idea, Hoppin interrupted. Too bad you're busy raising money for the library. I might give you money to write it yourself.

You've confused me with my sister, Helen said sternly.

Huh? said Hoppin.

That's my sister who does the fund-raising, said Helen.

Oh right sorry sorry, said Hoppin.

Helen announced the need to check on the outcome of an earlier "crudités emergency," then threaded her slim way through a pair of overly lipsticked women still wearing their clear plastic rain kerchiefs.

I love a woman with a dark side, said Hoppin, tracking Helen's retreating behind. Everyone's so cheery these days.

Not the youth, I said. They're more darkly inclined. Energetically so.

Darkly energetic, said Hoppin, head bobbing. I like that.

In fact, I said, I've been wanting to write about—

How did you say you knew Roz? Hoppin leered at my name tag.

We're suite mates, I said.

Suite mates, enunciated Hoppin suggestively.

I don't know what Roz has told you about me, I began.

Roz has never mentioned you, Hoppin said. Roz is out for Roz and only Roz. That's why I funded her. Egomaniacs are the best self-promoters. I make money in the end.

Roz is very talented, I said.

She evidently thinks you're a moron or else you wouldn't be here. Do you want another drink?

I followed Hoppin numbly to the drinks table. Apparently the crudités emergency had been a dire one. There were no hors d'oeuvres on the hors d'oeuvres table and no shortage of drinks, thus the atmosphere in the library had grown commensurately garbled and giddy. Hoppin downed a vodka tonic and ordered a second, then gestured toward the flagstone patio beyond the bar. I freshened my drink and exited through the French doors to the right of the piano to find Hoppin seated on a wrought-iron bench. Though the rain had stopped, the bench's underside still dripped a pattern of darker drips onto the flagstones.

Torture, he said, smacking the bench. Haven't they heard of cushions? Maybe I'll earmark my donation. Drop your ham.

I brushed the water from the seat. I sat.

So, he said. No affairs with the suite mates. No skeletons in your closet. Nothing to offer a prurient fellow at a dull-as-dust gathering of women who have had their genitals cremated and stuffed in the family urn.

That depends, I said.

Depends, said Hoppin. Depends is for leaking old people.

Hoppin removed his wire rims. He burrowed his index finger into his eye and rotated it manically. He was growing bored with me.

Well, I said. There was this one patient.

A female?

A girl, I said. Fifteen.

I told him about Bettina, how she had lied to me, how I had broken patient-doctor confidentiality in order to help her and in the process of helping her had fairly well screwed myself and a few other people, how I had been encouraged to take some time off from my doctoral studies during the investigation, how I had eventually dropped out of school and returned for a certificate in therapeutic social work, how I had always felt inadequate around colleagues like Roz whom I believed took pity on me and welcomed me, however marginally, into their folds, because it underscored their feelings of superiority.

Did you imagine her naked? said Hoppin.

Roz?

The girl.

Never, I said.

Hoppin squinted at a bird feeder, wildly swinging beneath the weight of two squirrels.

I learned from Bettina that the female imagination is a beautiful yet dangerous force of nature, I said, struggling to hold his interest. That imagination and sexuality for young girls are inextricable. I'm committed, now, to exploring that boundary between the beautiful and the dangerous. I'm committed to do whatever it takes to explore that boundary.

Hoppin sighed, scraping the metal heel plate of his loafers back and forth over the flagstones like a match over flint.

I've been investigating this boundary with another patient of mine, I said.

I told Hoppin about Helen's niece. I told Hoppin about my theory of hyper radiance. I told him how Helen's niece was connected to Bettina. I told him about the climate of Puritan repression. I told him about the witches.

Is she a virgin? he asked.

She's fantasized her abduction, I said. There is no abductor.

So she faked her abduction, Hoppin said impatiently. But where did she go? To her boyfriend's parents' ski house? Maybe this abduction was just a good occasion to have a lot of sex.

She doesn't have a boyfriend, I said.

But is she a virgin, Hoppin said. Yes or no?

I couldn't bring myself to tell Hoppin about the medical exam. She hadn't been a virgin. But I found Hoppin's virginity fixation tiresomely predictable for a man of his type (compensating for other lacks with an overdetermined masculinity) and totally beside the point. I didn't want to lie to him, nor did I want his inexpertise to forbid the future of my project.

I'm planning to write a book about this theory, I said. That is, if I could secure some monetary support.

Cutting to the chase, said Hoppin. I like that. Tell me more about the witches. Witches are a nice touch. Witches sell second only to Nazis.

We'd have to front-load a lot of details about witches, and maybe include a chapter about modern-day satanic worshippers.

I'm afraid that's a tangential and unrelated phenomenon—

My brother-in-law is a publisher but he's cursed with a tacky art director, also known as my sister. We'd have to retain design control. I'm seeing a cover with a sun and inside of it a girl's face, her imagination burning out of control, a girl, her hair in flames, tied to a stake, smiling . . .

Technically, no witches were burned at the stake in New England, I said.

I could give a crap about technically, said Hoppin. I'm talking deep cultural perceptions.

Misperceptions, I said.

In terms of death, burning women sell second only to suicides. Ask Helen's sister about the dollar value of suicide. If the flames in her hair resembled snakes, we could subconsciously introduce the Medusa theme. The girl who turns men to stone. Renders them impotent. Or perhaps it should be the opposite?

I don't think there's room for a Medusa theme, I said curtly.

Just a taste of Medusa. A barely perceptible undercurrent of Medusa.

If I were a strict Jungian, which I'm not, I'd probably say—

Nobody knows from Jung or Freud or goddamned Horney. It's your job to tweak those parts of their brains that are waiting to be tweaked. You've got to scare them, make them fear the undiscovered menace. Best sellers are created through fear.

Of course, I said.

But not real fear, said Hoppin. Fake fear. Fairy-tale fear. Fear that lasts only as long as a book. Did you say the girl was a virgin before her abduction?

According to her medical exam . . .

I don't care about medical exams. You're the doctor. According to your *professional opinion*, as it pertains to the writing of a good book, was she? Or wasn't she? Readers won't feel any pity for a slut, you know.

Hoppin stared me down with his gunmetal eyes.

She was definitely a virgin, I said.

Mary appeared for our eighth appointment looking extremely thin. Possibly it was a trick of her clothing; she had a tendency to wear oversize shirts and sweaters, shapeless blouses. Today she wore an old college sweatshirt, a tattered crewneck with the words WORCESTER TECH across the chest. I made a note to phone the physician, the one she saw once a week for a basic vitals check and medication adjustments.

You seem tired, I said.

Mary didn't respond. Besides the sweatshirt she wore brown corduroy pants, the thighs rubbed bald by a repetitive activity I couldn't conjure from the size and location. She picked at the outer edges of these napless patches with her fingernail.

Are you taking your sleeping pills?

They give me bad dreams, she said.

Can you describe the dreams, I said.

It's the same dream. The one with K and the fire and my mother and the empty jewel case. What are you writing, she said.

I turned my pad toward her.

Recurring dream of lost virginity, I said.

She nodded. So we're agreeing that's what it means.

That's what you've decided, I said.

I didn't decide anything, she said. Things happened.

Things, I said.

With K, she said.

In the dream, I said.

Does it matter? she said.

Dreams are a distortion of reality, I said.

If you dream of losing your teeth it means you're sexually frustrated. If you dream your jewel case is empty it means . . . you know what it means.

Dream images are not standardized, I said. Often the most obvious interpretation is simply that: the most obvious interpretation. Many more layers of significance may lie beneath it. To stop at the obvious would be—to badly misinterpret the dream.

K used to be a smoker, she said. He hadn't smoked for months but he still smelled like cigarettes when he kissed me.

This is in the dream, I said wryly.

This is what I remember.

So you remember now, I said.

She shrugged. Just parts. I remember feeling very itchy. Like there were tiny splinters of glass in my skin. And tongues. Lots of pink tongues. They licked me all over and it hurt.

Mary sneezed.

I handed her a tissue. She blew her nose feebly. I closed the window above the radiator. When I returned to my chair, Mary still held the tissue over her face.

Mary, I said.

Her shoulders shook imperceptibly. She exhaled, sobbing into the tissue.

Sleeping pills can cause mood swings, I said. I'm making a note to call your physician.

OK, Mary said into the tissue.

Her voice, despite her apparent crying, was neither gutteral nor choked.

Her shoulders continued to shake.

Mary, I said. Look at me.

Mary peered from behind her used tissue. Her eyes were red and dry.

I held out a handful of clean tissues.

Thanks, she said, sniffing aridly. I'm sorry.

No need to be sorry, I said. Unless you've done something . . . wrong.

She stared at me.

Define *wrong*, she said acidly.

I only meant—there's no harm in crying if it's for a good reason.

And who will determine whether my reason is good or not? You?

Tell me why you're crying, I said.

I don't know *why*, she said. But I promise you there's a good reason. I just don't happen to know it. Is that OK?

Your emotions are always valid here, I said. We're not questioning the validity of your emotions.

It sounded like you were.

I'm sorry if it sounded that way to you, I said. I was urging you to talk about the source of your distress.

The dream, she said. I wake up from that dream and I feel . . . ashamed. I don't want to see my mother. If I avoid my mother, the shame is less.

What are you ashamed of, I said. Ashamed that K stole your jewels?

Ashamed because . . . I'm not myself.

Who are you, I said.

I'm a character in a story. I'm a real person but I'm not a real person. The things that I've done aren't the things that I've done.

Why would that make you ashamed? Your representative in the dream did something shameful. Not you.

But maybe it's not a dream, she said.

Exactly right. It's a fantasy. A fantasy that you've entertained while awake. Thus you cannot blame your subconscious. Perhaps this is why you're ashamed.

No, no, it wasn't a fantasy, Mary said. It wasn't a dream. I'll tell you what happened but you have to promise not to tell my mother . . .

I cut her off. I knew what she was doing. She rightly sensed I was about to call her on her deception, and she was trying to divert me with more promises of fake confessions.

What if I told you I don't believe that K exists?

Mary didn't respond.

What if I told you I thought you'd made him up? What would you say?

What *would* I say? Mary said.

I nodded.

Why don't I just say it? she asked.

Fine, I said. Say it.

You're exactly like my mother, Mary said. That's both what I would say and what I am saying.

How am I like your mother, I said. Because you're ashamed in front of me? You're ashamed of your conscious fantasy life?

You can't see what's happening right in front of your nose because it doesn't fit your worldview. In this way you are exactly like my mother.

What is my worldview, I said.

Your worldview, Mary said, is only about your world.

And that makes me different from you? That makes me different from anyone?

Yes, she said.

Interesting, I said.

Mary picked at the bald patches on her pants with a newfound neurotic intensity.

Your worldview makes you intrinsically deaf to my worldview. To explain the difference would be a waste of both of our time.

So you think you're more empathic than me.

I might be, she said. Your head is ossified. I still have a flexible head. I still have hopes.

I wrote on my pad. *Ossified Flexible Hopes.*

I rested my pencil lengthwise along my thigh.

You're diverting the focus from you to me, I said. As usual, the minute I strike close to a valuable vein of inquiry you divert the focus. What I am suggesting, Mary, is that you've been lying to me.

But aren't you also the focus? she said. Aren't your needs as important as my needs? Aren't you a person too?

Real tears appeared. She laid a finger sideways beneath her bottom lashes, catching the overflow and flicking it away. The skin beneath her eyes had reddened and swelled, the result of her harsh dabbings with the tissue.

Suddenly, I understood.

I *am* a person, I said.

Mary didn't respond.

That's why you're upset, I said. You've realized that I am a person.

I know you're a fucking person, Mary said. It's you who forgot.

How did I forget?

I told you I was ashamed and you responded with hostility.

I don't think I responded with hostility, I said.

You responded with disinterest, and because it means a lot to me, this admission that I feel ashamed, I read it as hostility. How's that?

Fine, I said. But I want to hear *from you* what you feel ashamed about. Deceiving people is a shameful business, isn't it, Mary?

Mary's eyes teared up again.

You're attacking me, she said. I'm trying to tell you something important and you're attacking me.

I'm not attacking you, I said. You're in *therapy*. Did you think it was going to be easy? Did you think you'd be able to fool me the way you've fooled your parents?

The only person I've fooled, she said, is myself.

God! I said. I threw my pad to the floor. Don't be so self-pitying.

I'm sorry, she said, sobbing now. I'm sorry.

Don't apologize, I said. Tell me the truth. Tell me the *truth*.

I don't know, she said. It's so complicated all of a sudden.

You do know, I said. People do not forget the shameful events of their life. It's all they can do not to think about them constantly.

Mary's eyes overflowed. She wept without sobbing. Her face dissolved.

I allowed her to cry without interruption. Her distress had developed an engine of its own; she was distressed by her distress now, and the true cause would be impossible to unearth until she'd exhausted herself. I walked to the window and reopened it. I needed air. I stared at the dull streets, the dormant trees, the dirty snow. The early-April overcast sky. The ugliest day of the year and yet I felt inured to its ugliness—*ossified*, perhaps—in a giddy way.

In my pocket I could feel the business card that Craig Hoppin gave me on the patio of the Dibble Library.

Call me, he said. Call me and we'll discuss your future over lunch.

And so we had lunch, martinis and cobb salads at a bistro on Newbury Street. I told Hoppin more about Helen's niece. I sketched out my hyper radiance theory on a series of cocktail napkins: her family's witch relative at the top, a black dot, Bettina Spencer below her, another black dot, and Helen's niece below Bettina, an X. The two dots and the X were connected by arrows, the whole structure surrounded by concentric circles, each applying inward pressure indicated by many shorter arrows beaming in from the perimeter: Semmering Academy; the patient's mother; the town of West Salem; the larger inherited Puritan mind-set of sexual repression; the even larger cultural distrust of women, which, I pointed out, could be traced back to mythological times and thus could even include Medusa.

Hoppin liked this. He smoothed the crumples from the napkins with the backside of a spoon.

I'm a visual man, he said. Now I understand. Yes, the arrows point inward, but they could just as easily point outward.

That's exactly right, I said to him. These girls—these hyper radiants—they reverse the energy flow of the arrows.

I drew arrows pointing from the center X toward the outermost ring.

The increased pressure under which they've existed either crushes their spirit, or, as I suspect is a trend, their spirit rebels, it ingests this negative energy and reflects it outward as an act of intensive, even destructive, creativity. I can help them harness what currently manifests as a destructive tendency and transform it into a positive tendency. A work of art.

We ate our uninspired lunch, we ordered coffee and no dessert. Hoppin, as he signed the check, promised to get me a contract by the end of the week and the first installment of my "research grant." Outside the bistro's plate-glass windows, a collection of schoolgirls gathered. They stared at themselves in the windows, fixing their lipstick, pretending to forget that people sat behind their makeshift mirrors, observing them from inside their own reflections. One girl stared at me. Her lips gathered into a glossy pink sneer.

A slight uneasiness mixed with my excitement. *Was this wrong?* As the girl sneered at me, I wondered whether what I was signing up to do was justified. Hoppin had too many expectations that clashed with the truth. I would be saddling my professional reputation to a real girl who might not, when I was through with her, exist.

The girl's mouth circled into a fishlike "O."

I asked Hoppin whether, ethically, I had the rights to Helen's niece's story. Could I tell the story if it's hers? Could I claim it as my own?

Who says it's hers, said Hoppin. She's a liar. There *is* no real story. We'll just change the salient details. Her name. Where she lives. Even personal details that don't fit the hyper-radiant profile. Everybody does it.

But ethically, I said.

Is it more ethical to co-opt the story of one lying girl, or is it more

ethical to utilize a version of her story to help the many others who suffer from her condition? You're doing the world a favor.

Right, I said.

It's a matter of bravery, Hoppin said. You'd be surprised how brave
you have to be to do something of note. You have to be willing to be a
bastard. *Pour faire une omelette il faut casser des oeufs.*

Indeed, I thought. This opportunity came, as did most opportunities,
at a price to somebody. I tried to soothe my conscience by thinking about
famous case studies. Because Mary had been fascinated by it, Freud and
Dora came first to mind. I reminded myself that great case studies were
made, not reported. I reminded myself that Dora was just the name of a
fictional girl based on a real girl. The real girl had scarcely figured in the
final product. That was the mistake of feminists like Roz, I thought. To
defend Dora was to defend a fictional creation. To defend a fictional creation was to miss the point.

Girls' lives don't have points, I heard in my head. *That's why they do what
they do.*

The girl in the window put the back of her hand over her mouth.
With a brusque motion she spread the lipstick across her cheek like a
slash of war paint.

I experienced an impulse similar to the one I'd experienced in the
company of Mary's Aunt Helen; as I'd wanted to make the cigarette case
disappear, so too did I want Mary to disappear.

I was not proud of this impulse.

I was proud of this impulse.

Her name, I said, wondering if Hoppin had seen the girl, too. But
when I turned to the window again she was gone.

Her name, I repeated, suddenly fixated. I wanted to cleave Mary and
her fictional representative in two. What shall we call her?

Our waitress returned to collect the bill. Her silver name tag flashed
in the sunlight shining through the plate glass window, blinding me.

Miriam, Hoppin said. We'll call her Miriam.

What Might Have Happened

T he girl was bored. An improvement, the man thought as he soaked the encrusted soup bowls in the sink. Better than sad or despondent or demeaned. But he changed his mind when he returned to the living room and found the girl rummaging through a drawer in the Bavarian sideboard. Who knew what was in the drawer of the Bavarian sideboard. Certainly he didn't know, and so he found himself wishing she'd grow sad again. He found himself thinking *bored was the new curious.* He'd begun to settle into his pre-nighttime routine, a blankly suggestive period in which sentences entered his head—*the silence rang sublime; dinner was a squalid affair; bored was the new curious*—and repeated themselves endlessly, refusing to leave until he celebrated the artificial beginning of the next day with a cup of coffee. Often these sentences were nonsensical variations on some oft-uttered phrase (*defenestration was all the rage*) or statements in the past tense, narrative non sequiturs that might or might not pertain to his day. He wondered if this new narrative impulse was a residue of his wife's reclamation therapy. Reclamation therapy insisted on the past tense, the third person; in truth it was a creepy exercise that he'd endured only because it meant he'd have something to do. Bored had not been the new curious, he'd learned after the accident, bored was the new bored. So his wife had dragged him to this exact house and said, respecting the third-person recommendation of his doctor: *He was a bugaboo for pressed shirts and shoe trees. He was deathly scared of infestations.*

Then they had had sex. He and his ex-wife, on the guest bed, without sheets, to maintain the feeling of past-tense temporariness, the inviolability of a story that already had an ending. His wife said, as he entered her, *The man never could satisfy his wife because he was preoccupied by the possibility of bats.* He did not tell the girl about this encounter on the guest bed, but he worried she would discern it nonetheless. She'd divine it from random clues found in the Bavarian sideboard, from a paper clip and a coin of candle wax. Soon she'd be telling him a story in which he was having sex with his ex-wife on the guest bed while his ex-wife told him that he was too worried about bats to be a good lover. The girl would laugh at him and use this as another prod to suggest that he should kiss her or engage in some other form of sexual misconduct with her, so then she could prove to him that he was the illicitly passionate man she claimed he was.

The man looked at the girl as she sifted through the contents of the drawer. He found her very beautiful at that moment—her hair, ever dingier, catching the light from the nearby lamp and seeming to gleam, even to sparkle. But he quickly redirected this impulse toward the critical: *Her outfit tires me,* he thought. The field hockey uniform. The sweatpants. How could she expect him to fondle her while she wore a uniform? It was too much of a porn-movie cliché, to the degree that he understood the highly clichéd world of porn.

You know, he suggested, you might think about changing out of those clothes.

What? the girl said. Her head was practically inside the drawer. Her voice echoed woodily.

Those clothes, the man said. Do you really think I would molest you in those clothes?

The girl raised her head from the drawer.

Who says I want you to molest me? she said.

The man rolled his eyes. *Dinner was a squalid affair.*

Don't roll your eyes at me, the girl said. Eye rolling means you don't respect me. If you're going to molest me, I demand your respect.

There are clothes in my ex-wife's bedroom, he said. Feel free to wear anything.

Even her underwear? the girl said.

Your comfort level with a stranger's underwear is something I can't regulate, the man said.

You used to make me wear your ex-wife's underwear, the girl said.

The man rolled his eyes again.

Sorry, he said, catching himself. But I respectfully think you've lost your touch. Your stories are becoming clichéd.

Your life is a cliché, the girl said. Who gets amnesia about their whole life? Who believes that cheesy plot twist any longer?

The girl dropped cross-legged on the floor and flicked at the hardened sole of his ex-wife's sheepskin slipper with her fingernail. Click click click. The sound was repugnant to him.

Are you saying you don't believe me, the man said.

I'm saying I don't believe in forgetting, the girl said. Which is different from saying I don't believe you.

Huh, the man said. I'm not seeing the difference.

I'm sure your amnesia feels real to you, the girl explained. I'm just not certain it exists.

The man didn't respond. He decided it was time to have a drink.

Scotch? he said, busying himself at the wet bar behind the couch. I can also offer you peppermint schnapps, white rum, coffee liqueur, flat tonic.

I don't drink, the girl said. But I'd take a cigarette.

Ex-wife didn't allow smoking in the house, he said. Log cabin. Fire trap. Etc.

You smoked when she went skiing, the girl said. You hid in the attic and opened a window. You lit incense to mask the smell.

The man shrugged crossly. You'd know better than I, he said.

The girl took this as permission to forage for cigarettes. She scurried up the staircase which was carpeted in a rust-brown shag that, when trod upon, released the smell of mildew.

While you're up there, he called after her, change your clothes.

Because if I'm dressed like an adult, she said from the landing, you can forget you're molesting a child.

That's right, the man said, raising his glass. Cheers.

The girl disappeared around the landing.

The man threw back the scotch while standing at the wet bar; the rule of drunks, he knew, dictated that each trip to the bar equaled one drink, even if each trip to the bar equaled three drinks. He refilled his glass, emptied it, refilled it a second time, returned to the couch. The scotch surged and settled around his heart. He was a threatened man. *Threatened man.* A redundancy. He was a man. A redundant man. He felt the need to stoke the fire with the poker, he felt the need to growl in a throaty, mucusy timbre, he felt the need to run upstairs and teach the girl a lesson. *A redundant man with bats in his attic is nobody's fool.*

Upstairs, he heard the sounds of resistant drawers opening, the swelled wood popping loose with a mortally wounded rodent squeak. He imagined her holding up his wife's clothing, item by mothbally item, trying to select an outfit he'd like. Or an outfit he'd dislike, an unsettling outfit. Or maybe the girl would opt for something predictable—now that she was fatigued her story lines were starting to fray—and emerge in a silky bathrobe and nothing beneath. She'd forgo the old sheepskin slippers in exchange for something less mutton-footed—his ex-wife's leather sandals, perhaps, college-era hippie thongs that she wore around the house when the fire was too hot.

But most likely, he thought, the girl, if she wasn't predictable in one way, would be predictable in another. Instead of mocking him via the overtly sexual, she would mock him through its opposite. She would descend the staircase with pajama pants turbaned on her head, the bunchy terry-cloth robe his wife stole from the Copley Plaza Hotel, an inherited pair of rubber waders, grotesquely interpreting adulthood like the child playing dress up that she was. The man tried to prepare himself for anything, because he was sensing that this evening had turned into a serious game. It had been a game from the second he'd opened his car door for her, but he'd taken it lightly—a larkish opportunity pursued by a bored man. But the evening's larkish aspect had long ago expired. In the parking lot of the twenty-four-hour rest stop on the highway. As he hurried toward the pay phone and hurt his hip—which, now that he thought about it, hadn't hurt at all since the parking lot. A side effect of his subterranean panic, which had since left his muscles, shifted to the surface, now made plain by his vibrating hands holding an empty scotch tumbler. Momentarily empty. He refilled it, listened to the no-noise of the girl in his ex-bedroom. Where was she? He shot a worried glance at the stairwell, half expecting her head, or rather her eyes, like those of a bat in the rafters, to be spying on him with unblinking animal disinterest. But no. The landing was empty. He waited for the clinking of his ice cubes to subside. Far above him—in the attic—he heard a hull-like creaking, a furry thump. Looking for cigarettes, he thought. That's where she was.

He sipped his scotch economically. Usually the ironclad awakeness of insomnia prevented alcohol from affecting him, but tonight was different. Tonight his brain was muzzy, the hyperalert state that made every object appear spotlit and coated in titanium had rescinded its hold on him. This worried him. He worried that, muzzy-brained, he wouldn't be up to the challenge of beating the girl. *Beating the girl.* As in *defeating* the girl, he said to himself, mentally squaring away any potentially misunderstood double entendres as if he would be called to the stand to testify against himself. Really this was all just a game; to consider it a game made him both less and more anxious. A game was fun. A game could be lost. He started to wonder if perhaps the girl had been put up to this game by his ex-wife. She was the kind of woman who laughed when people vomited into their laps on planes. It wouldn't be beyond her.

Yes, he decided, his paranoia growing, his ex-wife had put the girl up to this. How else to explain it? What kind of girl would engineer her own kidnapping by a strange man? It didn't make sense that a girl would do a thing like this. Who would intentionally put herself at risk? Who would purposefully cause such alarm back home? Unless that was the point. She was using him, and in return, she was giving him what she thought any man his age would want. Sex. Yes, she'd figured, any man would want to have sex with her, particularly if it were being forced upon him as a natural part of his past.

Upstairs he heard a door open and close. In the silence that ensued he heard what he interpreted as the sound of her interim nakedness as she shed the field hockey uniform, the sweatpants, the slippers, and re-draped herself with the overtly sexual or patently ridiculous outfit she'd fashioned from his ex-wife's drawers. Almost as though her nakedness triggered it, a continent of wet snow slid from the roof and landed outside the door with the dense thud of a body striking ground. He started, thinking maybe she'd thrown herself from the window. *Defenestration was all the rage.*

He opened the door—it was completely dark now—and stared past the cabin's glow into the indistinguishable murk beyond. The night was so evenly and inertly chilled that the effect was akin to staring into a refrigerator whose bulb had burned out. In the distance he heard a coyote, and the desperate noise of some clawed animal scratching itself.

Don't turn around, the girl said.

She was behind him. How had she gotten behind him?

Can I close the door? the man said.

Were you leaving? the girl said.

No, the man said. I was thinking.

You think a lot when you're about to abandon me, the girl said. What were you thinking about?

I was wondering if you'd thrown yourself from the bedroom window, the man said.

Why would I do that? she said.

I have no idea, the man said. I don't know you well enough to say.

Do you believe that knowing a person means they can't still surprise you? the girl asked.

The man could hear the girl breathing. Raspy. Maybe she'd been crying upstairs. Maybe after all those hours in wet clothing she'd caught a cold.

I guess not, the man said.

Would it scare you if you were the person who knew me better than anyone else in the world?

We're wasting heat, the man said. I'm shutting the door now.

He didn't wait for her to condone his plan. As he closed the door he heard her scurry, sock-footed, into the kitchen.

Lie on the couch, she said. With your feet facing the door.

Can I freshen my drink? the man asked.

No, the girl said. You've had enough to drink tonight.

She's been spying on me, the man thought as he extended his body on the couch.

Would it? the girl said. She'd positioned herself now behind his head. In the window opposite, he caught her reflection. Momentary, because she caught it too. She flicked the row of switches by the stairwell, extinguishing the lamps and the upstairs hall light. He shivered on the couch, the outside chill still clinging to his sweater. She looked like no one he recognized.

The house was dark, save for the meager glow of his struggling fire.

Would it what? the man said.

Would it scare you if you knew me better than anyone else in the world, the girl repeated.

Scared, the man said. I don't know about scared. Maybe sad. Sad for you.

You shouldn't be sad for me, the girl said. You should be sad for yourself.

I am sad for myself, the man said. Not actively. But atmospherically, I am sad for myself.

Poor you, said the girl.

I'm not asking you to pity me, the man said. I'm being matter-of-fact. If I know you so well, you should know me well, too.

But I do know you, the girl said. Better than you do. You forget.

Right, right, the man said, growing tired of this charade.

Have you ever gone to therapy? the girl asked. I've always wanted to go to therapy. Maybe I'll go when I get home. I'll probably need it.

The man didn't ask her why.

Don't you think I'll need therapy? the girl prodded.

I say this respectfully, the man said, but it's my hunch you needed therapy long before you met me.

Could be, the girl said thoughtfully. But I didn't have a reason to go. Now I'll have a reason.

Do you need a reason? the man said.

In my family, the girl said, yes.

So that's why you're here? the man said. You want a reason to go to therapy?

Maybe, the girl said.

Seems a lot of trouble to go to, the man said.

But we're having fun in the meantime, the girl said. We're having an adventure and we're learning a lot about ourselves.

Why do you want to go to therapy? the man said.

The girl laughed. Why does anybody want to go to therapy? she asked.

The man did not know the answer to this seemingly obvious question.

I've always had a fantasy about going to therapy and saying not a single true thing about myself.

Why would you want to do that? the man said.

Because, the girl said. I could become anyone.

You could become your own most impossible person, the man thought.

I'd imagine that's difficult, the man said. Saying not a single true thing. The truth creeps in. Every good lie is founded on a truth.

Then I'll tell bad lies, the girl said.

So when you get home, the man said, what bad lies will you tell about us?

Behind him, he heard the snip of a lighter.

I don't know, the girl said through her exhale. That all depends on what happens.

Chadwick

She stood at the threshold to the man's house. I am dreaming this, she thought, I am surely dreaming this.

The man slipped behind her to shut the door. It latched meaningfully with a chunky, no-going-back sound that echoed through his foyer.

She should have been shocked by the man—by the mere fact of him standing here before her—but instead she felt seized by a more pressing panic. *Her mother had met the man.* Impossible, unthinkable. In all her many imagined permutations of the past, she had never once entertained this scenario. But if her mother had met the man then her previous theory, supported by her vision of her mother and Dr. Hammer sitting around his living room drinking coffee liqueur, was violently upstaged. The table overturned, the image ignited from the sides and consumed itself. In the bright blankness, nothing new coalesced. Her head was a stunned and newly empty space, the hole from which a wisdom tooth had just been pulled, the pain dulled by Novocain and a dense plug of gauze.

She was struck by the smell of cooking fish.

Sorry, the man said, gesturing toward the kitchen. I'm making dinner.

She stared at him numbly.

Fish, the man explained.

He smiled uneasily. His face had changed so little that she was confident she'd have recognized him on a plane or in a hardware store, she'd have experienced that electrocuted vertigo sensation that attended all unexpected meetings with people you'd relegated not only to the past but to your imagination. He had ceased to exist for her.

I'm not hungry, she said.

No no, he said, it was just that—when I imagined seeing you again, I didn't factor in the possibility that my house would smell of fish.

I love the smell of fish, she said.

Nobody loves the smell of other people's fish, he said. Drink? Vodka? Wine? Vodka?

Vodka, she said.

They remained awkwardly in the foyer. His house reminded her of a hotel business suite—functional and striving to offend no living creature. The walls were painted a drab khaki, the at-attention living-room furniture upholstered the color of an unexceptional dog, a generic gray-tan-brown that would, she imagined, appear browner in the sun, or more tan, or more gray. A kaleidoscope of blah is how she would describe his decor if asked; she repeated this phrase—*a kaleidoscope of blah a kaleidoscope of blah*—as a way to calm herself.

The smell of fish became the smell of burned fish.

So then, the man said. Can you hold on a minute?

He abandoned her in the foyer without inviting her farther inside. She considered leaving. She'd dreamed of seeing the man again, of course she had, but this reunion was not as she'd imagined it would be. She'd imagined they would fall back into an easy rapport tinged with hostility and a slight erotic promise that no real-world concerns would have spoiled in the interim. She'd imagined her insides would flutter wildly, as though she had swallowed a small and giddy bird. She'd imagined that she would discover that all these years she'd been waiting for an unspecified *something* to happen to her, and that this *something* was embodied by the man. The loneliness of this realization was overwhelming.

The man returned, face sweaty, hands fumbling with a dish towel.

That's that, he said. Tossed it to the cats. Figure of speech. Wouldn't want you to think I'd become a cat person. Oh. I forgot your vodka.

The man disappeared again.

Make yourself comfortable, he called from the kitchen.

This, she wanted to inform him, would be an impossibility.

She slung her coat over a chairback and sat rigidly on the couch amidst his kaleidoscope of blah. If she'd known she'd be seeing the man tonight, she might have taken more care to appear as the remarkable girl he'd once known, rather than the invisible woman she'd become. Maybe, she reflected, her disappointment upon seeing the man had nothing to do with him; maybe her disappointment was inspired only by herself, and her own failure to be instantly transformed by his appearance. But at least, she thought, at least she could still be upended by a person, even if the upending was due to a disappointment. Better than seeing Bettina Spencer and experiencing nothing except the nostalgic sensation of lack, a distant muscle memory of what it used to be like to succumb to the magic pull of a stranger.

Here's your vodka, said the man. He held his glass in one hand, the vodka bottle wedged under his arm.

He sat in an easy chair opposite her. The coffee table, a glossy blank slab between them, supported no books or magazines. No photos lined the fireplace mantel. The framed paintings on the walls—reproductions—were of gray harbors and gray piers and distantly gray lobster boats, not depressing exactly, more meditative and sober, portraits of bland stolidness.

He placed the vodka bottle on the coffee table.

Can I offer you something to eat? the man said. Nuts?

She shook her head.

The only thing worse than the smell of other people's fish is the smell of other people's burned fish, he said apologetically.

It's not the fish, she said. To be honest I don't have much of an appetite.

Me neither, he concurred.

Amazingly, she thought, he had barely aged. Yes, his skin had turned more sheeny and hidelike and it was stretched tighter over his face as though he had shrunk it one day at the beach. She was relieved to note that his lips had not retracted into his mouth, lending him the inwardly seething puppet look so many men his age suffered from. They remained on the exterior of his face, more darkly red, concentrated in color and thickness like a dried cranberry.

He still had very nice lips.

How about a fire, the man said, slapping his thighs. I've gotten better at building fires since you last saw me.

He stood beside the fireplace, its marble mantel so highly shined it could have been made of molded plastic, and flicked a light switch on the wall. She heard a *click* and a *whump!* Blue flames jagged upward through a symmetric crisscross of fake logs.

He smiled at her proudly, but she could tell he feared that he appeared silly, or incomplete, or somehow lacking to her.

That's better, he said, rubbing his hands together in anticipation of the heat headed his way. Who knew it would snow in early November?

It's been a week of unexpected occurrences, she said, training her gaze toward the fire and holding it there. She wanted to give him the chance to examine her privately, to assess how she'd changed—hair more coarse and gravity-bound and less an iridescent nimbus, cheeks less voluptuous, nose longer and more prominent, total face effect verging, in her opinion, on that of a fancy spook-eyed hound—so he could gauge whether the girl he'd known before had hearkened her at all.

So, he said, thrusting his glass over the coffee table toward her. Cheers.

Cheers, she said.

If she were narrating this, she thought, she would say an uncomfortable silence descended. She would say the problem with fake fires is that they don't crackle and snap, they don't make noises to relieve an awkward silence nor do anything unexpected that justifies a pretend diversion. All she could hear was the steady, numbing rush of gas into the perforated metal floor of the hearth. What had run through her mother's mind when she'd met the man? Had she thought: *This man maybe had sex with my daughter.* Had she thought: *This stranger is a memory touchstone that reminds me of no one so much as her.*

She pushed her mother away and she easily evaporated. Her mother did not belong here.

She tipped back her glass, finished the vodka in one swallow.

Are you married? she said, holding out her glass for a refill.

The man raised an eyebrow.

Is that too personal a question to ask? she said.

It's nice to be asked a personal question, the man said as he filled her glass. Rather than told the personal answer.

I've lost my touch, she said. Unlike you—she gestured toward the fireplace—I haven't been improving my skill set.

I doubt you've lost your touch, the man said. Too quickly, she thought. Almost eagerly. She allowed herself to plainly stare at him. What was the point in coyness? She was too old. He was too old.

Be that person, she could see him pleading. *Be that person so that I can be that person.* If she was disappointed in her ability to be transformed by him, he was equally fearful of his inability to be transformed by her.

She could not be that person.

Are you married? she repeated.

No, the man said.

You never remarried?

No, he said. Does that upset you?

Why would it upset me, she said.

He shrugged. Because it's upsetting, he said.

Better than remarrying five times unsuccessfully, she said. Better than remarrying your ex-wife.

The man chased a small object—lint or a bug—around the inside of his vodka glass. He wiped his finger on his pants.

Maybe I did remarry my ex-wife but I'm too embarrassed to tell you, the man said.

You shouldn't care what I think, she said.

Does that seem plausible to you? he persisted. That I remarried my ex-wife and lived miserably ever after?

She could not be that person.

Endings never were my forte, she said, more sharply than she intended.

The man appeared pained by her remark. But he pushed this reaction away.

But you're here, he said, as though her being here represented an ending of some kind, and in his view a successful one.

I'm here, she agreed.

Good, he said. I mean it. I'm glad.

You were expecting me, she said. That's what you said when you answered the door.

I've been expecting you every day for the past fourteen years, he said. Weren't you expecting me?

No, she said.

He appeared puzzled.

But *you* found *me*, he said, somewhat defensively.

Roz Biedelman gave me your address, she said.

She realized how this sounded.

But I came here because I wanted to, she added.

Ah, he said.

I don't suppose you want to explain, she said.

How Roz got my address? he said.

She nodded.

How do you think she got it? he said.

She stifled another barbed retort by returning her gaze to the whooshing gas jets and the five blue flames. The fake fire was so absurdly fake; whoever had designed it had *tried* to make it look fake, as though the whole enjoyment behind a fake fire was the fake part, not the fire part.

She was sick to death of fakeness.

You know what they say, he said, prodding her. Hesitation is the modesty of cowards.

You know what they also say, she said. Sarcasm is the lame humor of assholes.

He smiled, evidently pleased.

See? he said. Found your touch and it's only been two minutes.

I have no idea how Roz got your address, she said stonily.

No? he said.

No, she said.

Pah, he said. You're no fun.

He polished off his vodka, hiding his face in his glass to mask his displeasure. He set the empty glass dramatically onto the coffee table. His face aged ten years with no forced smile to scaffold it. She could sense that he was no longer scared of her, and that this was what scared him. In desperation, he was goading her to toy with him again, even if, deep down, he knew the effect was pointless. His life, she assumed, was defined by a soul-deadening certainty. Today the paper will come. Today I will have lunch alone, today I will want to eat spaghetti for dinner but will wisely opt for a salmon fillet that will stink up my house because nobody unexpected ever appears.

More? he said, pouring himself a hefty, practiced slug. Or I could fix you a cocktail I learned from my ex-ex-brother-in-law. He calls it the meerkat fizz. Brings warmth to the belly.

More vodka is fine, she said, suspecting he had become a high-functioning alcoholic. It would explain the drab order of his house, the late and ultimately expendable dinner.

It's not like you're driving tonight, the man pointed out, as though she needed further convincing. It's not like you're going anywhere.

Prophetic words, she said.

Aren't you gloomy, he said. And if you weren't expecting me to answer my door, whom were you expecting?

Dr. Hammer, she said, seeing no reason not to tell him the truth.

I believe he lives in Colorado Springs.

I have no idea where he lives, she said. Obviously.

He's in Colorado Springs, he said. He works as a physical therapist.

You've been keeping better tabs than me, she said.

Does that seem crazy to you? he said, somewhat hopefully.

More pathetic than crazy, she said.

The man smiled.

The insult posing as for-your-own-good honesty, the man said. You must have really missed me all these years.

She didn't reply.

I'm just trying to get you to talk, he said.

Why don't you talk for a change, she said. Why don't you tell me about Roz.

You're wondering how I know Roz, he said.

She nodded.

I don't, he said.

She gazed at him ruefully.

I know Roz through my ex-wife, he said. My ex-wife joined ZAIRE.

RWANDA, she corrected. You beat your ex-wife?

Wishful thinking on her part. She just wanted to belong to a group.

Seems everyone's joined that group at one time or another, she said.

Cult is more like it. That Roz is some kind of brainwasher.

She had the strange urge to come to Roz's defense. But she remained quiet.

My ex-wife started to leave messages on my machine, he said. Accusations like "Your ego-driven love style has scarred my wellspring of self-regard." But occasionally she was more circumspect. "I forgot to tell you about the time we played boccie with a dwarf. I forgot to tell you what a bastard you were in Milan."

And you told your ex-wife about me, she said, hastening him toward a logical connection that mattered to her.

I did, he said. And she told Roz.

When was this? she asked.

Just after the trial, he said. I figured what was done was done.

You figured your life had become unrelentingly dull and you needed some attention, she wanted to say, but didn't.

I needed to talk to someone, he offered lamely.

I've found something that might be of interest to you.

Her heart prickled. He was an idiot, she thought. She wanted to say to him: *You are an idiot.* But she wanted to grind his face into his idiocy by spelling it out.

And what better person to tell your story to than your ex-wife, she said, your ex-wife who was involved with a therapist who knew me and my family—is that what you were so innocently thinking when you "needed someone to talk to"?

The man sipped his vodka meditatively.

You're extremely cynical about people's motivations, he said. You know that, don't you?

Actually, she said, refilling her own glass this time, I cling to an extremely simplistic and infantile way of viewing the world. I'm a grudge holder. This is because I haven't properly separated from my mother. Or so I've recently been told.

She realized, afterward, that she sounded more bitter than she'd intended. More self-pitying. But maybe she was bitter and self-pitying, and if she was, what was the harm in behaving that way? He was a stranger. She didn't need to keep up appearances for his sake.

I'm sorry about your mother, he said. Her death must have come as quite a shock.

Her mother. And there she was again, her mother, a genie summoned from the fake hearth, a propane sprite available at the flick of a light switch. *Her mother.* Again she tried to conjure the evening when her mother had rung the man's bell. *That* must have come as quite a shock, she wanted to respond. And then what? Probably the man was impressed by how much her mother looked like her and yet how much not like her. As though she and her mother had once been identical twins, but she had been raised in a vatful of warm milk and her mother on an uninhabited coastal rock among puffins. Since her mother wasn't one for stalling, she would have asked the man, point-blank, if he knew her daughter. I am dying, she would have told him, but not out of any need for pity am I telling you this. I want you to feel badly if you lie to me.

She searched the man's face for confirmation of these unspoken suspicions, but the man's face belied nothing. He was an empty person, he'd always been empty and that was why she'd chosen him. He was easy to fool. He wouldn't be able to see that she was as empty as he was.

She was overcome by the most unexpected urge to kiss the man.

Before I forget, the man said, I have something for you.

He disappeared into the foyer. He returned, holding something behind his back.

I didn't get a chance to wrap it, he said. Close your eyes.

Annoyed, she obeyed. He stood at a distance from her, she could tell without seeing, reaching only as close as he needed to in order to place the unwrapped object in her hands.

Open them, he said.

She stared at the familiar cover.

Miriam: The Disappearance of a New England Girl, by Dr. E. Karl Hammer.

Very funny, she said.

It's a great read, he said. Though I admit also a bit of a letdown. I didn't recognize myself in K.

You'll just have to fake-abduct a more reliable narrator, she said. The night is still young.

It's a great read, the man repeated.

I wouldn't know, she was about to say, *I've never read it.* But the book had fallen open to the endpapers.

For "Miriam," she read.

Her vision reeled and she realized that she was suddenly, irreparably drunk. She slid out of her chair and extended her body along the warmed hearthstones. A fake log glowed next to her head.

I have beds, the man said.

No no, she said, I just need to lie down.

You're welcome to sleep here if you want, the man said.

I just have a headache, she said. Where did you get this book?

Can I offer you some peas? he said, ignoring her question.

I'm not hungry, she said. But the book—

—for your head. Nothing like a bag of frozen peas to help a headache.

He hopped out of his chair, seemingly relieved for the excuse to leave her. She lay motionless on the carpet, listening to the hiss of the gas. Above her, the unpainted rafters cast spooky whalebone shadows across the ceiling. *They are pulsating,* she thought. She was inside a whale, swallowed and afloat in its capacious middle on a cushioned shred of flotsam. Her hand had drifted toward the coffee table, on which she'd left the book. The book that, she had to assume, her mother had given the man. How else would he come to have it? She remembered as a teenager touching the spine, feeling that complicated thrill of shame, pride, magic, radiating from the cover. It was true—she had never read the book. The cover showed a photo of a girl with brown hair and bangs, the presumed Miriam, prettier than she was, or at least she appeared prettier from the fraction of her face that was visible as she strained toward a diffuse light source overhead. Her hair blew about, a loose strand here and there, like snakes from Medusa's head. Wind was implied. Heaven was implied, or salvation, or abduction by probably friendly aliens. The overall whiteness of the world threatened to erase her.

The man returned with a bag of frozen peas. He kneeled by her shoulder and draped the bag over her forehead. She smelled the metallic vegetable odor of a long-unthawed freezer.

Thanks, she said.

I don't want you to think I'm pathetic, he said, sitting back on his heels.

Because of the peas? she said.

Because I still think about you, he said. There are times when a person is susceptible to human meaningfulness. When I met you, I was susceptible.

Again, she was overcome by the urge to kiss him. This urge was not sexual, this urge was taunting and mean, it initiated from a vicious place. She turned her head toward the glowing ceramic logs; her lips felt blistered from the heat.

It helps that you never saw me again, she said. The need to kiss the man was momentarily supplanted by a migrainous confusion—wincing and debilitating.

That's true, the man said. But seeing you now, I'm not disappointed in you.

Thanks, she said.

You were a person worth remembering.

I was a person worth imbuing with an unwieldy amount of meaning-less symbolism, she said. Flash flash flash—*life-changing encounter.*

I'm going to say it again, the man said. You're being cynical.

She managed an awkward sip of vodka. Her knees parted, her mouth grew sloppy. *Kiss me,* she thought. *Shut up and kiss me.*

The man withdrew from her and sat on a mushroomy ottoman. He lit a match and extinguished it with a violent flick. He did this repeat-edly, tossing the used matches toward the fake fire.

Stop it, she said.

Sorry, he said. Bad habit. Do you want to hear more about Roz Biedelman?

I want to hear about my mother, she said bluntly, tired of the conver-sational foreplay. The man, even though she wanted to kiss him, was really just a means to an end. He was a means of communicating with her mother who had always, whether alive or dead, been a mute inhabi-tant of another world.

Your mother, he said. What do I know about your mother.

Don't play stupid, she said, the vodka and the headache flaring her impatience. Really, don't do it. It will make me hate you.

Hate, he said. You're not made for hate.

Nothing like a sweeping pronouncement about one's emotional inca-pacities to lessen the hatred impulse, she said.

She raised herself onto her elbow, her shirt falling open to expose the edge of her bra; in trying to arrange herself, she knocked *Miriam* from the coffee table to the floor; the book sprawled indecently in a wide split, spine so floppy from overwork that the extended pages lay flat against the rug.

So my mother came to see you, she said.

If you say so, the man said.

What did you tell her, she said. Her knees wove back and forth. She propped her temple on her palm, her fingers mussing her hair into a girl-ish tangle. She was asking for it, she certainly was.

The man remained impervious.

What would you have told her if you were me?

Fuck you, she said.

The man filled her glass with more vodka. To do so he had to lean over her body. His closer-up smell yanked her backward, through her present self to a limpid, more dangerous time.

If you want to play, we might as well *play,* the man said. You haven't asked, but I still suffer from chronic, incurable insomnia. My night, as you already pointed out, is still young.

I don't want to play, she said.

That's too bad, isn't it, the man said, smiling. But the smile was a false smile; behind it the man was tense, even furious. Because I want to play, he said. And I know something you want to know. And besides, he said, softening slightly, this is for your own good.

Is it, she said.

At the conclusion of my ex-wife's ZAIRE involvement, he said, she was told to write down everything she remembered about her life with me so that she could move on. "If you write it down yourself," she told me, "then it belongs to you."

Am I supposed to be writing this down? she asked him, praying he'd sink beside her on the floor, curl himself around her, and allow her to disappear into sleep.

I'll give you the beginning, he said. The girl's mother received a letter. From a certain doctor. "I've found something that might be of interest to you."

This is stupid and I'm drunk, she said.

Indulge me, he said.

Fine, she thought. One last story. One last golden-spun piece of bull-shit. What was the harm in it?

She hates the doctor, she said. She'd rip the letter up.

But let's say she didn't rip it up, he said. Let's say she read the letter and put it in a drawer. Until she became sick.

Until she became sick, she agreed.

And? he said.

Overhead, the whalebones wavered. She exhaled, irritated with him for trying to force the evening back into a claustrophobic ski cabin where their lives could no longer fit.

As with many sick people, she said, she admitted only to herself that her curiosity was finite and would soon be reduced to a hard lump of carbon, unable to absorb anything new. To all outward appearances she behaved no differently than she ever had; looming extinction would not pressure her into altering her exterior. Is this what you had in mind?

But inside she felt differently, the man said. Inside, she had to know. So she contacted the doctor.

She contacted the doctor, she said. The doctor, being a doctor, proceeded to doctor her. The girl's mother, though she wouldn't admit it, began to enjoy the conversations with the doctor. She tried very hard to continue hating the doctor, because hating her had become an identity for the girl's mother. But the doctor was strangely helpful and understanding. Finally, the doctor handed the girl's mother an address. Beneath the address the doctor wrote, "He will want to see you." The girl's mother's time was running out. So she went to see the man in the middle of the night.

Did he want to see her?

Yes and no, she said. His life, he liked to believe, had taken him past this incident, and he had no need to revisit it. But a part of him felt confused by the girl, and this confusion had evolved into an unresolved hurt. Her mother represented an opportunity for him.

He was using the girl's mother, he said.

It was a mutual using. So he invited her inside his house.

And they talked, said the man.

They talked.

What did the man tell her, asked the man.

I . . . I don't know, she said, her imagination rearing back to the threshold. This was wrong, she thought. Wrong wrong wrong.

Maybe the girl's mother didn't talk to the man, she said. Can I change the beginning?

Of course, he said. It's your story.

She rang his bell, not in the middle of the night, but in the daytime. When he answered the door she handed this copy of *Miriam* to him. Then she left.

Without talking to him, he said.

No, she said. No, she talked to him. She said, "Give this to her."

Why would she do that? he said.

Because she was a terminally ill conflict avoider, she said, her voice tightening. Did I tell you that she refused to see me before she died?

But why would she give me the book? the man said.

Because, she said, if I managed to find you, then I would know.

You would know that she had found me, the man said.

I would know that she knew about you, she said. And the book would mean that she forgave me.

She started to cry. She didn't feel ashamed. She stared again into the fire, the tears running sideways over her cheek and spooling their tickly way into her ear. He didn't speak and neither did she. In the middle of this silence, she sensed his mood change. For some reason, who knew the reason, maybe because she was crying. The man felt badly.

I'm sorry, he said. I thought this might be fun. But now I realize, I'm being cruel.

You're not, she said.

No, I am, the man said.

Tell me what you told her, she said. I did what you asked. Now you have to tell me.

The man didn't respond.

Tell me everything, she said again. Her tears became less urgent as her composure began, once again, to seize her insides. She glanced at the book jacket, at the girl with the snake hair, and thought: *YOU. You are turning me to stone.* She shoved the book away. She wanted to prolong this moment of watery messiness. She wanted to cry more and more and more.

I didn't tell her anything, the man said.

You could have, she said. I wouldn't have minded. You could have told her everything.

I really couldn't, the man said.

Because you feel guilty? she said. There's no need—

No, the man interrupted. No. I couldn't tell your mother anything because I've never met her.

She raised up on her elbow.

Stop it, she said.

He stared into his vodka, avoiding her.

I did what you asked me to do, she said, starting to cry again. I *did* what you *asked.*

And I said I was sorry, the man said. But I've never met your mother.

A wild violence gripped her. Honestly, she thought, if she had a knife she would plunge it into his chest. When would he stop with the stories? When would he realize that lying was pointless, that even very bad lies were founded in some way on the truth? Her heart raced as if she were under attack and she spun through ways to protect herself: Speak her mind? Stab the man? Kiss him? Leave? But this decision lost its urgency. Her chest filled with that altitude-dropping queasiness she experienced on turbulent planes. She could tell by his face—he wasn't lying to her.

He had never met her mother.

I'm sorry, the man said a third time.

He had tricked her, she thought. *He* had tricked *her.* She laughed. A short, self-mocking laugh. If she weren't drunk and exhausted she might have had the energy to be furious with him, but instead she found herself overwhelmed with admiration. *Good for him,* she thought. He had succeeded where everyone else, including herself, had failed. He had tricked her into revealing to him her most private hopes.

She dried her face brusquely on her sleeve. A fucking fool is what she was. Her mother was dead. What she failed to tell Mary while she was alive is what Mary would always fail to know from her. But there are other ways of knowing things, she reminded herself. There are other ways. She just couldn't come up with any more ways. She had run out of possibilities.

Why are you sorry? she said. It's hardly your fault.

I encouraged you, the man said. I let you go on longer than I should have.

Stop blaming yourself, she said. It's ... *self-involved.*

I'm just saying, he said.

Everything I did was done because I wanted to do it, she said. Do you understand?

The man didn't respond.

If my mother had come to see you, that is what I would have wanted you to tell her. *Everything I did was done because I wanted to do it.*

The man still didn't respond. She could tell that he wanted her to leave.

So, she said. How did you get the book?

It's a long story, he said.

A secondhand bookstore, she guessed. Or wait. Is your ex-wife involved again?

The man didn't respond.

I thought you wanted to play, she said nastily.

Really, he said. I think we should probably end this.

End, she said. Is this the end?

I think the ending happened some time ago, the man said.

She wanted to kiss the man so badly that it was like an urge to vomit. Kissing a person, she understood then, was not about desire, kissing a person was just a way to make them stop talking. He had called her Scheherazade and yet, she reflected, Scheherazade's story rang so falsely to her now, the idea that one told stories in order to avoid harm; by telling stories Scheherazade was asking for it. Stories were a way of asking for it—to be killed, to be kissed.

He stood from his chair; he picked up her coat and handed it to her from a safe distance.

She struggled from the floor, brain throbbing bloodily in her ears. She put on her coat, her hat, her scarf.

Don't forget that, he said, pointing to the book.

I don't want it, she said.

But it's yours, he said.

Actually, she said, it's yours.

I'm sure your mother *would* have wanted you to have this book, the man said. What I'm saying is—I'm sure she forgave you.

You have no idea what she thought, she said.

She stared at the book. She didn't want it anymore. The book, she thought, was just another book that she had never read.

But I have a hunch, he said. She sounded like a nice woman. A forgiving woman.

You don't know anything about my mother, she said.

I feel as if I do, the man said, staring at her searchingly.

She shook her head, dislodging his gaze.

You're so, so mistaken, she said. She wasn't anything like me.

Really? the man said.

Really, she said.

But your aunt told me that you were your mother's daughter, he said.

What? she said, felled by a sudden wave of dizziness. She kneeled on the floor, hands braced on the coffee table.

When she gave me the book, the man said. Your aunt sat on that couch for hours and told me all about you two.

She stretched out on the floor, hand gripping her head. Above her the

quavering rafters closed in, beside her the fake blue flames made a tim-
panic snap so deafening it might have been her own veins bursting and
flooding her brain. The bones thundered everywhere. *Where am I?* she
thought, but she knew the answer. She had paddled through the whale's
organs, its veins, sliding her way into the flammable chambers of its
wooden heart.

Tell me everything she said about me, she said. *My aunt.*

What Might Have Happened

The girl blindfolded him with a dinner napkin and led him up-stairs by the hand. She guided him around the narrow banister, wincing as he missed, barely, knocking his knee against the small bureau in which she'd found the movie reels. He had very little sense of caution, she noticed. He followed her willingly even though she'd done nothing to gain his trust; she might as readily push him backward off the second-floor balcony as onto the stale eiderdown puff covering the master bed. She found herself growing angry and irritated with him, a response that she interpreted as misplaced fear. She was a girl, he was a man, she was, in the parlance of her mother's worldview about all things sexual, *asking for it.* She was asking for it and if she was asking for it, she wanted to want what she was asking for. But anger was easier to entertain than desire at the moment, it heated her body up just below the skin and might even, in a darkened attic, be mistaken for desire.

She quickened her pace down the hallway, leading the man up the pinched staircase at the hall's end. *Oops,* she said, insincerely, as the man cracked his forehead against the attic doorjamb. *Hunch down,* she ordered. *Step up.*

She arranged the man in the center of the rugs she'd found rolled into musty tubes and piled in the attic corners. She unrolled them but still they humped up in the centers, clinging to their former shape.

Sit, she said.

The man sat. Above him, swaths of loose insulation, stapled between the rafters, spilled like a stop-time pink avalanche over his head.

He fumbled with his blindfold.

Absolutely not, she said. Keep that on.

Keep it on? he said. He sounded drunk to her, and this redoubled her anger. What an idiot, she thought. Allowing his guard down to such a degree that he'd become drunk. She found it hard to muster anything but disgust for him.

She fiddled with the cord on the old projector, a two-ton dinosaur the blue-silver shade of an institutional folding chair she'd managed, not without risking the loss of her toes, to heft atop a stacked set of Reader's Digest books about geology. She flipped the power switch, igniting the rattle-hum exhale of the exhaust fan. The light through the lens hit the center of the white bedspread she'd wedged into the sash of the attic's only window.

What is this, said the man, his head turning toward the sound. Are you vacuuming?

We're watching movies, the girl said.

The man licked his lips. With his blindfold on she found herself more attuned to his other features. His nose was too large, his mouth a nervous twang of flesh that appeared to vibrate even when he was speechless.

His lips disgusted her.

She pretended he was a soldier; she pretended he was a soldier who'd had both of his eyes blasted out by a hand grenade. She pretended he was a man in need of her help and general loving assistance.

I'm going to prove to you I'm not a liar, said the girl, which is why I wanted us to come to this cabin.

Was it *you* who wanted to come to the cabin? the man said. I thought it was my idea.

I made it look like your idea.

Ah, he said. Every idea I've ever had was your idea.

Nice way to deny responsibility, said the girl.

No no, said the man, his docile good humor making it hard to imagine him as a soldier who'd had his eyes pulverized, minusculized, pummeled, beshattered. I just didn't want to take credit where credit wasn't due.

The girl resisted an urge to kick the man.

She attached the first reel to the projector, removed from a canister marked KALAHARI I. The film ticked and stuttered. A bearded man appeared on the screen wearing aviator sunglasses and a khaki jumpsuit. Wherever he pointed his gangly hand, the camera followed. A gang of meerkats twittered on a cracked mud surface, their little claws upraised, their ears flicking backward and forward as though they could hear the sounds of people from a different decade and on a different continent watching them.

Let's begin at the beginning, she said. Here we are standing outside my family's brownstone.

All I see are shadows, said the man, his face turned toward the bedspread.

This is all part of the process, said the girl. Didn't your ex-wife tell you?

No, he said.

A person is better able to remember through abstract prompts to the memory, she said. If you are told exactly what to remember, you'll never trust it was *your* memory. It will exist as a story somebody told you. It won't feel like *yours*. This is all about you reclaiming your story.

Fine, said the man tightly.

So here we are standing in front of my family's brownstone, said the girl. How old am I?

How should I know, said the man. I can't see a goddamned thing.

Look harder, she said. How old do I look.

The man didn't respond. He rubbed at his eyes through the napkin.

Do I look twelve, said the girl.

The man raised his head.

Sure, he said.

Say it, she said.

You look twelve.

What are you thinking?

Right now?

In the movie. What are you thinking *in the movie.*

I'm thinking that a person is watching us.

You're paranoid, she interpreted.

I'm wondering about logistics, he said. If I'm on film, a person is filming me.

Two meerkats began to chase each other around a spiky, shrublike cactus.

Your ex-wife is filming you, said the girl.

Then I'm feeling badly for my ex-wife.

Because you're attracted to me, said the girl. Because you're experiencing inappropriate sexual feelings toward a young girl.

Because my ex-wife couldn't have children, he said.

Why was that?

She had an abortion before she met me, he said. She was no longer able to have children. Isn't that what you told me?

So your interest in me is purely paternal, said the girl.

At first, said the man. That's how it always begins.

The khaki-jumpsuit man was joined by a stubby, dark-skinned man. The stubby man wore a pair of soccer shorts; he carried a small flute. Both men smiled that wide, awkward smile of strangers being observed with nothing to say to each other.

So we became father-daughter friends, she said. Here we are in the Commons, going for a row. I'm waving to the camera so enthusiastically that I lose my balance and fall between your legs.

I am rowing, he said.

You are rowing, but you drop your oars and catch me. This is the first time it occurs to you that a father is only a father if he wants to have sex with his daughter.

How does my ex-wife respond to this?

She's oblivious, said the girl. What I just described to you happened offscreen.

Oh, he said.

Your ex-wife, who is a secret racist, was filming a biracial couple on a park bench having a fight.

Oh, he said again.

Fast-forward now. Are you getting tired?

What?

Tired.

I never get tired, said the man. Which doesn't mean I'm not bored.

So you're bored, she said. Not my fault. It's your life we're watching.

I didn't say it was your fault, he said. I have been bored and not tired my whole new life.

Here I am outside your window, she said. You are in your attic. You're filming me from above as I skip rope on the sidewalk. What are you thinking?

You're outside on purpose, he said. You're outside my window skipping rope and wearing—let me guess—your school uniform.

Is that what you'd like me to be wearing?

The man scoffed.

Answer the question, she said.

What I want has nothing to do with it, he said.

Which is why we're doing this act of reclamation, she said.

The man frowned.

What am I doing, the girl prodded.

You know what you're doing, the man said.

Tell me, she said. In your own words.

The man paused. She sensed that he was closing his eyes, not literally, since he was blindfolded, but now he was actually seeing images on
the backs of his eyelids.

You parade back and forth in front of my window, he said. You hike
up your skirt, you behave in a cartoonishly seductive manner to make me
pay attention to you.

Interesting, she said.

Don't flatter yourself, he said.

If I were a therapist, I might say that you're blaming me for what's
about to happen, she said.

I am blaming you, the man said hotly. Should I not blame you?

I was a girl, she said. An innocent girl.

You're a transparent and not very subtle tease, the man said.

Fuck you, the girl said tonelessly.

I was just *sitting* there, the man pointed out, growing riled beneath his
blindfold, his cheeks and chin covered in an anxious sheen. I was just sitting there in my stupid car reading my stupid paper and waiting for
something less stupid to happen to me. I was bored. I was bored and I
was so, so awake.

The girl fell silent. The khaki man's and the stubby man's heads
moved in unison as they watched a bird overhead. The bird's silhouette
flitted across their upturned faces like a fast-moving cloud.

So that's your excuse, she said. You were bored.

I'm not trying to excuse myself.

Then you're fine with being a pervert, she said.

The man with the soccer shorts blew his flute. Across the cracked mud expanse, a meerkat rolled onto its back, legs jerking. The khaki-jumpsuit man's smile froze.

The man's upper lip curled into his teeth.

He didn't respond.

You're a *pervert*, the girl goaded. Don't you have anything to say to that?

The man blinked, his fists clenching and unclenching.

He didn't respond.

The girl laughed meanly.

What, he said.

Nothing, she said. I take it back. You're not a pervert.

The man in the khaki jumpsuit stared at the camera.

You're too boring to be a pervert, she said. You say you're bored, but you're not bored, you're *boring*. I've tried my best, but I give up. I can't save you from yourself.

The man blinked rapidly beneath the napkin, little cloth shudders.

Fine, he said, voice tightening. I'm a pervert. Is that what you want to hear? Is it?

What do *you* want to hear, the girl corrected.

Me?

You're not talking for my benefit, she said. You're talking for your own.

The man in the khaki jumpsuit stared at the man with the killer flute.

Are you beyond? she asked, sweetly mocking. Are you beyond beyond?

The man pinched his head between his hands so forcefully that his forearms trembled. He was, she feared, committing some kind of strange suicide.

When he spoke, she did not recognize his voice.

I spied on you outside my window jumping rope, he said, a ridiculous activity for a twelve-year-old, but fine, that's how you enjoyed spending your afternoons, jumping rope outside the house of a married man you loved like a father. You wriggled and hopped and fiddled with your too-short skirt, the waistline rolled up a few sleazy turns, and bingo, it occurred to me that I desired you not as a daughter—because, let's say it, you're *not* my daughter—but as a girl, or a girl-woman, and I decided to molest you.

Nice, the girl said, though she felt spritzed, suddenly, by a nervous layer of sweat, the backs of her hands and her cheekbones tingling in the overheated attic.

The khaki-jumpsuit man ran into the center of the meerkat tribe folded around its dead. He opened and closed his hands, flashing his white palms at the sky.

Go on, she said.

Of course "molest" wasn't the word I used—I didn't use words, because when I tried to articulate my desires to myself all that materialized was your naked body. So one day I invited you up to my attic, and because you believed that you had engineered this invitation, you accepted. This was *your* show, this was your doing, this was all under your control.

The meerkats raised their heads one by one. Their noses quivered.

But then you had to shuck your school uniform for a pervert, then you saw that desire is an ugly force all its own, it cannot be controlled and certainly not by the object that inspired it. And so you learned a hard lesson.

The meerkats turned on the man like attack birds, flying at his pants legs and clawing his arms.

Or maybe not, the man continued. Maybe not because now you think, *I'm older*. Now you think, *I can control the situation*. But I wonder about that. I can sense you're scared.

Am I, she said.

Not of me. Of you. You can inspire desire, but you can't feel it your-self. How lonely that must feel. How terribly, terribly lonely.

The man with the killer flute smiled his wide smile.

The images ended, spooling into an unfocused burst of white.

The end, said the man. He did not remove his blindfold. He re-mained in the center of the carpets.

He stretched out his legs, massaging his kneecaps.

I'm right, aren't I, he said. I get it now. I understand why we're here.

And that makes you feel superior, she said, her heart beating angrily. Or nervously. All her emotions combined indistinctly, like a Morse code message so rapid it fibrillates into nonsense.

More than you do, the man said.

At least I wasn't such an idiot that I stopped to light a cigarette in the middle of a street. At least I didn't hate my life so much that I was will-ing to nearly kill myself to become another person.

And you aren't? the man said meanly. What a disappointment.

Above the man, the pink tongues of insulation waggled at her mock-ingly.

The girl coughed. The insulation tongues shed tiny iridescent fila-ments made visible by the projector's lights. She breathed them in and they burrowed like quills into her throat. She would cough for years, she thought.

Aren't you willing? the man taunted. *Scheherazade?*

Shut up, she thought, trying to work up her nerve. *Shut up shut up.*

She coughed again, a timid, exploratory cough, nothing involuntary about it. But soon it became involuntary. Soon she found herself so over-come by the quilled sensation in her throat that she could barely catch her breath and even, in a strangely becalmed fashion, felt herself begin-ning to lose consciousness—the white blankness of the projector breathed onto the bedspread, the white blurriness caused by hyperventi-lation—as she stumbled over to the blindfolded man, who, clumsily, caught her between his outstretched legs.

Apparently, she began, ignoring the throat scratchiness that made her eyes water so profusely she worried he might think that she was crying. She pushed her face into his face, her hands braced on his inner thighs.

Apparently, she repeated, her lips over his, I am.

West Salem

She took the Mercedes because the keys were in the ignition, parked on a side driveway that skirted an orchard of apple trees besieged by silhouetted vines; the predawn sky pushed through the diamond-shaped gaps and created a menacing landscape of points and tangles. The Mercedes was salt-scarred to the point of looking frostbitten in places, the baseboards were filigreed with rust, and the heat, when she cued it, stank of charred mice nests.

Sleepy still, drunk still, hovering on the bruised edge of a hangover, her brain was strangely suited to the task of driving. She passed through the gate without incurring further damage to either cars or the wall. Driving down Water Street and toward the empty town, however, her hands started to shake, her stomach yawning acidly as the vodka dregs were suctioned up by her capillaries and distributed to the only parts of her not already saturated with alcohol. Her body was in shock, not yet ready to register the damage she'd done to herself last night as she revisited, again and again, the bottom of her glass.

Though she'd gotten less than two hours of sleep, she was giddy—practically manic. This was the starry limbo period that followed a shock; she allowed her as-yet-unprocessed night with the man to stun her into this strange, dreamy happiness. She fiddled with the radio dial and found a newscast that pinged off her eardrums but grounded her to the predawn day outside her windshield, a grounding that was challenged by her distorted take on her surroundings. To her right she saw a woman in a white bathrobe walking a dog in a white bathrobe, a tiny dog in a tiny white bathrobe—how ludicrous!—a dog in a tiny white bathrobe that transformed, as she passed closer and the woman entered the dimming circle of a streetlight, into a normal Pomeranian, just fur and eyes and little black feet. Normal Pomeranian is an oxymoron, *hah hah hah*, she thought, but still she repeated it in her head, *normal Pomeranian, normal Pomeranian*, and this repetition anchored her to a day that seemed determined to feel unreal.

Given her failure with shortcuts, she stuck to the main roads and spent the drive concentrating on the salt- and snow-scummed yellow line while mentally deliberating over what she would tell Aunt Helen. The truth was out of the question, so she tried to conjure a plausible reason to explain why she'd needed Aunt Helen's car in the middle of the night, why she'd failed to return with the car, why the car was unreturnable for the foreseeable future. Usually she excelled at this sort of challenge but bending her head around what might have happened, rather than what actually happened, felt as ridiculously impossible as animal shapeshifting; she could sooner transform herself into a normal Pomeranian, so entrenched in her own queasy self did she feel.

Two miles from her house she saw, driving toward her, her father's car. As he passed her she caught the mercury flash of his face through the streetlight-reflecting windshield, neither tired nor sad nor relieved. He looked blandly dead to her, void of the pinch and scowl of everyday humanness.

She slowed the Mercedes and turned into the next available driveway, thinking she would follow him. Not to spy on him but to make sure that he hadn't died behind the wheel, or died last night, or died earlier in the week without his daughters noticing. She owed him this much; the man needed some reminding that he was, at least technically, alive. Or maybe it was she who needed the reminding.

Her father drove under the speed limit and so she caught up with him quickly, just as he began his counterclockwise trip around the West Salem rotary. Three-quarters of the way around he pulled into the diner lot. She pulled in after him, parking near the Dumpster.

She waited in the Mercedes until he'd gone inside. She watched him order a cup of coffee and make a joke that the waitress laughed at out of politeness. She walked quickly to the diner's door, passing just outside her father's seat.

She saw him notice her through the window. She saw him pretending that he hadn't.

When she slid into the booth opposite him, he was busy reading the menu.

He didn't glance up.

"You're out late," he said.

"You're up early," Mary said.

The waitress appeared. Mary ordered a coffee. Her father ordered eggs and bacon and toast.

"I'm not hungry," Mary said.

"Make it two," he said to the waitress.

They sat in silence; sizzling noises exploded from the kitchen.

Her father was dressed for the outside, wool pants and a chamois shirt, a down vest, a wool hat. He reached into the pocket of his down vest and placed the plastic baggie filled with ashes on the table.

The baggie, Mary noted distastefully, had become creased from multiple handlings and transfers; the plastic had turned cloudy and begun to look like trash.

"And here I thought you were dining alone," Mary said.

Her father tore open a sugar packet, added it to his mug, failed to stir it.

"You don't think much of me, do you?" her father said.

"What?" Mary said.

"You heard me," he said.

Mary reddened.

"I was just making a joke," she said. "I'm sorry. It was inappropriate."

Her father didn't reply. She'd clearly upset him.

"Interpret it as the strangled sign of affection it's meant to convey," she persisted. "OK?"

She smiled beseechingly.

"No need to tell me how to interpret strangled signs of affection," her father said. "I've been doing it for thirty-seven years."

Her father turned his attention to the large plate-glass window to their right, to the mostly empty parking lot and the mostly quiet West Salem rotary. Frost veined the perimeter of the glass; rather than signaling the death knell of autumn, the tendrils looked to Mary like the hopeful beginnings of something, a crystalline root system surviving against all odds.

"Fine," Mary said. She gestured toward the baggie. "So then. What are you two getting up to after breakfast?"

Her father scrunched his face ruefully at the window.

"Golf course," he said.

"The country club?" Mary said.

"No," he said. "The public course."

Mary nodded. The coffee had begun to infiltrate her system, failing to awaken anything but her awareness that she'd recently, like two minutes ago, been drunk.

"Mum hated that club," she said.

He shrugged. "Could be," he said. "Could be she just liked to pretend that she hated it."

"Keeping up appearances," Mary said, her mind flashing to the book, wrapped in a plastic shopping bag and sitting on the passenger seat of the Mercedes.

"It wasn't easy," he said.

"I doubt it was," Mary said.

"What I mean is," her father said, "it cost her."

Mary nodded knowingly, though she had no idea what her father was talking about. Did he mean it gave her mother cancer? It made him love her mother less?

"We never told you girls," her father said, "but your mother and I talked about separating. More than once."

"You were married for a long time," Mary said, not at all surprised to hear this. She'd received the occasional guilt-inducing letter from Regina detailing the tension in the house, so much more thick and stagnant now that the three sisters, and their erratic energies, weren't around to destabilize the air.

"When I thought we'd reached the end of our marriage, I'd go golfing. I'd go to the place she pretended most to hate. When I got home I'd feel better."

He stared at her searchingly, as though wanting confirmation that he'd done a brave and unusual thing. Mary didn't know how to respond. Her father's meager form of rebellion was touching, but also sadly pathetic.

"So," her father said, changing the subject, "I won't ask what you've been up to."

"You don't have to ask," she said. "I'll tell you."

"Your mother used to disappear on me," he said, ignoring her offer. "Those last few weeks. When she could still drive. I never asked her where she went."

"Maybe she wanted you to ask," Mary said, considering for the first time the emotional hardships her mother must have suffered in this marriage—a happy enough marriage that was, like all permanent arrangements, an occasional prison for both parties. Her mother was obviously the more difficult personality, yes; but her father had made it easy for her to be difficult. He'd made it easy for her to be strangled by her own worst tendencies.

Her father stared at her balefully. "You think you know what she wanted," he said.

He was still angry with her, she thought. But then she more correctly read his expression: he was sincerely curious.

"I like to think so," she said. "But it's hard to distinguish what she wanted from what I want her to want. To say *she would have wanted this* is really to say *I want this*."

The waitress arrived with their food. Her father replaced the baggie in his vest pocket to make room for the plates.

"So then," her father said, salting up his eggs, "how about you come with me to the course."

Mary played with her eggs. They wobbled unappetizingly at the touch of a fork tine.

"What about the whale watch?" she said.

Her father shrugged. "That's just a lot of silliness, don't you think?"

Mary smiled.

"It is pretty silly," she said.

"Your mum's ashes won't know the difference between a whale sighting and a swamp view, and we won't have to get seasick."

"Fair point," Mary said.

"So what do you say," her father said. "Eat up and we'll go to the course together."

Her father stared at her with his rumpled bulldog eyes. Whatever she wanted from him, she realized, he wanted so much more from her. They had reached that parent-child turning point where she knew, or so she believed, what was better for him than he did. This realization flat-out broke her heart. Equally heartbreaking was the realization that she didn't want, or rather *need*, to scatter her mother's ashes. She had the book.

"I think," she said, putting a hand on his hand, "I think Mum would have wanted you to go alone."

As she pulled onto Rumney Marsh, she was greeted by the calming sight of Ye Olde Bastard walking his schnauzer, his wool coat over his pajamas, cuffs bunched inside the emerging fleece linings of his boots. He stared at her as she drove past, his face absent his usual extra helping of scorn. Maybe he was more friendly in the morning, she thought. Maybe he suddenly saw her as a colleague of the dawn. She waved to him—it seemed only polite—and his expression shifted from neutral to mystified, mystified to dubious, dubious to skeptical. She averted her eyes before his skepticism reverted back to scorn, because she wanted to locate a meaningful sign in Ye Olde Bastard's comparatively affable reception; she was different today, she'd sunk back to her common-denominator self and it took a man of gourmet derision like Ye Olde Bastard to detect it.

She parked the Mercedes where Aunt Helen's station wagon had been parked last night. She snuffed the engine and closed her eyes, inhaling the mildewed skank of floor mats. As she stepped into the street, a car slalomed past her, bulleting her face, her jacket, her pants with a gritty gray slush.

She yelped involuntarily. Ye Olde Bastard glowered at her from beneath his tam-o'-shanter.

The jerk, she thought. The crabby, controlling, heartless old jerk.

"Take Umbrage!" she yelled at him.

Ye Olde Bastard's schnauzer squatted to take a dump.

"Take Umbrage!" she repeated.

Ye Olde Bastard stooped awkwardly, his hand clad in a white surgical glove.

Her outrage stunned her awake more bracingly than the corrosive diner coffee, and she entered the kitchen feeling giddily refreshed. The kettle on the stove released a leisurely thread of steam through its snout. She heard, from the living room, the crumple of paper. Somebody was packing. Or somebody was unpacking. Maybe, she thought with a jolt of hopefulness, her father—since he was embracing his rebellious side— had decided not to sell the house. Maybe in a fit of predawn regret he'd enlisted Regina to unpack all the items meant for donation to the historical society, because he'd realized, from the gloom of his sleeping-pill coma, that total erasure of a person did not achieve total erasure of a person.

She heard a thumping noise and a high-pitched screech. Seconds later, a tail-tucked Weegee appeared, his nails skitching across the linoleum as he ran for the bathroom-cum-storage-closet. Mops and broomsticks toppled as he tried to mash himself into an invisible ball behind the toilet. She waited for the avenging form of Aunt Helen to appear, too corpse-colored for this hour, but nobody came to Weegee's rescue, a fate he'd obviously intuited by the fact that he'd lapsed into total silence in hopes that his enemy, whoever it was, might not discover him.

In the living room, Regina, still in her nightgown, kneeled before a pyramid of knotted newspaper balanced on the center of the shiny fireplace grate.

"*There* you are," Regina said. "I was worried."

"You were?" Mary said, out of breath, her mind's needle stuck in a manic groove. *Take Umbrage! Take Umbrage!*

"You've been gone for hours," she said. "Of course I was worried."

Mary, a tingle spreading under her chest, was just tired enough, just susceptible enough to be touched. Regina, she thought, was worried about *her*. This was the upside to losing your mother. Sisters rallied behind other sisters they once hated in new and supportive ways. Families, freed from the inevitable string of bad chemical reactions, were forced to regroup in formerly untenable molecular clusters.

"About me?" she said.

"*Yes* about you," Regina said.

"That's so sweet," Mary said.

Regina regarded her scornfully. "If you were dead I was going to have to deal with Aunt Helen myself."

"Oh," Mary said stupidly. *Take Umbrage!* "Is she awake?"

"God no," said Regina. "Pass me the sports section."

Mary passed Regina the sports section. She found herself wanting to tell her sister about her night with the man. She wanted to show her the book. She wanted to ask her: *What does it mean? What do you think it means?* She wanted to force her sister to entertain a question to which she'd already decided the answer.

"I drove Aunt Helen's car into a stone wall," Mary said.

"Did you total it?" Regina said.

"It found a higher calling," Mary said.

"Who found a higher calling?" Gaby asked from the hallway.

She appeared in the living-room archway, her nightgown streaked with rust and grease, her hair tucked into Regina's long-lost ski cap with the blue-and-red pompon.

What have we all been up to, Mary thought.

"Aunt Helen's car," Regina said.

"I couldn't find the ax," Gaby said. "Do you think it's in the attic?"

"Why would it be in the attic," Regina said.

"Because it's not in the garage," Gaby said.

"Why do you need the ax?" Mary asked.

"We don't have any kindling," Regina replied. "Did you *see*?" She pointed to the hat on Gaby's head.

"Congratulations," Mary said.

"I found it in Mum's old suitcase along with a pair of ice skates. I didn't find your book."

"Thanks for remembering to look," Mary said, slipping her hand inside her coat pocket to feel the chill sheathing of the plastic bag.

"Don't you think we should have one fire in the new fireplace before we sell the house?" Regina asked, snatching the hat off of Gaby's head and pulling it onto her own. "Especially since Dad is off scattering Mum's ashes without us?"

Regina stared at Mary challengingly, as though she'd had a hand in their father's decision.

"I . . . no," Mary said.

"And you don't care," Regina said. Her pompon bounced as she talked.

"She was his wife," Mary said.

"I mean about the *fire*," Regina said. "You don't object."

"I don't think so," she said. "Should I?"

"Not in my opinion," said Regina. "But I can never predict with you. Can you help look for the ax?"

"Can you wait five minutes?" Mary said.

Neither Regina or Gaby responded.

"Great," Mary said. "I need to change." She gestured at her mud-spattered pants.

"Don't wake up Aunt Helen," Regina warned.

"I won't," Mary promised.

"I mean it," said Regina.

"She's not going to like what she sees," said Gaby.

"She won't see it," Mary said.

"That's the plan," said Gaby.

"It's stuck in the wall," said Mary.

"What?" said Gaby.

"*The car*," said Regina.

Still wearing her coat, Mary ascended the front hall staircase. The darkened second floor had a vacant and depressing feel, it bleated the way hotels bleat with a squalid loneliness after the guests have left but before the maids have arrived, each door opening onto a room with furniture and a messy bed and no other sign of committed human inhabitation. Mary could scarcely believe this was her house, the house she'd grown up in—and it wasn't. The people made the house, and when the people were gone, well, the house was just a shelter in the crudest sense. What had she been thinking, offering to live here? Before long she'd have moved to the attic, spread out the remaining rugs, stocked the wardrobe with vodka, occupied her days reading *Famous Canadian Shipwrecks*. She realized that she'd be flying back to the West Coast, probably the day after tomorrow. She was done here.

Through the gap of her bedroom door she could hear her aunt's slow, regular breathing, like an intubated patient on a hospital respirator. Aunt Helen was dead out. Still, Mary didn't want to risk waking her. She'd have to find a change of clothing elsewhere. Regina's clothes were off-limits; she didn't want to bother with the politics of wearing Regina's clothes. Gaby's clothes were always funkily unwashed, dotted here and there with stains and smelling like old juice. Which left whatever wearable items she could drum up in her parents' bedroom. She still thought of it as "her parents' bedroom" even though the room had already suffered the effects of her mother's absence. Empty cardboard boxes near the closet, bills on the bedside table, multiple glasses of water on the bedside table, multiple water rings from multiple glasses of water scarring the bedside table, the bed unmade for so long that the fitted sheet had come undone on her mother's side of the bed, exposing the askew mattress pad and, beneath that, the actual mattress. Her mother's smell—grapefruit leather sawdust—lingered among the blankets.

Inside her mother's walk-in closet her smell redoubled, and redoubled yet again as Mary flipped through the hangers, searching for an inoffensive shirt and pair of pants. Her mother's style had been trending toward all-purpose golf for years, but she'd never realized how thoroughly this transition had been made—white and khaki and black the predominating colors, everything collared and pleated. Mary pulled all of her mother's clothes off their hangers and sweaters off their shelves in an attempt to find something—what exactly? She couldn't say. Soon the shelves and hangers were empty, the clothing piled in an awkward heap of arms and legs on the closet floor. Dutifully, her hangover gathering its ill forces, she loaded the clothes into the waiting cardboard boxes. She stripped the bedsheets, hid the pill bottles in the drawer, covered the water stains with a lace doily, bussed the water glasses to the bathroom sink. She held her breath as she carried the sheets down the hall to the laundry room, then muscled them into the washing machine, added a long pour of soap, turned the machine's knob to the most intensive setting.

Back in her parents' bathroom she washed her face and stripped her clothes, dressing in a pair of her father's old jeans and his WORCESTER TECH sweatshirt. She removed the shopping bag from her coat pocket and tucked it into the jeans' oversized waistband. On the way downstairs with the dirty water glasses, she dumped her slush-spattered outfit, which additionally smelled of vodka, on top of the washing machine.

Now her headache had begun a cyclical attack, the nauseaous spiral inside her head interrupting its orbit once each dizzying turn to smack the inside of her left temple. She had about thirty more functional minutes before she'd have to lie down in whatever room was vacant and sleep off the rest of the day. From the living-room doorway she could see her sisters hovering around the fireplace in their matching nightgowns, each wielding a poker and appearing to her, in her glazed state, like two elderly forest sprites trying to prod a reluctant animal out of a smoldering cave. On the floor beside them lay the remnants of a large wood frame.

"You're just in time," Regina said.

Mary's brain scrambled to patch together the disparate elements into a cohesive scenario.

"We're having our own ash-scattering ceremony," Regina said. "But first we need some ashes."

She gestured toward the scroll of canvas beside the hearth, its edges hacked away, presumably by the serrated bread knife that lay, as though Abigail Lake were being framed for a crime against herself, over her own lumpily rendered hands.

"Who wants to do the honors?" Regina said.

"I'll flip you," said Gaby. "Got a quarter?"

"Check inside the piano bench," Regina suggested.

Gaby shook down the piano bench while Regina, with the jerky nervousness of a first-time firemaker, tossed the remaining frame splinters into the flames, retracting her hands fearfully from the sparks. Abigail Lake withstood her impending injustice stoically. Her face appeared sadder and more elongated than usual—like the countenance of a fancy, spook-eyed hound. Mary had never seen herself in Abigail Lake before, but now the resemblance was so startlingly obvious, she couldn't believe she'd ever been able to convince herself otherwise.

"This is a bad idea," Mary said, still too stunned to appropriately respond. *Take Umbrage!*

"I told you she'd be a killjoy," Gaby said. "Mimsy can only disrespect Mum when it's her idea."

"We're not disrespecting Mum," Regina said. "We're pissed off and we're expressing that we're pissed off."

"To whom?" Mary asked, trying to keep the quaver from her voice. Why did she care what happened to Abigail Lake? Why did she fucking care? "To whom are you expressing yourself? Mum is dead."

"Would it have been so hard to leave us each a brooch?" Regina said.

"And you would have liked that better," Mary said, "being a big fan of brooches."

"I don't mind the occasional brooch," Gaby said.

"I hate brooches. That's not the point," Regina said.

"What is the point?" Mary said acidly.

"The point isn't that Mum left us something she knew we'd hate."

"Mimsy's trying to stall," Gaby said. "She's stalling until the reinforcements wake up."

Mary bit her index finger between the two lowest knuckles, the skin rolling away from the bone and leathering between her teeth.

"Maybe Mum hated Abigail Lake as much as we did," she said finally.

"Which excuses the fact that she gave her to us," Regina said. "Come on, Mimsy. We've been waiting for the joke to end. Gaby and I, we've been waiting for Dad to give us the check, or the pearls, some meaningless symbol that she loved us or wanted us to have, even a stupid fucking *brooch* to remember her by."

Mary's brain, her poor stupid brain, struggled to action. She'd been so fixated on her own solitary quest, the search for the book, that she'd failed to consider how her sisters felt after that disappointing afternoon in Buzz Stanworth's office. It wasn't just her—they'd been left out, too. And yet there had to be a reason for this, she thought. A reason that her mother, not a cruel woman, had behaved in a manner so seemingly cruel toward all her daughters. There had to be a reason. Mary's nausea intensified as she forced her brain to accelerate and search for this reason. If she was good at one activity, she thought, it was this: creating a plausible story out of disparate details; it seemed only fitting that she would, after all these years of selfishly applying her talent, finally discover a way to put it toward more philanthropic use. Yes indeed, she thought, with a surge of purpose that overrode her queasy lethargy, she could help people make sense of the senseless; as in the game of props, she could take these seemingly unrelated objects or details and weave them into a convincing story that would alter a depressing landscape into one slightly more saturated with hope.

"Maybe," Mary said, thinking aloud, "maybe she knew we'd burn Abigail Lake."

"Mum?" Regina said.

"Maybe that was the plan all along," Mary said.

"*All along*," mocked Gaby.

"She knew you both dislike me," Mary said.

"Not true," said Regina.

"Moderately true," said Gaby.

"Moderately true to true," said Regina. "But not for any good reason. I mean not any *recent* good reason. Anyway. Fine. I dislike you."

"It's fun to dislike you," said Gaby. "It's sporty."

"Mum gave us Abigail Lake for a reason," Mary said. "She gave us Abigail Lake so we would have someone to hate."

"Abigail Lake?" Regina said.

"No, Mum. We'd hate Mum," Gaby explained.

"By burning Abigail Lake we're expressing our anger toward Mum," Mary said. "This would be cathartic for us. We'd also, on a secondary level, be destroying the symbol of me as the unpardoned family member."

Regina nodded. "OK," she said. "And then what. We're supposed to forgive Mum for being a whimsical bitch?"

Abigail Lake appeared, in her usual eerie way, to be eavesdropping. Mary swore, in her half-hallucinating state, that Abigail Lake started to smile.

"She's dead," Mary said quietly. "Why do we need to forgive her?"

Gaby and Regina eyed each other. Mary's forehead buzzed and she could feel a crying jag start its electric descent from the top of her head. Her sisters, too, were about to cry, she could sense it in the room like her elbow could sense a rainstorm.

She waited for the sobbing to erupt. Regina and Gaby, she thought, were both holding their breath.

Mary staved off her dissolve; she didn't want to be the first.

Cry now, she silently urged her sisters. *Cry now.*

Gaby snorted.

"That's some corny therapy talk," she said.

"Really a stretch," Regina agreed. "But a nice try."

"You always were a lousy liar, Mimsy," Gaby said. "Regina, heads or tails?"

Regina chose heads. Gaby flicked the quarter and failed to catch it. It landed soundlessly on the carpet.

"I *am* the oldest," Regina said, taking Abigail Lake by her sawed-off ends and stuffing her, awkwardly, into the fireplace.

The three of them watched. They waited. But the canvas didn't catch. Abigail Lake seemed impervious to extinction.

Finally, the painted surface turned slick and bubbly.

"There," Gaby said.

"Fuck you, Mum," Regina said.

"Adieu, symbolic portrait of Mimsy in a bonnet," said Gaby.

Abigail Lake's hands curled up into themselves like actual witch's feet receding beneath a house foundation. Exhausted, hungover, weirdly tweaked by Abigail Lake's imminent forever disappearance, Mary started to cry. Quietly, so that no one would notice. Was she sad? Relieved? Just really unbearably tired? She couldn't say.

Regina pulled off her ski hat; her hair crackled audibly with static. She reached around Mary's ears and pulled the hat over her head.

"This doesn't make me like you," Regina said to Mary as Abigail Lake burned. "Or you either," to Gaby.

"I definitely don't like either one of you," Gaby said, handing Mary a scrap of newspaper with which she was presumably meant to blow her nose.

Mary watched as Abigail Lake's eyes and cheeks slid and muddied, the fire's serrated edges sawing through the canvas edges and exploding into green-tinted flames. She should listen to her own advice: Mum was dead. Why did she need to forgive Mum, and vice-versa? What mattered were the people who weren't dead yet—her sisters, her father. What mattered was that she was being given a chance to rectify things, as Roz had pointed out, and she didn't want to fuck it up.

Mary reached into the waistband of her father's jeans and withdrew the bag, pulling *Miriam* from its interior. Symbols of forgiveness were worth what, anyway? *When I say what she would have wanted I am saying: this is what I want.*

Mary didn't wait for the book to catch. Her final vision of *Miriam* was a black silhouette quivering between states of matter, that stunned moment when a flammable object can seem stubbornly immune to flame.

"Take Umbrage!" she announced. She so desperately wanted her sisters to cry, or show some kind of vulnerability, but she knew better than to expect the impossible. Expressing indignation, or sarcasm, or anger was the only way of exhibiting love in her family, and really what was so wrong with that?

"Take Umbrage!" she repeated.

Her sisters didn't respond, or if they did, Mary didn't hear them as she climbed the front stairs and entered her parents' bedroom, shutting the door softly so as not to wake Aunt Helen. She stretched out on her mother's side of the bed, taking no umbrage herself while thinking of the time she'd found her mother asleep in her own bed once, that confusing and glorious time, thinking of the time—just this morning, in fact—when she'd gazed up at the insomniac man, snoring in his armchair, the girl from his past serene and asleep at his feet.

Notes

Mary did not show up for what became our final appointment. Later, I would admit to my own analyst to feeling a powerful sense of relief when she failed to materialize in the waiting room at 10 a.m., 10:10, 10:30. At 10:35, I decided to go for a walk, to buy a coffee and sit on a bench in the Commons. It was the first warm day of the year and my office, for many reasons, had become small and oppressive to me.

The Commons teemed with airily dressed mothers and unjacketed businessmen, the emotional gloom of a winter-bound populace exposed by the sun to be as seasonally fragile as ice. To say that I was drawn to one particular end of the duck pond over another would be to attribute too much power to my subconscious; but I was drawn to the southern end of the pond where the sun was most vicious on the brown water and the glare so intense that I couldn't discern people, only black scurrying shapes.

I sat on a bench. I dumped two sugars into my coffee. I shaded my
eyes against the sun with my paper bag. I watched the silhouette of a pair
of boaters, a father and a daughter from the looks of their outlines, glide
past me in a rental skiff.

I guess I'm late, she said.

I turned to my bench mate. She wore sunglasses and a weathered canvas beach hat, as though she were a celebrity striving, in an extremely con-
spicuous way, to achieve invisibility.

I tried to remain unsurprised.

Forty minutes late, I said. If sitting at a duck pond counts as showing up at all.

What makes an appointment, she asked. The doctor or the office?

It's a nice day, I said, ignoring her pithiness. Better that we're outside
anyway.

She didn't respond.

What a tacky way to meet for our last time, she said.

Is this our last time? I said. When did you decide this?

A fortnight ago. I think we've reached the end, she said. I think we've
used each other up.

Have we been using each other? I said.

This was a topic she'd circled in the past—the notion that we were
exploiting each other, or, as she'd stated it, that we were helping each
other further our careers. At the time I'd dismissed this preoccupation of
hers as another of her false leads, but now saw it as incredibly prescient,
almost as though she'd known, from the beginning, that she was bound
to be my muse. We had not helped each other out—no, no, to her mind
we had *used* each other. But still.

I used you, I said. Is that what you think?

She pushed her sunglasses—too big for her face, not her sunglasses—up the bridge of her nose.

Wouldn't you rather be used than unused? Personally I would rather
have a use.

You'll have a use, I said.

You promise? she said.

I promise, I said.

We lapsed into silence.

I've seen this in movies, she said. Girls and old men on park benches. They have meaningful exchanges. When the conversation stalls they feign interest in ducks. When they depart each will be eternally touched by the other—the old man by the girl's wise innocence, the girl by the old man's innocent wisdom.

You've never been touched by my innocent wisdom, I said. Any reason you plan to start today?

She didn't respond.

We sat in silence. We feigned interest in ducks.

He took me rowing here, she said.

Who? I said.

K, she said.

Kurt, I said.

Whoever, she said.

But K is Kurt, isn't he? I said. He was Kurt, symbolically castrated for your imaginary purposes.

Everyone should have a purpose, she said.

And so he did. You symbolically castrated him because he kissed you when you were younger. You symbolically castrated him because, despite what you've wanted me to believe, your imagination does not permit the inclusion of genitalia.

Don't say *genitalia* so loudly, she said loudly.

K was Kurt, I insisted.

Whatever, she said. You can call him what you like. It's your story now.

My story, I said. Am I the patient? Are we switching roles again?

She tossed me an irritated look. Or was it a knowing look? What *did* she know? Did she know I'd already taken her story as my own, did she know, hyper radiant that she was, a girl able to intuit, with her stealthy imagination, that I'd begun to type up my notes and that her name was already Miriam?

You know what you're doing, she said, standing to leave.

She smiled at me, and I sensed in her smile a knowing sadness, a woundedness, a palpable regret and uncertainty of the sort she'd never revealed to me during our sessions together. It occurred to me then, as it had briefly when her aunt visited my office, that Mary's fantasies weren't fantasies at all. But this suspicion didn't disturb me. This suspicion did not, as it had over lunch with Hoppin, initiate pangs of guilt. I recalled what Helen said at the library fund-raiser—*the tragic lives of the untragic.* Mary had been a useless girl, and I was putting her to use with her permission. Subsequently, we had long since passed the point when the truth was of any consequence between us. As I watched her disappear into the intensifying glare radiating off the pond, her small black figure swallowed by the sun, I understood that it did not matter to me anymore what was true and what was not, because while Miriam remained with me, the girl who had inspired her was gone from my life for good.

Acknowledgments

S ince the city of Boston inarguably exists for some people, I have tried to do geographic justice to its portrayal (though there is not, to my knowledge, a two-block concentration of mental-health professionals located on a small street northwest of the Commons). The towns of West Salem and Chadwick do not exist for anybody, and thus all street names, schools, train stations, hockey rinks, stone walls, minimalls, and other landmarks will hopefully be granted the immunity of fictional places. Abigail Lake is a fabrication and not one of the accused witches executed in Salem in 1692, despite the claims of this book. There *was* an Alice Lake executed around 1650–1651, but while her last name has been nicked, she is otherwise not to be considered a historical inspiration for this character.

A debt of inspiration is owed to the following writers and books: Janet Malcolm (everything she's ever written but particularly *Psychoanaly-*

sis: The Impossible Profession and *In the Freud Archives*); Adam Philips; Jeffrey Moussaieff Masson (*The Assault on Truth* and *Against Therapy*); Leslie Farber; Alice Miller; *Remembering Trauma* by Richard J. McNally; *Sybil* by Flora Rheta Schreiber; *You and Psychiatry* by William C. Menninger, M.D., and Munro Leaf. Dr. Hammer and his theory of hyper radiance owe a great conceptual debt to historian Mary Beth Norton and her book *In the Devil's Snare: The Salem Witchcraft Crisis of 1692*. Bruno Bettelheim, from beyond the grave, kindly did not forbid the second-hand use of his title.

Immeasurable gratitude is due to early reader Amanda Gersh for her subtle suggestion that the then book should be burned at the proverbial stake and to later reader Jonathan Lethem for his help with less terminal problems. Henry Dunow is thanked for donating his incisive, beat-around-no-bush insights and for applying psychic compresses via telephone when someone became ridiculous. Bill Thomas is thanked for his unwavering smarts and early support—I've tried to deliver an end product deserving of his confidence in me.

The people at Doubleday (in particular Melissa Ann Danaczko and Alison Rich) have been sublimely nice, intelligent, flexible, and efficient. I greatly appreciate this.

I would like to thank Donna Bassin for in no way being a model for any character in this book. A hefty check is owed to Andrew Leland for picking up my *Believer* slack in perpetuity. Ben Marcus is thanked and thanked and thanked and thanked.

Finally, I would like to acknowledge the therapists whose priceless inspiration was purchased at great hourly cost. This book is, in some roundabout, and I hope not entirely insulting, way, an appreciative nod to you.